A CLASSY AFFAIR IN THE COUNTRY

MARGARET AMATT

LEANNAN
PRESS
INDEPENDENT PUBLISHER

LEANNAN PRESS

First Published by Leannan Press 2024

Book Cover designed by Margaret Amatt

eBook ISBN: 978-1-914575-51-8

Paperback ISBN: 978-1-914575-50-1

Prologue

Ophelia

February

Ophelia Chattan-Blythe slammed the BMW into a gravelled parking area in front of Glenvorneth House. Her blood chilled at the thought of what she might see inside. She gripped the car's keycard tight in her palm and ran up the wide stone steps to the front door. Why did this remind her so much of the day her grandfather had died? He'd been taken too young and too soon, and so much had been lost. Her father had been thrust into a role he wasn't ready for, and Ophelia's childhood had changed irrevocably. She shoved open the heavy door, and it creaked like something out of an old horror movie. Hastening into the small, flag-stoned outer porch and through a large stained-glass door to the main entrance, she called, 'Hello!' Like anyone would hear her in this vast house unless they were hanging around the hallway, which, clearly, they weren't. She shivered as she crossed the worn and faded carpet. One of her ancestors had built this gothic mansion in the nineteenth century and once upon a time she'd seen so much charm and history here, soaked in her grandparents' stories about the place, and loved its quirks. Those days were unlikely to come again.

Where was her father? If Jacinta's messages were anything to go by, he was in a bad way. Ophelia couldn't afford to have him doing anything crazy – like dying. Dramatic maybe, but as heiress to this place, the thought often invaded her mind. She wasn't ready. Just as he hadn't been when his father died. And come to think about it, she really *couldn't* afford it. Glenvorneth cost an absolute fortune to maintain, but one day she'd have to find a way. *Please, not now.*

'Hello!' she shouted, heading down the hallway that shot off to the left of the grand stairs. A long fancy rug ran the length of it, with side tables up against the walls, covered in antique vases. Ophelia shoved open the double-doors to the main drawing room. She froze in the doorway, staring around at the scene of perfect domesticity. 'Er...?'

Jacinta, her stepmother, sat on a chaise reading, while her six-teen-year-old half-sister, Francesca, was curled in a window seat scrolling through her phone. Her father, Rupert, was sipping a large whisky, reading a magazine, and chortling to himself. Both Rupert and Jacinta looked up. Warm relief flooded Ophelia at the sight of her father, who looked in perfect health, but she rubbed her forehead. What was going on... or not? Francesca glanced around, almost like an afterthought, then returned to her phone.

'Nice of you to drop by,' Jacinta said. Ophelia ignored the hint of a jibe. Water off a duck's back these days. Jacinta was one of the main reasons Ophelia lived in Edinburgh and had given up living at Glenvorneth. Had things been different, she would have found a way to live on the estate, nurture it and make it into a place for people to enjoy – not just her family. That was how her grandparents had wanted it, but Jacinta had quickly put a stop to that.

'So, what's going on?' Ophelia's heart was still racing from what was obviously a false alarm, but even seeing her father looking as normal as ever didn't take away the sense that something wasn't right. 'I thought you were on death's door?' She frowned at her father before making her way over, planting a kiss on his cheek, then sitting on the edge of an elegant sofa next to his armchair.

'What?' He shook his head. 'Me?'

'Your message...' Ophelia turned her attention to Jacinta. 'It implied he wasn't going to make it.'

'Really?' Jacinta lifted an eyebrow and made an innocent expression. 'That wasn't my intention. You must have misread it.'

'I assure you I didn't.' Ophelia pulled her phone from her Dior saddle bag, but before she could open it, Jacinta cut in.

'Good timing though, because there is something we need to talk to you about. Isn't there, Rupert?' She gave him a pointed stare.

'Ah, yes. This is quite serendipitous, as it's probably some-thing I should say to you in person, though it's not easy.'

Ophelia's stomach lurched. What now? Adrenaline shoved her brain several steps ahead. Was he ill? Or planning on stepping aside and handing over the estate? Or had Jacinta found a way to disinherit her, so that Francesca, or one of her two sons from her previous marriage, could inherit instead? Ophelia couldn't allow that. Her grandparents had fought hard to ensure the estate would go to her instead of the closest male heir, as happened with the majority of estates. How could she let it go? It might be the easier option, but not the right one.

'Unfortunately,' Rupert said. 'The estate has reached the point of near bankruptcy.'

'What?' Her heart sank. That couldn't be right, surely?

'It's so often the way these days. We're not the only estate in the area that's struggling. The old workers' cottages are in a terrible mess. This house needs work and now, with the damage at the stables, things are worse than ever.'

'What damage?'

'A roof collapsed,' Jacinta said.

'What about the horses?'

'They were all fine.' Rupert held up his hands. 'But we've had to stop running the livery as it simply isn't viable.'

'And Conker?' They better not have got rid of her horse.

'He's still there, but we had to move him into temporary accommodation.'

Ophelia frowned. 'What temporary accommodation?'

'The back of Dagmar Ingenfeld's trailer,' Jacinta said.

Ophelia let out a sigh. At least Conker was safe, but she'd neglected him for too long. He was in good hands though; Dagmar was the best when it came to anything equine. 'She's still working here then?' They hadn't laid her off, at least.

'Not for much longer, the way things are going.' Rupert dipped his chin to his chest with a hefty sigh. 'We've had to let so many of the staff go. Dagmar still does the horses and Barbara has stayed on as estate manager, but that's it.'

Ophelia raised an eyebrow. 'That's it? Who cooks and cleans?'

'We manage with the cooking, and we have a cleaner who comes once a week.'

Her father and Jacinta cooked! It must be bad. Even her imagination couldn't supply images to fit.

'So... Is there something you want me to do to help?' Ophelia twisted a silver bracelet on her arm. She ran her own design business, which had become quite successful. It paid for an apartment in Edinburgh, and she'd put some money by, but she couldn't bail out Glenvorneth.

'Actually, yes. We have the perfect solution.' Rupert clasped his hands on his lap and beamed like an over-excited schoolboy.

On the window seat, Francesca looked up with a smirk.

'What solution?' Ophelia pressed.

'I believe there's a man who could save us,' Rupert said. 'His name is James Charlton and his family own Duchan Fayre; you know that wonderful shopping place you and Jacinta both love?'

'Yes, I know it.' She brushed invisible lint from her Harris tweed blazer; she'd bought it at Duchan Fayre sometime last year. Everyone in the area knew the place. It was a premier venue for country clothes, homeware, luxury gifts, and food. The restaurant was well known too, and it was situated in extensive grounds, surrounded by hills and waterfalls, all making for a perfect out of-town shopping experience. 'How can this man save the estate? Is he going to invest in it?'

'That's the eventual outcome I have in mind.'

Ophelia frowned at Jacinta. Why was she making that smug face? Something else must be going on here. 'So how will this investment come about?'

'That's where you come in.' Jacinta fluttered her lashes. Experience told Ophelia that when Jacinta wore an expression that saccharine, something extremely unpleasant was coming.

'You want me to approach him?'

'Not exactly.' Rupert gave a fake little cough. 'We want you to marry him.'

Francesca sniggered from the window seat and started tapping at her phone, no doubt relaying what her father had said to an entire class of teenagers.

Ophelia got to her feet and shook her head. 'You want me to marry him? It might have escaped your notice, but this isn't the Victorian era. Why do I feel like I've just walked onto the set of Bridgerton?' She strode to the window opposite to where Francesca was sitting and stared over the grounds. This was a joke, right? 'You might not be on death's door, but you've clearly lost your marbles.'

'Oh, come on, Ophelia.' Jacinta clapped her hands on her thighs. 'Think about it. You're single, and you don't have to marry him straight away.'

'Or at all, if you don't like him,' Rupert said. 'But why not meet him and see? You must be lonely living on your own.'

Even if that was painfully accurate, she wasn't about to admit it.

'By all accounts he's a delightful man.' Jacinta waved an airy hand.

'Marry him yourself then,' Ophelia snapped.

Rupert chortled. 'Now, now. Let's not be silly.'

Ophelia half closed her eyes at her faint reflection in the window and took a deep breath. *Let's not be silly!* That was a good one coming from the man who was proposing to marry off his eldest daughter to the highest bidder.

'Why don't you just come up with a business plan?' Ophelia turned back to face them. 'There used to be so much more going on here.' She didn't want to point fingers, but in the seventeen years her father had been married to Jacinta, and more specifically the ten in which he'd been in charge, everything her grandparents had put into action had fizzled out and died. 'The estate used to be a hub for community events. Remember the gala days and garden parties? We used to open rooms and show off the costume and furniture collections to the public. Why not start some of that again?' Before Jacinta even opened her mouth, Ophelia sensed the resistance. Jacinta hated 'the public' interfering in her life.

'We tried that a year or so back. We opened up one summer for a display of costumes, but we barely made a penny.'

'It can't be a one off. You have to keep it up.'

Jacinta wrung her hands, pouting, and didn't make eye contact.

'We don't want to do anything that'll rock the boat too much.' Rupert eyed Jacinta with a slightly furrowed brow. 'That's why we're putting forward the gentlest solution.'

Ophelia raised her hand to her forehead and pressed her fingertips into it. She forced herself to maintain steady breathing. *Do not rise or react. Just stay calm.* But really. The 'gentlest' solution was her marrying a perfect stranger for his money? Surely there had to be a better way? But what?

CHAPTER ONE

Ophelia

March

A branch loomed over Ophelia like the sword of Damocles. She stared up at it as Barbara, the estate manager, pulled up the hood of her waxed jacket and frowned.

'Be careful. I don't think it's safe.'

Ophelia picked up a few fallen slates in her path, moving from under the dodgy tree and making her way towards the door of a dilapidated building beside a beautiful little lochan.

'This old house used to be beautiful.' She peered in through a grimy window, seeing little but junk. 'How long has it been like this?'

'Oh, ages now. None of the estate cottages are inhabited any-more.' Barbara let out a hefty sigh.

'No wonder the estate isn't making money.' Ophelia remembered a time when all the cottages were inhabited. Someone had even lived at the boathouse for a while, and she'd had to stop hiding there. She'd resorted to the stables, confiding in the horses when she needed a friendly ear.

'Exactly.'

'I always thought this would make a beautiful place to live.' She gazed around, recalling the times she'd escaped the main house for the solace of this little boathouse – when her parents had quarrelled, when Jacinta came on the scene, and when her grandparents died. 'But it's too rundown now.'

'Could it be done up as a holiday rental? Would that work? It's in such a perfect place, after all.'

'It's a good idea in theory. I've been drawing designs for it since I was six.' If Jacinta hadn't been so beastly, Ophelia saw herself doing up this place and living in it, but she couldn't bear the thought of being so close to her. Somehow, she'd landed the cliched wicked stepmother for real. In the beginning, she'd tried to get on with her, but no matter what she did, nothing changed. 'I have plans and designs ready to go. I'd love to put them to good use, but without money, it's a low priority.' She toyed with the phone in her pocket and sighed. 'Have you heard my father's plan for how he thinks he'll save the estate?'

'Hmm. Yes.'

'And what do you think of it?'

'Well, it sounds very old-fashioned to me. Unless you happen to know James and want to marry him already.'

'I've never met him and if I go throwing myself at him, it'll look blatantly obvious what I'm doing.'

'Possibly, but the Charltons expressed an interest in meeting your father. I think this is where he's got the idea from.'

'It still sounds like we need a much better plan.'

'Indeed. There's potential on the estate, but, well, your father doesn't want to see it. He's afraid of change. I fear it's caught up on him. As for Jacinta...' Barbara inhaled deeply. 'She needs to—'

'Stop spending money?'

Barbara chuckled. 'Yes. That. But also understand the need to diversify, the way your grandparents did. She wants to do everything in a way that won't interfere with her lifestyle, only I'm not sure that's possible.'

'I wish I knew what to do for the best,' Ophelia muttered, more to herself than Barbara.

'I hope you don't mind me saying, but I believe your grandfather wanted this place to go to you for a reason. He saw, even at a young age, that you had what it takes to make it special again. Sadly, I don't think your father does. Perhaps if you were to come back for a little while.'

'What for?'

'Start the ball rolling on some projects. Maybe it wouldn't do any harm to meet James Charlton. What if he's nice?' Barbara gave her a cheeky grin.

'I might be able to stay for a short while.' And what if James turned out to be exactly the man she'd been waiting for? Not that she hung about waiting for men to fall at her feet, but she genuinely believed there was someone for everyone and she just hadn't been lucky enough to meet the right person yet. Sad, because her father had inadvertently hit the nail on the head; she was lonely. She wanted a partner. A real one who could fill the gap in her soul. No one she'd dated so far really fit properly. Whenever she was on dates, it felt like trying to put a jigsaw piece into the wrong puzzle.

If she agreed to meet James, though, it had to be on her own terms, not her father's and definitely not Jacinta's.

'Your input would be very welcome,' Barbara said. 'Meaning no disrespect, but sometimes it's like banging my head against a wall with your father.'

'I can imagine. Let me chat to Lucinda, my deputy. She's very good and if she thinks she can keep everything ticking over in the office, then I'll stay for a while.'

'Wonderful.'

'I'll call her now, if there's reception.' She checked. Two bars. *That should be enough.*

'I better get back to work.' Barbara jumped into the old Range Rover and drove off down the track through the woods towards the main house.

Ophelia called Lucinda, pacing and gazing at the stunning scenery around the boathouse. Was that someone walking on the other side of the lochan? People occasionally walked through the woods here. It used to be part of a bridle path from the stables, but with them out of action, she doubted anyone would bother now. She squinted into the dense wood, waiting for the call to connect to the Timeless Butterfly Interiors office in Edinburgh. She'd started it as a one-woman interior design business with money her grandfather left her when she was straight out of uni, but it had grown and grown. More than she'd intended.

'Darling, hi,' she said as Lucinda picked up. 'Got some news, and it's not all good.'

'About your dad?'

'Oh, golly, Dad's fine. That was a story Jacinta made up to get me here so they could tell me their other crackpot plan. Just wait until you hear what they want me to do.'

'You are joking,' Lucinda said, when Ophelia told her story.

'Sadly no. But that brings me to the real problem. I should stay for a while to see what's going on and maybe start a few upgrade projects. I have to accept that nothing will happen unless I do it. Would you be ok with that? I'll do as much as I can from here, but you'll be the main person in the office.'

'I'd love to. You know I've always been after your job.' She giggled and Ophelia laughed too. Lucinda was a sweetheart. She'd been the first person Ophelia had hired as the business expanded. She'd not expected it to get quite so big in such a short time.

'Well, I'll upgrade you to acting manager and pay you accordingly for the next few weeks. And thank you. I really appreciate this.'

'Any time.'

With that settled, Ophelia returned to the house to break the news to her father and Jacinta. She wasn't overly delighted at the prospect of staying in the house with them, but it would be the easiest thing to do. Her mother, Edith, lived in the nearby town of Glenbriar, which was a twenty-minute drive along the side of Loch Briar from the estate. If she really couldn't stand it, she could always bunk with her, though Edith was fond of her own company, and it wouldn't be as convenient as being here.

But Ophelia made a point of dropping in to see her as soon as she could, for a brief visit to update her on the plans. Edith wouldn't like to be left out.

'Utterly outrageous!' she said, when Ophelia told her what Rupert and Jacinta were plotting. 'They really don't get any better, do they?'

'Unfortunately not. I don't know what to do.' Ophelia hugged her mum, inhaling the comforting scent of her mum's perfume.

Edith patted her back. 'Your father is still in the dark ages. It's one of the reasons I divorced him. Don't you go marrying anyone you don't want to. That decision is up to you. I know how important the estate is to you, and how responsible you've felt for it since losing your grandfather, but don't sell yourself for someone else's dream.'

'I won't.' Though that little voice wouldn't be silenced completely. *What if I'm missing a trick?* What if James was the man who could fill the hole in her heart and ignite the dormant spark inside her? Sometimes her heart raged so hot she wasn't sure how to tame it, but she kept it forced down behind her public face. The guys she'd dated previously weren't exactly high on the passionate scale. They were usually too gentlemanlike, which was ok, but she craved so much more. Not that she would ever confess that to anyone.

Edith checked her watch. 'I'm running late for yoga, darling. But I'll see you at my birthday lunch.'

'Ah, yes, of course. I'm looking forward to it.' Ophelia kissed her mum goodbye and jumped in her car. *Bugger.* She'd forgotten to buy her a birthday present, but she could nip into the Glenbriar Gallery on the way home. Her mum was a big fan of modern artwork.

She squeezed the car into an on-street parking space and headed inside. Sweeping back her long fair hair, she cast around the open-plan room, screwing up her nose at the odd chaotic artwork, curvaceous sculpted wood and bizarre metalwork. This wasn't her kind of thing at all. She liked the classical landscape paintings, wildlife studies, and, most of all, portraits. Her grandparents had told her stories of all the portraits in Glenvorneth and Ophelia tried to remember everything they'd said, but she'd been too young to fully appreciate them, and now it was too late to ask. Her half memories were all that was left because her father and Jacinta didn't care.

Her phone buzzed. *Barbara Strachan* flashed on the screen. An assistant peered over from the desk.

'Hi.' Ophelia moved out of sight, inadvertently stepping into a darkened alcove containing what was presumably supposed to be erotica. She blinked, tilting her head. *Good lord.*

'Ah, Ophelia, I'm glad to have caught you,' Barbara said. 'Can you meet me at the boathouse?'

'Um... Possibly. Why?' She averted her eyes from the extreme close-up of droopy breasts lolling before her.

'Because I—'

Ophelia frowned at the screen. Barbara was still talking, but quieter and obviously to someone else in the room.

'Hello?' She glanced around as she waited. Would her mother appreciate something like this as a gift? Unlike herself, Edith loved the abstract, finding hidden meaning in even the oddest pieces, but this stuff? The name Camilla Woodcroft was scrawled in the corner of the pictures. Ophelia had a vague notion Jacinta had mentioned that name. Was she aware that a friend of hers painted stuff like this? Surely that wouldn't sit well with her.

'Sorry.' Barbara finally reappeared. 'Listen, please meet me. If you could be there at two... Pardon?' Barbara vanished again.

'Can I help you, madam?' The assistant's voice made Ophelia jump.

'Actually, yes, I need a gift for my mother. She's dreadfully hard to find anything for. If I choose artwork for her, it would be like imposing my taste on her, and my mother's taste is very different from mine. I've no idea what she'd fancy in here...' Her eyes lingered on the droopy breasts; did anyone display pictures like that in their house? 'Do you sell gift cards?'

'Of course, madam. We have them in tens, twenties or fifties.'

'Hello!' Barbara yelled in Ophelia's ear.

Ophelia held the phone away. 'Hi.'

'I'll meet you at the boathouse at two.'

Ophelia still had no idea why, and it would be tight. Barbara obviously assumed she was coming from the house. She'd need to put on some speed, but she had a lingering feeling her afternoon was about to go tits-up, unlike the saggy boobs on display around her.

CHAPTER TWO

Ophelia

Fog patches spread over the glen, obscuring Ophelia's vision as she took the lochside road towards the estate. Her BMW cut a crimson slash through the gloom. Squinting ahead, she flicked the full beam on and off as she moved in and out of the misty sections. Low clouds hovered above the loch like steam from a boiling cauldron.

Her phone rang, making her jump. Jacinta. Ophelia pressed the speaker. 'Hi.'

'When you're in town, would you pick up something for dinner, please?'

'Sorry, I've already left.'

'Can't you go back? You're not here, so you must still be close to the town.'

'Not really.'

'Please, Ophelia, help me out here.'

'It's not a case of helping out, I—'

'Always an excuse.'

'It's not an excuse. I have an appointment.' Ophelia ground her teeth. The fog had lifted a little and a white van was moving along in front of her.

'Well, god knows what we'll eat then.'

This was a straight section and without thinking it through, Ophelia sunk the pedal to the floor, racing past a van. Before she got by, a foggy patch engulfed her again. Unable to fully see, she held her foot down, a sudden panic gripping her. What if a car materialised through the fog? She would smash it head-on. Her fingers were numb, and she clenched the wheel. The van slowed, and she cut in front of it. Her grip relaxed, and she sped ahead, heart thumping. *What a stupid thing to do. Shouldn't let Jacinta get to me like this.* Honestly, that woman was one of the few things that ever made her mad.

'Ophelia! Are you still there?'

'I'll see what I can do.' Ophelia forced the words out, hardly able to breathe. 'There's another call coming in that I need to take.'

She wasn't lying. Barbara's name was flashing up. She shut off Jacinta, hitting the button with fingers still shaking. 'Hello.'

'Ophelia, hello. I'm glad I caught you. I'm running a tad late.' The line was crackly and Ophelia screwed up her face at a metallic squeak. 'I meant to say earlier, if you arrive before me, be careful...' Barbara's voice crackled off again, then burst back. '... scruffy man lingering not far from the boathouse...' More crackling. '... Mhairi from the house down the way told me he stole a moped...' The crackling continued. '...spare key in the flowerpot, but...'

'What? There's a scruffy man at the boathouse who stole someone's moped?'

The call cut out before Barbara could reply. 'Seriously?' What was going on?

She hit the brakes and pulled up a side road. It rose steeply and wound around the back of the estate. At the back gate, she pulled in and trundled down a track to the small lochan. Mist almost fully obscured it and if she didn't know it was there, she might have thought it was nothing but a big empty space. She steered the BMW into a gravelled layby beside a low wall. Ahead was the forlorn old building, long and low, with a curious tower looming on one side. Poor shabby old boathouse.

She exited the car, bleeping it shut, and slung her Dior saddle bag up her wrist. The cold air nipped her face as she scanned around. The surrounding tall trees were dark, and she shivered. Was someone watching through the low hanging mist? She recalled seeing something moving over there the last time she was here. Was this safe?

Giving herself a shake, she turned her attention to the dilapidated ruin. She hadn't been inside for so long. Had Barbara said the spare key was in a flowerpot? A brief thrill gripped her as she lifted a pot by the door and saw the rusty old key. Not great security. She unlocked the creaky door. What if the scruffy man Barbara had mentioned was using the place as a squat? A stench of mould hung in the chill air. Fumbling for the light switch, she stifled a scream as she touched a cobweb. *Yuck.* She shook it off, then picked her way through a jumble of old furniture to the back room. It seemed like her father was using it to store piles of unwanted junk. From the windows should have been a stunning view on a clear day. Instead, layers of grime obscured everything.

An engine and a banging of car doors made her jump. What was that? Barbara? Her pulse quickened at a scuffling sound – mice, rats? *Oh no.*

A hefty clanging reverberated outside. *What the...?*

Ophelia rubbed a view hole in the filthy window with a tissue and saw a white van parked beside her car. A tall man with floppy, sandy coloured hair and a dusting of stubble was next to it. He bent and picked something up. Ophelia's eyes goggled as she spied what he was holding. A crowbar. *What the hell? Is he about to jemmy open my car?* 'No way.' Without another thought, she ran to the door, grabbed an old set of antlers from the top of a cupboard, and stormed out. She marched to within three feet of the man, wielding the antlers like a shield.

'What do you think you're doing?' The chill wind snapped at her cheeks.

'Whoa.' The man turned around, no longer with anything in his hand, and gave her a quizzical look. His eyebrows were high on his face, and he held his muscly arms up in surrender, displaying the wide expanse of a muscular chest under his work-worn, faded shirt. *Holy crap.* A man like that could charm his way into anything with those inviting eyes and that crooked grin. *Don't be fooled*. This could be the scruffy moped-stealing conman upgrading to car theft. And now she was standing in front of him, trying to take him on with a set of old antlers. Like that would do any good. She wasn't short, but she couldn't match his muscle power; he was built like He-man.

'I saw you about to break into my car.'

His eyes held hers for a moment, and she didn't move. Her tummy did a weird little flip.

'What are you talking about?' He seemed on the verge of laughing. Ok, so the antlers must look pretty silly.

'I'm calling the police.' She wrestled the antlers to one side so she could reach her mobile.

'Listen, lady, put that away, and those things. They'll take someone's eye out. This is—'

'I saw you.'

'Saw what? I'm Brann Duthie the builder.'

'Who?' She blinked, trying to process what he was saying.

'You called me.'

Her heart raced. His crooked smile didn't fade as he waited for her to speak. Some women, even amongst her friends, would go for his type: muscly and rugged, with make-love-to-me eyes. *But not me*. Well-groomed, smart men were her thing.

'I didn't call you.' Had Barbara? Was that what this was all about? 'If you are who you say, then you better prove you're bona fide.'

'I'm boney what?' He pulled a face.

'Show me your I.D., please.' She clung to the antlers, knowing how stupid she must sound as soon as the words were out of her mouth. If this guy was a thief, wouldn't he knock her on the head and be done with?

'Er.' His brow furrowed. The van door opened, and a younger man got out, but hovered on the far side. Was this some kind of gang hustle? Maybe she should get in her car and go.

'Um, ok. I've got my driver's license somewhere. Hang on.' He pulled a wallet from his back pocket. 'My name's also on the van, if that works.'

Her eyes darted to it, and she saw the words clear as day. Brann Duthie Builder.

'Well...' She gave a little shrug. 'How do I know you didn't steal that van and are just using the name?'

He let out a snort laugh. 'Smart thinking. You should be a detective.' Opening the wallet, he stepped closer. The fine hairs on her neck rose. Despite what should be a sense of impending danger, that wasn't the only vibe she was getting. Something else built in her chest, a burning heat. It spread through her body. Perhaps she could attribute it to being annoyed or panicky, but that didn't quite explain it. It seemed to have more to do with the proximity of his chest and the heady scent of citrus, spice and raw man. 'Are you going to put those antlers down?' He quirked his lips at her again.

She realised her knuckles had gone white clinging to them and she'd rather unfortunately aimed them at his crotch. 'I.D. first.'

'As you wish.'

Ophelia tightened her grip on the antlers, not sure if she trusted him or not.

A vehicle sound alerted her attention. She spun around to see Barbara pulling up. Dazzling headlights blinded her. Then Barbara, in her tweed suit, hauled herself out of the old Range Rover, grinning.

'Good afternoon.' She raised her voice as a strong gust shaved across her grey bob. 'Ophelia, you made it. Excellent.' She frowned at the antlers for a second, then turned to the man. 'And you must be Brann Duthie.'

'Yes,' he said.

'No,' Ophelia said, at the same time.

'Oh dear.' Barbara laughed. 'There seems to be a mix-up.'

'Whoever he is, I saw him with a crowbar about to break into my car.'

Brann shook his head at the younger man who'd walked around to stand next to him. 'Some tools fell as I was driving. I was about to tidy them up, but the crowbar fell out when I opened the car door, that's all. I'm here because someone called Barbara phoned me to look at some work needing done.' He glanced at Ophelia, and she had a strong sense that he was checking her out. Her hackles rose. 'I assumed that was you.'

'No, that's me,' Barbara said, 'and yes, I called you both.'

'So why *did* you call me?' Ophelia turned to Barbara, blocking the two men. 'You didn't say why.'

'Oh, gracious yes, let's step inside and I'll explain, it's far too cold out here.'

Brann still had a trace of that annoying smirk on his face. He stood back to let her in. 'Ladies first, and just in case you're still in doubt.' He held up a little pink card and Ophelia saw his name and photo on his driver's license.

She gave him a stiff smile, feeling like a total idiot, still clinging to the stupid antlers. She dumped them back on the top of the low cupboard and tried to avoid Brann's gaze. *Why is he staring at me like that?*

'Now.' Barbara clapped her hands. 'This is Ophelia Chattan-Blythe, she's the daughter of Rupert, the owner of this estate, but to all intents and purposes she's in charge for now.'

Ophelia wasn't sure that was true in any shape or form. Running Timeless Butterfly Interiors had been hard enough. But that had been a task she'd grown into alongside the business expanding. Being in charge of something as big as Glenvorneth was so much more daunting and not something she wanted to do alone – or soon. No wonder her father struggled. Perhaps that was why he'd kept Barbara on instead of a cook.

'Ophelia has come to our rescue,' Barbara went on. 'She knows, as I do, the estate needs to diversify. Rupert doesn't like that idea, or his wife doesn't – but Ophelia understands. She's our heiress.' Barbara patted her arm. Brann gave her a definite once over, his crooked smile widening. What did that look mean? Why was he staring? *Hell. Why am I?*

'There will have to be some significant changes,' Barbara went on. 'We need to make a start, and this place is in the perfect location for a holiday rental. Not that it looks it today, but it could be. You agree, Ophelia, don't you?'

'Well, yes, but...' Much as she loved the place, it was low on her priority list. There were more urgent parts of the estate needing attention.

Brann peered around. 'It's definitely got potential.'

'So you can do it?' Barbara said.

'Depends what it is you want. I could make it structurally safe, but if you're talking about extensions or significant changes, then I can't just start knocking down walls. You need plans and a building warrant. You might need a structural engineer. It depends how strong the structure is.'

'Yes, yes.' Barbara swept off his words. 'Ophelia and I can sort all that.'

'I... what? I'm only here for a couple of weeks.' She didn't want to leave Timeless Butterfly Interiors for too long. But then, this was her heritage and her future. Her beloved grandparents had gone to a lot of trouble to ensure the estate would come to her. How could she let them down? Especially when it felt like letting herself down too.

'Well, it looks like a fairly stable old building.' Brann moved closer to Ophelia and tapped on a wall. 'Though I'd need to check it properly. And obviously there's a lot to be cleared out.' His eyes roamed over the mouldy furniture and piles of junk. 'Those antlers should definitely be moved out of reach of some of us,' he muttered sideways at Ophelia.

'What? I—'

'Don't worry about that,' Barbara said, clearly not having heard fully. 'I know a couple of lads who'll clear this place out for a bit of pocket money.'

Ophelia ground her teeth and narrowed her eyes at Brann. Barbara rattled on. At first Brann kept his focus away from Ophelia, then slowly he turned to her, raised his eyebrow, and quirked a little grin.

'Listen.' Ophelia wasn't sure what Barbara was talking about. She'd lost track and the heat in her neck was making her annoyingly flustered. 'I can't hang about.' Not if she was to go back into town and get some food for dinner.

'Me neither,' Brann said. 'I'm a busy man. Come on.' He clapped his silent sidekick on the arm. Surely, that had to be Brann's brother. The resemblance was too uncanny. 'If I'm lucky, I might find another heiress to rob before dinnertime,' he added in a low voice as he passed Ophelia.

'What?'

'Yes, yes, let's sort a date for you to give this place a thorough inspection.' Barbara flicked through her phone.

Brann winked at Ophelia before exchanging dates with Barbara.

What the...? Was he for real?

Barbara opened the door, and they filed out. 'Gosh this wind. Let's move. And thank you for coming, Brann. I'll see you at the house, Ophelia. We can discuss this further.' Barbara climbed into the Rover. The fog had blown away, and narrow rows of waves skimmed the top of the lochan. Brann Duthie's sidekick jumped into the van and slammed the door. Icy rain drops pelted Ophelia. Brann folded his arms and blocked her. She couldn't get to the car without sidestepping him.

Barbara drove off with a toot and a wave.

'So that's your BMW, is it?' Brann examined it, seemingly unperturbed by the adverse weather, even though strands of wet hair were sticking to his rugged face. Ophelia shivered. Her riding jacket wasn't waterproof. She wanted to get into the car.

'Yes.' She made to sidestep him.

'That was a dangerous piece of driving earlier,' he continued quietly. His face had a magnetism about it that held her eyes fixed on him. It gave her an electric shock. 'Even more dangerous than letting you loose with those antlers.'

'Seriously, that is already way too old. Just what are you talking about?'

'You went past us at crazy speed on the road in the fog. You could have killed someone.'

Oh god. That was him? She stared at him, knowing fine what she'd done, but not about to dig herself in any deeper. He was right; she'd let Jacinta get to her and done something stupid. Of course she wished she hadn't done it, but she had, and she didn't need a lecture.

'I've a good mind to report you. You nearly put us off the road. If someone was coming towards us, we'd all be dead. Fancy heiress or not, you've no right to drive like that.'

'I really don't need this. I'm not sure I want you working for us. We're not... You're not a good fit, for me... Us.' The words almost jammed in her throat and a stupid little voice inside her tried to tell her all the ways he might be a perfect fit, but she ignored it and shut it down.

'Sure. Have it your way.'

Jumping into the car, she slammed the door and drove off. Her ears buzzed, and her head spun. Guilt crept in and she cringed at the memory – Brann was right; she'd been driving like a lunatic. As she drove sensibly back, her breathing calmed a little and her eyes frequently strayed to the rear-view mirror. He didn't catch up. Hopefully, she'd never see him again and she could erase this from her mind, but a part of her wanted to see him, and soon. It felt like they had unfinished business, though whether it was good or bad, she wasn't entirely sure.

CHAPTER THREE

Brann

Brann swung the van into the Glenbriar High School car park and cranked on the handbrake. A lot had changed with this building since he'd been here. Hardly surprising as he'd left twenty years ago and, truth be told, he hadn't exactly had a good attendance record. Make that a good record full stop. No need for his daughter to know that, however. Just as there was no need for her to know that when he was only a couple of years older than her, he became a dad for the first time. No doubt she could do the maths, but he didn't want to draw attention to if he could help it.

He made his way to the front door, which now had a security entry system. How things had changed. The world had gone safety mad. Like the carry on he'd had yesterday with that posh woman threatening him with antlers and demanding I.D. She might have been one hell of a looker, but what a headcase.

After working out which button to press, he waited until the door clicked, then entered. The reception area was all new. This had been a gathering ground for pupils before assemblies when he'd been here, but now it had a large desk with a Perspex window separating him from the receptionist.

'Hi.' He ran his fingers through his hair. 'I'm Caitlin Duthie's dad. I had a call saying she'd hurt herself and I've come to get her.'

'Of course.' The receptionist smiled at him and got to her feet. 'I'll just buzz you through. She's waiting on the blue seats.'

Brann smirked. 'Ah, the blue seats. Still got them, yeah?' They were the place where anyone who was waiting to go home was sent to sit until someone showed up to get them. 'They've been there since nineteen oatcake.'

'Oh, really? Were you at school here?'

'About a hundred years ago.'

'I know the feeling.' The receptionist hit another security pad with a card on her lanyard and opened the door for him. 'Caitlin, your dad's here.'

Brann peered at his daughter, and she looked back with wide eyes and a pained expression. Her left leg was extended in front of her and she rubbed at her knee.

'What happened to you?' Brann asked.

'I think I sprained it when we were doing cross-country.'

Quite impressive that she even took part. He remembered bunking off cross-country, along with almost every other subject. After he left school, he'd started to enjoy sports, but on his own terms. Running wasn't his jam. He liked weights and the tug-of-war at the Highland Games was his big thing. Now he was captain and determined to get the team a win this year, but it was a big ask for a group of amateurs.

'Come on then,' he said. 'Let's get you home.' He lifted her bag from the seat beside her and helped her to her feet.

'I hope you're feeling better soon,' the receptionist said. 'The first aider reckons rest will do the trick. Nothing seems to be broken.'

'No worries.' Brann smiled at her. 'I'm sure she'll make a full recovery. Thanks for taking care of her. You're a breath of fresh air compared to the dragon of a receptionist we had when I was in school. I think she scared people off more than helped with anything. Have you been here long?'

'Three years now, but only part time.'

'Well, you do a great job. Thanks.'

'Oh, you're welcome.' The receptionist gave him a huge grin as he helped Caitlin through the door. 'That's nice of you to say so.'

'Not at all. You have a great day.'

'Seriously, Dad,' Caitlin muttered when they were out of earshot.

'What?'

'You didn't have to flirt with her. She's married.'

'I wasn't flirting. We were just chatting.'

'Yeah, right.'

Brann looked away and rolled his eyes at a bush beside the path. Heaven help Caitlin if he ever got a girlfriend. She was paranoid if he even spoke to another woman. Of course, he'd had other women since breaking up with her mum, otherwise it would have been a barren six years, but he'd never brought anyone home when Caitlin was around. He'd never introduced her to anyone, and she was a big part of the reason new relationships didn't last. The split had hit her hard, and she'd already suffered bouts of childhood depression. The last one had landed her in the hospital when she'd harmed herself. That had been a year ago, and she'd just finished counselling. Touch wood, she seemed to be on the mend, but Brann didn't want to rock the boat too much. Hence leaving a job so fast to get her. Hearing the words 'Caitlin's hurt herself' had a profound effect on him.

'Can you get into the van ok? Do you want me to lift you?'

She glanced around to see if anyone else was about. 'Ok.'

He opened the door, then lifted her in. She may be almost sixteen, but she was still his little girl, his baby. As a toddler, she'd had almost white-blonde hair that was so wild and curly it looked like she'd stuck her finger in a socket. Now it was darker, sandy coloured like his own. She tamed the frizz with conditioners and sprays – several bottles of which filled his bathroom for the days she was with him. 'You ok?' he said as she settled herself in the seat.

'Yeah. It's still a bit sore. I twisted it when I was running down the bank near the duck pond. I had to walk all the way back. That made it worse.'

'Do you want to go to the surgery and get it checked?'

'Na. If it gets bad, I will, but I'll try rest first.'

'Ok.' Brann nipped around to the driver's seat and jumped in. His house wasn't far from the school, neither was Kristalee's – his ex. But she didn't drive, so he was on duty whenever transport was needed.

'Where's Harrison?' Caitlin asked.

'Still working. We're putting in a new kitchen in a flat on The Back Wynd.'

'Are you going back to work after you drop me off? Or is he walking home?'

'I'll go back for a bit if you're ok, but I can stay if you prefer. I'll need to get Harrison later though.'

'Why? The Back Wynd is like five minutes away.'

'Yeah, but I need to load the tools in the van. I'm not leaving them at a property overnight.'

'Well, I guess I'll be ok on my own. Can I watch Netflix?'

'Yeah. As long as it's appropriate stuff.'

'Dad, I'm not six.'

'I know, just saying. Don't freak yourself out like that time you watched a horror movie on a sleepover and wouldn't sleep with the light off for months after.'

'Seriously. It was only like a few days, not months.'

He raised an eyebrow. 'If you say so, but it sure felt a lot longer than that.'

She leaned her head on the glass and let out a sigh. 'It's not fair, you know.'

'What's not fair?'

'All my friends go horse riding and most of them have their own horses. Why can't I do that?'

Where had that thought come from? The randomness of teenagers was hard to work out sometimes. 'Because it's expensive. And where would you keep a horse? Who would look after it?'

'I would, and there are loads of places around here to keep horses. Some of my friends ride at Ross McPherson's farm. He has horses and you can borrow them.'

'Who's Ross McPherson? Is he your boyfriend?'

'No, Dad! He's like some old guy.'

Brann tapped the steering wheel, wondering if the man was actually his age. Being thirty-seven was ancient in the eyes of a teenager.

'And my friend Aria got a retired racehorse for like nothing. They would have had it put down otherwise, so she pretty much got it for free.'

'Well, I'll have a think, but it's a big commitment, you know.'

'Obviously, I know.'

'Good, because you're still young and it's not something to take on lightly.' If only someone had warned him at seventeen what a commitment parenthood was. Not that he'd have listened. It wasn't like he and Kristalee had meant to have a child. They were stupid kids who spent too much time fooling around. After Harrison was born, they'd tried to stick together and be a family, hence having another kid, but there were times they'd had such big bust ups it felt like they'd never overcome them, and latterly they hadn't. By the time Harrison was fourteen and Caitlin was ten, their relationship was dead. Both Brann and Kristalee were wise enough to realise they wouldn't pick each other now. What they'd seen in each other as teenagers had passed and they couldn't keep things going. After years of arguing, it was kind of ironic they'd split amicably, though Brann wasn't sure that was ideal for Caitlin. She couldn't understand why they wouldn't get back together when they were still friends. She couldn't grasp the fact they were only friends because they were apart.

With Caitlin back home, Brann went to his desk and opened his laptop. May as well catch up with a bit of paperwork. He was getting used to this part of the job and just as well because the business was expanding since he'd built a fancy new house for the CEO of a local whisky distillery. He was making a name for himself in the town, and he'd taken on Harrison as his apprentice. Usually, he worked on the larger contracts with trustworthy friends in the trade, but eventually he wanted to employ them himself. He'd reached the stage he could afford to hire a couple of workers and pick some bigger contracts. His inbox was full and several requests for work had come in.

After he'd replied to his emails, he checked into the living room where Caitlin sat, flicking through TV channels, with her ankle resting on the coffee table. 'Are you ok for a few hours?'

'Yeah. I'll be fine.'

'Ok, baby girl. Take care and call me if your ankle gets worse. I'm not far away.' He leaned over the back of the sofa and kissed her. 'Love you.'

'Love you, Dad,' she said, still pointing the remote at the TV. He ruffled her hair and left.

When he got to the van, he sent a quick message to Kristalee to tell her Caitlin was resting at his house but seemed fine, then started the engine.

An unknown number rang, lighting up the van's console. 'Hello,' Brann answered.

'Ah, hello,' a rather pompous female voice spoke. 'It's Barbara.'

Brann frowned. 'Um... Barbara who?'

'Barbara Strachan. I work for the Glenvorneth Estate. We met yesterday at the boathouse, if you recall.'

'Oh, yeah.' How could he forget? Why was she calling him though? Had the killer-heeled 'heiress' decided they were a good fit after all?

'Ophelia has made a list of jobs to add to the boathouse project. Some of them are quite urgent and I'm hoping to get some rates from you and also some dates for when you could look around at the work.'

Ophelia had made the list. She must have changed her tune. 'What kind of jobs are we talking about?'

'So, there's repair works to the stables, plus Ophelia thinks extending them by converting the old steading would be a good plan. She's also written here, upgrades to the workers' cottages, restoration of the Factor's House, extension of the Boathouse. General repairs to the main house. Fencing needing replaced.'

Brann frowned. 'And you want me to do this work?'

'Absolutely.'

Brann felt a smirk growing. He couldn't help it. This was an opportunity not to be missed. Those jobs would keep him going for a while, and this would be another prestigious job to add to the company résumé, but did that mean working with Ophelia? Hopefully not.

'Now, when would be a good time for you to show me around? Let me get my diary.'

Brann drove towards the Back Wynd as he waited for her to find a suitable date. He'd heard Ophelia saying she was only there for a couple of weeks, which suited him fine. He couldn't start the work until after that anyway, so he wouldn't have to see her again. What could be better? Apart from seeing her again... Did he really want that? Bizarrely, he kind of did. Experience told him it was just as well she wouldn't be about then, because he had a bad habit of doing things that weren't good for him. He'd worked hard to get his life on track, and he didn't need a distraction like her causing him any trouble.

CHAPTER FOUR

Ophelia

'Ophelia! Ophelia!'

Ophelia ground her teeth as Jacinta's voice got louder and shriller. *Why is she calling me like I'm her servant?* Feigning deafness was an option, but it would be quicker and easier to find out what Jacinta wanted. Leaving the smart oak and leather desk strewn with papers, Ophelia got up and crossed the hallway to the drawing room. When she was a child, this room had been the height of taste and style. Her grandparents had maintained the period glamour effortlessly. Now the estate was crumbling.

'You called, milady.' She gave an ironic curtsey.

'Oh, don't be silly.' Jacinta laughed and flapped her hand. 'Are you going into town this afternoon?'

'I am, but not to the shops. It's Mother's birthday party.'

'Oh yes. Is it at the Cross Keys?'

'No. It's at the Loch View Hotel.'

'That pink place?'

'Yes.'

'I haven't been there for years. It wasn't that nice, as I recall.'

'It's been done up and by all accounts is very nice, so no need to stress.'

'Oh, I never stress.' Jacinta gave an airy little wave.

Ophelia barely held back a scoff. 'Is that all you wanted me for?'

'Francesca is running low on some horse supplies. Can you nip by the feed store and grab a bag of alfalfa?'

'You want me to go to the feed store, which is nowhere near where I'm going, and get a large bag of alfalfa in my new car when I'm wearing my party clothes?'

'Would you, darling? That would be so wonderful.'

'Oh sure, milady, your wish is my command.' She returned to the study, shaking her head.

It would be quite nice to tell Jacinta to stuff the alfalfa, but Ophelia knew better. She also happened to like the horses and hated the idea of them being short of food. Of course they wouldn't starve but still. If she wore her coat and borrowed her father's pickup, she could do it, though it would mean a detour into town.

The feed store was around the back of a furniture shop that Ophelia loved. It was named Wood 'n' Chic and always had the most amazing upcycled pieces in the windows. She'd bought things from there online for work and she really must call in soon, but she didn't have time today. She pulled into a concrete quad surrounded by industrial-looking buildings. The feed store was in one section next to a DIY-type outlet and a garage. The parking situation wasn't great and there weren't any free spaces except one right in front of the feed shop. How lucky was that?

She backed into it and jumped out. The store was busy, and she ignored the funny looks she was getting. Obviously she didn't usually shop dressed in a red floaty jumpsuit and high-heeled silver sandals. Her coat was a padded Joules that didn't match her outfit and made her look even more ridiculous.

'I'm heading to a party.' She tapped her card, feeling the need to explain.

'Somewhere nice, I hope,' the assistant said.

'The Loch View Hotel.'

'Lovely. Would you like someone to carry the alfalfa to your car?'

'Yes, please.'

Ophelia opened the boot, and the assistant lifted it in, giving her an odd look before returning to the shop. As she went to close the boot, her eyes drifted past the assistant to two men who were chatting on the pavement outside the DIY shop.

Oh hell no.

One of them was Brann Duthie. Even though he appeared immersed in his conversation, Ophelia knew he'd seen her. She could tell from the expression on his face.

Eyes elsewhere! But it was impossible. Something pulled her focus. He glanced her way and when his gaze met hers, a little smirk grew on his lips.

Jesus Christ.

She slammed the boot shut and her eyes settled on the post behind her car. It had a disabled parking sign on it, a little faded, but still there. *Crap.* She hadn't noticed it, but no doubt that assistant and Brann had made their own assumptions about her. *Oh god.* Time for a quick getaway. But before she'd got to the driver's door, a female voice called her name. Frowning, she checked where the sound had come from.

A woman with short salt and pepper hair locked a white Mercedes close to the back door of Wood 'n' Chic and waved to Ophelia. *Help.* It was the Countess of Dairvin, a second cousin of her father's, someone who couldn't be ignored.

'Hello.' Ophelia returned her wave. She tugged off her coat and tossed it onto the passenger's seat, still with half an eye on the countess. Could she get in and drive off now she'd acknowledged her?

Apparently not. The countess beckoned Ophelia by waving her white leather bag. With a deep breath, she made her way over, shivering and rubbing her arms. Without her coat, it was Baltic.

'Ophelia darling, wonderful to see you.' The countess mock kissed her on both cheeks, then patted her arm. 'You look exceptional, young lady. You always do, but you're absolutely shining today.'

'Oh... Thank you. I'm just on my way to my mother's birthday tea.'

'Lovely. I'm looking for some furniture. We're doing up the sunroom and I adore the pieces in this place.'

'Me too.'

'Terribly difficult to park in town these days, isn't it? I got this space just as someone was pulling out and I'm very glad because I detest public car parks. All this phoning numbers and using apps to pay. It's quite ridiculous.'

'Yes.' Ophelia glanced back at the pickup. She needed to get back and move it out of the space.

'I was talking to your father the other day. Wonderful news about you and James Charlton, the Duchan Fayre boy.'

'What?' Ophelia almost choked. 'I haven't even met him.'

'Oh…' The countess frowned. 'How odd.'

'My father's plan is a little archaic. I'm not a commodity he can marry off to the highest bidder.'

'No, that's very true, though James Charlton is a delightful man from what I've heard. But if you don't like him, there's always Rafe Harrington. Do you know him?'

Ophelia wracked her brain. 'I don't think so.'

'His father has a big business up here and Rafe has his own. He's a very wealthy and eligible young man these days, so I'm told.'

Did anyone ever talk about her as a wealthy and eligible young woman because of Timeless Butterfly Interiors? Or did all her eligibility come from being heiress to Glenvorneth?

'He has been married before,' the countess went on, 'which isn't ideal, but there are no children to complicate matters.'

Ophelia kept her face dead pan as years of training had taught her. The countess was blunt, but in some ways, she was right. Being the child of a blended family herself, Ophelia knew it wasn't always plain sailing, especially when she and her stepmother had such a personality clash.

'I'll bear that in mind,' she said. 'But I'm not here for long.'

'Pity. We were hoping to have you over one afternoon.'

'If I'm still here, I'd love to.'

'Wonderful. Now off you go, looks like someone's interested in your vehicle.'

'What?' Turning, she saw a man in a uniform pinning something to the front of the pickup. She hastened over. 'What are you doing?'

'Parking fine, madam. This is a disabled badge-holder space, and I don't see a badge on your vehicle.'

'I was literally just leaving, and I'm sorry, but I didn't see the sign. It's a little faded.' How cringe did she sound?

The man picked up his walkie-talkie. 'Consider this a warning.'

Ophelia jumped in the car and took off. In her rear-view mirror she saw Brann still talking to someone, only he looked like he was laughing. Had he reported her? Double cringe.

She muttered to herself as she drove out of town to the Loch View Hotel. Why hadn't she spotted the disabled sign? And that bloody builder. Why did he linger in her thoughts more than he should? And why was she always on the back foot every time she saw him? When she arrived at the hotel, she grabbed a short fur bolero and pulled it around her shoulders, ready to meet her mother's friends. Who were they these days? When her parents had been together, they'd all moved in the same set, but her mother was so independent she made friends all over, in cookery classes, the choir, through volunteer work. But Ophelia had never met any of them.

'Hello, darling.' Her mother greeted her with a kiss. 'Come and get a drink.'

'Happy birthday.' Ophelia handed over the gift card and scanned around the bar restaurant that was filled with women, mostly around her mother's age.

'Are you Ophelia?' a short woman with an asymmetrical bob asked.

'I am.'

'Your mother talks about you a lot. We're in the choir together. I hear you run Timeless Butterfly Interiors.'

'Um... Yes.'

'Your mother told me about it. I looked it up because I had no idea what it was. I see you have a shop now too.'

'Yes, I do.' She hired a manager and a retail team to run that, while she, Lucinda and two other designers oversaw the design part.

Edith pinged a glass, calling for them to go into the dining room. She was elegant and smart in a simple navy suit, with a large, handmade necklace. Her short hair was coloured a shiny chestnut shade. Ophelia half wondered why she'd never remarried, but didn't complain or dwell on the idea. Her father's second marriage had caused her quite enough issues. The other guests looked like some choice pages from a vintage *JD Williams'* catalogue, sipping their cocktails in gold lamé, velvet trousers and patent Mary-Janes.

Ophelia took a seat opposite her mother.

'Hello, I'm Nancy.' The woman beside her smiled, adjusting large glasses. 'You must be Ophelia. You look like your mother.'

Ophelia nodded in agreement. Edith glanced over at them somewhat contemplatively.

'Are you enjoying being back?' Nancy asked.

'Not really.' Ophelia wasn't sure what had made her tell the truth and not spout one of her well-rehearsed replies. Possibly because Nancy had a down-to-earth face and a trustworthy air. 'My father wants to marry me off to a rich man I've never even met.'

Nancy shook her head. 'Edith told me about that. It's quite appalling.'

'I honestly think he believes it's a good idea.'

'And do you?'

'Absolutely not. I want to choose for myself.' But every night when she closed her eyes, she imagined herself walking down the aisle with a faceless, very rich young man. It was definitely one way to save Glenvorneth.

Except that night when her eyelids fell shut, the man had a face, and it wasn't a stranger or someone resembling the photos she'd seen of James Charlton. It was Brann Duthie.

Bloody hell.

April

How had Ophelia ever thought two weeks would be enough time to sort of the Glenvorneth mess?

'It's fine,' Lucinda said, when Ophelia called her to relay the news that she was staying on for yet another week. 'We're coping perfectly well here.'

'I miss you all. Working from here isn't the same, but I need to be here. Even making a comprehensive list of everything that needs done is taking forever. Barbara is nice, but she's impatient and sometimes she doesn't see the bigger picture. She wants to start itty-bitty jobs here and there.'

'You've got more business sense than any of them, by the sound of things.'

'Nobody at Glenvorneth thinks that. They all think I'm stupid, except maybe Barbara. My father is still determined I should meet this James person. I'm getting sick of hearing about him.'

'You should meet him and at least make a proper judgement.'

'I suppose. But if I don't like him, I can see them still wanting me to marry him.'

'What if you do like him?'

'Oh golly, I don't even know. I mean, I can't just like him, then marry him. It'll take time one way or another.'

'That's true. And you're never one to rush into things.'

'Oh, Lucinda.' She sighed. 'I miss having you and my other friends around. I don't know anyone here.'

'What about your mum?'

'It's not the same. She's a busy woman and we don't really have a lot in common.'

'I think you should treat yourself. Get your hair or your nails done.'

'I'm not sure the salon here is any good.'

'Just get a style and blow dry to test it.'

'I suppose so. I could do with getting out of here for a bit. It's a big house, but it's so claustrophobic with Jacinta breathing down my neck.'

'Haven't you been riding?'

'Not yet. All my riding clothes have mysteriously disappeared. Jacinta has probably thrown them out. I've ordered some new jodhpurs and boots. Once they arrive, I'll take Conker out. Hopefully, the weather will be a bit better by then too. It's so grim just now.'

Taking Lucinda's advice, Ophelia booked herself into a local salon with a stylist called Hayley McBride. The local salon,

Cutting Edge, had a good name in the town and when Ophelia arrived, she checked in the window first. Seemed like a clean little place, with bright lights and lots of mirrors around the walls. She pushed open the door. A woman about her age with dark eyes and matching hair got to her feet from behind the reception desk and greeted her with a broad smile that put her instantly at ease.

Even before she spoke, Ophelia sensed this was someone she could like. Her face relaxed, and she returned the smile. The first genuine one she remembered having for weeks.

'Hello. Are you Ophelia Chattan-Blythe?'

'Yes.' She ran her fingers through her hair.

'If you just take a seat here, I'll get your jacket safely away and fetch a gown.'

'Thank you.' Ophelia smoothed her hands down her white jeans and put her feet on the footrest. These long boots were smart, but they nipped a bit. She stared at her reflection. The immaculate face she put on every morning stared back. Who was the real Ophelia and where was she hiding? A bizarre question maybe, but Ophelia often felt like this. Like she didn't really know herself, or that a part of her was missing and hadn't been discovered yet. But how could she change that, when she didn't know what to look for?

'Are you just visiting the town?' Hayley draped the gown over her.

'Kind of. My family live nearby and I'm visiting them for a while.'

Hayley started combing through her hair, and it calmed Ophelia. She allowed the stress of the past month to drift away. The salon bell rang and a woman with short, dark hair and glasses came in with a large bag. She chatted at the door with another stylist. Was the delivery person Nancy? The woman from her mum's birthday party? Before Ophelia could be sure, the woman turned and left. The stylist carried the bag towards the back of the salon. As she passed Hayley, she muttered, 'It's for you from the flower shop. You got a secret admirer?'

Ophelia caught Hayley's eye and saw the trace of a blush on her cheeks. This was intriguing.

'I don't know,' Hayley said.

'I think you should find out,' Ophelia said. 'It's not every day a girl gets sent flowers out of the blue. Not in my experience anyway.' No one had ever done anything remotely romantic for her. Her past boyfriends had all been so flat they'd have fit through a letterbox. Somewhere deep down she wished she could let go of the public front and do something more spontaneous – have some fun, some passion, and not just date the same type of man over and over.

'I should finish your hair first.'

'You've hardly started yet and I'm curious.'

'Well, ok.' Hayley put the comb away in her pouch and pulled open the bag. Inside was an enormous bouquet of roses and a card.

'Shall I read this?' The other stylist pulled it out.

'Seriously?' Hayley stared at her.

The other stylist handed it to her and smiled. Hayley read it and Ophelia watched her sucking on her lower lip, then smiling.

'Well?' Ophelia said. 'Do you know how invested I am in this?' It was so enjoyable compared to the tension in the house she'd had at home since her return.

Hayley giggled and passed her the card.

Ophelia read the note from someone called Oliver, who was clearly mad about Hayley.

'Wow. Sounds like you're onto a winner.' Ophelia handed the card to the other stylist, who read with her mouth open.

'Oliver? Isn't he that grumpy divorce lawyer guy you hate?' she said.

'The very same.'

'You hate him?' Ophelia watched her in the mirror. This was like being on the set of a soap opera.

'We used to not get on so well.'

'Oh my god,' the other stylist said. 'This is hilarious. Are you dating him?'

'Yep.'

'Good for you,' Ophelia said. 'And he's a divorce lawyer?'

'Yes, but I'm trying not to hold it against him.'

'Does he do prenups?'

'I don't know.' Hayley frowned at Ophelia in the mirror. 'I could ask him. Do you need one?'

'If my father has his way, then I might.' And she wasn't kidding.

Rupert and Jacinta had shown no let-up in their plan to introduce her to James Charlton, and perhaps she should go along with it for now. At least until she discovered what he was like. No point discarding him without even meeting him.

She arrived home later with beautifully styled hair, thanks to the wonderful Hayley, and almost dropped dead at the sight of a police car in the driveway. Was this something to do with Brann the builder? Had he finally reported her for speeding? But two months had passed since she'd had the run in with him. *How has time flown so fast?* And surely, he wouldn't have waited this long? If he had, she would seek him out and disembowel him. That would give the police good reason to come after her.

She headed inside and found a large policeman sitting in the drawing room, looking totally out of place, speaking to Jacinta and her father.

'Everything ok?' she asked, hoping she sounded casual.

'Fine,' Rupert said. 'We've been hearing about a couple of thefts in the neighbourhood. Some strange things have been going missing. A moped and a lawnmower.'

She raised an eyebrow, and a wicked thought crossed her mind, nudging her to suggest Brann was behind it, but she didn't. That was Jacinta-level of mean and she wouldn't stoop that low. 'Barbara mentioned the moped, but that was a while back, wasn't it?'

'We have reason to believe the thefts might be related, and they both took place near here. You should be vigilant,' the policeman said.

Ophelia nodded with an internal sigh of relief. Moped thefts were a lot less to worry about than being done for dangerous driving – even if she deserved it. Apparently, Brann hadn't reported her after all. But she'd quite happily run him over with that moped if it got him out of her thoughts. Why the hell did she keep thinking about him? It was beyond annoying.

CHAPTER FIVE

Brann

Brann took a swig of water from his steel bottle. 'It's so stuffy for April.'

'Yeah, and this fucking straw isn't helping,' Harrison muttered. 'It stinks.'

'Yeah, the idiots in charge of this place haven't got a scooby what they're doing. I don't get why we're to start here before repairing the damaged stables first. This'll take much longer. I told that Barbara woman, but she's so scatty.'

'Yeah, and the owner. Fuck my life. What does he look like? I know it's Scotland, and it's the countryside, but really? Who the hell wears plus-fours and that sort of get-up these days?'

'You're not wrong.'

Rupert Chattan-Blythe, as he'd introduced himself, may as well have been called Sir Pompous d'Aristocratic Twat. He seemed like a nice enough person but had so much bluster it was like he'd stepped straight out of a period drama. Brann's phone rang and his chest tightened. The school. Again. What was it this time?

'Hello.'

'Is that Mr Duthie?'

'Yes.'

'I'm just calling to say that Caitlin's taken a wee turn in class and isn't feeling very well.'

'Oh really? Does she need to go home?'

'She's been to the matron for a wee lie down and she's gone back to class for now, but I've said I'll call you and let you know, because if she's still feeling bad at lunchtime it might be better if you came for her.'

'Right, ok. Thanks. I'll call back at lunchtime and see how she is.'

'What's up?' Harrison asked as soon as Brann ended the call.

'Caitlin's not feeling well.' He frowned. 'Is something going on with her again that I don't know about?'

'Like what?'

'I dunno. That's the second time recently the school's called about her. The last time, she seemed better the minute we got home. She never mentioned her ankle again.' Hopefully, she wouldn't relapse and start self-harming again. Not when she'd seemed so much better.

'Who knows?' Harrison said. 'She's pals with lots of little rich girls who like ponies and places like this. She doesn't really fit in.'

'Hmm.' Brann slung his phone into the back pocket of his jeans. He knew exactly how that felt. He and Kristalee had stuck out like sore thumbs when they were at school. 'I need air. This building is making my skin crawl.' He left through the rickety door of the old steading. Some of the straw smelled like it had been there for a hundred years, which was maybe when this place was last used. It would take days to clear it before they even started on the building work. Such a waste of time and resources. He ripped off his t-shirt and threw it carelessly onto the ground, sure it was crawling with all sorts of bugs. The weather was warm, if not baking, but a creepy sensation was making him itch.

He grabbed an empty wheelbarrow and pushed it towards the door. It might be better to subcontract some people just to clear out the mess. He had better things to be doing. The news about Caitlin was unsettling, and a helplessness besieged him. What could he do? She hated him interfering, and it was her life, but he wanted her to be ok.

Before he returned inside, the sound of hooves on the track caught his attention. He spotted a chestnut horse on the path. Its rider was slim and elegant, wearing a lilac top and tight jodhpurs.

Oh shit.

It was her. The snooty heiress. Wasn't she supposed to be gone? *Get inside quick! Before she notices.* But he couldn't move quick enough.

'What are you doing here?' She narrowed her eyes, and he winced.

'Er... Working.'

'Working? Here?'

'Yeah.'

'Why?' She towered over him from atop her horse, eyeing him up and down, taking in every inch of his muscle, the celtic knot-work tattoo on his left bicep and his wide chest. Did she like what she saw? He was no stranger to exercise and was in good shape, but he still felt exposed, like she was x-raying him inch by inch. Why had he discarded his shirt? 'We agreed you weren't going to be working here.'

'I don't think we agreed on anything. You said we weren't a good fit.' He raised an eyebrow. 'But Barbara called and offered me work, so I assumed you'd changed your mind.'

The heiress slowly looked away. 'But why here? This area isn't a priority. If you're working, why aren't you at the fallen-in sta-bles?'

'I suggested that to Barbara. To be perfectly honest with you, this is a total waste of my time.'

'What do you mean?'

'She's got me cleaning up mess that's possibly been in there since the nineteen-fifties. I doubt that's what you want to be paying me for.'

'I shouldn't be paying you for anything because you're not even supposed to be here.'

'My contract says otherwise, your highness.'

'Don't call me that. It's rude.'

'Rude, am I? I'm not the one who parks in disabled parking spaces and drives like a bat out of hell, putting other road users in danger.'

She ground her teeth and seemed to be letting out a slow breath from her nose. 'Neither of them is what you think, ok? I didn't realise the fog was so bad, because I wasn't concentrating. I stupidly let someone get to me and made a bad decision. And I didn't notice the disabled badge on that parking place until I was about to leave... And then...' she groaned, glancing away. 'Of course it all sounds like a stupid excuse now and I don't expect you to believe me or let it drop, but I've said my piece, and that's that.'

For a moment, the sharpness in her irises dulled, and a hint of vulnerability flashed there, but she blinked it away.

'Who called you about this work?' Her gaze bored into him again. 'Barbara or my father?'

'Barbara.'

'I need to speak to her.'

'You do that. I've got to get back to shovelling shit.'

'Probably what you're best at,' she muttered. 'And for the love of god, it's not *that* hot.' Her eyes lingered on his chest again and her cheeks went slightly pink. 'Put some clothes on.' She nudged her horse and rode off back down the path. The horse swished its tail with a dismissive flourish.

'You won't believe this.' Brann marched back inside.

'What?' Harrison frowned at him.

'Do you remember that posh heiress who thought we were car thieves? She's here. She's just had a moan at me. Cow.'

'What did she say?'

'That I'm not that hot.'

He snorted.

'Ok, not that exactly. But she demanded I put some clothes on... Christ.' Brann dug his hands into his hair.

'I bet she leads a sheltered life. She's probably never seen a topless man before.' Harrison smirked.

'Well, she was definitely having a good look.'

'Oh please,' he groaned. 'That's gross.'

'Why?'

'I don't want to think about some posh bint leching over my dad.'

'Don't call her a bint.'

'Seriously, why not? You called her a cow.'

'Suits her better.'

'What's her name, anyway? Wasn't it something that sounded like "awful"?'

'Ophelia. What a name... eh? O-feely-her-arse.'

'Dad! That is much worse than calling her a bint. And please tell me you don't want to do that.'

'Course not. Now shut up and let's get back to the shit.'

They worked on until they couldn't take much more of the smell, but at least it distracted him from thoughts about princess Ophelia.

Staring around, Brann sighed. 'It doesn't look like we've done anything. This place is such a frigging mess.'

'Can we stop for lunch?' Harrison said. 'I need out of here for a bit.'

'Yeah. Let's get the food and we'll sit out.' Brann got their lunches from the van and they slumped down next to the paddock fence. A woman was in a lower field carrying a bucket. She had extremely long fair hair, pleated down past her bottom. At least it wasn't Ophelia, though Brann was certain he hadn't heard the last from her. Just the thought of her wound him up and made his blood overheat, though he wasn't sure if it was irritation causing it, or something completely different.

He glanced up. 'Uh-oh.' Footsteps on the path and they were getting louder. 'I hope that's not her again.'

'Bet it is.' Harrison stuffed the remainder of his roll into his mouth. 'She'll be coming for another ogle.'

'Shut up.' Brann jumped to his feet, grabbed his shirt from the ground and pulled it on. Even if it was infested with fleas, it was better than facing her half naked.

Gravel crunched under riding boots, and Brann looked up to see Ophelia marching towards him. She stopped, eyed him up and down and ran her fingertips up her riding crop.

'Ditched the antlers for a new weapon?' he asked.

'Oh, very funny.' She flicked her long, elegant ponytail over her shoulder, and blinked several times like she was trying to clear an image from her mind. Cow or not, she was bloody beautiful. She scanned around. 'What exactly are you doing here?'

'Nothing.'

'Nothing?' She frowned at him. 'Then why—'

'It's my lunch break.' He winked at her.

She gave him the smallest of smiles, before it faded and she smoothed back some stray hairs, like she was gathering her thoughts. Or perhaps she was annoyed with herself for daring to send a smile his way. 'There was something on the news about that.' Her eyes met his again.

'What? My lunch break was on the news?'

'It was about how much time and money the public waste paying builders to sit about drinking tea and eating donuts.' Her smile returned, only this time her pupils flashed with a wicked glint.

He barked out a laugh. 'If you think I'm shovelling all that shit without my tea and donuts, then you've got another think coming.'

She smirked and sailed past him through the open door. 'Oh Jesus.' She pulled back.

'Yeah, not pleasant, is it?' Brann said. 'Fancy a sticky bun to take the taste away?'

She rolled her eyes. 'No, thank you.'

'So, are you here for a particular reason, or to check if you and I are a better fit these days?' He linked his gaze with her. A crackle of electricity sparked inside him. She maintained eye contact, but her expression faltered ever so slightly. She was feeling this too. It was obvious. The tension thrummed, and neither looked away.

She took a step closer. 'Dream on. I'm here to make sure the work is done efficiently, that's all.'

'Oh yeah? Well, if you think that means me working through lunch, forget it.'

'Not what I meant, but you can pack up here.'

'You're firing me? Because I have a contract and I haven't breached it, so I'd like to know on what grounds.'

'I'm not firing you, just moving you on. This isn't the job I want you doing right now.'

'And what would you prefer me to do?'

She raised an eyebrow as if contemplating something, and he silently dared her to say what was going through her mind. 'I have a whole list.'

'I bet you do.'

She narrowed her eyes. 'Are you always like this?'

'Like what?'

'Oh, never mind.' She shook her head. 'Just follow me.'

'Yes, your highness, though why should I do what you say? Have you got proof you're in charge now? How do I know you're not messing with me, so I get sacked?'

'I guess you'll have to trust me, won't you?'

'I'm not sure that'll do. After all, when I say I'm Brann Duthie, you think I'm some car-stealing criminal. Now it's your turn; show me the proof. In fact, why not go the whole hog and get a DNA test? Come back and speak to me when the results are in.'

'Oh, how amusing you are.' Ophelia flicked her crop against the wall. 'But none of that will be happening. You're free to go and ask my father. I'll even come with you if you want someone to hold your hand.'

'I don't want you holding anything of mine.'

She raised an eyebrow and her lips twitched. *Fuck's sake.* She obviously knew he was lying. Of course he was. He wouldn't object to her putting her hands anywhere she wanted. Her expression said she got the memo loud and clear.

'Don't worry, there's no danger of that.'

He shook his head, biting his tongue. 'So, what do you want me to do? Or are you going to toddle back to daddy first and tell him what a bad man I am? Maybe you'll get me sacked before my next tea break.'

'I'm perfectly capable of doing that myself.' Her eyes ran him over from top to bottom.

'I don't doubt that.'

'Come with me and you'll see where I want you to start.' She beckoned him.

'Ladies first.' He smirked. 'I'll follow like a good boy.'

'Indeed.' She glanced over at Harrison, who stood next to the fence, gaping. Brann cringed and half closed his eyes. Hopefully Harrison hadn't heard any of the barely disguised innuendo.

'So, where are we going?'

'I'll show you where I need you to concentrate your skills.'

'With pleasure.'

She stared at him, and her eyes flashed. 'I'm talking about the damaged stables.'

'Me too.'

'Well, you can start there ASAP. That's the priority. But you and I will need a proper meeting at some point to discuss the work schedule and timeline.'

'I can't wait.'

'Oh, me neither. It'll be the highlight of my year.' She led the way to the stable, which was a short walk from the steading building they'd wasted the morning on. 'It's fairly self-explanatory what needs to be done. In fact, I'm sure you understand it better than I do.'

'Yeah. I know what to do.'

'Right. Well, I'll leave you to it. That's quite enough fun for one day. Just let me check my diary for when we can meet. Can't do tomorrow. Got a date.'

'Lucky you. Lucky man,' he added with an ironic lift of his brows.

She threw him a withering glance. 'Wednesday morning looks clear. Does that suit you?'

'Sure. Wouldn't miss it for the world.'

'Got yourself a date then.'

'And here was me thinking I'd dodged that bullet.'

'Oh, don't worry, you have.' She left with a flick of her ponytail.

Brann stared after her.

'Oh my fucking god.' Harrison craned his neck to check she'd gone as he approached. 'What the hell was that all about?'

'Search me.'

'Ha! She totally fancies you.'

'Shut it.'

'Yeah. Cause you fancy her too.'

'No, I don't.'

Harrison laughed. 'It's so bloody obvious. She wants to get down and dirty with you in the hay.'

'I said shut it.' But he grinned because Harrison was right. 'She's so maddening.' Brann balled his fists. 'My god, I'd like to...'

'Smack her with that crop?' Harrison suggested.

Brann snorted.

With all the unresolved sexual tension building inside him, he couldn't focus. But Christ, he had to let his mind be free of her. This was a job. It could potentially be a big job, one that could build the company's reputation. He mustn't blow this opportunity chasing some fantasy woman he enjoyed a bit of verbal sparring with. His seventeen-year-old self wouldn't think twice about fooling around with her, but twenty years of experience had taught him a few things. Things he had a funny feeling he might have difficulty remembering when Ophelia was around.

CHAPTER SIX

Ophelia

Ophelia stood by the window in her room, watching Brann speaking to her father in the gravelled front driveway. What the hell were they talking about? Hopefully Brann wasn't actually asking her father if she had permission to be dishing out orders, because she wasn't entirely sure she did. Barbara seemed to think she did, but was her father onboard with any of it?

Brann laughed and ran his hands through his hair before heading to his van. What was it about him that made energy ping around her body like manic flies bouncing off walls? *Just count to ten.* She had to focus. Today was the day she was meeting James Charlton, and she couldn't let thoughts of Brann get in the way. Whenever she was near him, she emerged from the cocoon of her normal life and let herself go. All the stuff they'd said to each other the previous day. It had felt a bit like arguing, but it wasn't. Was it banter or flirting? She'd never done either before. Not like that anyway.

Rupert had arranged the meeting with James. That was her 'date'. Wouldn't it be amazing if he was built like Brann and induced the same sensations in her? Why did that seem unlikely in the extreme? And yet she was never attracted to men like Brann... Never. Until now. Now, she couldn't keep him out of her head and every particle in her body was urging her to go down to him and do what she had to do. Which was what? Kiss Brann? Strip Brann? Strip herself? Get close to Brann? Have hot sex with Brann? All of the above really, which brought her back to just how utterly ridiculous this was.

Must stop. Must stop. Must stop.

She played the words in her head like a mantra as she moved away from the window and sat down at her dressing table. She had a burning desire to tell someone and maybe get advice, but at the same time she couldn't confess this to anyone. It was a guilty little secret she wouldn't dare share. What would people make of it? She tried to imagine some of her friends' reactions. They'd be shocked and tell her to keep a lid on it. Her friend, Florence, would laugh herself silly; they'd always joked about how they didn't understand women going for these muscly types. Florence was now engaged to a city banker with a perfectly average physique. Ophelia had always thought she'd go for the same type... Until she started drooling over the builder.

And what about her colleagues and employees at Timeless Butterfly Interiors? They wouldn't believe their totally together boss had fallen apart so thoroughly. She had to channel some of her professionalism. And she could.

'Yes. I can.'

She fixed on her smile and went downstairs to help Jacinta make a buffet lunch for when James arrived.

On the stairs she stopped, gazing around at the portraits. Her eyes landed on the one of her grandparents, painted just a couple of years before they died. It was so realistic she almost felt they could dust themselves down and step out. *I wish they would.* If only she could talk to them now. What would they advise? Would they expect her to marry James for his money? Her grandmother had told her she'd married because of her parent's wishes, but it had turned out to be perfect for her. *Could that happen for me?* She touched her hand to the frame, taking a deep breath to stall the sadness bubbling inside her, then carried on to the kitchen.

Jacinta wiped her brow as Ophelia entered. 'Cooking is not my scene. I wish we could get rid of Dagmar and get the cook back.'

'No, we need to keep Dagmar. She's been loyal to us, and she's always been so dedicated. We were chatting about the stable upgrades, and she has lots of great ideas.'

'Well, I'm not sure we can keep her on. Money should be spent wisely.'

'I agree.' Ophelia opened the fridge door. 'And we're managing with the cooking, so we'll keep Dagmar.'

'But she's such an oddity.'

'That's not very nice. She's just quiet.'

'I'm sure she only likes working here so she can practise for all the competitions she enters.'

'Well, at least she wins.' Ophelia and Dagmar were close in ages and Dagmar was unbeatable in everything, every year, and always had been.

'Oh gosh, yes. She wins everything, doesn't she? Including the Who Looks Most Like Their Horse competition.'

'Seriously, no.' Ophelia shook her head. 'That's a horrible thing to say. She's very pretty and looks nothing like a horse. Even if she did, it's not ok to badmouth her.'

'I hope Francesca is ready.' Jacinta peered into the hallway, ignoring Ophelia. 'The taxi will be here soon. Which reminds me, I need to ask the driver if he can drop her in Glenbriar on Thursday for the musical theatre club. I can't take her as I've got a massage therapy booked for the same time.'

'Such bad planning,' Ophelia muttered. And how was Jacinta paying for all this stuff?

'Here's the taxi.' Jacinta peered out the window. 'Francesca! Where is she?'

Jacinta ran out to catch the driver. Francesca strolled in wearing the tartan skirt and blazer all the Kinroy Academy girls wore and shoved some books from the kitchen table into her schoolbag. Ophelia had attended the same school what seemed like a long time ago, though she was only twenty-eight.

'I hope you've got some good subjects today,' she said.

'Not really.' Francesca flicked her long hair. 'History is a drag last period.'

Jacinta returned. 'Hurry up. The driver is waiting. He'll drop you off in Glenbriar on Thursday. You remember where to go when you get there?'

'Well, sure, Mum. I'm fifteen, not five.'

'Indeed. Now, hurry up.'

Francesca opened her bag and put in another book.

'I wonder if we should put together something of an action plan for how best to approach James,' Jacinta said. 'Where's Rupert got to? He should be part of this. And get a move on, Francesca.'

'An action plan?' Ophelia shook her head and laid out some slices of bread. Francesca sniggered as Jacinta bustled into the pantry. 'You can laugh now,' Ophelia said, 'but in a few years, don't be surprised if the same thing happens to you. And if I don't like James, they might even save him for you.'

'Ew, no thanks. He's like far too old for me.'

'He's the same age as me. Only thirteen years older than you. That's about the same as Father and your mum.'

'Oh my god, that is so gross.' Francesca slung her bag over her shoulder and headed for the taxi, looking like she might throw up.

Ophelia zoned out to Jacinta's master plan. She was going along with this for now, but on her own terms – not theirs.

'Remember, we're not forcing you to like him.' Rupert patted her on the back later that day as they waited for James to show up. 'But I've heard so many good things about him. Give him a chance.'

'You know I will, father, but let me do this myself.' Ophelia checked the time. She had so much she could be doing.

'We will, but we can't completely ignore him.'

Perhaps James Charlton would take one look at the mad bunch that was the Chattan-Blythe family and run straight home.

She'd built him up in her mind to be charming, maybe a bit flashy and completely self-assured. The photo she'd seen of him on the Duchan Fayre website was too generic to make much of a judgement from, but he appeared well-groomed and handsome in that businessperson kind of way she was so used to. She'd dated men like that in Edinburgh, though none of the dates had gone far. They just didn't click. Where was the fire?

As James crossed the threshold, Ophelia sized him up. He shook her father's hand with a brief smile, then turned to her and met her eyes. He was tall, dark-haired, and not bad looking. His expression was one of easy charm, but Ophelia didn't feel moved at all. He was yet another Mr Nice Guy she didn't see herself ever falling for. Still, he didn't seem threatening either, which was definitely a plus.

'This is my daughter, Ophelia.' Rupert ushered her forward, and she gritted her teeth at being moved around like a doll.

'Nice to meet you.' Ophelia held out her hand.

James shook it somewhat stiffly, his palm very warm. 'And you.' He turned his attention back to Rupert directly. 'My parents are very keen to meet you as well. Perhaps you'd consider dining with them?'

Ophelia frowned slightly. His voice was low and gentle, but his words had a rehearsed air about them.

'Of course. We would love that. Wouldn't we, dear?'

'Absolutely.' Jacinta beamed at James. 'They sound very much like our kind of people.'

James caught Ophelia's eye, and he gave her a little smile, almost like he was apologising. Was he in the same boat? Had his parents sent him here to 'court' her?

'Why don't we get lunch?' Ophelia fiddled with the gem on her silver tennis bracelet.

'Sounds good to me,' James said.

'Capital plan.' Rupert clapped his hands.

Ophelia led the way to the dining room, Rupert and James followed. Jacinta was in full flow, telling James about the latest curtain fabric she'd found. Ophelia glanced back. His face was a picture. The poor man.

'It's a buffet.' Ophelia opened the dining-room door. 'We weren't sure what you'd like.'

'I'm sure it's excellent, thank you.'

Although Jacinta's subjects for conversation were terrible, at least she kept the chat flowing, which was something.

'We should take a walk around the estate after lunch,' Rupert said.

'Um... right.' James's eyes strayed to the grandfather clock in the corner. 'That sounds nice.' He couldn't have sounded more unenthusiastic if he tried.

Rupert got to his feet. 'Come on, Ophelia. You can show James everything he needs to see.'

She pulled out her best smile, containing every urge to make a smart remark. 'Do you play polo?' she asked James as they left via the main door.

'Er, no.'

'It's one of my favourite sports, though I don't do it as much as I like anymore.'

'I'm more of a golf man.'

'Golf, hmm. I've never tried that.'

Rupert beamed as though this conversation was a proposal. Ophelia's insides squirmed. She couldn't imagine herself being married to this man. He did absolutely nothing for her. Pleasant, yes, but she didn't feel the slightest thing.

'I'm sorry about this,' James said quietly to Ophelia as they strolled along the path by the horse paddocks.

'About what?'

'Us being thrown together like this. It's so fake and awkward.'

She smiled and gave his arm a little pat. 'You're not wrong.'

'Tell us about your role at Duchan Fayre.' Jacinta sped up to butt in, and Ophelia ground her teeth.

'I'm one of the executive managers, along with my parents,' James said. 'They built it up from scratch. It's worked out well. We found our lane and stuck to it.'

'I'd say you've nailed it,' Ophelia said.

'Much like you have with Timeless Butterfly Interiors. It's wonderful.'

She blinked and opened her mouth. He knew about her business? That meant he'd done his research. Wow. It was something she rarely talked about when she was at Glenvorneth. Mainly because no one here cared, or they got annoyed when she mentioned it, like they didn't think she should tout her business out of the workplace. 'Thank you.'

'I love Duchan Fayre,' Jacinta interrupted. 'I'm probably one of your best customers.'

Ophelia ground her teeth. Typical. Jacinta would adore Timeless Butterfly Interiors if anyone other than Ophelia owned it.

'I could arrange a tour for you if you like?' James turned his attention to Jacinta.

'Oh, I would,'

'I wonder if it would spoil the magic for me,' Ophelia said. 'If I saw behind the scenes.'

He smiled, and actually he was rather cute. 'Maybe it would enhance the magic.'

Rupert grinned from ear to ear. Would he and Jacinta just go away? Their presence was making this so difficult. Her constant interruptions were annoying and his manic smiling at every little exchange made him look insane.

'The stables are up here.' Rupert pointed up the hill. 'They're a bit of a mess. We've got some people in fixing them.'

'Yes, let's not go that way.' Ophelia didn't care if James saw the stables in that state, but she didn't want to risk seeing Brann.

'Oh, come on.' Rupert marched ahead. 'We must go this way so I can explain the ideas for the steading.'

'But...'

He was already halfway up the path and James was following with Jacinta, though he seemed more worried about getting mud on his shoes than anything else.

The closer they got, the more Ophelia's senses tingled. Wooden planks clattered and the scent of sawdust wafted up her nose. All of it pointed to Brann. He was there somewhere. Just out of sight.

As they rounded a bend, she spotted his van. Beside it, his sidekick was sawing at a workbench. The brotherly resemblance struck her again. Brann had got the majority of the rugged sexiness. His brother was good-looking too but was obviously younger and a bit more boy-band than swarthy warrior.

What the hell was she doing?

Fantasising about him – again!

It was genuinely impossible to get him out of her mind. Was she even trying? Having him there filled a space where before there was nothing. But she desired something there. And now she'd seen Brann, it seemed like the space was made to fit him.

How crazy am I?

She barely knew him. But that didn't matter. It wasn't knowl-edge of him she wanted – well, only in the biblical sense. She was so hot for him it was insane. Properly insane because she didn't even like him. Did she?

'Ophelia,' Rupert said. 'What do you think?'

'What?' She'd missed the conversation, almost forgotten they were there, in fact.

'I thought I could ask the builder if he could put on those little wooden eaves like they have around the market stalls at Duchan Fayre. It's a small thing, but I think they're great.' He patted James on the arm and Ophelia cringed. His sucking up was hideous.

'Yeah, sure.'

'Let's go ask him now.'

'What?'

Rupert headed straight towards the stables. Brann's sidekick must have seen them coming because he'd disappeared inside the van and the doors were shut. Sensible.

Ophelia hung back. Maybe she could hide too.

But too late. Brann appeared, carrying a large plank. His tight black t-shirt showed every muscle on his chest. His celtic-knot tattoo just showed on his bicep at the edge of his sleeve.

Too hot for words.

Ophelia loosened her neckline and looked away as Rupert approached him.

'Hello-hello,' he said. 'This looks smashing.'

'Morning,' Brann said, and Ophelia couldn't prevent her focus from snapping back to him. He was looking at her too. Those eyes inviting her to do all sorts of things she shouldn't even be thinking about.

'This is James Charlton, an executive manager at Duchan Fayre.'

'Hi.' Brann smiled, adjusting his focus, still holding the plank of wood.

'I think you've met my wife, Jacinta, and my daughter, Ophelia, already. Haven't you?'

Brann's gaze flicked straight past Jacinta and back to Ophelia. His lips twitched. 'Yeah. We've met.'

'We were just passing,' she said. 'You're very busy and we don't want to keep you, do we, Father? Time's money after all.'

'Indeed.' Rupert winked at James, who was fiddling with the cuff of his suit jacket. How out of place did he look? This must be so torturous for him. 'So, Brann. We were wondering if you could add on those wonderful fancy eaves they have around the market stalls at Duchan Fayre. I think they'd look marvellous on this place.'

Ophelia clenched her jaw, willing herself anywhere but here.

'I'm sure I could, if that's what you want. Get some pictures and add it to the job list.'

'Ophelia will sort that.' Rupert waved an airy hand at her.

No, I won't. She wasn't paying for frivolous nonsense, and the designs she'd done for this place were equal to Duchan Fayre any day.

'It might mean altering some of the other designs though,' Brann said. 'Which would be a shame, cause they're really cool.'

A little tremor coursed through Ophelia. He probably didn't know the designs were hers. But he liked them, and that sent a gush of pride through her bloodstream.

'I'll leave Ophelia to sort it.' Rupert tapped James and pointed to the door. 'Let's carry on up.'

Jacinta gave them a sour look before going too. Brann moved closer to Ophelia before she headed off. He swung the plank around so she couldn't go past.

She glared at him. 'What are you—'

'Is that your date?' He waggled his eyebrows. 'Very you.'

'What would you know about it? Honestly, you're so rude.'

'Only for you, Princess.'

'Don't you call me that.' But her insides had woken with a bolt of electricity. She pushed the plank and Brann laughed, moving it out of her way. She caught up with Jacinta, Rupert and James, but her head was back with Brann. As they carried on walking, the buzz inside her grew so loud she was on the verge of exploding. If she didn't do something, she'd break. She couldn't keep up this public face without getting rid of some of the tension.

'Father, I just remembered something else I have to talk to the builder about. I'll be a few minutes. I'll catch you up.'

'The builder?' Jacinta said in a scandalised voice. 'Why on earth do you need to talk to him precisely now?'

'Don't be long,' Rupert said.

Ophelia ignored them and marched, almost ran, back to the stables. Brann's brother was back at his workbench, and he froze when he saw her. She gave him a brief smile, then headed for the stable door.

Before she got in, she heard singing... Like an actual proper voice and for a moment she thought the radio was on. Was that Brann?

She entered, and he turned like he was about to speak. The singing had stopped. Presumably he thought she was his brother. He stared at her.

'Well, hello again. What do you want this time?'

She marched straight up to him, put her hand on his chest, and pushed him against the wall. He held up his hands and didn't resist, though he could throw her off in a second if he wanted. A smirk creased his face.

'Nice singing.' She fixed him in her gaze. The heat of his body scorched her palm as she pressed it into his hard wall of muscle.

'You need to pin me here to tell me that? Do you want me to shut up or sing for my supper?'

'Neither. I need you...' She took a deep breath. 'To back off and get out of my head.'

He burst out laughing. 'You're telling me to back off? When you're the one doing this? And how the hell do you expect me to get out of your head? I can't help it if you can't stop thinking about me.'

'Are you sure it's not you thinking about me?'

'So what if I am?'

'I knew it.'

He gave a little shrug. 'So we're both thinking about each other then. Feel free to invade my mind whenever you like. I could do with the company, and I have a vivid imagination.' His eyes raked her over.

She pulled even closer, so close she could kiss him. His lips were slightly parted, like they were ready to return the favour. How reckless would that be? But it was what she wanted. An untameable desire like nothing she'd ever experienced before fired up inside her, pushing her forward. 'You can keep on imagining because that's all you'll ever get.'

'Oh really?' His palm landed on her hip and drew her towards him. She inhaled sharply. 'Tell me why I can't have what I want when I know you want it too.'

She stared at him, and he stared back. Her breathing was heavy, and so was his. His chest rose and fell noticeably. His hand was fastened to her hips. At the same moment, they leaned into each other. Ophelia clamped her hand around his neck and their lips met. Burning heat ripped through her. She opened her mouth to him, moaning and embracing the fire as their tongues touched. Never had such unbridled lust overpowered her like this.

She pulled back. 'Don't ever do that again!'

'Don't worry. I won't.' His eyes didn't leave hers and he gave a little smirk.

She wrenched him forward and kissed him again. He put his other arm around her and pulled her close. The heat of his mouth and the strength of his body set her on fire; she wanted him. All of him. Here and now.

Bloody hell! She couldn't do that.

This was bad enough.

'I mean it,' she breathed onto his lips. 'Never again. That's it. You understand?'

He laughed. 'Whatever you say.'

With a huge effort, she broke free of his hold and stalked off, almost running to catch up with the others.

I'm not stupid. I know how insane that was. But the buzzing energy inside her had exploded.

She controlled her breathing as she walked, fanning her face and loosening the neck of her shirt. Yes, that had been stupid, but also completely wonderful. She'd done something spontaneous and passionate. Her insides were gooey, and her head was light. How insanely good did it feel?

She needed to keep riding that wave because when reality kicked in and she analysed what she'd just done, it would hurt. Levels of awkward from here on in would be off the charts.

CHAPTER SEVEN

Brann

Brann leaned on the frame of his front door. Somewhere upstairs, Caitlin was shuffling about, hopefully getting ready for school. On the doorstep stood Kristalee talking – with her hands as much as her mouth like she always did. Rings and bracelets glinted in the early morning light as she gesticulated.

'I'm not really used to getting up for work this early,' she said with a yawn. A new job hadn't subdued her unique dress sense. She'd always liked goth style but was also a fan of floral prints, making for a combination all her own. Her black eye pencilling and dark lippy, plus the shock of burgundy hair and thick Doc Martens, were somewhat at odds with her blue and white flowery dress. When they'd been together at school, she'd been black-haired with make-up to rival Alice Cooper; the new look was almost soft in comparison, but she still looked like a rockstar.

'Listen.' He glanced upstairs, then stepped outside and closed the door. His house was a semi in Rowan Way, a street that had long had a bad rap in Glenbriar. But he kept his place nice and, thanks to his building skills, it had a neat front porch and a conservatory at the back, which made it stand out from the others in the street. 'We need to talk about Caitlin. Is everything ok with her?'

'Aw man.' Kristalee let out a sigh. 'I really don't know. She won't talk to me. She says everything's fine, but then she has these mystery illnesses and injuries.'

'Has she mentioned horse riding to you?'

'Yeah. But it's not like we can afford that. No way are we getting a horse.'

'I agree we shouldn't just go out and get her a horse, but what if we try and get her riding lessons or something? She mentioned a farm where some of her friends go.'

'Ross McPherson's place?'

'Do you know it?'

'I know where it is, but I've never been there. It's out in the sticks. You'd have to take her because I couldn't walk her there and it's not on a bus route.'

'I wouldn't mind that.'

'Well, fine. Let's see how much it costs. I've persuaded her to join a musical theatre club too. She likes singing and dancing.'

Brann nodded with a little grin. Both he and Kristalee enjoyed singing and dancing too, and could both play the guitar. It was what had brought them together at school. But that shared love had got them into all sorts of trouble, and the big ideas they'd had about starting a band had ended with a teenage pregnancy.

Hopefully Caitlin had more sense. She'd definitely had more parental input than he or Kristalee ever had.

'Let's hope that works out. When is it?'

'Tomorrow after school.'

'I can pay for half. How much?'

'I'll message you. I can't remember, but it's not that expensive.' She checked her phone. 'I better go.'

Brann opened the door and Kristalee shouted upstairs. 'See you later, Caitlin.'

'Bye, Mum.'

'And have a good day, Harrison,' she called into the kitchen.

He came into the hall and hugged her. 'See ya, Mum. Enjoy the new job.'

'I'm sure I will.' She waved goodbye and headed off.

Brann checked the time. 'Caitlin! Have you found whatever it was you're looking for? I need to leave.'

'Yeah, just coming.'

'Hurry up, will you? I've got a meeting this morning.' He rolled his neck to dispel the tension building in his body. 'Meeting' might be an understatement. After yesterday's encounter with Ophelia, who could tell what to expect? This was a dangerous road. One he'd thought he'd left behind long ago. Some words came to him – words an old boss had said years ago when he'd got his first apprenticeship.

The problem with having kids so young is that you miss part of your own growing up. The good thing is, by the time they're grown, you're still young enough to have fun and regain some of your youth.

Was that what he was doing? He wasn't sure he wanted to regain his youth. What he did want was something raw and more basic than that. Kissing Ophelia yesterday might have been a jackass move, but she'd started it. A proper, repressed lady after a bit of rough. And fuck it, he'd enjoyed every second. Possibly a bit too much, and it had satisfied a carnal ache inside. Something that had been growing for a long time. Except the satisfaction only seemed to last as long as she was there. Now the ache was back, making him fidgety and uncomfortable. He wanted to see her but at the same time didn't.

The worst of it was, he didn't even get it. Why her? She was a posh princess from another world, not someone he'd be attracted to in a million years.

Ridiculous.

'Ready.' Caitlin appeared at the bottom of the stairs. 'But you don't need to wait. I can walk to school myself.'

'I know that,' Brann said. 'But I want to make sure everyone is out, and we're all locked up.' He opened the door for her, and Harrison grabbed his backpack and left too. Getting them out of the house in the morning hadn't got much easier over the years, though at least neither of them was having a tantrum or refusing to put on their shoes. Brann flicked off the lights and locked the door.

'Have a good day.' He gave Caitlin a hug and kissed her forehead. 'You're at Mum's later, so I'll see you on Saturday.'

'Bye, Dad. Bye, Harrison.'

'Bye-bye.' Brann jumped into the van, and Harrison followed.

'Do I have to come to this meeting?' Harrison asked.

'No. You can keep going with the stables.'

'Thank Christ for that. Those Chattan-Blythe people are weird. That Ophelia is scary, and Rupert is like the toad from *Wind in the Willows*, and that film totally freaked me out.'

Brann laughed. 'Yeah, he is a bit like that.'

'You better watch out if you're meeting with Ophelia alone.'

'Why?'

Harrison raised an eyebrow. 'Because she totally has the horn for you. And you never actually told me what she wanted when she went into the stables to speak to you. What were you two up to?'

Harrison was clearly trying to provoke a reaction, but did he realise how close to the truth he was?

'Business.' Brann kept his eyes on the road. 'Now, shut up about her or you can go to the meeting with her instead.'

'She wouldn't like that. She only likes you.'

'I said shut up.' But he couldn't help a little grin.

When they arrived at the stables, a note had been pinned to the wall inside.

Venue for meeting has changed. Meet me at the workers' cottages at ten. Ophelia.

Harrison ripped it off the wall and smirked. 'I'm guessing those cottages have a nice bed for you to get cosy in.'

'Oh, ha-ha.' Brann looked away and swallowed. What if he was right? Ophelia would be an idiot to suggest that though, especially when she'd left a note that anyone could see. Or was that part of a double bluff?

Isn't my life complicated enough?

He collected what they needed for the morning and set Harrison some jobs. He was a good lad who worked hard, and Brann trusted him to work sensibly. At ten to ten, Brann left him and wandered down the path to where he remembered Barbara showing him the cottages when she'd given him the initial tour. The estate was large and rambling, with paths crisscrossing it and wooded areas dividing it from other sections. Far too big for one family though.

A bright red BMW was parked outside a row of little stone cottages. They were probably tiny inside, but their location was stunning, with tall trees to the back and pretty gardens to the front, overlooking a field and the wider countryside.

Brann had reached the gate of the first cottage when the door of the BMW opened and Ophelia got out. Brann's insides flipped over. It was like watching a celebrity exit a limo. Her long legs in their tight riding boots came first, followed by jodhpur-style tan trousers and a pale pink shirt. She closed the door and raised her sunglasses to the top of her head, pinning back her sleek blonde locks. Brann's insides were on fire again.

'Morning.' She gave him a brief smile.

'Morning. Why did you want to meet me here?'

'I want to show you something.'

He raised an eyebrow. 'Oh yeah? Is this legit, or have you lured me here so you can have your wicked way with me?'

'Oh, get over yourself. I've got a job for you.'

He huffed out a laugh.

'Not that kind of job,' she muttered and opened the gate to the first cottage. A gentle breeze played with her hair as she fumbled with a set of keys, then unlocked the door.

The ceiling was a little low for Brann's liking and he almost collided with a lampshade in the hallway. 'What's the job you want me to do?'

'Well, as far as I can see, these cottages are in quite good shape. Would you agree?'

Brann glanced around. Everything appeared old and dusty, but there was no visible damage. 'I'd say so. I can have a proper look if you want?'

'Yes, do.'

'Ok. Give me a few minutes.' He moved through the rooms, checking the walls for signs of cracks, damp or anything else that might be a problem. 'Five more minutes and I'll have a look outside.' He nipped out and did a visual check before returning to Ophelia. 'I'd say this one looks fine apart from a few loose slates. I can check the others if you want.'

'Not now. If this one is fine, that's all I need to know.'

'Why?'

'Because I want to move in here for the time being.'

'You?'

'Yes, me.'

'Ok.' He frowned at her. 'It doesn't seem like your kind of place.'

'You don't know the first thing about me.'

He held up his hands. 'True.' But he couldn't help smiling. He knew one thing. How she liked to be kissed. 'So, is that the job you wanted me to do? Check this place over?'

'Kind of.' She let out a sigh. 'Would you do something else for me?'

'Maybe.' What the hell did she want now?

'Will you help me clear this place out? I really need somewhere of my own to stay. You'd think in a house as big as Glenvorneth, there would be somewhere, but Jacinta is everywhere I go. She's always nosing in to see what I'm doing, and it's impossible to work. I'm trying to help out with the estate, but I also have my own business.' Her face fell. She wasn't the cool heiress anymore or the fiery woman who'd caught him in the barn yesterday. She was a vulnerable human being. The same one who'd asked him to believe her stories about the driving and the parking place. He found that he believed her, and now she was asking for help.

Asking me.

Why would she ask him? But he didn't need her to answer that. His reply was automatic. 'Sure, I'll help. What do you want me to do?'

'Rip out all this old stuff and take it to the skip, then I can clean it, put some furniture in and voila.' She made an arc with her fingertips.

'I can do that, no bother.'

She let out a sigh. 'Thank you. I appreciate it.' She blinked but didn't break eye contact. 'I'm sorry about yesterday.'

'I'm not.' He quirked a grin. 'I enjoyed it.'

'I did too, but that's not the point. Behaving like that was really stupid. Just like my driving.'

'Hey, we all make mistakes. And don't worry. It's not like I'd tell anyone about yesterday.'

'Good, because I won't either.'

He couldn't shift his gaze from her. His body wanted to move forward, seize her, kiss her, make love to her and never stop, but he mastered every urge and stayed where he was. 'Should we discuss the building plans?'

'Yes. Let's do that. But not here.'

'Why not? If we go back to the house, won't... I can't remember her name... find us and annoy you?'

'Jacinta.'

'Yes, her.'

'Probably. But we can't stay here. It's too dirty.'

He covered his mouth.

'Don't even go there.' She rammed her fists into her hips. 'No, I don't want to play dirty in here with you before you ask.'

'I didn't say a word.'

'You didn't have to. I can read you like a book.'

He let out a laugh. 'How about we sit outside? There's a wee picnic table out there and it's a nice day.'

'Fine. Let me get my laptop.'

They left the cottage and Brann squeezed himself onto the bench under the picnic table. When Ophelia returned, she took the seat opposite. Whether purposely or not, her knees brushed against his. The first contact stole his breath, but she didn't move or flinch and after a moment, it became warm and comfortable. The urge to kiss her and hold her was still present, but with a contact point established, it tempered the fire.

She looked over at him and her eyes silently asked if it was ok to remain as they were. He replied in the same way and Ophelia opened her laptop.

'Let's start by ignoring everything Barbara told you. I've spoken to her and she's fine for me to sort this out. She would have come this morning, but my father has her doing something else, god knows what. Anyway, it's probably easier this way.'

Definitely more pleasurable. Brann shifted his leg slightly so more of it brushed Ophelia's. She inhaled sharply but returned the favour by subtly moving her ankle, so it caught the back of his shin. Without drawing attention to the fact they were engaging in a version of footsie, she carried on.

'I've drawn up a priority list and costed it out against your rates and our projected income figures. Some of the work is reliant on us making money, so I can't put in fixed dates. Once we get the stables back in action, we can get the livery restarted.'

'Do you do riding lessons?' Brann asked.

'Not anymore. We used to. That's why we originally employed Dagmar Ingenfeld. She's wasted looking after a few horses.'

'Why's that?'

'Because she's one of the best amateur riders in the county. She's a good teacher too. I'm surprised she hasn't left us to tell the truth.'

Brann liked the idea of someone like that teaching Caitlin to ride, but he probably couldn't afford her and if she wasn't doing lessons anyway... Well, maybe that was a good thing. He didn't want to start coming here on weekends too... Did he?

Ophelia carried on talking through her plans and emailing him the relevant documents. He downloaded them onto his phone and added dates to his calendar. For all her fancy airs, she was a very organised businessperson, though their continual leg rubbing was completely unprofessional – but necessary. A charge was building inside him, so powerful it might blast him all the way back to Glenbriar when it blew. Neither of them mentioned it, but nor did they stop.

'So, are we good with that?' Ophelia shifted her laptop to the side and gazed at him with her piercing blue eyes.

'I'm good with it.'

'Then that's settled.' She closed the laptop and leaned forward. 'Now, we should get back to work.'

'Yup. You got anymore hot dates on the horizon? That guy yesterday was—'

Ophelia held up her hand. 'James is a nice man. Don't insult him.'

'I wasn't going to. So, will you be seeing him again?'

'What's it to you?'

'Just plain curiosity.'

'You have no idea, do you?'

'About what?'

'About what it's like to be me.'

'How could I?'

'He's a man I met for the first time yesterday, but already Father and Jacinta have just about bought me a wedding dress, hired a venue and spent James's fortune at least three times over.'

'Seriously?'

'Yes. They're desperate for me to marry him, so that his money will save this place.'

'Do you like him enough for that?'

'No.' She threw out her hands. 'But that doesn't matter. If it's not James, it'll be someone else. That's what's expected of me.'

'This isn't Victorian times.'

'Oh, don't get me started. I've told them that already, but the more I think about it, the more I see doors closing. We need his money.'

'What about him? What does he get out of the deal?'

'Me and my crazy family. Who could ask for more?'

Brann smirked. 'Yeah, greatly appealing.' Well, one bit of it was. 'But if you'll accept a word of advice from your pain-in-the-butt builder. I've never been married, but I have had a long-term relationship. And, well, I wasn't exactly forced into it, but circumstances made it carry on a lot longer than it should have. You shouldn't stick with anyone for the wrong reasons. Being in a relationship you're not one hundred per cent sure about isn't healthy and I wouldn't recommend it.'

She looked away and seemed to be chewing her tongue, perhaps biting back words. 'I... Ugh.' She threw back her head. 'I hear what you're saying, but it's not that easy.' Lifting her laptop, she wriggled out from under the picnic table and got to her feet.

Brann missed the caress of her legs instantly.

'Listen, I need to get some work done. Work for my own business. There's so much admin I have to get through.'

'Sure.'

'Thanks.' She met his eyes. 'For... Well, just thanks. I'll catch up with you later in the week.' She exited through the little gate, got into her car, and drove off. Brann watched with his chin resting on his hands. Inside his chest, beneath the raging desire fire, his heart squeezed. Ophelia's issues were bonkers, but in her world, they were as real as anyone's. Poor girl. He scoffed. What was this? Him feeling sorry for someone in her position.

Yeah. That.

He got to his feet and strolled to the cottage door. Had she locked it? He didn't recall seeing her doing it. Whistling to himself, he tried the handle, and it clicked open. It wouldn't take long to clear the place out. He could even give it a clean and check out the plumbing and electrics. *Ah, why not?* Maybe he was a sucker for a pretty face, but the idea of making her smile sent a shot of deep heat through his veins.

CHAPTER EIGHT

Ophelia

Tucked under the front wiper of Ophelia's car was a folded piece of paper. She pulled it off and read the message.

I hope you remembered to lock the door of the worker's cottage yesterday, because you never know, a local car thief might break in and clear the place out.

She narrowed her eyes and flipped the note over. The message she'd written to Brann about meeting her at the cottage was on the other side. What did he mean by this? She frowned. *Had* she locked up yesterday? Not that it mattered. What was worth stealing from there? If a thief had got in and taken something, then they were doing her a favour. But hang on. Was that what he meant? Surely he hadn't cleared the place out already. She had to find out, even though she was already running late for her appointment with the financial advisor. She jumped in her car and whizzed down the track to the cottage.

The door wasn't locked. *Bugger.* She pushed it open and ducked inside. All the old furniture had been removed, the floor swept and, although it still had a dated look with the dull wallpaper and the ancient kitchen and bathroom, it was a lot better than it had been yesterday.

'Wow.' She let out a sigh. Brann must have spent the whole evening doing this. With a quick time-check of her phone, she went to return to her car. As she got to the door, she saw another note nailed to it.

Dearest, fanciest heiress Ophelia,

I've cleared out the cottage as requested (got an awesome price on the black market for all the crap too!). Also checked out the electrics and plumbing while I was here. Looks sound to me, but obvs I'm not a sparky or a plumber, so you might want a second opinion.

Enjoy decorating the place.

All my undying, devoted, and passionate love,

Brann (your most favourite builder in the whole wide world)

A small smile crept onto her lips. She kind of wished she could be annoyed about something in the note, but how could she? Sure, it was sarky and cheeky, but beneath the smart words was something else... The fact he'd done it at all.

She must thank him, but there wasn't time. This appointment was too important. Barbara was meeting her there, and she didn't want her arranging anything without her – not after the last time. Brann would have to wait.

Spring sunlight reflected in the loch as she drove towards Glenbriar. What might the advisor's prognosis be? Her stomach churned a little. Hopefully he wouldn't serve up bad news and tell her the estate was terminal and only had a few months left to live. Selling it had to be a last resort, but she couldn't deny it had crossed her mind. Money didn't grow on trees and finding it would be impossible... Unless she tried harder with James Charlton. Perhaps his family believed the Chattan-Blythes were as rich as them. Maybe they thought this would be a financially beneficial arrangement.

She ground her teeth at the thought. Why was her life so irritating?

Barbara was in the waiting room of Astral Finance when Ophelia strode in.

'Ah, you made it.' Barbara dropped a magazine onto the glass coffee table and sat back.

'It's such a nightmare parking in the town.' Ophelia had been very careful in her choice of space this time. She sat down next to Barbara.

'The tourist season is starting up,' Barbara said. 'They'll all be flocking back.'

A door opened off the waiting room and a tall man with dark hair came out. 'Morning. I'm George Wylie.'

'Hello.' Ophelia stood quickly and slung her bag over her shoulder. 'I'm Ophelia Chattan-Blythe and this is Barbara Strachan. We're here about the Glenvorneth Estate.'

'Of course.' George nodded at them both. 'If you come into the office.'

Ophelia went in first. Her stomach unclenched slightly when her gaze landed on the homely furniture and flowers on a side table. Not the austere, typical office she'd expected. It was the kind of thing she might have designed.

'Please, take a seat.' George closed the door behind Barbara, and it snapped rather ominously.

Ophelia sat but couldn't relax. She leaned forward, resting her wrists on her knees.

'So,' Barbara said. 'What's the verdict? May as well give it to us straight. Are we doomed?'

George took a seat opposite them at the low table and opened an iPad.

'It has taken a while to go through all the documents and get any kind of projected figures.' He put the iPad on a stand and angled it so they could all see it. 'There seems to be a lack of consistency over the past few years, which means it's difficult to work out what the income for the estate will be. It also seems that some of the income generated from the cottages and the stables will be missing, as they're no longer working. Is that correct?'

'Yes.' Ophelia nodded and the knot in her stomach tightened. She didn't require George to say anymore. All the tiny hopes she'd had that he might have spotted a loophole or some way to save them were dashed against hard rocks. He kept on talking, reviewing the documents they'd sent him, but it was all worthless. The bottom line would be the same no matter what.

'So, all in all, the estate isn't bringing in even forty per cent of the needed expenditure. And that's basing it on generous calculations that would allow only the bare bones of these projects to be completed. Once you add all the proposed extras, you're talking about figures that exceed your income by a percentage so high you'll struggle to get loans to cover them, and I would caution against even trying.'

'Right.' Ophelia glanced at Barbara.

'Oh dear,' Barbara said.

'What can we do then? How do we finance projects that are meant to bring in more money if we don't have the money to start them in the first place?'

'Good question.' George pulled up a screen on the iPad. 'Firstly, you have to narrow down the places that will make the biggest income. I've listed here where I think you should start for the best profit. Take small steps. Before the closure, the stables seemed to be a steady earner.'

'We've started work on that already,' Barbara said.

'That's good. The cottages haven't been let for some time.' George checked his notes. 'So those figures will be vastly different as rates have changed. Rental income could be good, but I imagine there's a lot of work needing done to them before they can be used again.'

'There is.'

'The other options are to find investors, though I suspect that would be very difficult in this case. Or you could sell the estate cottages and land. There are two substantial properties mentioned on here: the Factor's House and the boathouse. They seem to be of reasonable size and in a sought after location like Glenvorneth, they could be worth something.'

'The Factor's House is in a terrible state,' Ophelia said. 'And the boathouse isn't much better.'

'I think it would be a wonderful place to live.' Barbara smiled rather sadly and cocked her head to the side. 'We got a builder to look at it, but the cost is against us.'

'If there's a dwelling place already there, it's easier to get planning permission for a new building,' George said. 'You might be able to sell it as prime real estate. The other option is that you sell your business, Timeless Butterfly Interiors, as a going concern. That would raise substantial funds you could use to finance the estate.'

Ophelia's heart almost stopped. 'No way. I can't do that.'

'Understandable, but I have to give you all the options.'

She let out a sigh. How could she sell the business she'd worked so hard to build up? Was it the only way to save Glenvorneth that didn't involve marrying James Charlton? Convincing her father and Jacinta to sell land would be almost impossible. Her father was so possessive of it.

'What do you make of that?' Barbara asked as soon as they'd left.

'I need to fully digest it. But do you want to be the one who tells my father he has to sell part of the estate?'

'No.' She shook her head. 'That'll go down like a lead balloon.'

'Don't I know it? I wouldn't mind getting the land around the Factor's House valued though. Can you organise a land agent? But say nothing to my father yet. Once we find out how much it's worth, we can present figures to him and that might soften the blow, rather than slapping him with an airy-fairy idea.'

'Good idea. I'll get onto that as soon as I'm back. What about the boathouse?'

'Let's not touch that for now.' She'd always liked that place, more than the main house really. As a child, she'd cycled up there with stolen food, had picnics and fed the ducks. Selling it off would mean it wasn't hers anymore. And she was precious about it.

She wasn't going straight home. She had errands to run in town. One of them involved going to Wood 'n' Chic, the upcycled furniture store. She still hadn't paid it a visit. Today was the day. She waved goodbye to Barbara and headed off up the street.

As she approached it, she passed The Drip Drop Coffee Shop, another place she really must try. The scent of coffee wafted from the door as some people came out. She could murder a cup after the gruelling morning she'd had, but maybe later.

Wood 'n' Chic had large glass windows showcasing the repurposed treasures. As Ophelia peered in, she smiled. She'd quite happily go and live in the window display. The collection of vintage suitcases stacked artfully to form a makeshift coffee table was so up her street. Glenvorneth had heaps of cases like that in the attics. She was skilled at using designs in arrangements and loved the artistic placement. Her Timeless Butterfly shop sold soft furnishings that complemented this stuff to a T.

The refurbished dressing table next to the packing-case table was stunning with ornate details and perfect teal paintwork. So unusual but eye-catching. It would look amazing in the bedroom at the cottage, though it possibly wouldn't fit; the rooms were tiny.

She pushed open the door and spotted a corner adorned with hanging plants in teacups and pots. Trellises were fixed to the wall beneath, and smaller items hung from them on little hooks. A woman with a mass of curly blonde hair pulled into a messy updo smiled at her from behind the counter, which was also an upcycled table.

Ophelia approached her. 'Hello. I wonder if there's someone who can help me?'

The woman put down a small box she seemed to be attaching fabric to and gave Ophelia her full attention. 'I can do my best. Is there something particular you're after?'

'I've actually bought a lot from here in the past, though only online. I run Timeless Butterfly Interiors in Edinburgh.'

'Oh. Are you Ophelia Chattan-Blythe?'

'Yes.'

'We've spoken by email so often and I've always wanted to meet you. You're a very good customer. I visited your shop when I was in Edinburgh a couple of weeks ago. It's stunning.'

'Thank you so much…' Ophelia wasn't used to that kind of compliment from anyone around here. 'Are you Stella Wylie?'

'I am and it's so lovely to have you,' Stella said.

'What a coincidence that your surname is Wylie. I was at the financial advisor earlier and that was his surname too.'

Stella smiled. 'It is a coincidence, but he's also my husband.'

'Really?' Ophelia blinked away her surprise. 'Such a small world. Anyway, while I'm here to look around in person, I should also say, there's a ton of old furniture kicking around Glenvorneth, some of it in better condition than others. If you were interested in having a look at it with a view to buying, repurposing and selling it yourself, then I'd be happy to let you see it before I do anything else with it.'

'Sounds right up my street. I'd love to.'

Ophelia smiled. 'Wonderful. I might end up buying it back once it's all done up.'

Stella laughed. 'If it's something you particularly wanted repurposed, I could do it on commission. I do that a lot.'

'I don't want to overstep, but I can see lots of ways we could work together.'

'I agree,' Stella said.

'Maybe you would like to arrange a time to come for a chat and have a look at what we have?'

'Just let me pull up my calendar.' Stella got out her phone and Ophelia glanced behind the counter to a door into what looked like a warehouse. That must be the section backing onto the industrial quadrant near to the horse feed store. What an Aladdin's cave of furniture; some unfinished, some partly done and other bits maybe waiting for collection or to be moved into the main shop. She could use so much of it at Timeless Butterfly Interiors, but that had taken a backseat in her life. After spending so long building it up, she was little more than a glorified admin assistant at present. Lucinda and the others in the office were doing the consultations and visits. Ophelia's work was remote, doing the books, schedules, etc. and using photos and building designs on the computer if she needed direct involvement with projects.

A movement in the backroom caught her eye: a woman with burgundy hair and a very bright floral dress. Her thick boots, choker, piercings, and wrist cuffs didn't really match the look. She shifted her position as she painted a different section of the piece she was working on, and Ophelia caught her eye. That was some make-up she had going on. Gothic or heavy metal? That kind of thing anyway. She gave Ophelia a brief smile and carried on painting.

'Do you employ a lot of people here?' Ophelia asked Stella.

'No. It's just me and Kristalee. She's just started. She's covering Nina, my regular assistant, while she's on maternity leave.'

'Must be difficult to get people who can do this kind of thing. It's so tricky.'

'Yeah, it's not easy finding people with the right skills. Nina was great. She turned up one day as a customer and everything aligned. I'd been advertising for a long time before that. Kristalee, too, was in the right place at the right time. She's a very talented artist, but she'd never worked in the industry before. She underestimated herself.'

'Did I hear my name?' Kristalee looked around the door. She was tall, curvy, and kind of scary. The sort of person Ophelia would normally give a wide berth and not want to cross. A smile softened her features, and she was actually quite beautiful in a striking way, but with the thick eye make-up and burgundy lipstick that matched her hair, it was almost impossible for her not to appear intimidating.

'I was just saying how you underestimated your skills before you started working here.'

Kristalee pulled a face and ran her ringed fingers through her hair. 'I'm still not sure I can do half the stuff as well as you. I give it a go though,' she added to Ophelia.

'You do just fine,' Stella said with a little smile.

'Ta.' With a little grin she returned to the backroom.

'Now, I have some dates I'm available.' Stella held up her phone.

'Thanks.' Ophelia checked her own phone until they found one that aligned. 'I look forward to seeing you again.'

When she was back outside, she buttoned her jacket and headed for the Drip Drop Coffee Shop. Cradling a steaming mug, she sat at a high barstool at the window, looking out at the bustling main street of Glenbriar. With everything that had happened that morning, she'd almost forgotten about Brann. He'd cleared that whole cottage out for her. The thought started a tingling buzz inside her. She should get back to Glenvorneth and find him. Thank him.

She made her way back and went directly to the stables. A clattering, blended with low singing, reached her ears before she got to the door. Stopping, she leaned on the frame. This must be what watching porn was like. Those muscly forearms made her jaw tense. His too long hair fell forward as he sawed a thick plank on the workbench, crooning an almost sad melody with a deep, clear tone. He was a hot bastard alright. With a slight cough, she let her presence be known. He stopped singing and sawing and looked up.

'Oh, it's you. Is it time for the daily inspection? Shall I rally the troops and get them to stand to attention?' He raised his eyebrow.

She slow-blinked, then beckoned him over. How tempting was it to kiss him again in all his rugged, sweaty glory? But she wouldn't. She could master this.

He dropped the saw on the bench and came forward. 'What? Is there something else you want? Perhaps the daily kiss instead of the inspection?'

'No.'

'What then? You want to inspect my wood, or are you missing a good screw?'

'You're not funny.'

He chuckled.

'You have a good singing voice,' she said.

'Thanks.'

'You should try busking.'

'Tried it before. I've even sung at festivals.'

She raised an eyebrow. 'The cultured builder.'

'Just one of my many talents. So, is this why you're here? To compliment me?'

'No. I want to thank you.'

'Good god.' He let out a long, whistling breath and gently placed his fingertips on her forehead. 'Are you sure you're feeling ok? Should I call an ambulance?'

'Seriously, Brann.' She pushed his hand away. 'I appreciate what you did at the cottage. I didn't expect you to do it so quickly.'

'Do you know how many tea breaks and donuts I had to sacrifice for that?'

'I can only imagine.'

He smirked. 'Well, I'm glad it's to your liking.'

'Very much.' She eyed him over. Yeah, it was to her liking, but not as much as him. Crazy! Because she didn't go for men like him. This was a passing phase of lust, and she was dealing with it.

'I better get on,' he said. 'My boss is a tough one to please and I wouldn't like to get caught slacking on her watch.'

'Agreed.' Her eyes took a detour over his chest again. 'We wouldn't want you to get into trouble. I hear the punishment is very harsh.'

He raised his eyebrows. 'I'm almost willing to risk it.'

'Me too, but we really can't.' She shook her head and left him to work. The force of desire urging her to look back was so strong she almost couldn't bear it, but she fixed her eyes forward and carried on towards the house.

Chapter Nine

Brann

May

The weathered field, marked by patches of matted grass and thick ridges of mud, served as the training ground for the Brawny Briars, the local tug-of-war team. Brann dusted his hands together and sighed. Come August, just three months away, this crew would be competing in the Glenbriar Highland Games. They were up against it, as they were every year, being a group of amateurs. However, amateur teams were much more the norm these days. The Brawny Briars would also make appearances at other local games, but the Glenbriar ones were the biggest in the area and attracted large crowds from all over Perthshire, the lower highlands and beyond.

'Right, lads,' Brann said over the relentless patter of rain. 'Let's get started. We've got some new faces so let's go around and say a quick "hi" to everyone. I'm Brann Duthie, team captain.'

'Finlay McBride, deputy,' the man to Brann's right said.

'Aidan McBride, cousin of Finlay and newbie.'

'Nice to have you here,' Brann said.

'Rory Chubb, just call me Chubbs. Everyone does...'

And so it went on until everyone had introduced themselves.

'A lot of the training for tug-of-war is up to you. Go to the gym, pump some iron, work on that core strength. We'll do a couple of warm-ups, then we'll have a go. Tug-of-war isn't about finesse; it's about power and unity. You bring the muscle and together we'll work on the unity. We have to pull as one, understand the shifts, the ebb and flow.'

Brann crouched low, the muck squelching beneath his boots. He grabbed the muddy rope on the ground, the fibres coarse against his palms. 'Practice isn't pretty.' The word threw up an unexpected thought of Ophelia. She had a habit of creeping into his mind and playing games in his imagination. Nobody on earth was less suited to this muddy field than her and yet Brann's psyche had wandered off after her. If he caught her, he'd want to lie her down in this mud and do the dirty with her. *For fuck's sake*, he had a one-track mind. 'So, um... It's about muscle memory, about knowing when to lean back and dig in.'

He got to his feet, holding the rope. 'Right, warm up time. Finlay will lead this.' As a P.E. teacher, he was good at this kind of thing.

Before long, they were all deep in lunges and high knees.

'That's it,' Finlay called, 'Make sure you can feel the muscles working.'

When they were warmed up, Brann lifted the rope again. 'Right, let's try dividing up. This is trial and error, until we get the perfect order, so if we pick a side and place just now.'

The team mirrored Brann's stance, hands gripping the rope like a lifeline. Mud oozed between his fingers as he planted his boots into the damp earth. 'Ok, on my command. Are we ready?'

'Yes,' they shouted.

'Pull!'

The practice erupted in a chaotic mix of grunts and the squelching of mud. Each team member strained against the rope, muscles flexing. They spent half an hour at it until they were all too cold and wet to take anymore.

When training was over, Brann really needed a shower, but the training area didn't have one. Imaginings of Ophelia were back and the idea of having her in the shower with him made him even more hot and bothered.

He checked his phone as he strode up the road and found a message from Kristalee.

KRISTALEE: has Caitlin said anything to you about the theatre club? I thought she was really enjoying it, but I think something's happened there as she's saying she doesn't want to go back.

Brann's chest tightened. He didn't want to wish his kids' lives away – they'd already grown up so fast – but if Caitlin could finish high school and be done with, she'd be so much happier. He hated seeing her so upset, and it triggered ugly memories of his own. The urge to beat her bullies to a pulp burned strong.

But she wasn't great at talking about it, so he didn't know where to start. Sure, he got that too. She didn't want to rock the boat or make things worse.

As for what was wrong at the club, something small could have been blown out of all proportion, but unless she told them, how could they help?

BRANN: She's never told me anything about it. I wish we could get her to open up a bit more so we can help her out.

KRISTALEE: me too… I'll ask her again and see what she says.

God forbid she harmed herself again if it all got too much. He sent her a quick message to check in, but heard nothing back that evening. Work at Glenvorneth was ticking along. The stables were almost completely fixed and he would shortly be ready to start the next job on Ophelia's list. He hadn't seen much of her recently. Her visits had been infrequent, though he often saw her car outside the worker's cottage he'd cleared for her. She was probably busy decorating it.

Harrison knew nothing about his sister's problems at the theatre club. He had a new girlfriend and was so wrapped up in his loved-up world with her he was barely present at all. Brann knew the feeling. Though he wasn't loved up… Just lusted-up and obsessed. The fact Ophelia had stopped calling was probably a good thing for them both.

Perhaps she was now dating the posh guy.

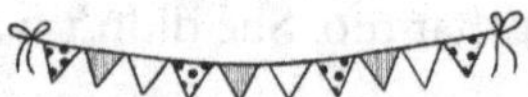

Brann hammered the trim around the front of the stable, and gritted his teeth from atop the ladder. Ah well. He'd have to get used to it even if it meant imagining every nail he smacked in was going into posh man's head. Poor guy. Brann didn't really wish him any harm. Ophelia was fun for a bit of banter, but that was as far as it would go for Brann and her. His life was messy enough. Somehow, among all the chaos, he'd managed to raise two kids. No mean feat really. Neither he nor Kristalee had had a clue back then, but they'd got this far. Sometimes, he wished he could go back, not to change things, because he loved his kids, but if he could use hindsight to iron out certain bits, so they were smooth and pleasant, not untidy and difficult.

He hummed to himself before turning it into a song. He couldn't read music and didn't have a clue about famous composers or anything like that, but he enjoyed singing and could pluck out a tune on a guitar. Sometimes he sang at the Autumn Gold festival on open mic night, usually just little things he made up himself. Nothing too complicated, just soulful stuff. People were usually kind and said he had a nice voice, but he did it because he liked it.

'Brann.' A soft voice caught his attention, and he stopped singing and peered down from the ladder. On the ground below was Ophelia, arms folded, looking up at him. Had she invaded his mind and heard him thinking about not seeing her for a while?

'Long time, no see,' he said. 'What's up?'

'Come down here a minute, will you? I need to talk to you.'

He rammed the hammer into his tool belt and climbed down. 'Yes, heiress in chief. How can I help you?'

'You can't, but I need to go over the timetable with you. There's been a development.'

'Oh yeah.'

'Come with me and I'll explain.'

'Ok.' Brann's eyes followed her neat figure as she marched around the back of the stable where her car was parked. The tight white jodhpur-style jeans got him every time. Her gait was like a supermodel on the catwalk.

She opened her passenger door and took out an iPad. 'I'm going back to Edinburgh at the end of the week,' she said.

'Why?'

'Business. Lucinda, my friend and colleague, has been running the show since I came back here, but she has a holiday coming up and so do some of the others, now that we're getting into summer. I can't fully cover everything from here, so I'm going back. I just want to make sure you're aware of the job timeline and what to do next.'

'Very aware.' But it wouldn't be the same without her around here.

'Good. You can discuss anything that comes up with Barbara and she'll contact me if need be.'

'Ok.'

She flicked through her iPad, though he wasn't sure what she was looking at. 'When do you think this will be finished?'

'I'd give it another couple of weeks to get all the snagging complete. I'm confident I can have it done by then.'

'Good.' She typed something in, closed the case and chucked it onto the car seat. Standing in the gap between the door and the roof, she leaned on them, with one heel resting on the edge of the footwell. Her gaze skimmed over Brann.

He glanced around and gave a little shrug. 'And is that all?' Their eyes met, and he knew it wasn't. When her focus dropped to his lips, he almost crashed forward and grabbed her. If she wanted it, he wouldn't say no.

She looked away and shook her head. 'You are the bane of my life.'

'Why?'

'You drive me crazy.'

'Likewise, Princess. But aren't you dating some posh guy now? Isn't he satisfying your carnal needs?'

'I'm not dating anyone, and he definitely isn't satisfying anything.'

'Would you like me to have a go?'

'I dare you to try.'

'Challenge accepted.' He moved closer, wedging himself in between the open door, so she couldn't get out. He snaked his arms about her, gliding his palms around her trim waist. So small and delicate. He ran his fingers over her tight bottom and planted his hand in the pocket of her jeans, pulling her close.

'You are the pits.' She slid her hand around his jaw, tugging his face down to meet hers. He opened his mouth to her, and their tongues met straight away, sending hot lightning bolts through his body. She wrapped her arms around his neck, and he tilted his head, kissing her firmly and deeply. Breathtaking and so risky. Anyone could see them here, but he didn't care. She didn't seem to either, returning his kisses fiercely – exactly what he liked. Strong, passionate women were his catnip. This woman may look like a princess, but she kissed like a warrior and he was here for it.

Ophelia broke off, but he carried on kissing her, figuring she needed air. He focused on her lower lip, moaning at the tightening sensation in his groin.

'You know I hate you?' she breathed, her hands pushing under his arms and slipping around his back.

'I know,' he said through the kiss.

She chased his lips again, and he let out another moan as her palms slid over his back. Her lightweight shirt and his t-shirt weren't a strong enough barrier, and the sensation of her body rubbing against his was almost too hot to handle, but he didn't let go.

'You... hate me too... Don't you?' she muttered in little breaths.

He barely broke the kiss to reply. 'With a passion.'

The kiss came to a crescendo. She tasted dreamy, like strawberry lip balm. So soft, yet powerful. Make or break time. Brann was almost willing to throw caution to the wind and take her up against the car, but she pulled away and he stepped back.

'For christ's sake,' she muttered, straightening out her top. 'I don't know what the hell is wrong with me.'

'I did ask.'

'You did. Which is another reason for me to dislike you. I can't even claim you took advantage of me.'

He ran his fingers through his hair. 'I can't imagine anyone taking advantage of you.'

'Oh, I don't know. Now, let's not make this any harder.'

'Easy for you to say. Some parts of my anatomy are finding that a problem right now.'

'Seriously?' Her eyes shot over him, and a smirk played at the corner of her lips. 'Looks like we've done enough damage for one day.'

'So, was that a goodbye kiss?'

'Something like that.'

'I look forward to you coming back then.'

She glanced away and sighed. 'I'm not sure when that'll be, so until then, be a good boy, won't you?'

He saluted her. 'But of course, your fanciness.' Standing back, he caught his breath as she shut the car door and went around to the other side. Was there any point trying to figure out what the hell had just happened?

Probably not.

Whatever it was, it had been insanely hot. Not to mention downright crazy. Not the first time he'd played with fire.

Ophelia zoomed off down the track, and Brann raked his fingers across his scalp.

Fuck's sake, I'm supposed to be a responsible builder. I'm someone's dad, an upstanding member of the community. And I'm behaving worse than a teenager.

He returned to the stables, humming his tune again. Something about that fine line between love and hate, just waiting to be crossed.

'There you are,' Harrison said. 'I've been looking for you. Where have you been?'

'I was talking to Ophelia.'

Harrison raised an eyebrow. 'Oh yeah? Talking? Does that mean you were snogging her round the back?'

'No. What?' The defensive voice gave away the lie. Hopefully that was just Harrison guessing. He better not have sneaked a peek.

'It's so freaking obvious the two of you fancy each other. I don't even know why you're trying to hide it. Why not just shag her?'

'That's enough. Don't be rude.'

'I'm not.' Harrison pulled an innocent face.

'She's off limits, ok?'

'For me? I don't want her... Jesus, she's way too scary for me.'

'I meant for me, though it goes for both of us. She's in charge here, so we behave.' The little voice beat on his head, reminding him how unsuccessful he'd been at that so far.

It should have been a relief she was gone, and he wouldn't have any more run-ins with her, but as the days went on, the old loneliness crept back. Somehow, the knowledge he might run into her each day had filled a gap in his soul. Even when he hadn't spoken to her, he'd seen her car or caught sight of her nipping in and out of the main house or the cottages. Now there was nothing.

He carried on until the stables were finished and got ready to start on the next job: fence repairs to the paddocks.

'I suppose we should tell Barbara we've finished here,' he said to Harrison.

'I'll leave that to you.'

That didn't surprise him. Harrison was young and inexperienced in dealing with people.

Brann downed tools and headed off to find her. Assuming she'd be in the estate office, he got to the door and knocked.

'Come in!'

He pushed open the door to see the top of her head from behind a computer and a mountain of paper.

'Ah, hello, Brann. Sorry I haven't been up to see you recently. It's been crazy here and I'm really struggling without Ophelia.'

'No sign of her coming back?'

'Not at the moment, sadly. But what a to-do. Just before she left, we had a land agent in to value the land. Well, her father went mad about it. I think that's partly why she left so quickly. Raging so he was. I've never seen him like that. Said he'll never sell land and didn't know why she would even have considered that as an option.'

Did he think the better option was to sell his daughter? Crazy family.

'Hmm. That's not good.' How could he empathise when he had no idea what it would be like to have this much land at his disposal? 'I just came to say the stables are done and we're ready to move on to the next job.'

'Well, that's the problem, isn't it? There's no money to pay you. No point in moving on to the next job when we can't even pay you for this one.'

'What? Wait a second, you can't do that. You have to pay me for the work I've already done.'

'I don't know how. There is no money.'

'You are joking me, aren't you?'

'Unfortunately not.'

CHAPTER TEN

Ophelia

June

'It's great to have you back. I honestly don't know if I'm coming or going.' Ophelia strolled through Timeless Butterfly Interiors main office room with Lucinda, who was newly returned from her holidays. 'I've never felt so disorganised.' She'd been back ten days, while Lucinda enjoyed time in France, and was only just finding her feet again. They made their way to Ophelia's office. Just being back here was like returning to a safe and happy place.

Lucinda shared a helpless look with her. 'What's happened?'

'Nothing bad. I just feel like my loyalties are stretched so thin between here and the estate.' She pushed open the door, and Lucinda walked around the desk to sit where Ophelia usually sat.

'Sorry.' Lucinda blinked and made to stand up again. 'Habit.'

'It's fine.' Ophelia took the other seat. She didn't see herself in that position much longer. 'Glenvorneth is a full-time job in itself. I think I'll have to spend a lot more time there in the future. I've been distancing myself from it while I'm here, but I'm worried about Barbara. She's good at bookkeeping, but the rest of it is beyond her.'

'I'm so sorry.' Lucinda put out her hand and took Ophelia's. 'I wish I could do something to help.'

'You are. You're looking after this place. I'm just terrified Glenvorneth will go back to square one with me being here.'

Now Lucinda was back from her holiday, it was an ideal time for Ophelia to return to the estate, but would she be abandoning her employees? What would happen to Timeless Butterfly Interiors if she was never here?

'Enough about me.' She gave herself a mental shake. 'Tell me about your holiday.'

Lucinda beamed as she recounted her trip. Ophelia tried not to feel jealous. She hadn't taken a holiday since last year when she'd gone to Cyprus with her friend Florence. Perhaps some people thought going to Glenvorneth was a holiday, but it wasn't. Not when she spent valuable work time hiding from Jacinta... and Brann – only with the added annoyance of not really wanting to hide from him at all. Her plan to move into one of the estate cottages hadn't come about in time and she'd ended up using it as an office; the only place she could escape Jacinta during the day.

With all the work at Timeless Butterfly Interiors, she'd shoved Glenvorneth further to the back of her mind. Returning to Edinburgh was fun. She had friends here and, with the long summer days, it was nice to meet people after work and sit outside the bars on the Royal Mile. Florence came up from London for a few days and Ophelia spent the weekend with her. As they were old school friends, Florence knew all about the history with Jacinta and was happy to listen to Ophelia venting.

'You should wash your hands of the lot of them,' Florence said. 'Concentrate on Timeless Butterfly Interiors. The shop is stunning. You could develop it into a chain.'

'I'd love to, but Glenvorneth isn't going away.'

'Not unless you make it. When you inherit it, just sell it. Does the history really matter? Loads of old houses change hands.'

'I know, but my grandparents fought hard to allow me to inherit. Otherwise it could go to an obscure relative and none of us will own it. It's my duty to preserve it. I don't want to let them down or be a failure.'

History lived in the walls of Glenvorneth. People with lives and stories. Her ancestors. Was it silly to want to save that, nurture it and grow something new from it as her grandparents had wanted to? They'd both been taken too soon, and if she didn't do something, who would?

July

The beginning of July arrived as something of a shock. Ophelia had decided to keep Lucinda in the office she'd used at Timeless Butterfly Interiors, and she'd taken an empty desk in the main room that looked out over George Street. With Florence's words rattling around her head, Ophelia realised how far she'd let Glenvorneth slip to the back of her mind; she really should call Barbara for an update. Lifting her phone, she hit the number.

'Hello, hello,' Barbara said almost immediately.

'Hi.' Ophelia tapped her pen on the desk. 'Sorry, I haven't checked in properly since I left. I've been so busy, but I assume everything is going fine as I haven't heard anything to suggest otherwise.'

'Yes, everything's ticking by as usual.'

'Great. So, where are we with the stable repairs? Is that all done now?' If Brann had worked to the timetable they'd agreed, it should all be complete. He should also have done the paddock fences, which would mean they could open the livery again and start making money.

'Well, not exactly. I mean, the stable repairs are done, but that's as far as we've got.'

'Oh.' Ophelia's grip tightened on her pen. 'Why?'

'Unfortunately, there was a hitch with the builders.'

Ophelia let out a sigh. 'Dare I ask what? Have they abandoned us?'

'No, no, nothing like that, and their work is excellent. Nothing to fault. It's, well, we don't have the money to pay for it, so unfortunately, they left.'

'What?' Ophelia gaped at her phone. 'The money was there to pay them not just for the stables but also for doing the paddock fencing, so we can get the livery up and running. I don't understand why they haven't been paid. I set aside money in the account for it.' The only money they had left.

'I know. But your father used it to buy a holiday for Jacinta's fiftieth birthday.'

Ophelia's jaw almost hit the floor. 'Excuse me? He did what?'

'You heard me.'

'He can't take money from the account for that.'

'Well, technically, he can. It's profit from previous years, so he can spend it as he likes, but he shouldn't have as you'd ring-fenced it for the stable upgrades.'

'I don't actually believe this. Does he honestly think a holiday is the priority?'

'No, he doesn't. He claims he didn't realise the money had been put aside when he used it. His plan is to repay it when he can.'

'And how will he do that? It's not as if he has a steady job.'

'He has investments. One or other of them will come to maturity this year.'

'That's absolutely ridiculous. I wish you'd told me sooner. We can't get a reputation for not paying tradespeople.' Ophelia sucked on the end of her pen, her stomach in knots. What the hell was she going to do? She had to pay Brann. This was despicable. 'Listen, I'll transfer money into the account to cover the stables and up front for the fencing. I want you to pay the builder with it straight away.'

'Do you mean you're going to use your own money?'

'I don't exactly have a choice, do I?'

Ophelia had deliberately not given Brann her number, telling him to contact her through Barbara. Now, she wished she hadn't been so silly. But that was a recurring theme where Brann was concerned. He seemed to bring out every silly bone in her body. She could, of course, call him whenever she wanted using his business number, but something about opening a private communication channel between them seemed even riskier than kissing him in broad daylight outside her car. *Yup. Silly. Just plain silly.* Even though it made sense in a small corner of her brain.

Barbara had assured her she'd spoken to Brann, and he'd agreed to come back and finish the fences, but Ophelia couldn't leave it to chance anymore. She needed to leave Timeless Butterfly Interiors and return to Glenvorneth. It was a wrench going again, but she had no choice. And with Lucinda looking so at home in the boss's chair, maybe the timing couldn't be better.

The old worker's cottage where she'd encamped before was cold inside, even though it was a bright sunny day and the grass and woodland surrounding the estate was luminous green. Flowers had burst into life. Red and pink rhododendrons had taken over and were like a giant hedge behind the back garden of the cottage. Compared to her Edinburgh office, it was so quiet and not unpleasant. It reminded her of times when she was happy here, with her grandparents. They'd walked in the woods, or taken her riding, and told her how Glenvorneth should be open to everyone, not just them, and how important it was not to isolate themselves from the community. Something they obviously hadn't told Rupert. Or perhaps they had, but he'd forgotten since Jacinta started giving her own counsel.

Guilt mites nibbled at Ophelia's conscience as she unloaded her laptop and notes onto a table she'd bought from Wood 'n' Chic. It was months ago she'd arranged for Stella, the shop owner, to come and look at the furniture stock, but she'd had to cancel that to return to Edinburgh. *Must rearrange that, and soon.*

First things first, though. She clenched her fist over the back of a wooden chair. Here was the never-ending nightmare of Glenvorneth. But where was Brann? She'd forked out a large portion of her own money to pay him, but when she'd driven up to the stables, he hadn't been there. Presumably he'd taken on other jobs after the one here had fallen through. Maybe he couldn't leave them to come back. Maybe he didn't trust her. Could she blame him?

The situation sucked, but what the hell could she do about it?

An image of James Charlton wafted into her mind.

He'd taken a backseat too, which was good, but if that was an option she wanted to follow, she'd have to decide how, and if it would be worth it.

What were her other choices? She wouldn't even entertain the idea of selling Timeless Butterfly Interiors. But she couldn't afford to keep bailing out the estate with her own money. She also couldn't stop her father and Jacinta from spending estate money, but she would try.

'I've already discussed this with Barbara,' Rupert said when Ophelia confronted him. 'It was a one off.'

'I won't have a big birthday every year,' Jacinta said.

'That money was supposed to pay the builder, not buy some extravagant holiday.'

'Listen.' Rupert held up his hands. 'Tradespeople work in a different way. They don't expect to be paid straight away. I'm surprised at him. I thought he was a pleasant sort, but he seems to have acted rashly by walking out. He should know the money will get to him, but often invoices lie unpaid for substantial periods. People are busy.'

Ophelia glared at him. He was completely impossible sometimes. 'That's not how it works. It may have been the case at some point in your life, but not now. He didn't invoice us because we'd already agreed on wages and when they'd be paid.'

'Well, that was a silly way to do it.'

'No. That's a fair way to do it.'

'Ophelia, when you have a big birthday, you'll understand. It's important to celebrate and make memories,' Jacinta said.

'I look forward to the one you'll be throwing me for my thirtieth next year then, just don't use estate money for it.'

Jacinta cast her a narrow-eyed glance.

'We must pay people for the work they've done,' Ophelia went on. 'That's business.'

She ignored Jacinta's scoff.

'We will pay him,' Rupert said. 'Just not as quickly as we first thought.'

Ophelia ground her teeth. She wouldn't tell them she'd paid Brann's wages. Not yet anyway. She didn't want them to think this was something she was going to do frequently.

'Barbara told me he's agreed to come back.' Jacinta brushed something from her skirt. 'So, he's obviously not that bothered. Or else he needs the work, which shows we're good employers really.'

'What absolute bullshit. Can you hear yourself?' Ophelia ran her fingers through her hair. Jacinta's warped logic was ridiculous.

'Really, Ophelia.' Her father frowned as Jacinta glared at her. 'There's no need for that kind of language.'

'That was tame, believe me.' She checked the time on the carriage clock. 'I have to go. I'm meeting Stella from Wood 'n' Chic. She's going to look through some of the furniture in the storeroom.'

'Oh, I could help with that.' Jacinta dropped her sour expression instantly. 'I'll show her what she can have and give her the best price.'

'No, thank you.' Ophelia inhaled slowly. 'I've already come to an arrangement with her.'

'What do you mean an arrangement?' Rupert said. 'This is a chance to make money. I hope you're not planning on giving it away. You could use some of the money to pay the damn builder.'

'The furniture in the storeroom isn't worth *that* much. Just leave this to me, ok?'

She caught Jacinta exchanging an irritated look with Rupert. Honestly, they had no idea. No wonder the estate was in tatters.

Stella arrived at one o'clock with an adorable little boy beside her and a smiley little girl on her hip. Both of them had the same wild curls as Stella, but now that Ophelia had discovered George, the financial advisor, was Stella's husband, she saw him in the kids too, especially in their big brown eyes.

'Hello,' she said. 'Welcome to Glenvorneth. And who do we have here?'

Stella followed her in the side door. 'This is Alex.' She nodded at the little boy skipping along beside her. 'He's three and a half, and this is Ava. She's nearly two. It's her birthday next week.'

'Aw, lovely.' Ophelia smiled at little Ava. 'I hope you have a brilliant birthday. And do you go to nursery or playgroup, Alex?'

'Nursery,' he said quietly.

'It's closed for school holidays at the moment. George's mum is great about looking after them, but it's a lot for her. I thought they'd like a trip today as the weather's so nice.'

'Feel free to take them for a walk around the estate after. There are lots of places to explore.'

'We'll do that, thank you.'

They'd barely been in the storeroom ten minutes when there was a knock on the door. Ophelia, suspecting Jacinta, went to open it, but was surprised to see Francesca.

'Oh, hi. I, um, have a favour to ask you.' She flicked her hair over her shoulder.

'A favour to ask *me*?' Ophelia couldn't keep the scepticism from her voice. Francesca might be her sister, but she rarely spoke to Ophelia, let alone asked for favours.

'Mum reckons you wouldn't mind giving me a lift into town. She says you're going anyway.'

'I'm not. I've got a meeting with Stella just now.'

'Yeah, mum said she could take over with that.'

Ophelia smiled and shook her head. 'That won't be necessary. I'm fine here and if your mum's free to do that, then she's obviously free to take you into town. If you want to wait until tomorrow, I'll take you then, but I can't today.'

'Right, ok... I'll wait until tomorrow then.'

Ophelia was quite sure she wouldn't, and returned to Stella and the children. They spent a while going through the furniture and chatting about how best to transport it. Stella had a van she used, but it was the lifting of heavy pieces that could be tricky. If only Brann was about. Ophelia could see him moving this stuff without breaking a sweat, but she was probably his least favourite person right now, so no point asking for a favour.

Seeing Stella's kids running about the grounds that afternoon made Ophelia smile. This was what should be happening here. Why not let people visit and enjoy it too? It was wasted otherwise. Her grandparents' vision had been for it to be a place everyone could enjoy. When they were alive, they'd hosted local events and community gatherings.

'This has been so great,' Stella said, as she loaded the kids into the car.

'Come again anytime.' Ophelia waved her off.

The following morning, Francesca surprised Ophelia by saying over breakfast.

'Can I come to town with you then?'

'Oh... Well, yes.'

Ophelia drove the car down the lochside, not entirely sure what to talk about with her younger sister.

'Who are you meeting in town?' Ophelia broke the silence after several uncomfortable moments.

'Oh, just some people from the theatre club.'

'Will you be putting on a show with all these skills you're learning?'

'The leaders want us to, but I don't know.'

'I'm sure we'll all want to come and watch.'

'Oh god. Sounds like a nightmare.' Francesca returned to her phone and silence reigned again. Seeing the first houses of Glenbriar was a relief. Ophelia wanted to claim her peace again.

'I'll drop you off down here,' she said. 'Then I'll go on the hunt for a parking place.' The town was crawling with tourists. Surely some of them would be interested in visiting Glenvorneth. They could walk, ride, even fish or take a boat out on the lochan. If only Ophelia could get Rupert and Jacinta onboard with the idea.

'Thanks.' Francesca unclipped her seatbelt and got out. She swished her long hair over her shoulder as she walked off down the street. Not so long ago, Ophelia had been just like her, desperate for lifts into town to meet friends and get away from the emptiness of Glenvorneth. Maybe she still was, only she didn't have anyone to meet up with these days.

Ophelia's trip was mainly to stock up on supplies for when she was in her office. Jacinta was still spending far too much on expensive deliveries, notably from Duchan Fayre; that had to be an attempt to impress James Charlton. So, Ophelia had to lead by example and get some nice normal stuff from local shops. Just some coffee, snacks, hand soap, loo rolls for when the bathroom in the cottage was finally done up.

'Hi!' a cheerful voice said, and Ophelia's eyes connected with a smiling face.

'Oh, Hayley, hi. How are you?'

'All good, thanks. Just taking a breather from the salon. It's roasting in there today.'

'I suppose hairdryers don't help on hot days.'

'Even with the door open, I'm melting.' Hayley loosened her shirt and wafted her neck with it. 'What are you up to today?'

'Just boring stuff. I might get a cold drink though. I'm a bit hot myself now you mention it.'

'Want to grab one with me? I was going to nip into The Drip Drop Coffee Shop. My mum works there, and they're doing some amazing frappuccinos and coolers at the moment.'

'That would be nice. I was just thinking how weird it is when I'm here that I don't have anyone I can go for a drink with or meet for lunch. In Edinburgh, I'm spoiled for choice, but I don't really know a lot of people here.'

'If you want a drinking buddy, give me a call and I'll see what I can do.'

Hayley's smile was so bright it was dazzling and infectious. Ophelia automatically smiled back. 'That's sweet, but aren't you busy with that man of yours? The one who sends you roses.'

Hayley giggled. 'Indeed, but that doesn't mean I don't have time for other people.' She pushed open the door to the café.

'I'll give you my mobile number. I don't like the idea of anyone feeling lonely.'

'You're very kind. I've just lost touch with people here.' She frowned as she looked around. Maybe she'd never really been in touch with that many people here. It wasn't because she hadn't tried, but she'd always been on the edge – sometimes literally. Like Francesca, she'd had to rely on lifts everywhere. She'd not attended the local school and her only clubs had been the pony club and a music group. But even there, she hadn't exactly made friends with local people.

'I can introduce you to lots of people if you want,' Hayley said. 'My job means I get to meet so many.'

'I always think of myself as someone with a lot of friends, but actually, I'm not super close to any of them. Maybe Florence, but she's so busy with her engagement. And Lucinda, but she's a colleague too.'

'That's ok. Colleagues are friends. Mine definitely are. Speaking of which, we googled you at work and were reading about Timeless Butterfly Interiors. It looks utterly brilliant.'

'Thanks.' Ophelia blinked, focusing out of the window, sensing that rush of heat she got whenever people complimented her on it.

'How did you do it?'

'Do what?'

'Get so successful?'

Ophelia gave a little shrug. 'I'm not sure I know. I don't feel like I am. It's just work that I enjoy, and it grew quickly.'

'I think it's amazing,' Hayley said. 'I wish you'd open a shop here. People in this town would love it.'

'That's not such a bad idea.' Though she wasn't sure she wanted to. Somehow, keeping that life separate from Glenvorneth worked better in her mind.

'It must be really hard trying to split yourself between the two places.' Hayley rubbed her arm.

'It is.' Ophelia let out a sigh. 'I appreciate you being so kind. It's rather lonely without anyone here to talk to.' The only other person she'd confided in here was Brann, which seemed quite ridiculous. But he'd helped her when she'd been stressed by Jacinta. Yup, her mind strayed off to him again. The most unsuitable man. The man who turned her from a well-mannered woman into a tigress on the hunt for a mate.

'I used to fancy myself as a bit of a matchmaker too.' Hayley giggled. 'So if you're lonely in that way, I could find someone to set you up with.'

Ophelia shook her head with a smile. 'Only if it's someone extremely rich.'

'Are you serious?'

'Deadly. Part of my life is the Glenvorneth Estate, and it can't survive without money.'

'That's sad,' Hayley said. 'What if you never meet anyone who fits the bill because your options are so limited?'

Ophelia laughed into her drink. 'Sounds very silly really, doesn't it?' Her whole life was a bit like that. But stopping for the drink with Hayley proved to be just the tonic. Ophelia was now friends with her on social media, and Hayley insisted she could message any time about anything.

It was habit, maybe, but Ophelia drove to the stables when she got back before going anywhere else. She liked to see Conker. Her heart flipped when she saw Brann's van parked near the paddock. A small field next to where Dagmar kept her trailer joined onto the larger paddock and Brann stood at the fence, leaning on it and chatting with Dagmar. What was he saying to her? Possibly something about not getting paid and Ophelia's stomach turned over. She had nothing to do with paying Dagmar's wages, but she couldn't remember seeing them in any of the notes or statements she'd read. Had the poor woman been getting nothing for months? How did she afford to live? She and Ophelia had never been best friends; that teenage rivalry still sat in the way of them ever getting close, but the thought of her working for nothing made Ophelia's skin crawl. This was what had become of the Chattan-Blythes. Hardly pillars of society.

Brann was laughing in that roguish way he had. Ophelia's jaw set and she was determined not to find him attractive... an impossible ask, of course. Dagmar was well known for being tight-lipped, closed-off, and quiet, but her pale face had lit up, her cheeks were rosy, and she was smiling. Ophelia couldn't recall seeing her smile much before – maybe with the horses, but not with people.

Seriously?

Brann and his way with women. Well, she'd have been a fool to think she was the only one.

She got out of the car and made her way towards them. Brann looked up, saw her, and said something aside to Dagmar before approaching Ophelia.

'Well, hello,' he said. 'Here's a person I didn't expect to see.'

'Hello.' Ophelia stopped in front of him. 'You're back, I see.'

'As are you, Princess.'

'I take it you got paid?'

'Eventually.'

'I'm very sorry about that.'

He raised an eyebrow. 'Yeah. It's not very pleasant after you've arranged a fee to not get it. Especially when the person you arranged it with goes off and insists you deal with someone else about it.'

'No, Brann, that's not what—'

'Save it. I'm not in the mood for games.' He stalked past her across to the other side of the field.

Ophelia took several calming breaths, forcing herself not to follow him. She looked around and caught Dagmar's eye. She was still by the fence a little way off, making a meal of untangling a bridle rope.

'Hello.' Ophelia approached her. 'How are you?'

'Oh... you know, fine.' She didn't meet Ophelia's eye.

'What was Brann saying to you?'

'Nothing much.' Dagmar kept her focus on the rope. 'Just something about the Highland Games.'

Ophelia frowned, her insides tense. 'Have your wages been paid since the stables closed?'

Dagmar shook her head. 'Jacinta says I'll get them backdated when the livery reopens.'

'What? Oh my god, Dagmar. That is not on.' Hot blood rose in Ophelia's chest and her brain might explode. She would have to pay the wages, but she wanted to find her father and Jacinta and knock their heads together.

Chapter Eleven

Brann

August

Brann strode through the crowd on the Highland Games field, dodging people, semi-aware of how good the attendance was this year, but his mind was elsewhere. *Get to the competitors' tent and make sure everyone is present and correct.* Dressed in his thick boots, kilt and tight t-shirt with the legend Brawny Briars printed in bold across the back, he flexed his fingers, eager to get on with the competition.

He'd almost reached the tent when he caught sight of a group of people laughing so loudly the sound carried over the other chat, the rumble of generators, and the distant sound of someone practising a tune on the bagpipes. Without giving them much of a thought, he made to bypass them, only to hear his name being called. He knew so many people in the town it came as no surprise to be claimed left, right and centre. Already, he'd said good morning to about twelve people. Turning to do the same again, his gaze landed on a portly man wearing tweed plus fours and a matching waistcoat. *Oh great.* Harrison's likening of Rupert Chattan-Blythe to Toad of Toad Hall wasn't far off. Beside him was a young man with dark hair, tall and slim but broad shouldered. He had on a white shirt and a pair of almost salmon-coloured trousers. Taking the piss out of someone's clothes was pretty low, but Brann couldn't help an internal snigger. These posh folks sure dressed in weird get-ups. Brann wouldn't be caught dead in trousers like that. The man looked about ten years younger than him. He couldn't imagine his ten-year younger self having any desire to dress like that.

Then it clicked. He'd seen that man before with Ophelia. He was the one they wanted to marry her off to.

Rupert was waving as if to beckon Brann over. He didn't really have time for this and was on the verge of walking on when he noticed Ophelia in the group, dressed in a slick riding jacket and her trademark tight jodhpurs and high boots. Her face was red, like she was on the verge of an explosion, but she wasn't looking at him. Her narrowed eyes and fixed jaw were directed at Rupert's wife. The one with the weird name. Brann had only met her once and had been treated to her death stare.

'Brann,' Rupert called again. 'Just want to wish you the best of luck today. I understand you're team leader for the tug-of-war team again this year.'

'I am... And, er, thanks.' He made to keep walking.

'You know my cousin is the Earl of Dairvin and chieftain of the games,' Rupert went on. 'He'd be delighted to have you in his tent for drinks later. I can arrange that with him.'

'Right.' Brann ran his hands through his hair. 'Maybe we should wait and see if we win first.'

'Last year's performance against the Highland Haulers was so close,' Rupert said. 'I have a good feeling about this year.'

'Let's hope you're right, I should—'

'I'm not sure you know everyone,' Rupert spoke over Brann.

Ophelia caught his eye and gave him a commiserating look. 'Yes, father, he does,' she said. 'And I'm sure he has training or something to do, so you should let him get on.'

'Have you met James?' Rupert waved his hand, ignoring her and indicating pink-trouser man. 'James, this is Brann, a local builder and team leader of the Brawny Briars tug-of-war team.'

'Yeah, we met vaguely a while back,' Brann said.

'James is the executive manager of Duchan Fayre,' Rupert said, then leaned closer to Brann and added quietly, 'Also my future son-in-law, with any luck.'

Brann's gaze met Ophelia's again and, although she couldn't have heard what Rupert said, she clearly got the gist. Her cheeks reddened and her eyes flashed scarlet. That look could slay someone from twenty metres, but no one else seemed to notice.

'Listen, it's good to see you, but I need to get the team organised.'

Rupert genially thumped him on the back. 'Off you go then, and good luck. We're counting on you to get a win for the town.'

'We'll do our best.' Brann glanced around the group and, as his eyes moved from James to Ophelia, he flicked her a quick wink. When he strode away, he sensed her eyes boring into him like a drill in his back.

Once he reached the competitors' tent, he pushed Ophelia out of his mind. Why the hell did he keep thinking about her anyway? She would marry that posh dude and that was that. Why should he care what she did? She'd shafted him with the wages, run off to Edinburgh, and not even had the courage to tell him to his face.

Forget about her.

'Ok, folks,' he said to the team. 'Let's get warmed up.'

'Your daughter came looking for you.' Finlay dusted his hands together.

'What did she want?' Brann asked.

'Not sure. But I don't think she was that thrilled about seeing me.'

Brann smirked. Finlay was her P.E. teacher. 'I'll message her later. She said she was coming to watch. She probably wants some spending money.'

With eight teams competing this year, there was potentially three matches to win, though they could be knocked out straight away. The first tug was less than twenty minutes away.

'It's good conditions so far,' Brann said. 'Not too sunny and no rain either, though it's forecast for later.'

They headed onto the field to cheers and shouts. Brann made a point of never looking at the crowd before a match. He didn't need to know who was watching and sometimes it was better to pretend no one was. His skin prickled with the same sensation he'd had earlier. Somewhere in the crowd, Ophelia's eyes had found him. He stayed focused; if he looked up, his gaze would land on her, though he didn't know where she was. A sixth sense would guide him there.

The tug started as a tussle and Brann yelled at the team to hold fast. The opponents tired first, and the Brawny Briars yanked them over the line, meaning they progressed into the semis. Two other teams waited to go on as the victorious Briars returned to the tent. Brann saw the muscly Highland Haulers striding out. They looked as unbeatable as ever.

'We've got ninety minutes before the next round, so let's take a breather. Go and have some fun with your families and we'll meet back here in just over an hour.'

Brann pulled out his phone to message Caitlin and wandered out of the tent. He headed around the arena, half watching the Highland Haulers in action and half looking out for Caitlin. If she'd been watching his match, she'd probably be around here somewhere.

After he'd hung around for a few moments, his phone buzzed.

CAITLIN: I watched your match, but I went straight to watch the horses. Some of my friends are in the competitions.

Brann winced, and his chest ached. If only he had the means to let Caitlin get riding lessons and a horse. He'd chatted to the woman who ran the stables at Glenvorneth, but the ballpark figures she'd given him for livery were sky high. He'd already investigated the other farm Caitlin had mentioned and while she could get lessons there, she'd have to wait for the new term.

He made his way towards the horse arena. A few marquees were set up behind it, with rows of trailers parked nearby. People on horseback rode by and others led horses. As he scanned the crowd, his gaze fell on exactly the person he didn't want to see but subconsciously knew he'd find no matter what. Wherever she went, he was drawn to her, even when he wasn't trying. She wasn't alone. Beside her was Dagmar, the stable worker from Glenvorneth, in a very smart riding outfit too, almost un-recognisable from the jeans, messy jackets and wellies she usually sported. Her extremely long hair was plaited and coiled into a low bun. Both she and Ophelia had spotted him. Ophelia tried to act like she hadn't seen him, but Dagmar gave him a flicker of a smile.

'Hi.' Brann focused on her, cold-shouldering Ophelia. Well, why not? She'd have walked past him if they'd been alone. He was sure.

'Hi.' Dagmar gave him an almost distracted wave.

'Are you competing today?' he asked.

'Yes. In several categories.'

'Good luck.'

'Thanks.'

A couple of people walked by and said hello. One of them caught Dagmar by the arm and started speaking to her.

Brann switched his attention to Ophelia and raised his eyebrows. 'And what about you? Are you in for the best in show heiress category?'

Ophelia narrowed her eyes. 'You think you're so funny, don't you?'

'I'm a damn sight more amusing than a woman who decides not to pay my wages for several weeks and then runs off, leaving some other poor minion to tell me. Wouldn't you say so?'

Ophelia put her hands on her hips and looked away, shaking her head. 'Is that what you think happened?'

'No, it's what I *know* happened.'

'Do you?'

'Yes.'

'Wrong again.'

'Oh yeah? Another of your games?'

'My games?'

'Yeah, it's how you get your kicks, isn't it?' He leaned slightly closer, catching a whiff of her sweet floral perfume over the strong horse smell. 'Playing your little games with me. Only this time you went too far.'

'No, Brann.' She gaped at him. 'That's not what—'

Dagmar tapped Ophelia's arm. 'I need to go.'

'Oh, sure,' Ophelia said. 'Can I catch you up? I have something important to tell Brann. It won't take a minute; I'll see you at the arena.'

'I can't hang about to play,' Brann said. 'I'm meeting someone.'

Ophelia waited until the crowd swallowed Dagmar, then took Brann by the wrist and tugged him in between two marquees.

'What's this all about?' he said. She let go of him, and he smirked. 'You trying to drag me somewhere private so you can kiss me again? This is a bit risky.' He nodded his head at the passing crowds.

'No, Brann!' Her jaw set like a bulldog clip. 'That's not what I want.'

'Really? That's surprising. I thought you were a regular little Lady Chatterley who couldn't get enough rough to satisfy you.'

'Shut up.'

'Or what? You'll get your pink-trousered boyfriend to come and kick my butt? I'd do it myself if I were you. You've got more balls than him.'

'Leave him out of it. He's a nice guy, and he is not my boyfriend.'

'I forgot. He's just someone you're going to marry for his money. Well, if you think I'm going to be your bit on the side, forget it. Once I'm done with the fences at Glenvorneth, you and I are through. I'm only doing them because I got paid upfront, but if money's run out, I can't risk not getting paid again.'

'That's what I want to talk to you about. That wage thing was nothing to do with me. I didn't know you hadn't been paid. As soon as I found out, I made sure you got your money.'

'So, you're telling me the money was sitting there, but no one bothered to pay me? Sounds pretty nuts to me.'

'No. I paid you from my own money because my father spent your wages... elsewhere.'

Brann stared at her and ran his fingers through his hair, his insides sagging. 'You shouldn't have to do that.'

'Oh, but I do. My life is wrapped up in the estate. Once the livery is running again, we should start making money, and I want to invest that into more repairs. So I am begging you not to leave us. I don't want to have to hunt for new builders or get a reputation as someone who doesn't pay.'

'You've changed your tune. A few months ago, you told me we weren't a good fit and you didn't want me working for you.'

'I was wrong.' Her expression lost its usual confidence. She seemed almost desperate. 'As I have been about a lot of things. You're good at what you do.'

Brann looked away, not sure what to say. 'How do I know your father won't do the same thing again?'

'You don't. And neither do I, but I think I got the message through.'

She didn't sound convinced.

'Ok. I'll do it, but I better keep getting the money upfront.'

She met his eyes and nodded, wrapping her arms about herself and shivering slightly. Brann's fingers itched to reach out to her, but he didn't dare. 'Thank you. I'll see that you do.'

'Ok.' He pulled an uncertain face, suddenly unable to find words to fill the silence. 'I gotta go.'

'Yeah. Good luck with the match.'

'Thanks.' He gave her a brief look, then marched off into the crowd, wandering about aimlessly for a moment or two, forcing himself forward because the urge to go back to her burned him like a blowtorch.

'Hey, Dad!'

He spun around, spotting Caitlin with a group of girls. With a groan, he approached. He hated being in the midst of her teenage friends.

'Took you long enough to find me,' she said.

'Yeah. I kept bumping into people.'

'See you in a bit,' she said to her friends.

Brann put his arm around her. 'Everything ok?'

'Yeah. Kind of. I just saw this girl from the theatre club hanging about. She's riding in a competition. I hate her. She's always spreading rumours about people, and she loves herself because she goes to some posh girls' school.'

'Well, keep out of her way. Leave the posh girls to mind their own business and you stick to yours.'

If only he could follow his own advice.

CHAPTER TWELVE

Ophelia

'**B**oo!'

Ophelia jumped as someone tapped her on the back.

'Hayley.' She turned around. 'You gave me a fright.'

'You look great.' Hayley admired her riding jacket. 'This is Oliver.' She tugged on the arm of a tall, very handsome, dark-haired man.

He put out his hand, and Ophelia shook it.

'Nice to meet you,' she said. 'I'm Ophelia. I met Hayley at the salon the day you sent her a wonderful bouquet of roses.'

'Oh, that.' He smiled a little awkwardly and his cheeks went pink.

'He's a real closet romantic.' Hayley cuddled his arm. They were a beautiful couple. That little twinge of jealousy Ophelia often got in the company of friends and family who were clearly in a happy, loving relationship reared inside her. The thought of trying to achieve this kind of bliss with James Charlton turned her stomach. She hated herself for thinking it because James wasn't a bad person. In fact, he was charming, polite and hardworking. Nothing about him should elicit such disgust in her, but she just didn't fancy him. Whenever he was close by, she felt completely flat, even when she tried really hard. It just wasn't happening.

'You're the divorce lawyer, aren't you?' she asked Oliver.

'Yes. That's me.'

'Well, I hope I never need to visit you in a professional capacity. Though as I haven't found anyone to marry yet, it's unlikely to be any time soon if I do.'

'I hope that's the case too.'

'Oliver, would you mind grabbing me a drink?' Hayley said. 'I could murder a coffee. Do you want anything?' she asked Ophelia.

'No, I'm fine, thank you.'

Oliver gave Hayley a quick peck on the cheek and strolled off.

'Are you ok?' Hayley asked.

Ophelia leaned on a fence and sighed.

Hayley stepped up next to her. 'Is your father still trying to set you up with the rich guy?'

'Yup. He invited James and his family here today. I still haven't met them yet, but they're coming home with us after. It's such a mess. I just don't find him attractive, but I know I should. I mean, he's nice, polite, handsome... What's not to like?'

'You can't help who you're attracted to and you can't force it. Sometimes it's the most unlikely people we're drawn to.'

'Don't I know it?'

Hayley leaned over and gave Ophelia a hug. 'You need to follow your heart a bit more. It's your life.'

Ophelia sat quite still; she wasn't used to being hugged by friends – not more than as a cursory greeting. This was quite pleasant really.

A little way off, Dagmar sat astride her steed; both looking completely poised. Ophelia had never mastered the perfect posture – she couldn't be bothered with the hours of practise.

'I should get ready.'

'What for?' Hayley said.

'I decided to ride Conker in the show. I wasn't going to bother, but why not? I'm hopeless, but it's more fun than hanging around with my family.'

'I'll come and watch,' Hayley said. 'I bet you're really good.'

'Honestly, don't get your hopes up. But by all means, watch. I should fetch Conker and get him ready.'

'I thought you had a groom.'

'Dagmar? She's competing herself. I can't expect her to do this too.' Ophelia cringed at the fact that Jacinta and her father thought it ok to leave her unpaid. Covering Dagmar's wages was something Ophelia was willing to do for a loyal employee and to ensure the horses were ok, but she didn't want her father and Jacinta to think this was something she could do indefinitely.

'I hope your ride goes ok.' Hayley hugged her again, and Ophelia went to get Conker from the trailer. She led him around the marquee towards the prep area.

A little way off, she saw Brann leaning on the fence, beside a pretty girl with long glossy hair, a similar colour to his own. Was that who he was meeting? She looked really young. Ophelia wasn't sure what age Brann was, maybe mid-thirties at a guess, but that girl looked no more than twenty. Her stomach squirmed at the thought of Brann dating people, especially beautiful young people. She knew nothing about his circumstances. *Christ.* She'd kissed him, not knowing if he was in a relationship. His flirting and the fact he'd kissed her back implied he was single. But it was crazy to think other people wouldn't find him attractive. Of course they did. He was a laid-back guy who happened to be super sexy.

Unbidden, he looked over. She couldn't help but stare at him. Her knees might actually have given way. She clung so tightly to the saddle strap it dug into her palm. As she mounted Conker, her foot slipped on the stirrup. Hastily, she rode off. Last-minute practice wasn't necessary. She wouldn't win or even come close, but she needed a warm-up and so did Conker.

Ophelia spotted other people she recognised and said hello to several as they passed. Dagmar was also in the practice area. She headed over to Ophelia. 'I saw your father going about with James Charlton. I was at school with him, you know?'

'Were you?' Ophelia raised an eyebrow. Dagmar hardly ever spoke about anything personal, so this was new. 'Was he a friend?'

'Not really.' She gave a little shrug. 'He was my neighbour for a while, but... Well, we weren't close or anything.'

'Ah.' Ophelia felt there was more to the story, but Dagmar said no more.

An announcer called the next three riders, and Ophelia was one of them.

'Good luck,' Dagmar said.

'Thanks.' Butterflies were unusual for her before a ride – mostly because she wasn't bothered enough to care. No one ever watched her, so it made no difference. They rarely had even as a child. She remembered Dagmar's mum religiously watching her at every competition, while Ophelia was dropped off and picked up at the end by one of her parents. She didn't make a thing out of it normally, but suddenly she felt sick. 'I better get to the start.'

She waited in the holding area as the previous competitor went over the final jumps before she rode into the arena. Conker managed the first jumps easily, and her queasiness subsided a little. Relaxing, her eyes strayed to Brann. He was still in the crowd with the young woman. He looked incredible – there was something so effortlessly attractive about him, especially in that tight t-shirt and the kilt. The nerves flooded back. Why was he watching? So he could take the piss? Her legs shook like jelly. Conker jumped awkwardly and the saddle became almost uncomfortable. It was Brann and his body she could feel. Nothing else. 'Come on, Conker.' A rail fell at the next turn. Maybe she was imagining it, but she thought she could hear Brann laughing. She and Conker got into a rhythm and the remainder of the course wasn't too bad, though he clipped the final fence.

'Well done.' She gave him a rub as they left the arena. Her heart was pounding. She didn't make eye contact with anyone. *Please do not let me see Brann again!* But at the same time, she yearned for it. He was probably in hysterics with his friend about her terrible miss, and her cheeks burned at the thought. This was like having a schoolgirl crush... On the boy who was all wrong for her.

Oh, get over him!

She took Conker for a cool down ride, before finally setting off to find her family and face the James-themed music.

Oh no!

Too late to change direction.

Brann was in front of her, standing in a crowd of people, laughing and joking. His arm was around the shoulder of the young woman, and she leaned in and rested her head on him. Brann hugged her close.

'Keep walking,' Ophelia muttered, but she wanted to vomit. 'And don't look.' She strode behind a hotdog stand to avoid passing him face to face.

'Ah, there you are,' Rupert said, when she arrived at the hospitality marquee. 'We were getting worried.'

James gave her a half smile and the guilt mites moved in as she spotted the older couple beside him.

'Oh, I was riding Conker in the show jumping, then I hung about and watched Dagmar while he was cooling down.'

'Dagmar?' James said. 'I think I was at school with her. I recognise the name anyway and it's not that common.'

'Yes, she said she knew you.'

His lip quirked up a little and Ophelia watched him. Was there some history here she should know about? 'I wish I'd known you were riding,' he said. 'I'd have come and watched.'

'I'm glad you didn't. It wasn't that good a ride, but Dagmar was brilliant as always.'

'I haven't seen her for years, but I recall she was very horsey.'

'Oh golly, yes. She's fab with horses.'

The announcer's voice droned from the speakers with stories and information.

'Sorry I missed you both,' Jacinta said with a smirk. 'We're going to watch Francesca's ride in the afternoon.'

Ophelia didn't waste a reply on her. She turned to James's parents.

'Let me introduce you,' he said. 'This is my father, Laurence, and my mother, Sherri.'

'Delighted.' Ophelia shook their hands, smiled, and made the right noises. She was well trained at this. James gave her a funny little look that she took as an upfront apology for anything they might say. Apparently, they were as keen to bring about a marriage as her parents. But they may as well have been speaking Greek, because all that kept rattling about in her head was Brann. Who was the woman he was with? His previous actions implied he didn't have a girlfriend, but it was unreasonable to think he was a perpetually single man who would be readily available whenever she fancied a kiss – just as he'd accused her of earlier. He wasn't wrong. Since when had she been like this? Even now, she could hardly believe thoughts like this were going through her head.

'Oh, I better be off.' Rupert checked his watch and got to his feet. Ophelia bounced back to the present. 'Got to get to the chieftain's procession.'

Thank god for the blaring sound of bagpipes and drumming. It drowned Jacinta's incessant babbling at the Charltons and also the intense silence between Ophelia and James. She couldn't find any words to cover it. The situation was so cringe. *I just don't fancy you.* She willed the message to him with a vague smile. He returned it like he understood perfectly and felt exactly the same.

They moved into a better spot to watch the procession, Francesca tagging along like a spare part. Ophelia stood next to her and smiled, not sure what to say, but maybe just being there would make her feel less out on a limb. The Earl of Dairvin led the way and Jacinta looked like she might break her neck to get a glimpse of him and the countess. What a spectacle: Jacinta, the groupie for a short, balding man and his shrew-faced wife. The Earl's taut face had turned beetroot in the heat of his full highland dress, as he marched ahead of the pipe band, swinging his sceptre.

'The countess looks stunning,' Jacinta said as they reached the stage close to the hospitality marquee.

Ophelia tried not to yawn. The Earl began his speech, thanking the usual people and praising the competitors for their effort.

When the speech was done, Rupert found them and took them to the Earl's table for lunch.

'Such an honour,' he said. 'But we're cousins, after all. The old boy sometimes makes a fuss, but he's on good form today.'

James rubbed his palms down his trouser legs, and his parents huddled around Jacinta, soaking up her stories about how close she was to the countess.

'Are you alright?' Ophelia caught up with James.

'I've never met an earl before.'

'Oh, no need to stress,' she said. 'He's pretty down-to-earth. His wife can have a sharp tongue, but Jacinta will entertain her, so nothing to worry about.'

'If you say so.'

Rupert introduced the Charltons, and they all took their seats. Jacinta almost did herself an injury trying to get next to the countess. But when the countess sat next to Ophelia, Jacinta's nose was shoved right out of joint.

'So, that's the Duchan Fayre boy, is it?' the countess said aside to Ophelia.

'Yes.'

'The family seems nice, but he doesn't look quite like how I imagined.'

'Oh?'

Perhaps the countess also wished him a bit more rugged, but Ophelia wasn't sure she dared comment. Usually, it was simpler to go along with what she said.

'But more to the point, are you engaged to him yet?'

'What?' Ophelia almost choked on her drink. 'No. We haven't even dated yet.'

'Well, you better get to it. Doesn't look like he'll be about for too long. If you don't grab him, someone else surely will.'

Ophelia smiled sweetly and let the words wash over her. The end of lunch couldn't come fast enough. Not only because she wanted away from the countess, but she really wanted to watch the final tug-of-war. She'd have missed the semis by now, but hopefully the Brawny Briars had got through and would have a chance in the final.

Thankfully, everyone else wanted to watch too, so when lunch concluded, they left the earl and countess and made their way to the athletics arena. On the way, Ophelia spotted her mum and a friend walking the same way.

'Dear, dear,' Rupert muttered. Jacinta took his arm and they and Francesca marched past. Laurence and Sherri Charlton followed, but James stayed with Ophelia.

'Your father showing his class, as usual,' Edith said.

'Hi, Mum.' Ophelia kissed her mum on both cheeks.

James gave her an awkward glance.

'This is James Charlton.'

'Oh, you're James.' Edith smiled and shook his hand. 'Delighted to meet you. I'm Edith, Ophelia's mother. And this is my friend, Nancy. Ophelia, you might remember meeting her at my party.'

'I do,' Ophelia said. 'How are you?'

'All good, thank you.' Nancy adjusted large red-rimmed glasses. 'We watched you riding, but I don't think you saw us. You went off very quickly at the end.'

'I didn't think anyone was watching, and it wasn't much to write home about.' Ophelia ran her hand over her forehead.

'It wasn't that bad,' Edith said. 'The one after you was much worse. She fell at the first fence and her horse practically completed the course itself before they could catch it.'

'Oh dear...' Ophelia laughed. 'We're going to the arena to watch the tug-of-war. Why don't you both come with us?'

'I'm not sure a bunch of sweaty men wrestling a rope is our cup of tea,' Nancy said. 'But you never know.' She exchanged a little smile with Edith.

'Let's go find out,' Edith said.

'We can get into the hospitality section. I have my pass.' Ophelia touched the badge on her lapel.

They took their place in the reserved area ringside. James slid onto the bench between Rupert and Ophelia. Rupert threw his ex-wife an unpleasant look but said nothing. Ophelia sighed. She should have warned James to sit somewhere else.

'The team leader is a sexy beast,' a voice from behind said, and Ophelia's heart stopped. They were obviously talking about Brann. And she agreed with them one hundred per cent.

Edith rolled her eyes, and Ophelia glanced around. 'What?'

'All this chat about Brann the builder,' Edith whispered.

'What do you mean?'

'He's got quite a following.'

'He's a very nice man,' Nancy said. 'He did me a new kitchen last year and he couldn't have been more helpful. Very efficient and left no mess.'

'Well, he is a good builder.' Ophelia kept her eyes on the arena for any sign of him. 'He's done work at Glenvorneth, and I can't fault it.'

'Your father was talking about the work he was doing when you went to ride,' James pipped in. 'He seemed to think he's exceptionally good.'

'Rupert talks a lot of shit most of the time,' Edith muttered to Ophelia. 'So I wouldn't take anything he said as a glowing recommendation.'

James eyed her like he wasn't sure how to respond, and Ophelia silently held her breath. Her parents were nothing like each other, but they both had their little foibles – sometimes not so little.

The team entered the arena and Ophelia's knees buckled. Thank goodness she was sitting down. Brann was so mind-bendingly attractive. Her face filled with heat, she fanned herself with her programme – despite the black clouds lingering, it was a warm day. No one would notice.

'He is totally hot,' the voice behind said.

Edith chuckled. 'Someone's got a crush.'

Someone did, and it wasn't just the woman behind them.

'Oh no. Rain.' Edith pulled up her hood.

More hoods and umbrellas shot up as Ophelia reached below her seat for her own brolly.

The teams stood facing each other, the rope taut. Ophelia couldn't take her eyes from Brann. It felt so wrong, even though everyone else was watching too.

The drizzly rain made strands of his hair stick to his forehead. His damp navy t-shirt clung to his sculpted chest, the words Brawny Briars emblazoned across his broad back. Ophelia re-called the feel of that chest, the heat of his embrace, and the sizzling kisses. The memories made her tingle all over. Her heart fluttered against her ribs like it was eager to take wing, fly to him, and take its place next to his.

A tap on the rope, a cry and the tussle began. He was like a mighty warrior engaged in mortal combat. A row of feet scraped the ground, heaving. Ophelia's heartrate sped up. They took the strain – and the fracas began. Willing them on silently, Ophelia watched Brann intently. His grim determination showed in every heave. The rain got heavier.

'Come on,' she muttered.

James glanced at her. She kept her face impassive until he looked away. Just as well they weren't together yet. Her eyes were having a virtual affair with the sexy builder.

Hiding beneath her umbrella, she watched. The opposing team, named The Highland Haulers, were mostly broad and beefy. They looked strong, and they seemed to have the upper hand. Slowly they pulled the Brawny Briars towards the line.

No!

Ophelia clutched her face, wincing.

The cheering and screaming hit fever pitch. Brann shouted so loudly Ophelia heard it. The sound brought renewed strength to the team, and they gained traction. The momentum shifted to them again. Now they were dragging the Highland Haulers closer to the line. *Come on.* Her eyes strayed past Brann to the crowd opposite. She saw the girl with the glossy hair clutching her face. Next to her was the guy who worked with Brann, the one Ophelia assumed was his brother. He was yelling and making fists. That was what it was like to have people who cared about you. Supportive people. Ophelia couldn't imagine anyone cheering her on like that.

It made her a little ill. That woman looked too young for Brann, but she clearly cared about him. *Who am I to judge?* Maybe love really was blind, and they'd stumbled into each other and fallen for each other.

How would it be if there were no expectations on me? Ophelia sighed. He was a man from a different background, sure, but did that mean he was wrong for her?

An almighty roar rose from the crowd. The Brawny Briars had pulled The Highland Haulers over the line. Tumultuous clapping and cheering ensued. Ophelia joined in, and James stood up to applaud.

'Marvellous,' Edith said.

Ophelia joined in the excited recounting of the match. Shortly after, the team was presented with medals. The Earl of Dairvin approached them, beaming. Gold glinted as he swung the medal around the first neck.

Oh god.

When Brann smiled, he was even more gorgeous than ever, even when covered in mud from head to foot.

The crowd began to disperse, Brann and the team vanished from sight to the competitor's tent. A crack in the clouds let through a ray of sun.

'That was quite something,' Edith said.

'It really was.'

'Shall we get a drink?'

'Let's.'

James came with them. Their route took them to where Brann's brother was standing with the young woman and a group of other friends gathered in a small huddle, all talking excitedly.

'Ophelia!' Hayley waved from amidst a group of onlookers. 'Did you watch that?' she burst out excitedly.

'Yes.'

'It was amazing, wasn't it? I can't believe they won!'

Cheers from behind made them look around. Brann emerged and was hugged, clapped on the back and congratulated by his well-wishers. He held his hair off his forehead, grinning. His t-shirt, arms and legs were covered in mud. The young woman ran up to him and hugged him. He laughed and hugged her back, lifting her off the ground and swinging her around.

Ophelia tore her gaze away from the embrace. Her eyes met with Hayley, who winked and grinned. She wasn't sure what the gesture meant and wasn't sure she wanted to.

Her head fizzed; she veered around Brann and his admirers. She hated him with a furious passion. Why did he mess with her mind until she couldn't think of anything else? How dare he make her feel this way? He was forbidden. He had no right to be in her mind at all. It was time to get rid of him. She'd enjoyed an afternoon of depraved entertainment watching him in all his masculine glory, but it must stop. She'd had her virtual fling and now it was over.

Chapter Thirteen

Brann

Brann levered off the remaining window frame of the old boathouse, using the crowbar that had offended Ophelia in this very spot when they had first met. There was something incredibly satisfying about the crack as the frame broke away. He grabbed it and tossed it aside.

Barbara had organised some people to clear the place as she'd promised all those months ago. It still stank of damp and would take some work to get it habitable, but what a location. Once it was finished, holidaymakers would pay big bucks to stay here. This was the place of dreams. Even working here this week had been nice. A retreat with its own loch, woodland all around and peace, perfect peace. He dusted off his hands and went inside, picking up the pieces of frame that had fallen in.

A clicking sound broke the silence and Brann checked around the doorway, back into the main room. The front door opened, and Ophelia nipped in, dressed in running shorts, a tight crop top, and very white trainers. Her long hair was tied back in a slick ponytail. Why was she here? By the looks of things, she hadn't noticed him. She tiptoed across the room to a window he hadn't knocked out yet and peered out. Was she hiding from someone?

Brann crept up behind her and put his hands on her shoulders. She shrieked, jumped a mile, and whipped around. He burst out laughing.

'What the bloody hell are you doing here?' She fanned her hand on her chest. 'You scared the living daylights out of me.'

Still chuckling, he patted her on the upper arm. 'Sorry. My bad, but why are you here?'

She gave a little shrug. 'I asked you first.'

'I'm doing the work I'm employed to do. This place was next on the list you gave me, so here I am.'

'I didn't see your van,' she said.

'Harrison took it to pick up some supplies.' He folded his arms. 'Now, your turn. What are you doing here? If you didn't know I was here, you can't be here to check up on me.'

She let out a sigh and rubbed her forehead.

'Are you hiding from someone?'

'My father invited James for another visit, but I can't face him today. I went out for a run to get away from them, but I saw the Land Rover on the track. My father must be giving him a tour of the estate and probably trying to find me at the same time.'

Brann smirked. 'You're a funny one, aren't you? Will you still be doing this after the wedding? Running into the woods and hiding from your husband?'

'I want this to work, but on my own terms. When my father sets things up, it's so horribly fake. Please, if they come looking, don't tell them I'm here.'

'I won't.'

'Thanks.' Ophelia gave him an appreciative nod and scanned around. 'It's looking good in here. You really are a good builder.'

'Um... Ok. I've barely started yet. Are you after something?'

'Why?'

'Because you're being so nice.'

She huffed out a little laugh, then squinted out of the window and frowned.

'Have they found you?' Brann asked.

'No. But come see this.'

Brann moved in close behind her. His carnal instincts pushed him to put his arms around her and keep her safe from her pursuers. He didn't want them to find her. The caveman inside him said, *she's mine*. Which, of course, was rubbish on so many levels, but he couldn't completely suppress the urge to take care of her. Standing behind her so he was almost touching her, he peered over her shoulder, following her sightline. A dishevelled man was staggering along the lochside, close to the edge of the trees.

'He looks a bit suss,' Ophelia said. 'Do you think he's a poacher?'

'Looks more like someone who's been sleeping rough for a while.' He resembled a homeless person crossed with a hippy.

'Should I confront him?' Ophelia said.

'Unfortunately, someone has taken your antlers, and it looks like a job you shouldn't attempt without them.'

She turned around and gave him a dry look.

'Let me.' He placed his hand on her shoulder. 'Just in case he's violent.'

'You think I can't handle myself?'

'I know you can, but you're too beautiful for this.' He raised his hand to her face and ran his thumb down her cheek, the raw urge to touch her winning over common sense. 'I wouldn't want him rearranging these features.'

'Brann, really.'

'Yes, really,' he whispered.

The sound of an engine made them both stop.

'Shit. That might be my father. I have to hide.'

'It might only be Harrison. Let me check.'

'I'm hiding anyway. And if it is my father, don't let him in here.' She disappeared through the doorway into the side room.

Brann opened the front door as Rupert heaved himself out of an old Land Rover. On the other side, James got out, adjusting his tie and looking like he'd just survived a ride across the desert in a dune buggy.

'Hello,' Brann said.

'Ah, you're here,' Rupert said. 'Where's your van?'

'Harrison's nipped to the hardware store. We need a lot of supplies to get started here.'

'I'm just popping in to show this place to James. It's quite rundown, as you see.'

James nodded.

'But the plans are very ambitious. This part would only be the living area and there's to be a full extension out the back for the rest of the house.' He stepped inside and James followed.

Brann moved to block the doorway to the other room, where Ophelia was hiding.

'It's a great location,' James said.

'Indeed.' Rupert looked at Brann. 'You haven't seen my daughter coming past, have you?'

'Nope.' Brann leaned on the door frame. 'I'm going to have to ask you gents to keep out of this room.' He pointed with his thumb over his shoulder. 'It's got... um, faulty electrics, and I can't guarantee the safety of it until it's checked properly.'

'Ah, right. No problem,' Rupert said. 'We'll leave you to it.'

Brann followed them to the main door and watched them get into the Land Rover. Once they'd driven away, he returned to the side room. 'You can come out now. They've gone.'

Ophelia sidled out and let out a low moan. 'This is such a nightmare.'

'Of your own making, I might remind you.'

'Don't. Is that man still hanging about?'

'Nah.' Brann checked out the window. 'Your dad might see him and tell him to clear off.'

'I should probably tell him.'

'I would have told him, but I was too busy hiding you.'

'Yeah. Thanks for that.'

Another engine sound caught their attention and Ophelia stared at Brann. 'Not my father again, surely.'

'Jump in, just in case.' Brann held open the door to the side room, then went to the front door and opened it. 'It's Harrison. You can come out.'

'Thank goodness for that.' Ophelia came out and dusted herself off. 'It stinks in there.'

'Damp.' He eyed her, and she smiled at him. The words he'd said before drifted back. He meant them. She was beautiful, and that smile made her even more so. Harrison's arrival made it impossible to say anything else. Just as well. Brann had betrayed more than enough – not only to her, but to himself. Whatever harmless obsession he had with her didn't need to get real. Not that it could... *Don't let the feelings get too deep.*

Harrison came in and glanced between the two of them. Heat rose in Brann's neck. *Explain yourself or he'll suspect.* And with good reason.

'So, you think it's, um, big enough then?' he asked, cursing himself straightaway.

Raising her left eyebrow slowly, she smiled. 'For what exactly?'

'The utility room.'

'Oh, it'll be fine. Size isn't everything, after all.'

Harrison smirked, shaking his head. 'So, I got all the stuff. I'm just gonna bring it all in. Do you need anything else from the van while I'm there?'

'Some more three-inch nails.' Brann picked up his hammer and play-smacked it on his hand. 'For my coffin.'

Harrison sniggered and went out. Brann turned to Ophelia. 'I—'

'Dad.' Harrison reappeared. 'Do you want the planks in too, or will I leave them there just now?'

'Leave them for now.'

'Ok.' He left again.

Ophelia was leaning on the windowsill. She let her arm fall nonchalantly, then slow clapped. 'Ha, ha, ha...very funny, I'm sure.'

'What?'

'Getting him to call you "Dad".'

'What?'

'I know he's your brother.'

Brann furrowed his brow. 'Um, no, he isn't.'

'Yes, yes, very good. You can keep this up all day if you want, but why bother?'

'Because it's true.'

She stared at him with narrowed eyes. Brann didn't flinch. Not the first time someone had mistaken Harrison for his brother, but somehow it bothered him more that Ophelia didn't know the truth. What had she taken him for? A baggage-free single guy? He'd have to disappoint. He was a single father of two, with a lot of baggage.

Harrison returned with armfuls of boxes.

'Who am I?' Brann turned to him.

'What?'

'What is my relationship to you?'

Harrison grinned. 'You're my dad.'

'Well, obviously he would say that.' Ophelia shook her head. 'Is this some little scenario you've cooked up between yourselves to make me look silly?'

'Not at all. I swear he's my son. I've got birth certificates and photos to prove it. I've also got a daughter, Caitlin. You maybe saw her at the Highland Games.'

'That was your daughter?' Ophelia's eyes widened. 'I thought she was somebody you were seeing.'

Harrison doubled over laughing.

'Are you kidding me?' Brann's jaw dropped. 'She's only sixteen.'

'Well, I could see she looked young. I thought she was about twenty. But so what? I don't know what age you are. You definitely don't look old enough to be his dad though.'

'I'll take that as a compliment, but I assure you I'm old enough. I'm thirty-seven, he's nineteen.'

'Wow... Well, that's... nice.' She met his eyes, and he read something new there – appraisal perhaps, or judgement. Definitely questions. Were her insides burning to ask for details? If they were, she kept her cool and said nothing. 'I better leave you to get on.'

He watched her go, then shut the door behind her as she left.

'Ouch,' Harrison said.

'What?'

'She's not happy about that.'

'What do you mean?'

'Because guys with grown-up kids aren't as attractive as rugged single blokes. She doesn't want to be my stepmum.'

'Shut the fuck up! Like there was ever any danger of that.'

'Stop denying it. You wanna do her. Why was she here? Were you two snogging in the backroom?'

'No, we bloody weren't. Now, stop talking about this.' He needed to rid himself of her, not keep going on, but whatever he did, every path seemed to lead back to her, and he couldn't find an escape route.

Chapter Fourteen

Ophelia

September

What kind of man was Brann Duthie? Ophelia asked herself the same question for what felt like weeks. And she answered it too... Trying to avoid any answers that made him sound good.

'He's the kind of man who had a child when he was a teenager,' she told Conker as she mucked out his stable. But that question brought up more. Who was Harrison's mum? Did he and his sister have the same mum? Did Brann still have feelings for this woman or these women? What had their life been like when they were together as teenagers? Was his partner younger or older?

'I wish I could stop caring,' she muttered.

'Hey.'

Ophelia whipped around, and her eyes widened. 'Brann.' Shit. What had she said out loud? Had he heard her muttering to herself? 'What is it?'

He leaned his arm high on the doorframe and his eyes raked her over in that way they often did. And yes, she was well aware she frequently returned the favour too.

'Just came to see you.'

'Really? Why?'

'I dunno. You've not been about as much lately. Did you tell your father about the man who was wandering about?'

'No, but I told Barbara. She thinks it might be the moped thief, and she called the police.'

'I thought I was the thief?' Brann smiled, but his eyes weren't as cheerful as his expression.

He'd definitely stolen something from her, but nothing as trivial as a moped. He'd gone straight for her heart. 'I don't know what you are,' she said.

'I'm just a regular guy. Listen, about that... I guess finding out I was Harrison's dad surprised you a bit.'

'A little.'

'Yeah. Thought so.' He moved his arm from the door and crossed the stables, leaning in and stroking Conker. 'I thought you already knew. It's not exactly a secret.'

'It never occurred to me.'

'Sorry.' He gave a little shrug. 'Guess I look different now, huh?'

He'd got that right, but why? He was still the same guy. 'Maybe, but that isn't necessarily bad.'

'I hope not.' His crooked grin was back, and it was so endearing she couldn't stop herself from returning it. 'Caitlin, my daughter, not my girlfriend' – he raised an eyebrow – 'really wants to learn to ride and get a horse. I'm struggling to find a place that can do it. I don't suppose you fancy teaching her?'

'Me? I'm not a great rider.'

'I saw you at the Highland Games and you looked pretty good to me.'

'Did I?'

'You sure did. That was a difficult course to even attempt, and I know you weren't exactly practising in the run up, because you were working here and doing your other job. You weren't the worst by any stretch. It seemed more like you'd lost concentration.'

'I did.' Could he guess what had caused that? The twinkle in his eye said he could. 'Maybe you should ask Dagmar.'

'Already did, but she was a bit vague.'

Ophelia sighed. 'I can certainly let Caitlin use a horse here. Conker is a good horse and doesn't mind who rides him. But really Dagmar is much better suited to giving lessons than me. I'm not patient enough.'

'Astonishing. I'd never have guessed.'

'Oh, be quiet.'

The sound of voices outside made Brann turn around.

'That might be Dagmar now. I'll speak to her.' But before Ophelia got to the door, in came Jacinta and Francesca.

'Hello, Ophelia,' Jacinta said. 'What are you doing in here?'

'Tending to my horse.'

'I didn't think you ever stooped that low.'

Ophelia rolled her eyes.

'I think you're talking about yourself. Dagmar has enough to do, and if you want her to carry on doing her job, then you need to make sure you keep paying her.' Ophelia glared from Francesca to Jacinta. 'Otherwise she might leave.'

'Wages are Barbara's department.'

'Yes, but the money has to be there for her to use. She can't authorise wages if someone has spent all the money on a fancy holiday, can she?'

'Change the record,' Jacinta said, then blinked at Brann as though surprised to see him. 'Are you fixing something?'

'No. I'm just leaving.'

Ophelia followed him out of the door. 'Listen, I'd like you to stop working at the boathouse for the next few weeks and help me get my cottage fully inhabitable. Get me a kitchen, bathroom and fittings. I need out of the big house now. I can't cope with that woman any longer.'

'As you wish, milady.' Brann tapped two fingers to his forehead in a salute.

That was the kind of man he was – a reliable, helpful one.

'I don't trust that man,' Jacinta said when Ophelia returned to the stable. 'There's something not quite right about him.'

When she'd first met him, Ophelia would have agreed and taken great pleasure in tearing strips off him, but now a furious need to defend him rose in her. 'What nonsense. It's not him with the issues around here.'

'I see you've joined his fan club. Honestly, the way some people go on about him like he's something special. He looks shifty more than anything else, if you ask me.'

'Thankfully, no one did. And it sounds to me like the lady doth protest too much. Perhaps it's you who should subscribe to his fan club. I can see you keeping a naked poster of him under your pillow.'

'That's revolting.' Jacinta's cheeks reddened, and Ophelia laughed.

'I think he's the dad of a girl I know in the musical theatre club,' Francesca said. 'He picked her up once. Rosie thought he was a hot dad.'

'Francesca, really.' Jacinta looked outraged.

'What? I mean, she wasn't wrong, was she? He's kind of alright.'

'This is a disgusting conversation.'

Ophelia smirked to herself, then winked at Francesca as Jacinta carried on muttering about how repulsive it was for a sixteen-year-old to be talking like that.

Ophelia stopped typing and drew in a breath. She might have been better off working in the big house and braving Jacinta, but even with all the hammering and banging, she preferred working in the cottage. Brann and Harrison had taken over all week, fitting a new kitchen and bathroom. Soon Ophelia would be living here as well as working here. The proximity to Brann was the main reason for being here and not in the big house, though she hardly dared admit it even to herself. Something about him being so close made her feel like everything would be ok.

That was the kind of man he was. *The kind who makes me feel safe.*

Today was her birthday, but she hadn't mentioned it to him. It seemed silly blurting it out. Rupert and Jacinta had given her a card and a pretty bracelet. Quite nice, except she knew it was a re-gift as she remembered Jacinta opening it the previous Christmas. Well, at least they weren't spending estate money. Lucinda had called to wish her a happy birthday and Edith had planned a lunch date for them at the weekend. For a twenty-ninth birthday, that was fine.

Come lunchtime, she was getting hungry, but she still had to get through a lot of designs for Timeless Butterfly Interiors. The trouble was, she couldn't make food here until the kitchen was in, but she couldn't face the main house either.

Voices caught her attention. A woman was speaking, and Brann replied. Who was it? *Please not Jacinta.*

The door to the spare room where Ophelia was working opened and a smiling face looked around.

'Happy birthday!'

'Hayley. What are you doing here and how did you know it was my birthday?'

Hayley tapped the side of her nose. 'You told me ages ago, and I remembered. I also got your message the other day saying you were getting this place done up, and I took a chance to pop over. I don't work on Tuesdays, so I'm free. And I brought lunch.' She brandished a bag from the Glenbriar Deli.

'You're actually a lifesaver,' Ophelia said. 'I was wondering what to do about food.'

'I bought loads because I didn't know what you'd fancy. There's enough here to feed the five thousand.'

'I'm sure you can use up the rest.'

'How about I ask Brann to join us? He's good for a laugh and I bet he eats a lot.'

'I'm not sure that's a good idea.'

'Why not? He's a real sweetie. He danced with me at a wedding when I was on my own.'

'Did you date him?'

'Nah. I never really fancied him like that. Probably because I always fancied Oliver. Here, let me ask him.'

Ophelia groaned internally as Hayley disappeared from the room. Secretly she wanted Brann to celebrate her birthday with her. *But that's not sensible.* And whenever they were together, things happened... The crackle of sexual tension was impossible to stop. Sometimes it was so powerful it must surely be visible to everyone.

'They're coming through in a few minutes.' Hayley beamed, returning to the room.

'I hope it doesn't make things awkward. I mean, I'm paying them to work here.'

'Yeah, but they're nice. I could give Brann the food and ask him to take it away if that would be better.'

'You can't do that now.' Ophelia made her way outside and sat at the patio table, so she was facing the small, sparse garden in front of the woods. A fleeting thought crossed her mind. What if the tramp they'd seen at the boathouse came wandering by when she was here alone? What if he came to the window or something? This cottage was a long way from anything.

Heavy footfalls told her Brann and Harrison had arrived.

Ophelia imagined how different she'd feel if Brann lived here too. She'd never be afraid at night if he was there holding her.

'Happy birthday to you,' Brann sang in his low, soulful voice. 'Happy birthday to you.'

'You told him.' Ophelia glanced at Hayley, then at Brann.

'Yup, she told me. And no, I don't have a birthday present. But I do have a question, or I can keep on singing.'

'What question?' she asked, though she quite liked his singing.

'Is this your real birthday or the official one?'

She tilted her head and blinked slowly. 'You're not in the least amusing.'

He grinned and flicked her a wink.

Hayley frowned slightly, then gave them both a puzzled look before sitting down and opening the deli bag.

Ophelia stared at the trees at the bottom of the garden, hugging herself so tight her nails dug into her arms. Those trees were very dense. Anyone could be hiding in there. A chair scraped behind her and she turned around and blinked.

Oh my god.

Why had Brann chosen to sit so close? Far too close, and yet not close enough.

'It's like *Upstairs, Downstairs*, isn't it?' He waggled his eyebrows. 'The servants dining with the upper class.'

'Seriously?' Ophelia said.

'Aren't the peasants revolting?' he said.

'You said it.'

'I did indeed.'

'So...' Hayley eyed them quizzically. 'I've got almost every filling you can imagine. Does anyone have any preferences?'

'I eat anything,' Brann said.

'Me too.' Harrison surveyed the selection. 'Except prawns. I don't like them.'

'Leave them for the birthday girl.' Brann gave Ophelia a gentle pat that made goosebumps erupt on her arm. 'Prawns are for the upper class.'

She shrugged him off, and he laughed.

'So, how's this place coming along?' Hayley asked.

'Good,' Ophelia and Brann said at the same time.

'Finally, something they agree on.' Harrison raised an eyebrow at Hayley.

She chuckled as she handed around the plate of sandwiches.

'First and last time,' Ophelia muttered, taking a sandwich.

'Have any of you ever been whitewater rafting?' Hayley said brightly. 'I've wanted to do it for a while. We thought about doing it for my brother's sten party, but his fiancée isn't really into that kind of thing. Oliver says he's up for it, as an adventure, you know.'

'Wouldn't you be better trying handcuffs or something a bit less life-threatening?' Brann said.

Hayley laughed. 'I didn't mean adventurous like that, cheeky.'

'I haven't tried it, but maybe I should.' Ophelia nibbled her sandwich.

'Which one?' Brann asked quietly. 'Handcuffs or rafting? I'd quite like to be a fly on the wall for either.'

'Dream on.' Ophelia barely opened her mouth, speaking so low no one heard except him.

'I'd try it,' Harrison said. 'I've gorge-crossed before, on an outdoor activity course when I was at school.'

'That sounds scary,' Hayley said.

'It was fun.' Harrison grinned at her, then at Ophelia. 'Were you two at school together?'

'No,' Hayley said. 'I went to Glenbriar High School.'

'Me too,' Harrison said.

'And Ophelia went to that girl's place, didn't you?'

'Kinroy Academy.'

'And where did you go?' Hayley asked Brann.

'Glenbriar too... though I didn't spend much time there.' He lolled back, folding his arms, and Ophelia tried not to stare. How dare he tease her with that godlike body? 'I skived most of the time and did whatever I wanted; not my smartest move, but hey...'

Ophelia swallowed. *That* was the kind of man he was... But not anymore. And somewhere along the line, he must have changed because he'd made good.

'How did you learn how to do all this stuff if you didn't go to school?' she asked.

He stretched a muscly forearm across the table to lift a sandwich. 'I did an apprenticeship later on.'

Her eyes couldn't stop their treachery, but how could she not look at Brann? She wanted him so badly it hurt all over. But he was from another world.

She stole a look at him, then Harrison. How were they father and son? Brann was eighteen when he was born; Harrison was nineteen now. *Imagine him with a baby...* Nope, she couldn't, but that was what Brann must have been like.

Having him so close set her blood racing. She would take him on for another fight in a second, though it wasn't really a fight she wanted. Brann Duthie, the epitome of rugged manhood, was sitting at her table, eating from her plate, smiling at her and her friend, invading every inch of her being. If only Hayley and Harrison would vanish, she'd sweep the detritus from the table and have him right there.

Her gaze was trained on him. For a moment, he stared in the opposite direction, then slowly shifted his focus back. Their eyes met for several highly charged seconds and the heat in Ophelia's cheeks rose to burning point. He knew exactly what she was thinking, didn't he? The tiny curl of his lips told her he did, and he wanted exactly the same thing.

Hayley was still chatting to Harrison, which was just as well because Ophelia wanted to use the moment to eye flirt with Brann... and a whole lot more.

'Well, we should get back to work.' Brann broke the moment, dusting his hands together. 'Our boss is a tyrant who gets ants in her pants if we take breaks too often.' He winked at Ophelia.

She gave him a withering stare. 'Then off you go or you'll find your P45 waiting for you tomorrow morning.'

He left with a chuckle, and Harrison followed with a wave.

'Such a beautiful day.' Hayley glanced around the garden, then behind her to the cottage. 'Tell me.' She leaned forward conspiratorially. 'What is going on with you and him?'

'Meaning what?'

'Oh, come on. The banter. All those looks. He's got the hots for you and...' Hayley pulled a face. 'It could be mutual.'

'You have an overactive imagination.'

Hayley raised a sceptical eyebrow. 'Yeah?'

'Yes.' She blinked and looked back at the trees. 'I can't.'

'Can't what?'

'Can't like him... In that way. In any way. He's an employee, and it has to stay that way.'

'Why? If you like him—'

'I don't. I just told you. He's good at his job and that's that.'

Yes. *That* was the kind of man he was. A builder who worked hard on the estate – not someone she could have anything more to do with than that.

CHAPTER FIFTEEN

Brann

'Tea break time again?' Ophelia marched through the door of the cottage kitchen, and Brann looked up from his phone with a start. Harrison almost cracked his head from under a base unit.

'Well, you're the boss,' Brann said. 'If you'll just grab my tools, I'll get off.'

'Oh, gross.' Harrison cringed under the base unit, and Brann laughed.

Ophelia held her hand over her mouth. 'Oh, ha-ha. I just thought it was very quiet in here.'

Shaking his head, still grinning, he replied, 'We're not naughty little school kids. If it suddenly goes quiet, it doesn't mean we're hiding in the corner plotting to burn the house down.'

'So what are you doing?'

'What does it look like?'

Ophelia scanned around, and Brann held his breath. Joinery was his real love, and he took pride in it. He called himself a builder because he worked on bigger projects now and had contracts with other trades, but when he got back to working with wood, his hands and his heart worked together. He'd brought the designs to life, and her scrutiny made him uneasy.

She smiled. 'It's looking good.'

'Phew.' He ran the back of his hand across his forehead in an exaggerated fashion, pretending to let sweat drip off it. 'You had me panicking there.' Joking, yeah, but partly true.

'So, what's the timeframe looking like?' she asked. 'When can I expect to move in?'

'Well, the plumbers are here tomorrow. They'll connect the water and finish the bathroom. Once we've got everything in, the electrician will come back and do the final fittings. That should be by the end of the week. You can decorate it after that, but it'll be ready to move in. If there's any snagging left, I'll come down next week and finish it.'

'Great. I can't wait to tell Jacinta. She'll be thrilled to get rid of me.'

'Bet she misses you.'

'Ha. Bet she does not.'

Brann smirked as Ophelia left and returned to work. A message from Caitlin caught his eye before he put his phone away.

CAITLIN: It's Take Your Child to Work Day next week on Tuesday. Can I come with you? I went with Mum the last time.

Brann half closed his eyes. He didn't mind her coming with him, but he wasn't sure he wanted her to witness his interactions with Ophelia... Harrison was bad enough.

BRANN: Sure you can. Remember Mum's got a new job though. It won't be the same as last time. Happy for you to come with me if you want but be prepared to work!

CAITLIN: I'm prepared. Still got the pink hammer you gave me for Christmas once.

Brann laughed, and a little bubble of pride swelled in his chest.

Work was done on the cottage by the end of the week, as he'd anticipated. Ophelia had gone to Edinburgh for a meeting, but emailed him to say she'd be back on Tuesday and would take a look with him to see if anything still remained. Great. The same day he was bringing Caitlin with him.

'This place is so cool,' Caitlin said when they rocked up at the boathouse. 'I want to live here.'

'Yeah, it's cute,' Brann agreed. 'We need to crack on. We got a bit side-tracked doing up that cottage.'

'For the heiress,' Harrison said.

'Is she like dead posh?' Caitlin asked.

'Oh yeah. Speaks in that plummy way. And she's got the horn for Dad.'

'Harrison, shut it,' Brann said.

'Are you serious?' Caitlin pulled a disgusted face. 'Isn't she like really young?'

'I'm not *that* old.' Brann put his hands on his hips; he was in better shape than a lot of guys younger than him.

'But you're not seeing her or anything?'

'Of course not,' he said. Caitlin's panic about him having relationships bubbled to the surface again. How to get over this? He didn't want to be single forever, but it scared him to think if he moved on, she might harm herself. 'She's way out of my league and she's marrying some posh man.'

'Is she actually?' Harrison said. 'She doesn't seem that into him... But you...'

'That's enough.' Brann glanced at Caitlin. Her face was white and her eyes wide. 'I've got a job for you.' He led her into the side room. 'This room is getting plasterboarded, but you see this corner has a tricky little section. Can you make me a template?'

'Um, how?'

'With this.' He held out his universal measuring tool. 'Use it to make the angles and cut a template from this card. Then I'll use it to cut the plasterboard.'

'Ok. I'll give it a go.'

Brann left her to it and returned to the main room. 'Don't scare her,' he muttered to Harrison.

'I wasn't. I just said it like it is.'

'Well, don't. I admit it, we've done some stupid flirting, but you know as well as I do nothing is going to happen there. Caitlin panics about stuff like that, so no need to worry her for nothing.'

'Yeah. Whatever.'

Brann went out to the van and breathed in the earthy scent of the air. The lochan rippled in the breeze and everything was quite serene. Across the water, where the trees were dense, was a large shape. He squinted. Was it that man again? Then it moved, and he saw it was a deer. It made him smile. This was like something from his imagination. He watched it for a while, his eyes roaming around. The leaves were starting to turn. Some yellow had crept in. The summer had almost passed.

The sound of an engine on the track ruined the perfect peace. A flash of red in the September sun announced the coming of Ophelia in her scarlet beamer.

'Morning.' She jumped out.

'You're back, I see.'

'Indeed, I am. How's work?'

'I only just got here. But it's fine.'

'Do you have a minute to come to the cottage with me? I had a look around and there are a couple of things I need to ask you about.'

'Yeah, sure.'

'I'll have a nose in here first though, if you don't mind?' She led the way inside and Harrison turned around. He threw Brann an *I-told-you-so* look and let out a snort.

'I heard on the radio on the way here it was Take Your Child to Work Day,' Ophelia said to Brann. 'I see you followed the brief.'

'Actually, about that...'

The side door opened and Caitlin came through. She stopped dead as her gaze landed on Ophelia.

'Oh,' Ophelia said. 'Are you actually taking part in Take Your Child to Work Day?'

'Yup,' Brann said. 'I am. This is Caitlin, my daughter.'

Caitlin's lips barely twitched. 'Hi.'

'Pleased to meet you.' Ophelia gave her a little wave. 'I'm Ophelia.'

Caitlin gave a brief nod, then glanced at Harrison, who shook his head, still with that annoying know-it-all smirk.

'Have you done the template?' Brann asked.

'Yeah,' Caitlin said. 'I think so.'

'Good. I'll have a quick look, then I need to go to the cottage and check the snagging. You can make a template for the other corner and help Harrison while I'm gone.' Brann went into the side room with her.

'Is she going to the cottage too?'

'Yeah. She owns it.'

'What are you going to do there?'

'Check everything is ok. Why?'

She shrugged. 'I dunno.'

Christ. He had to behave himself. Both his kids suspected him of misbehaving... Exactly like he had done. *Cringe.*

He left Caitlin in the side room and headed out with Ophelia, fully aware as soon as he left his kids were likely to start talking about him.

'Let's go in my car,' Ophelia said.

'Am I allowed in it?' Brann dusted off his work trousers.

'I have seat covers.'

He snorted. 'You're well prepared.'

'I have a horse. I often get messy.' She drove off down the track towards the workers' cottages.

'Next week, the guys are coming in to put on the extension to the boathouse,' he said. He'd ordered it so it would be delivered ready-made. They just had to put it up and clad it. Nice and easy, all wood, and a perfect blend for its surroundings, just as the plans had stated. Whoever had done them was fantastic. They'd been so detailed and clear he hadn't run into any issues.

'Oh, wow. Things are really moving now. It's exciting.'

'Is cash flow any better?'

'The livery is pulling some money in.' Ophelia steered one handed, her other hand on her lap, displaying her immaculate nails. 'So, that's eased the pressure a bit, but a lot of it's gone on paying Dagmar.'

'You realise it's completely outrageous that she was working for free?'

'Of course I do. That's why I paid her out of my own pocket.'

'You did what?'

'You heard me.'

'Well, now I'm furious on your behalf. Why do you put up with this shit?'

'For a long time, I didn't. That's why I left, but look what happened while I was away. The whole place has fallen apart.'

'Then dump them and leave them to fix it themselves.'

'I can't. My grandparents went to great lengths to ensure I was allowed to inherit. If I abandon Glenvorneth, their effort was for nothing. They wanted me to do this and I have a lot of respect for their wishes. They were good people and had big ideas for the estate, but they both died too young and before they could properly enact their plans. My father and Jacinta are clueless and resistant to everything, but if I want this place to succeed, I have to work with them.'

Brann put his hand over hers, and she took an audible breath. 'What happened to your grandparents?'

'My grandmother died first. Cancer. My grandfather went just over a year later from a heart attack, though it was more like a broken heart. He couldn't live without my grandmother.'

'That's sad. I'm glad you're here to honour them, but I really wish you didn't have to deal with so much shit on your own.'

Ophelia raised a finger and linked it with his. 'Thank you,' she whispered. 'You're actually ok sometimes.'

'You're obviously not yourself today. I think you need a long lie down.'

She pulled a pout like she was trying to stop herself from smiling.

Aye, with me, if you like, Princess. Any time. He squeezed her hand.

She raised her eyebrow and smirked. *Yeah, she understands.*

They got out at the cottage, and Brann followed her inside. 'So, what are the issues?'

'Nothing big. The box around the pipes in the living area doesn't look right, and can you look at the sealant around the bath? Is it meant to be like that?'

'I'll take a look.' She was quite right. The boxing wasn't finished properly, and the plumbers had been sloppy with the sealant. 'I need to come back and fix them both. I've got stuff in the van.'

'I'll give you a lift back.'

She stuck close to him as they went to the car, and he had a weird sensation like she needed him beside her. What was even stranger was how he felt it too, like his soul was only relaxed when it was close to her. This wasn't the same as those times they'd lusted over each other; it was much more profound. He touched his hand to her lower back as they reached the car, before they split to go to either side, and her lips twitched in a gentle smile.

'If the kids are ok, I'll nip back straight away and sort those two things,' he said as she drove him back.

'There's no rush. I've not got all my furniture yet. I'll be there though. I'm heading back to do some work.'

As soon as he got into the boathouse, he checked Caitlin and Harrison were still busy.

'Yeah, we're fine,' Harrison said.

'I'll take the van back to the cottage,' Brann said. 'Shouldn't take me long. Be back in an hour or two.'

Outside the cottage was Ophelia's car and an old-fashioned silver Jaguar parked behind it. He pulled in and cranked on the handbrake.

Three women got out of the Jaguar as Brann popped his belt. He recognised two of them. Barbara and Jacinta. The third one appeared around the same age as them but was wearing a somewhat wacky, bright fuchsia outfit.

He jumped out behind them as Ophelia opened the cottage door. She frowned and folded her arms. 'What's this? A deputation?'

'Hello, Ophelia,' Jacinta said. 'I've brought a visitor. You'll be very excited about this.'

'Will I?'

'Indeed. This is Camilla Woodcroft,' Jacinta continued.

'The mad artiste,' Camilla added with an over-the-top flourish of her hand.

Ophelia took a step back, and her eyes met Brann's. He tried not to smirk as Camilla beamed; she radiated like a neon light in a pool of candle-lit roses. Completely outré in a bright floral kaftan flowing in the wind. And *Christ*, it was shockingly see-through. A black-lacy thong wafted in and out of vision. Brann averted his eyes.

'Camilla needs a place to stay,' Jacinta said.

'I'm doing some new paintings.' Camilla mimed waggling a brush in mid-air. 'I might try to exhibit at The Gallery. I've done some kinky pieces for them before. They like that sort of thing,

but I'm not in the mood right now. I was inspired a while back –
I had this man; god he was sex on a stick. We bonked like rabbits.
It really got my creative juices flowing, but now it's all dried up.'

Brann didn't know where to look.

Jacinta cleared her throat. 'This cottage might help inspire
you.'

'Hang on.' Ophelia held up her hands. 'This cottage?'

'Yes.' Jacinta blinked, all innocence. 'Barbara tells me we need
to make money where we can and this cottage is ready now, so
we can start renting it immediately.'

'I'm living here.'

'Let's discuss this inside and not in front of the builder,'
Jacinta said. She and Camilla went inside directly, but Ophelia
blocked Barbara from going in and Brann was stuck behind her,
unable to get past.

'What is going on?' Ophelia said.

'Sorry, so sorry. She thinks she's helping. You know what she's
like.'

'I do, but I paid for this. This was for me to stay in while I'm
working here. Now, she's swanning in and snatching it.'

'I'm sorry, I really am. I tried to talk her out of it. Let me try
again.' Barbara gave her a commiserative look and headed inside.

Ophelia's jaw set and she glanced up at Brann. Her eyes seemed
a little glossy. Was she going to cry?

'What do you make of this?' she said.

'It's out of order, if you ask me, but I doubt they'll care what I think.'

'This is the story of my fucking life. I just want to go back to Edinburgh, where I have friends. I used to love Glenvorneth so much, but now...' She held her hand to her lips.

The urge to reach out and hug her burned strong, but he resisted. Flames licked his chest, and he balled his fists. Must stay professional. He couldn't risk anyone coming out and seeing them.

'Do you still want me to do the repairs?'

'Maybe better wait until they've gone. This could get messy.' Her phone buzzed, and she pulled it out. 'And what's this?' she groaned. 'James.'

'Are you and him dating now?'

She rolled her eyes. 'We're going on our first date this Friday.'

'Right.'

'We arranged it together, so we wouldn't have our parents around micromanaging every second. Let me listen to his message.' She raised the phone to her ear. Brann shoved his hands into his pockets, trying not to listen, but it was impossible not to hear it.

Hey, sorry. I'm not going to make it on Friday. Something's come up, but you keep the tickets. Take someone else, if you want. And, Ophelia, maybe we should take this as a sign. You and I aren't really going anywhere. I don't think we really like each other in the right way. Don't get me wrong, you're a nice person, but I don't think we're compatible.

Ophelia slapped the end message button and lowered her phone. 'Did you hear all that?'

'I did.'

'That's a first. I've been dumped before we even went on a date. Well, I better not tell Jacinta. She thinks after Friday night I'll be engaged.'

'Then tell her. Let her be disappointed. She deserves to be pulled down a peg or two, especially after this.'

'Actually, you're not wrong.'

'Where were you meant to be going?'

'A charity dinner dance at Scone Palace. It sounded like fun, but not something I want to go to alone. I even brought my favourite dress back from Edinburgh to wear.' She gave a sigh. 'Oh well, no ball for Cinders. No house either, by the looks of things.'

'How about I go with you on Friday? I won't be as suave as Mr Pink Trousers but I like dancing and food... and you.'

She stared at him. 'Brann, have you lost your mind?'

'Clearly. I'll take that as an emphatic no.'

'Take it as a yes. Just don't tell anyone.'

He smirked and saluted her. 'You got it, Princess.'

So much for behaving professionally. Well, he'd never been any good at behaving, had he?

Chapter Sixteen

Ophelia

Ophelia stepped out of the taxi into the gravelled drop-off area. The cold air nipped at her cheeks, and she pulled her faux-fur stole tighter around her shoulders. Scone Palace rose before her, its almost red brickwork and crenulations lit by glowing uplighters on the path. Distant strains of music from inside carried into the still evening.

Brann got out the other side and adjusted his jet-black kilt jacket. 'I see they've sent a welcoming committee.' He raised his eyebrow at a pure white peacock wandering along beside the path.

'They certainly have. Just for you.'

Brann smiled, stepped up beside her, and put out his elbow. 'Shall we, my princess? And I must say you are looking particularly delectable this evening.'

'That's a big word for a builder, isn't it?'

'I told you before, I'm a multi-talented builder.'

'I know you are.' She linked her arm through his and nodded. 'I've heard you singing many times and your woodwork is legendary. I've also heard you're pretty hot with a screwdriver.'

He let out a laugh. 'Naughty, naughty, but if you're looking for a good nailing, you've found the right guy.'

She play-slapped his hand as they made their way to the entrance. They waited for a moment on the steps, and Ophelia found the tickets in her clutch bag.

'I didn't think you'd need a ticket to get in here. Aren't you some relation to Lord What's-his-name?'

'We're distantly related to the Mansfields, but it's not them hosting. This is just the venue. It's some businessperson who's hosting it. Someone James knows.'

Her midnight-blue dress clung to her form, and she was quite impressed as she saw her reflection in the mirrors in the grand hall. She and Brann didn't look too bad together at all. No one who didn't already know would guess he was the builder. His kilt suit replaced his usual scruffy garb, and he looked like a model, not a workman. A flutter rippled through Ophelia. He was hot when he was tooled up in his workwear, drool-worthy when he was in the tug-of-war team, and just as sexy when smart.

She could forget about the fact she'd been forced back into her old room at the main house, while Camilla was entrenched in her cottage. At least here, she was free, living the moment, and not having to worry about anything else.

'You scrub up well.' She eyed over Brann's reflection.

He shot her a sidelong glance, the corner of his lips quirking. 'I never thought I'd find myself at a place like this.'

Ophelia met his eyes. 'And yet, here we are.'

'Indeed we are. The princess and the peasant.'

She nudged him, and they both laughed.

Glittering chandeliers picked out the sequins on her bodice as they stepped into the grand hall. She scanned around, wondering if she'd meet anyone she knew.

The large room opened up before them, buzzing chat mingled with soft piano music. Going to an event where she didn't know anyone was unusual, but probably for the best. She didn't really want to explain why she was here with Brann... Mainly because she wasn't entirely sure why. It had just kind of happened. And as undeniably pleasant as it was, she couldn't quite make sense of it.

'Brann, you know this isn't a date, don't you?' The sudden need to clarify and explain herself sent the words tumbling out. 'This is just—'

'Us being us. Yes.'

'I'm not sure I know what that means.'

'Don't you?'

'Bonsoir!' a loud, tipsy voice said. Someone gripped Ophelia's upper arm tightly. She turned to see a somewhat eccentric looking woman, dressed in a hideous baggy outfit that appeared to have been cut from an old pair of jacquard curtains. 'Flora

MacDonald, you remember me, yes? I know your mother very well and your stepmother, both very interesting women.'

For very different reasons, no doubt.

'Of course, I remember you.'

'Wonderful. And are you Mr Charlton?' she asked Brann. 'Jacinta told me all about you when I saw her last.'

'He's not. Mr Charlton couldn't make it.'

'How unfortunate. So, are you—'

'I think someone over there is trying to get your attention.' Ophelia pointed into the crowd.

'Really?' Flora asked. 'Oh, it's David Payton. I'll go see what he wants. Will catch you later.'

'Oh god.' Ophelia sighed. 'Has Jacinta told the whole world about James?'

'Have you told her you've split up with him?'

'Not yet. I'm keeping out of their way. That business with the cottage has really pissed me off.'

Brann put his arm around her shoulder. The heat from his palm on her skin was burning. 'Yeah. That's a piece of shit.'

The move was evidently meant to be comforting, and it was, but it was also possessive and protective. Normally, Ophelia would have objected to men doing this to her, but she found she didn't mind being under his wing like this. It added to her strength and made her feel like she belonged somewhere. With him? *Oh help.* That couldn't be good, but she liked the sensation, and she tilted her head slightly, so she was just leaning on him.

With a brief pat, he dropped his arm, leaving her cold and alone.

'Oh no,' she said. 'I've just spotted someone I really don't want to talk to.'

'Who?'

'Xander Davenport.'

'Who's that?'

'My stepbrother. Jacinta's son. God knows why he's here, but then, it's unsurprising. He loves himself and is always pushing himself forward. Just like his mother.'

'That's a bit harsh, isn't it? He must be quite young.'

'He's twenty-one, and he's at university doing a course he shouldn't have got on at all.'

'How come?'

'He didn't get the grades he needed at school, but Jacinta and her ex went to the school and kicked up such a fuss. They claimed they'd paid for him to get the right grades, so the school altered them and he got in.'

'That's outrageous.'

'Don't I know it? Oh bollocks. He's seen us and he's coming over.' Ophelia pulled a false grin as Xander approached. He was fair-haired like his mother and good-looking in a floppy-haired, boyish kind of way, but cockiness radiated from him, alongside a dazzling white smile. A similar young man was with him. He had darker, curly hair, and together they looked like they were ready to start their own boy band.

'Well, hello, sis,' he said. 'I didn't expect you to be here. Isn't this beneath you, like the queen attending the peasants' ball?'

She narrowed her eyes. It was the kind of thing Brann frequently came out with himself, but not this time. He wasn't smiling, and he drew closer to her. He was so tall and broad chested he looked like a bear next to these two ferrets. 'Scone Palace is hardly the place for peasants, Xander.'

'Very true. It's just that it's a business type thing. For professionals. We're here for the connections.'

Bully for him. Did he have any idea how successful her business was? Probably not. None of her family did, except her mother.

'I saw some peacocks out front,' the other man said. 'They might be attending the pheasants' ball.' He and Xander laughed.

Brann glanced at Ophelia and pulled a face.

'This is my friend Sean,' Xander said once he'd stopped laughing. He eyed Brann and frowned.

'Oh, this is Brann,' Ophelia said.

'Hello, Brian,' Xander said.

'Hi.' Brann didn't correct him on the name, and neither did Ophelia.

'Is this who mother is marrying you off to now?' Xander whispered.

'Not exactly. He's a... friend who stepped in last minute.' It was weird calling Brann a friend, but no other word seemed to fit.

Sean was listening in and smiled somewhat smugly as Ophelia finished. 'I wonder if you'd do me the great honour of dancing with me?' he asked in a pompous voice.

'Now?' Ophelia gaped at him.

'No time like the present.'

'Well, um...' She glanced at Brann, who raised an eyebrow.

'If you feel the need,' he said. 'But only one. The next dance is mine.'

Sean took her hand, his palms sweaty and hot, and led her to the dancefloor. She winced as they took their positions. He had to be Xander's age, and it was strange dancing with a friend of her younger brother.

'You and I should see more of each other,' Sean said.

'What?' Ophelia frowned, but her eyes were distracted. Brann stood at the edge of the dancefloor, talking with Xander, but his eyes were on her. Xander looked even more boyish next to him. Brann was red hot in his kilt and just dishevelled enough to be rugged without being scruffy. How Ophelia would love to prise back that lapel, drag him towards her by the bowtie, get her hands on his belt, his sporran...

'I hear your father is trying to marry you off to the highest bidder. Totally shocking in this day and age, I might add. But if you're looking for credentials.' Sean's cheeks were rosy as he blabbered, some of the cockiness momentarily gone.

'You're a little young for me.'

'You think? Oh...'

She was relieved when the dance ended, and she returned to Brann. With a brief goodbye to Xander, she pulled Brann onto the dance floor.

'What's up?' he said with a grin.

'I think that child has ruined my dress by clinging to it with his sweaty palm.'

'And now you want me to clean it off with mine?'

'Something like that.'

'Nothing would give me more pleasure.' He swept his arm around her and pulled her close. 'Well, something might, but right now, this'll do.'

Ophelia wrapped her arms around his neck, surrendering to him. 'Show me how real men dance.'

'Don't worry, I will.' His words were like soft kisses on her ear. 'That lad you were dancing with apparently has his sights set on you.'

'So I discovered.'

'Xander tells me he's got great earning potential, but he's got no chance of inheriting his family estate, which is apparently little more than a farm, because he has three older brothers. So instead, he wants to marry someone with lots of land. And Xander obviously told him about you, and tonight's his lucky night.'

'Oh, for god's sake. He's too young and I don't fancy him.'

'No?' he whispered. 'Who do you fancy?'

'Stop it,' she said through gritted teeth as he slid his palm over her bare back.

'Stop what? Talking or doing this?' He caressed her back lower with his other hand.

'I don't know.'

'Then tell me, who do you fancy?'

'Please, Brann, don't make me answer that.'

He nuzzled his cheek against hers. He'd shaved, but there was still enough stubble to graze her soft skin. If Sean was watching, he'd surely realise he had no chance of competing with this guy. She only hoped Xander didn't report back to Jacinta. She didn't want to have to explain this.

The dancing continued until the meal was served. Ophelia stuck to Brann like glue and was pleased to be at a table with strangers where they could talk freely and not have to pretend to be this or that. Brann was fun to talk to and easy company. The food was good, and they both had several drinks as they were getting a taxi home. James had already booked and paid for it. Ophelia let a moment of guilt wash over her.

The dancing resumed after the meal, but the air was stuffy and too warm.

'Should we go outside?' she said. 'It's hard to breathe in here now.'

'Ok. But it'll be cold out there.'

'You'll have to keep me warm.'

'Sounds like the perfect job.'

A few other people were outside in the courtyard. Brann put his arm around Ophelia, and they walked towards a little chapel on a hill close by. It was much darker here, and the air was cold. The palace looked stunning all lit up and, beyond it, the lights of Perth shimmered in the distance.

'Can I kiss you?' Brann's softly spoken words in his low voice broke the silence.

Ophelia's breath hitched. She wanted it more than anything, but where was all this going? 'Why?'

'Because *I* fancy *you*.'

'I know that, Brann. But where is this leading?'

'Nowhere. That's the point. That's why we should do it while we can, before you go off with some rich guy.'

'Alright.' She wrapped her arms around his neck again and they resumed their position from the dance floor earlier, only this time no one was watching. The darkness hid them, and Brann's arms were like a safety belt. Nothing could harm her while he held her like this.

'You're so very beautiful, my princess.' He dipped in, pressing his lips against hers.

Ophelia relaxed into him, savouring the soft warm kisses before delving deeper. Soon their tongues met, and she clenched her arms so tightly around his neck, she thought she might break it. But she wanted him, needed him. Every part of her connected with him on a spiritual as well as physical level. This was a meeting of body and soul. Brann held her tightly, perfectly cocooning her body. She didn't want to be anywhere else. These were the only arms she wanted around her… Ever. But how the hell would that be possible?

Chapter Seventeen

Brann

October

Brann watched as the crane lowered the side panels of the boathouse extension. He held his breath. This was where he became a control freak and wanted to do it all himself. The rest of his life could be as messy as fuck, but with this kind of work, he hated the thought something might go wrong, and it was out of his control.

'I'm sure the operator knows what he's doing,' Harrison said, obviously picking up on the vibe.

'I'm sure he does. We just can't afford any mistakes.'

When the last panel was in place, Brann exhaled slowly. He and his team got to work, hammering everything into place. The boathouse had a whole new look. The quirky, original bit was now a feature front with a cabin-style lodge out the back giving ample living space and three upstairs bedrooms. This was the type of modern miracle Brann loved. Flatpack houses.

Back in the main part of the boathouse, he opened his laptop and worked on some admin while the team brought everything together. He used to scoff and moan about his superiors spending more time in an office than onsite. Now he understood why. Paperwork was a necessary and time-consuming evil.

A knock on the door. He looked up as Ophelia's head poked around. He suppressed the raging hormones that fired up at the sight of her. Since their soiree at Scone Palace, they'd been well-behaved and were trying to stay businesslike. Not an easy ask, especially after that kiss they'd shared. That'd been something else, a union of souls.

'I'm stunned,' she said. 'The extension is up already. How did I miss it?'

'It's quick once it arrives.'

'No kidding.'

'Obviously, there's still work to be done, but with the shell on like that, you can see how it'll look.'

'It's incredible.'

'Glad you approve. We all know how hard you are to please.'

She huffed and raised an eyebrow. 'What are you doing now?'

'Admin.'

'The boring stuff.' She sat on the plank of wood he'd balanced on two reels to make a desk for himself.

'You guessed it.'

'I've just had a heap of that to do for the business. I miss meeting clients and working on designs with them face to face.

Lucinda's been doing all that. I get the brunt of the admin work and some of the online meetings.'

'What is it you actually do?'

'Don't you know?'

He shook his head.

'Oh... Well, I'm an, um, interior designer.'

'You'll be in your element here then.'

She gave an odd little half laugh. 'Knowing my luck, Jacinta will swoop in and get her mad artist friend to decorate this place too, before I get a chance.'

'You should move in here.'

'That's not a bad idea, especially as she stole the cottage. This could be perfect. We won't get as many holidaymakers over the winter months, but will it be ready?'

'For you, Princess, I'll move heaven and earth and make sure it's ready.'

She quirked her lips up and patted him on the shoulder. 'I don't dislike you quite as much as I used to.'

'Good progress then.' He winked at her.

She peered out the window, then got to her feet and went over to it. 'Come here a minute.'

He followed, moving in behind her, his hand dropping instantly to her lower back.

'It's that man again,' she said.

'I'm going to talk to him.'

'I'll come with you.'

They nipped outside and strode around the lochan. The wind whipped up, and the trees swayed.

'Hey there,' Brann called to the man.

He stopped moving and turned to face them. His beard was very long and Brann suppressed an urge to call him Gandalf.

'Are you ok?' Brann asked.

'Mmm.' The man nodded.

'Can we help you?' Ophelia asked. 'We've seen you here before. Are you looking for something?'

'My house.' He pointed at the boathouse. 'Used to live there.'

Brann flicked Ophelia a little glance, and she pulled a helpless face.

'You used to live here? I think I remember you, but that was a long time ago.'

'A long time, yes.'

'Listen,' Brann said. 'Are you sleeping rough out here?'

The man nodded. 'Got a camp.'

'Do you also have a moped?'

'Borrowed it, but it ran out of fuel and can't get it back.'

Something stirred in the back of Brann's mind, a long-forgotten memory. He was just a boy and his dad had thrown him – almost literally – out of their house one night when he wanted to have some unsavoury guests over. Their wacky old neighbour had almost knocked Brann over on his motorbike, but instead of losing his shit as a lot of their neighbours would have, he'd taken him in for the night and given him a drink and some mouldy biscuits.

'Are you Donald Struthers?' Brann asked.

'Huh?' the man frowned at him from under his bushy eyebrows. 'Donald, yes.'

'You know him too?' Ophelia blinked at him.

Brann nodded, then turned his attention back to Donald. 'You used to live next door to me when I was a lad. I'm Brann.'

Donald peered forward. 'You've grown.'

'I hope so. I was about ten when I last saw you. We should get you somewhere safe.'

'Nowhere safe these days.'

'You can't stay here. It's dangerous with winter coming.' Brann stepped closer and put his arm around Donald's shoulder. 'I could run you to a hostel. Do you want me to help you collect your belongings?'

Donald fidgeted with his tatty sleeves. 'Yes. That might be best. I like the woods, but it's very cold.'

'Come on then. Let's get you some help.' He turned to Ophelia. 'Can you go back and tell the guys where I am?'

'Sure. Will you be ok?'

'Yeah. We'll be fine.'

Donald's camp was deep in the woods. If Brann had to choose somewhere to sleep rough for several months, this wouldn't be a bad choice. But the poor guy looked thin and malnourished. His speech was slow, and so were his movements. It seemed a little cruel packing up his life and moving him on, but he needed help, and he wouldn't get that out here.

'How did you end up here?' Brann asked.

'Walked when we all fell out.' Donald was moving so slowly it was taking ages to get back to the boathouse. Brann didn't remember Donald's family or much about him. Only the motorcycle and that night of kindness when otherwise he'd have been sleeping in the garden while his dad had a drunken orgy. 'Worked here for a while, then I had to go. No money to pay me.'

'I know the feeling. I'll get you somewhere safe.'

'Too old for this. A long time ago, some nice people lived here. They helped me. And a little girl. She could draw.'

'Was that Ophelia?'

'Ophelia yes. Strange name.'

When they finally got back, Brann put Donald's stuff in the back of the van and let him climb in.

'Wait there and I'll let the others know where I'm going,' Brann told him.

Ophelia was inside at his makeshift desk on her phone.

'I'm going to run him into Perth,' Brann said. 'There's a homeless shelter there.'

She put her phone down. 'Can I come too?'

'You can, but I'm not going to sugarcoat this. He smells bad. If you think you can stand it all the way to Perth, then fine, but you'll be sitting right next to him.'

'It's fine. I'll do it. I remember him. He lived in the old worker's cottages for a while when my grandparents were still alive, then my father moved him here. I'm not sure why. Goodness knows how he ended up in the woods.'

'Apparently your father didn't pay him.'

Ophelia groaned. 'Get's worse and worse, doesn't it?'

'Not half. But he remembers you. Apparently you were good at drawing.'

She gave him a half smile. 'I should certainly hope so.'

'Come on then, but don't say I didn't warn you.'

Brann put the heating on in the van and opened the windows, driving with his head facing away from Donald. Poor guy clearly hadn't washed for many months. Ophelia seemed to be coping well with the smell, though she was having more trouble keeping her hair in place once they hit the dual carriageway and the wind whistled in.

'Do you remember me?' she asked. 'I saw you sometimes with my grandparents when I was little.'

'Yes. You did pretty pictures. Do you still do them?'

'Yes, I do.'

Brann was impressed she made out anything from his words. They were quite garbled.

By the time they got him to the hostel, handed over his belongings and told the receptionist as much information as they could, it was a lot later than Brann had anticipated.

'Bye, Donald,' Ophelia said as the receptionist went over to him.

He gave them a little wave.

'Take care,' Brann said. 'I never thanked you for that night when I was a kid, but maybe this will repay the favour.'

Donald gave him a weak smile. 'You're a good boy. You did good. Shame about your parents.'

'Yeah, well, never mind. They're both gone now.'

'Thank you,' Donald said. 'Stay safe. Ophelia is a beautiful wife. So kind.'

Brann covered his mouth to hide his laugh as he left. Ophelia raised her eyebrow. 'Only someone who'd been living rough for years would think that we're married.'

'So true.' Still chuckling, he got back in the van. 'I hope the house hasn't collapsed.'

'I'm sure it'll be fine. I don't suppose you're going to tell me how you know him? What did he do for you when you were a kid?'

'Helped me escape my dick of a father for a night.' He started the engine and drove off, not looking at her. 'My childhood was pretty shit. Dad liked to have women around, just not with me in the house, so he'd kick me out. Who knows what he wanted me to do? I just wandered about.' Sometimes he'd cried. Until he got tough, then he kicked off and got into trouble. Nothing serious, but it got him a reputation he never really deserved. Having his own kids had helped with that. He'd stopped messing around for their sake. 'Donald nearly ran me over one night when I was hanging around. Even then, he was a bit odd, but he was kind hearted.'

'That's how I remember him too. I guess I was lucky growing up. I used to think my childhood was bad, always hiding from my parents when they were arguing, but at least I never got kicked out to fend for myself.'

He shifted his hand to rest on her thigh, and she linked her fingers with his. 'It's all relative. Your hurts were just as painful as mine.'

'Not really, but you've done so well considering what you came from.'

'Thanks.' He let out a sigh. 'Maybe you could ring the police and explain about the moped. It's still in the woods, though it's in pretty poor shape now.'

'Sure.' Ophelia pulled out her phone as he drove. 'Oh no,' she groaned, after ending the call.

'What's wrong?'

'Hayley's booked to go whitewater rafting this weekend with her boyfriend. Apparently her brother and his wife were supposed to do it too, but they have the sick bug and can't make it. She wonders if I'll go instead and take James. Get this, because it would be a good bonding experience for us.'

Brann chuckled. 'I guess she doesn't know you were dumped before the first date.'

'No one knows that.'

'Except me.'

'Yup.'

'And do you want me to stand in for him again? I can become Brian and go rafting. Except Hayley already knows who I am, of course.'

'Exactly. There's no way I can take you.'

'Why not?'

'Because Hayley already thinks I fancy you.'

'Got that right, didn't she?' He raised his eyebrows but kept his eyes on the road.

'Seriously, Brann, you need to stop saying things like that.'

'Just saying it like it is. Tell her we're going as frenemies or something like that.'

'Frenemies?'

'They're all the rage at the moment, according to Caitlin.'

'It's risky.'

'So what? Since when has that bothered you? You took a risk leaving your business and coming here. You're contemplating getting thrown off a waterfall into plunging rapids, but you think it's riskier being seen with me... In case someone discovers the truth. God forbid you were caught liking someone like me.'

'Alright. You've made your point. Fine. Come with me.'

He chuckled. 'I really put my foot in it there, didn't I? I've just volunteered to be thrown over a waterfall this weekend.'

'Yes, you did. And you can't chicken out now.'

'Neither can you. I can't wait to hear what you tell Hayley.'

Ophelia let out a low moan and sank back into her seat. Brann smirked. This could be an interesting weekend.

CHAPTER EIGHTEEN

Ophelia

Ophelia opened the door to Wood 'n' Chic and a little bell rang. Camilla Woodcroft and Jacinta followed her. Ophelia had privately arranged to help Camilla furnish the cottage – with proper payment for the privilege, none of which would be going to the estate – unaware that Camilla had also invited Jacinta. Now Ophelia wished she hadn't bothered. With the rafting later that day, this was something she could do without, but she didn't dare leave Jacinta here alone in case she decided this was a service Camilla should be getting for free.

'Good morning.' Jacinta muscled her way forward and straight to the desk, where Stella was smiling. 'You might remember me. I'm Mrs Chattan-Blythe of Glenvorneth.'

Camilla tipped Ophelia a wink and pulled a face, indicating she thought Jacinta's introduction a bit hoity-toity. But that was Jacinta to a T. Lording it over everyone.

'How are you?' Stella smiled at Ophelia. 'It's nice to see you again.'

'And you,' Ophelia said. 'We're looking for a few pieces for the cottage.'

'I know exactly what we need,' Jacinta said. 'So, let me see.'

'Actually, I'll decide that. I'm a designer, I know what'll work and I'm also in charge of the budget. Camilla's set it and I doubt she wants it to go too high.'

'Indeed, I don't.' Camilla held up her hands.

'Ophelia is a little bit sore about this,' Jacinta said in a hushed voice. 'She labours under the delusion she has some right to authority over me but, at the end of the day, I own the cottage. She's in charge of nothing yet.'

Stella blinked a few times, then smiled. 'Everyone is welcome to look around.'

Kristalee, the woman with the heavy metal make-up and alternative dress sense, came in from the backroom and said something to Stella.

'I'll have a look,' Stella said. 'You stay out here and help these ladies.'

'Sure.' Kristalee wandered around the desk, running her heavily ringed fingers through her burgundy hair, and came over to Ophelia. 'I didn't realise before you were related to the Chattan-Blythes.'

'For my sins, yes.'

'I know Edith a little. She's your mum, right?'

'Yes. How do you know her?'

'I cleaned her house for a while after she moved away from her husband. Your dad, I suppose.'

'Ah, I see.'

'I see her about quite a bit with her partner. They look so happy together. Good for her.' Kristalee smiled with a little nod.

'What partner?' Ophelia frowned. Her mother didn't have a partner; she'd never seemed interested in anyone since the split.

'The woman from... Wait a minute, you didn't know she was seeing anyone?'

'No, and I didn't know she was into women, either.'

'Oh... I didn't mean to say anything out of turn.' Kristalee clapped her hands to her mouth. She and Ophelia were similar in height, both tall, though Ophelia was Willowy, where Kristalee had curves. Her appearance usually made Ophelia feel small beside her, but now Kristalee seemed to diminish. 'I thought it was common knowledge.'

'But...' Ophelia frowned, pushing her mind into places it had never gone before. The wonderings she'd occasionally had about why her mum had never remarried. The friends she had. Nancy... Could it be Nancy was more than a friend?

'She told me years ago she'd never felt right with your dad and hoped she could bring her true self out in the open soon. It seemed obvious to me what she meant. I mean, she wasn't always alone at the house, and when I saw her out recently, I assumed she'd told people.' Kristalee pulled a helpless face. 'I'm really sorry if I've put my foot in it.'

'It's fine.' Ophelia took a deep breath. If it was true, so what? She didn't mind, but to hear it from someone else made her a little sad. Why hadn't her mum told her?

Her mind wouldn't focus on the furniture after that, and she wanted to get out. The desire to call her mum and discover the truth was like heartburn, but she didn't want to barge in and be tactless. Also, the uncertainty as to why her mum hadn't already told her niggled away like a brainworm.

With the rafting later, she didn't have enough time to visit her. And her mum was always so busy, there were no guarantees she'd be there.

She returned to Glenvorneth to change, after making sure she chose all the furniture, Camilla paid for it, and Jacinta did nothing but pull faces as she looked on, trying to add helpful suggestions that Ophelia ignored. She'd arranged to meet Brann in the car park of Heather Glen Water Sports Centre twenty minutes before she was due to meet Hayley – deliberately giving them time to psych themselves up for this.

His van was already there when she got out. Rain was drizzling now and the autumn colours on the surrounding trees and hills were stunning.

Brann got out wearing a tight t-shirt, showing off his sculpted abs and biceps. He lifted a jacket from the seat before he closed the door and swung it around his shoulders.

'Lovely day to get wet,' he said.

'Yeah.' Ophelia shook her ponytail out from under the collar of her windcheater jacket.

'Everything ok?' Brann frowned. 'You look a bit off-colour. Are you nervous about this?'

'I suppose so, but it's not that. I've had a really weird morning.'

'Jacinta?'

'Surprisingly no. Not entirely, though she was part of it.' Ophelia rubbed her forehead and glanced around, trying to straighten things out in her mind.

'Tell me.' Brann put his hand on her upper arm. 'Sharing is caring.'

She flicked him a wry smile. 'Well, only if you swear not to tell anyone else. This is totally unconfirmed, and it's already making me edgy.'

'Cross my heart.' He drew imaginary lines on his chest with his fingertip. 'My lips are sealed.'

'Well, an assistant in the shop I was in this morning started talking to me. She said she knew my mum, then she said something about my mum having a partner.'

'And does that bother you?'

'Not exactly. Apparently, her partner is a woman though. And, well, I just didn't know. But I feel like I should know, and I can't understand why she wouldn't tell me.'

He gently rubbed her shoulder, and the motion soothed her. 'Maybe she's scared to.'

'Maybe.'

'It's hard to tell your kids important stuff if you think it might hurt them, or if you don't know how they'll react.'

'I guess.'

'What would you have done if you were in her shoes?'

'Probably the same as her.'

'Exactly. Hey, come here.' Brann gently tugged her closer and wrapped his wonderful arms about her. She placed her hand on his broad chest, the soft fabric of his t-shirt warm beneath her. Her forehead rested perfectly against his neck, and she nuzzled into the heat of his skin. He ran his fingers down her cheek in a soothing motion. 'It's ok,' he said quietly. 'I'm sure she'll tell you when she's ready. Just give her the chance.'

'You're actually a wise man.'

'For a builder.'

'For anyone.'

He shifted slightly and placed a kiss on her cheek. 'And you're a strong woman with a big heart. Sometimes it's hidden under your hard shell, but it's there.'

She shut her eyes for a moment, sensing her heartbeat, aware it was close to Brann's and how right that felt. 'Well, today's the day you've been waiting for.' She patted his chest, then pulled back, steadying herself with a deep breath.

'When I get to see you in a wetsuit?'

'I was thinking more that you get to shove me off a waterfall.'

He chuckled. 'Except I don't. I'm coming with you.'

'That's kind of how it's meant to be, isn't it?'

'Absolutely.'

Another car pulled in and Brann moved away from her, under the cover of the shop porch.

'That's Hayley.' He nodded his head at the car.

'Now for the tough bit. The rapids will be a cinch compared to this.' Ophelia didn't follow Brann into the porch but waved to Hayley as she got out of the passenger side of a car.

'Hi!' Hayley ran over and hugged Ophelia. 'So, did you bring James? Are we getting to meet him? Ready for the bonding session?'

'Um, no.' Ophelia glanced behind her and realised Brann was keeping out of sight. 'James and I aren't a thing anymore. In fact, we never got as far as being a thing.'

'But we need him,' Hayley said. 'To balance the raft.'

'It's ok. I brought... The builder.'

'Brann?'

'The very same.'

'Do you want a bonding session with him?'

'No. He was... In the right place at the right time.'

Oliver came up behind Hayley and put his hand on her back. 'Everything ok?'

'Fine, yeah. Ophelia's brought Brann instead of James, but that's ok. As long as he shows up.'

'He's here already. Brann!' Ophelia called to him.

He strolled out with his hands in his pockets. 'You called, Princess?'

'Just wanted to show Hayley you're here. She's worried the boat won't balance.'

Hayley laughed. 'Well, this is unexpected. But good to see you. This is Oliver, my fiancé.'

'You're together now.' Brann smiled. 'That's good news.' He shook Oliver's hand. 'I'm Brann.'

'The builder, not the boyfriend,' Hayley said.

He put his hands up. 'Definitely the builder. And the boat balancer.'

Hayley took Ophelia's arm and let the guys walk ahead. Ophelia was prepared for this. 'So, you and him...' Hayley cocked her head in Brann's direction. 'This is new.'

'He's here for the rafting, that's all. It's something he's always wanted to do.'

'Is it? I didn't think he sounded that keen before. Must be something else that's made him want to do it... Or someone.'

Ophelia smiled at her, then put her finger on her own lip. 'Shh. Stop speculating. There's nothing to see here, ok?'

Hayley's expression told her this wasn't the end by a long stretch.

As Ophelia wrestled into her wetsuit a short time later, she caught Hayley grinning again.

'I'm not sure I like wearing this,' she said, before Hayley started questioning her again. 'It's kind of like being naked with only a layer of rubber on top.'

'That sounds all kind of dodgy.' Hayley giggled.

'Seriously? You're like a high school kid.' Ophelia lobbed her rolled-up top at her, which only made Hayley laugh more.

After pulling on the ugly over-jacket, Ophelia sat back on the wooden bench in the changing cabin beside Hayley and the other rafters.

'So, class three rapids,' Ophelia said. 'Should I know what that means?'

'Nice try,' Hayley said. 'But why not tell me about Brann?'

Ophelia groaned. 'Why won't you believe what I already told you?'

'Would you if you were in my position?'

'Probably not.'

She was saved from having to continue as several of the other people started filing back into the main room.

'We should go too.'

'Ok,' Hayley said. 'But this isn't over.'

Brann and Oliver were waiting. Both of them looked a lot better in their wetsuits than Ophelia felt. Brann was all-levels of hot, almost superhero style with the tight suit showing off his body shape – broad shoulders, muscly chest and tapered waist.

Ophelia deliberately made no reaction as she approached. Hayley greeted Oliver with a hug.

'You look edible,' she said.

Brann edged closer to Ophelia. 'Do I look edible too?'

'Oh yes. I'll happily feed you to any sharks we see on the way.'

He barked out a laugh, and Hayley turned to him with a quizzical expression. Ophelia rolled her eyes.

'Come on, we're going.'

Logan, the instructor, was waiting with some of the group already assembled around him. He smiled easily, talking with wide hand gestures. They approached, and he welcomed them.

'Once we're all together, we can head off in the minibus. Let me do a quick head count.'

The minibus had a trailer with a rack of rafts on the back. Ophelia's stomach lurched. Why was she doing this? She never did anything like this, and those rafts didn't look very secure.

'We got this.' Brann patted her on the back as they made their way into the minibus.

'It's a bit nerve-racking, isn't it?' Hayley clipped her seatbelt.

'You chose to do it,' Oliver said with a smile.

'I want to and I'm not chickening out, but I'm nervous.'

'Me too,' Ophelia said.

'I didn't realise you were keen,' Hayley said to Brann.

He pulled up one shoulder. 'Ah, you know me. I'll try pretty much anything.'

When they arrived at the starting point, Logan explained the safety issues to the group. He helped them into the boats and instructed them on how to paddle at the shallow edges of the river. Ophelia, Brann, Oliver, Hayley, and another couple were in a boat together. Logan demonstrated the technique – everyone seemed to know what they were doing except Ophelia; she couldn't get it right.

'What you're doing is fine,' Logan said. 'You just need to make larger movements, stirring rather than stabbing.'

'Remember that.' Brann leaned closer. 'No stabbing. Especially if you ever get the urge to pick up a pair of antlers again.'

'Just shut up, will you?' Ophelia narrowed her eyes as she saw Hayley laughing.

Half an hour they practised before Logan jumped on the boat with them. A couple of other groups seemed more experienced and were going alone. A fourth boat had another instructor with them.

Ophelia was very relieved someone was with them. She could see herself mucking this up. The boat lunged into the current, and they were off. All seemed calm. They dipped and bobbed along the river. A few small peaks pushed them up before they smacked back down.

'Ok everyone,' Logan called. 'This is the first stage. Everybody ready, remember to stay calm and listen for my instruction.'

As they coursed forward, Ophelia's heart was almost ripped from her chest. She couldn't draw breath. They plunged into a deep trough, only to be flung high onto a mountainous crest. As they slammed back down, she lost the feeling in her limbs. Logan's shouts were indistinct. Her face was wet. She wanted to wipe the water from her eyes, but her hands were stuck to the paddle.

Suddenly the tumult became a softer bob. Her senses were recovering. Lessening her grip on the paddle, she realised she could breathe again. She blinked the water from her eyes as they reached a calmer point, but they were still racing along.

'You ok?' Brann asked.

'What? Oh... I think so.'

He smiled and gave her a wink, dipping his paddle at the same time. Anyone would think he was a seasoned pro. *Show off*.

'Ok, everyone,' Logan called. 'A little while until the next rapids, sit tight, and enjoy some of the terrific scenery. This is the Dairvin wood on either side of the river. Lovely walks in there, especially with these autumn colours – and we're coming to the soldier's leap. After that, we approach the next set of rapids.'

Ophelia didn't want to do it again. Her stomach was still back at the first set, and suddenly she heard Logan's voice alerting them to the soldier's leap. The boat dashed forward, speeding into the current, then lunged. A blur of red and gold sped past on either side.

'Ready everyone?' Logan shouted.

She didn't hear what he said next; she was too petrified. They were approaching a waterfall.

A hand rested on her arm. 'It's ok,' Brann mouthed. 'You'll be fine.'

She nodded. Then the breath left her body as they careered over the edge. She shut her eyes, clinging to the paddle.

A moment of utter silence.

She must have died.

The boat smacked the river below; it spun for a few seconds. The noise of screaming and laughing hit her alongside the tumultuous gush of the water. Logan shouted at them all to paddle.

She instinctively stabbed at the water, forgetting everything about 'stirring'.

Another set of rapids was in sight. The boat raced towards them, drawn with stealthy speed and unseen force. They plunged in, were thrown back up, and again. The boat spun; Logan yelled at them to paddle. Another dip, Ophelia's stomach was left behind. She wanted it to stop, but at the same time there was a thrill in every peak and tumult. Finally, they swirled into an area of open calm. The river widened and despite its speed, it got gentler; they eased along until Logan instructed them to paddle to the bank.

Ophelia couldn't move. She was shaking all over.

'Come on.' Brann helped her up. 'You've done it.'

She let his strong arms and powerful body guide her out of the boat. So cold. She shivered, barely aware his arms were around her. The van was waiting to take them back to the centre. Hayley and Oliver were huddled under a blanket, laughing.

Ophelia curled in next to Brann, and he pulled a blanket over her and put his arm around her shoulder.

Teeth chattering, her whole body shaking, she became aware that the low sound she'd taken for the engine was actually Brann. He was humming a soft melody. As she tuned into it, it soothed and comforted her like a magical healing song. The relief that the rafting was finished subsided, and a bubble of pride swelled in her chest. She'd done it. Done something anyway. Maybe not exactly what she'd set out to do. She'd been seen with Brann and by the biggest gossip ever. No way would Hayley be able to keep a lid on this. The box was well and truly open. Except what exactly was inside? Ophelia wasn't sure.

The changing cabin was only slightly warmer than outside, but Ophelia was very glad to get back into dry clothes. Brann's singing had fed her soul and kept her going, but now it had stopped, it left her empty.

'That was brilliant, wasn't it?' Hayley said.

'I might think so in a month's time.' Ophelia towelled her hair, pushing away the odd loneliness. 'Right now, I'm still too shaky.'

'Just as well you had a strong pair of arms to fall into.'

'Yeah. That's why I brought him along. He's the scaffolding.'

Hayley snorted. 'So, do you and him want to get some food?'

'No thanks,' Ophelia said. 'Well, I can't speak for him, but I have stuff to sort out with my family tonight.' A little white lie, but she couldn't face anything else – because if she went, Brann was sure to follow, whether in the flesh or in hundreds of questions. Of course, she couldn't prevent him going if he wanted to, but she suspected he wouldn't want to be a gooseberry, so would likely decline.

'No worries, we'll get together again soon, for something a bit less dramatic.' Hayley sat on the bench as she pulled on her socks. 'But for now, you can spill the beans.'

'About what?'

'Brann! Why was he here? Are you two a thing, or what?'

'Of course we're not. He's here because he heard me talking about it and invited himself. That's all.'

'Looked quite cosy on the way back.'

'Yeah, well, I was cold.'

She smiled. 'You could do worse, you know. He's a nice guy, steady job.'

'Listen.' Ophelia plonked down next to Hayley. 'This is all lovely and I'm sure for most people what you just said is true. But it's not going to happen. Nothing can happen with him and me. Ever. I have to marry someone a lot richer. Maybe it's old-fashioned and sounds stupid, but it's my reality. Money doesn't grow on trees. Without money, my family home will be lost. And I'm not just talking about a house. It's a place with a soul where generations of us have lived. I owe this to my grandparents and their memory. It's not something I can give up lightly or walk away from. Seeing Brann would be nothing but a stupid fling, because nothing can happen in the long run.'

Hayley cocked her head and let out a sigh. 'That's sad.'

'Maybe, but it's also true, and I can't lose sight of that.'

Hayley reached out and pulled her into a side hug. 'I get it and I'm sorry. It can't be easy for you. I bet people laugh at you and think it's silly, but when you're living the reality, it's different.'

'Exactly.'

'And I guess it's almost impossible to find a rich man... Not only that, but a rich man you actually love.'

'Completely impossible, I'd say.' Which was why she hadn't made any progress for months.

'Especially if you happen to fall for someone else while you're looking.'

Ophelia leaned down, breaking Hayley's hug, and picking her wet swimsuit up off the floor. 'Just as well that hasn't happened then.' She stuffed the swimsuit in her bag, not looking at Hayley. She couldn't. If she did, her face might betray the truth, and she didn't want to face it. If she'd fallen for Brann somewhere along the line, she would never admit it. Not to Hayley. Not to him. And definitely not to herself.

Chapter Nineteen

Brann

The front door slammed and Brann cringed, midway through stirring a pot of chilli.

'Don't slam the bloody door! You'll knock it off its hinges.'

'It's not like you couldn't fix it in like five seconds.' Caitlin smacked a leather bag onto the kitchen table.

'That isn't the point. I'd rather you didn't damage my property.'

'Whatever.' Caitlin flicked her hair over her shoulder and slumped into a seat.

'What's rattled your cage?'

'Nothing.' She shrugged and pulled out her phone. Her eyes were slightly red, and Brann watched her for a second until she looked back and pulled a face. 'Why is your hair wet?'

'I went white-water rafting today.'

'What?' Caitlin gaped at him.

'Yup.'

'You never told me you were doing that. I'd have come and taken photos. Who did you go with?'

'Ah, just some... mates. It was a last-minute thing.'

'Did anyone get pictures?'

'I don't think so. We couldn't take phones on the boat, and it would have been difficult to find a place to stand for photos.' Logan had taken some official snaps before they started, but Brann wasn't about to share them. That would lead to too many questions. Some he didn't want to answer. But he was glad he'd gone along. Ophelia had looked so petrified. Not that he'd helped much, but some moral support was better than nothing.

'You're crazy,' Caitlin said. 'I'd never do that.'

'I never thought I would either, but it was a good experience.'

She let out a sigh and rested her chin on the back of her hand.

'Are you sure you're ok?' Brann sat opposite her. 'Talk to me. I know it's not always easy, but sometimes it's better to share.'

'Ugh.' She groaned. 'It's just this annoying girl from the theatre club. I thought she was a right snob, then she seemed ok for a bit, and we were like quite friendly.'

Brann nodded, not daring to speak in case he said the wrong thing and she clammed up again.

'I was going to meet her in town today, 'cause she's not at my school, see. But she didn't show, then I got all these photos from her friend, saying she didn't want to tell me herself, but she thinks I'm a loser. In the photos, she's...'

Brann tilted his head. 'She's what?'

'She's with this boy I like from the club. I can't believe she's going out with him when she said she wouldn't. I never want to go back there.'

Brann reached over and took her hand. An urge to storm out of the house and hunt down everyone who'd hurt his baby girl surged through him, but he mastered it. 'I get it. I totally get it. It's your call whether or not you go, but it seems a shame to give up on it because of a couple of people.'

'I know, but it's so awkward.'

He squeezed her hand. 'Yeah, I know. You're a strong girl, but if you don't want to fight this battle, I completely understand. Sometimes walking away is the best course.'

She pulled a face that was almost grateful, though a little annoyed.

'At least if she's not at your school, you won't have to see her there.'

'I guess.' She pulled a pout, then glanced at him. 'I think you know her.'

'Me?' Brann frowned. 'How do I know her?'

'Because she lives at that place you're working.'

'At Glenvorneth?'

'Yup.'

'What's her name?'

'Francesca Chattan-Blythe.' Caitlin put on a fake posh voice, dragging out the name like it was totally boring.

'Hmm.' He tried to recall if he'd met her or not. Whenever he was at Glenvorneth, his mind was always on a different Chattan-Blythe.

'Her sister is that posh woman we watched riding at the highland games. The bossy one who was there when I came up for the work experience day.'

'Oh, right. Her.'

'Yeah. I don't think any of them are very nice. Got more money than sense and the reason they all walk so upright is because they have so many silver spoons rammed up their arses.'

Brann sniggered. 'That's not very nice.'

'Yeah, well, she hasn't exactly been nice to me. And I know you were thinking about getting me riding lessons there, but I don't want to go now.'

'Understandable.' He let go of her hand, got to his feet, and went to stir the pot on the stove. A niggle worked its way from his chest into his gut. He'd have been pissed off about anyone bullying Caitlin, but the discovery of the culprit unsettled him. He didn't need any further connections to that family. Good or bad.

Letting Caitlin speak in her own time was usually best, so he didn't push her for anything else. She was happy to take her dinner into the living room on a tray and they sat side by side, with their feet up, watching *Strictly*. Brann wouldn't have watched it on his own, but these dad-and-daughter moments didn't come around that often. Soon she'd be too grown up to want to do this kind of thing with her dad. He had to take them while he could.

She was with him all weekend and they spent Sunday together, going for a run in the morning and Brann pottering about the house while she did her homework in the afternoon.

He was doing up his bedroom, a long overdue job. When he'd split with Kristalee and moved here, he had to provide a house with a bedroom for each child. Such was the rule for different sex children. Made sense, but finding an affordable three-bedroom house in Glenbriar wasn't easy. This town didn't come cheap. Thanks to his DIY skills, he'd been able to convert a two-bedroom house into three by partitioning the largest bedroom. It wasn't ideal and made for two very small rooms, but it complied with the guidelines. Now, Harrison was at his girlfriend's house more than anywhere else, and they were looking at places together. Caitlin wouldn't be at school much longer and Brann could see a time when he might sell this house and move somewhere else. He'd always fancied a doer upper. A proper one, like an abandoned cottage in the countryside. The kind of place he was always doing for other people. Like the boathouse. It was stunning, but he'd never be able to afford anything like that.

If he was to sell this house, it needed some changes. The décor was tired. Starting with his own room seemed like a good plan. He'd never really done anything to it. As it was the smaller bedroom, it didn't have a lot of space and it looked woefully like a teenager's bedroom, not a grown man's. Not that it mattered.

He didn't exactly bring people back here to see it. If he hooked up with people, he went to their houses. Only once he'd brought a woman back here and she hadn't been greatly impressed by the place. Who would be? Nineteen-sixties, two-bedroom, mid-terraced houses weren't exactly much to look at.

He'd ripped out an old shelving unit and was in the process of carrying the bits downstairs when his phone buzzed in his back pocket. Dropping the planks outside the backdoor, he pulled it out. *Kristalee*.

'Hi,' he said.

'Hi. Is Caitlin there?'

'Inside, doing her homework.'

'Ah, ok. I messaged her, but she didn't reply. I wondered if she'd gone into Perth.'

'She put her phone on silent and left it out of reach, so she can concentrate.'

'Sensible. I was gonna ask her to pick some stuff up, but I'll get it another day.'

'She went to Perth yesterday.' He glanced inside. The living room door where Caitlin was working was still shut. 'Listen, I need to tell you something.' He stepped into the garden and sat at the little round bistro table on the tiny patio area.

'What's up?'

'She told me about some girls who are bullying her. One of them is from the Glenvorneth Estate, where I'm working at the moment.'

'The Chattan-Blythes?'

'You know them?'

'Do you not remember? I cleaned a house for one of them when she split with the posh bloke from there.'

Those days seemed so long ago sometimes, but at other times were like yesterday. 'I vaguely remember you cleaning houses, but I'd never have put two and two together. I'm not sure I ever knew the names of most of the people you cleaned for.'

'Yeah. It's weird, because they were in the shop the other day.'

'Who was?'

'The Chattan-Blythes. The new wife and one of the daughters. I bloody hope it's not her who's doing the bullying. She's an adult.'

'No, it's someone Caitlin's age. From the theatre club.'

'I knew something was happening there. Well, I don't care if she doesn't go back if it's filled with snooty-nosed bullies. The Chattan-Blythe woman was right up herself.'

Brann bit his tongue. Sometimes that was true, and he'd told her so himself, but he didn't like hearing it from other people. She was his to insult; no one else was allowed. Even inside his head, that sounded totally nuts, but it didn't take away the irritation.

'Hmm,' he muttered.

'I assume she's the mother of the bully.'

'No, she's her sister.'

'What? I'm talking about the older woman.'

'Oh... I thought you meant... Never mind.'

'The sister wasn't that bad. Ophelia. She's friends with my boss. But, oh my god...'

'What?'

'I went and told her that her mum had a gay partner. And she didn't know.'

Brann raised his eyes to the heavens. Kristalee had done that? His ex? Somehow the web got even more tangled around him. 'Oh dear.'

'Yeah. Me and my big mouth. Anyway, how did we get onto this?'

'The bullying.'

'Well, I think keeping as big a distance from these people as we can is about the best thing we can do.'

And wasn't that the truth? Only Brann couldn't keep away. He had to work there. A good enough excuse for now, but he wasn't convinced he wanted to keep away anyway. Something about Ophelia always lured him back, even though he knew he shouldn't, and it wasn't good for him.

Brann and Harrison turned up at the boathouse on Monday morning, as usual. A message popped in so uncannily, he checked around to see if Ophelia was watching for his arrival from the bushes.

OPHELIA C-B: Now the boathouse has walls and floors, can I start moving stuff in or will that get in the way? I don't think I can stomach the main house much longer.

BRANN: The painters are coming today and tomorrow. If they get the main rooms finished, you can start moving stuff into the living areas and bedrooms while we finish the kitchen.

*OPHELIA C-B: Thanks. I might need your help to move furniture... You being the brawn after all. *wink emoji**

He smirked as he replied.

*BRANN: Just tell me where you want me and I'll oblige. *two wink emojis**

*OPHELIA C-B: I can think of a few choice places. *three wink emojis**

Brann looked up and was confronted by Harrison with folded arms, his eyebrows raised. 'Messaging your girlfriend again?'

'I don't have a girlfriend.'

'Who are you messaging then?'

'It was Ophelia asking about the progress.'

'Uh-huh. Like I said. Your girlfriend.'

'She isn't—'

'Yeah, so you say, and yet, that look on your face when you're messaging her... Well, didn't look like you were writing a progress update.'

Brann glanced away, chewing his tongue.

'And I don't suppose you're going to show me those messages, are you?' Harrison said.

'No, I'm not. Now, let's get to work. She wants to start moving in here.'

'Are you moving in with her?'

'No. Of course I'm bloody not.'

Harrison laughed and Brann threw him a look. Thankfully the painters arrived before either of them could say anything else.

Ophelia didn't appear in person that day, and Brann was glad. Keeping up their pretence took its toll. Where did they stand? How did he really feel? How much easier was it when he didn't have to see her? Except, a strong ache in his chest developed throughout the day when he realised she wasn't coming. It got worse the next day when she didn't show up again. She messaged, asking how the painters were getting on, and he hid in the van to reply in case Harrison spotted some look on his face again.

After he sent it, he checked his reflection in the rear mirror. *Christ.* He rubbed his face. *I look rough.* It went with the territory in this job, but he hadn't shaved since Saturday and his hair could do with a trim. He quite liked it longish – surfer style, as Caitlin called it – but it was starting to look more like tramp style. He frowned, wondering if old Donald was ok. Probably better off than out here in the wilds with November approaching.

On Thursday – finally – Ophelia called, summoning Brann to the back door of the main house. He took the van as ordered and rocked up to find her outside in a pleasant little courtyard area, surrounded by some small items of furniture and boxes.

'Ah, good, you're here,' she said. 'I need this stuff taken to the boathouse. And I have a bed.'

He raised his eyebrows. 'Are you having a laugh? You want me to get a bed out of the house and up to the boathouse? I'll have to dismantle it.'

'It's new, and it's not made up yet. It's just been delivered.' She opened a door to a small room. Some large boxes were piled at the side, along with a mattress covered in plastic.

'Couldn't this stuff have been delivered directly to the boathouse?'

'I tried. But they couldn't find it and when they came to the door, Jacinta answered and told them to put it in here.'

'Great. Well, you better get out of the way and let me get it out.'

She stepped back, eyeing him over as he lifted the first box.

'You sure you didn't get them to put it here so you could have your own little peep show?'

She smirked and gave a little shrug. 'I guess you'll never know.'

'Oh, I think I do.' He shoved the box into the van, dusted off his hands, and came back for the next one. 'You recovered from the rafting then?'

'Yes, but I'm never doing that again.'

He lifted the next box. 'What? The rafting or being seen in public with me?'

'Both.'

'Nice.' He returned for the mattress. 'How big is this bed? Are you planning on filling it with lots of men in loincloths to feed you grapes or something?'

'Maybe.'

'You'll have to help me with this. I don't want to drag it.'

She went inside and put her hands on the sides of the mattress.

'Together,' he said. 'Lift.'

'Bloody hell. This is heavier than it looks.'

'No kidding. Tell me if you need to put it down and I'll stop.'

Maybe she was trying to prove a point because she didn't say anything and they made it to the van without stopping. He balanced it on the edge, then moved around the back to push it in.

'Ready?' He put his hands close to hers and she pinned him in her gaze.

'Let's do it.'

Together, they shoved it into the van. As soon as it was in, Brann slammed the back doors shut and leaned on them. 'Team-work makes the dream work, huh?'

Ophelia let out a puff, then held a flat palm up to the side. Brann high-fived it.

'I was thinking about old Donald,' he said. 'I wonder if he's doing ok.'

'I could phone the hostel and see if they'll tell me how he is. I told my father I'd met him, but I'm not sure he even remembered who I was talking about.' She rolled her eyes. 'He's so out of touch.'

'Yup.'

Brann wanted to ask about her sister, but didn't. It would mean explaining about Caitlin and he didn't want to tell anyone about what had happened. It wasn't his place.

He ignored Harrison's look when he returned with Ophelia and the full van. Ophelia, however, started chatting with him. Brann smirked at his son's red face. Served him right for all his speculation.

'So, your strapping young son is going to help you get that mattress upstairs,' she said. 'I'm sure he'll be a lot better at it than me.'

'We Duthies are built to grind.' Brann pulled a bicep like Popeye.

'You said it.' Ophelia looked away with a little smile.

He and Harrison wrestled the mattress up the stairs and let it fall onto the wooden floor. The view from up here was incredible. The glass wall with its view over the lochan was like something from a magazine – kind of unreal.

'Why the hell was she laughing at you saying you were built to grind?' Harrison muttered. 'Have you had sex with her?'

'No, I fucking haven't and keep your voice down.' Brann glowered at the door. Harrison flopped onto the mattress and lay like a starfish.

'Bet you want to though. You could be next on this mattress.'

'Get off that and help me bring the boxes up. And behave.'

When they got back downstairs, Ophelia was on her phone. She excused herself and flattened it to her shoulder. 'Listen, can you give me a lift back to the house to get the rest of my stuff? I've got sofas coming tomorrow and I want to make sure they come straight here.'

'Hell yes. I don't want to try and get sofas in the van.'

He and Harrison took the bed boxes upstairs, then Brann ran Ophelia back to the main house.

'You will never guess what,' she muttered.

'What?'

'Jacinta's son, Xander, that little sneak, has gone and told her that his friend Sean and I are a couple waiting to happen. She's wetting her pants over him, because she thinks he has cash. And because he's friends with her little darling.'

'That boy we met at the dinner dance?'

'Exactly. He's a child. I'll never date him. I could have stomached James if I had to. He was nice and around the same age as me. But Sean. No, just no. But Jacinta wants to invite him for dinner. Oh, she is so irritating.'

Brann shook his head, trying to listen with an immune, possibly concerned ear, but it wasn't working. Raging bile was bubbling in his gut. The thought of her with any of these men made him want to smash something. But this was the kind of person who would get her. Not him.

He dropped her off at the house and went back to work. Harrison had already started unboxing the bed, and they began putting it together.

By Friday afternoon, the house was almost habitable. The bedroom had a bed. Ophelia was upstairs adding her soft furnishings. The living area had the new sofas, and the kitchen was almost done. It only needed a few finishing touches – things Brann could have done if he hadn't been running about helping Ophelia move furniture and making beds in between, but he wasn't really bothered. She was paying him to do it and he liked her company. He'd like to deny it, but he couldn't.

'I need to go back to the house and get a few more things.' Ophelia appeared in the kitchen. 'Then I'm going to spend my first night here.'

'Enjoy,' Brann said.

'Well, in case you're gone before I get back, I'd like to say thank you. To both of you.' She glanced at Harrison. 'You've really helped me out this week. I know it's part of your job, but I appreciate it nonetheless.'

'Um... Ok,' Harrison said.

With a little wave, she left.

'What's got into her?' Harrison asked. 'When's she ever been that nice?'

'Not a clue,' Brann said. 'Let's finish sealing these worktops, then get home for the weekend.' Brann refilled the sealant gun and pointed it into place. He was so well practised at this, he hardly looked at what he was doing as he zipped around the edge.

A knock on the door startled him and he lifted the gun just in time to avoid a wobble. 'Who the hell's that?' he muttered.

'Another sofa delivery?' Harrison suggested.

'Open it and see, will you? I want to finish this bit, so it doesn't go wonky.'

Harrison trotted into the hallway, which used to be the side room of the old part of the boathouse, and Brann heard him talking to a man at the door. The voice was vaguely familiar, but he couldn't place it.

'Who was it?' Brann asked when Harrison returned.

Harrison pulled a weirded-out face. 'Well, knock me down with a feather,' he said quietly. 'She's got a boyfriend, and it's not you.'

'What are you on about?'

'That was her boyfriend at the door.' He pushed his thumb over his shoulder. 'He's gone upstairs to look around. Looks like a right ponce,' he added in a whisper.

'What did he say his name was?'

'Sean somebody-or-other. Looks like he's my age. Bit young for her, no?'

'Seriously?' Brann put the sealant gun down.

'Where are you going?'

'We can't just let anybody come in here and wander about.' He stormed up the stairs and into the newly decorated bedroom. It looked incredible with a thick fur rug on the wooden floor, white lined and chunky knit throws on the bed. All with a view of the loch.

Sean turned from gazing out the window and put his hands behind his back when Brann appeared.

'Hey,' Brann said. 'What are you doing here?'

'Come to see Ophelia.' Sean held his chin high. 'You're Brian, aren't you? What are you doing here yourself?'

'I'm the builder.'

'What?'

'Yeah. And she didn't mention anything about you coming here.'

A little smirk played on Sean's lips. 'I'm sure she doesn't share her private life with her builder.'

'True enough, but we were just talking about her plans, and you didn't feature in them, so it's a bit suspicious to find you up here sneaking about in her room. Not to mention creepy.'

'Hold on a minute.' Sean moved his hands from behind his back to reveal a bottle of wine. 'I wasn't being creepy. She doesn't know I'm here because it's a surprise. I wanted to give her this.'

Brann raised an eyebrow. 'In her bedroom?'

'I was just looking around, ok? It's a good view.' Sean eyed him over. 'And if you're the builder, why were you at a party with her?'

'That's irrelevant.' Brann shook his head. 'And no. It's not ok. I'm leaving shortly and you're leaving too. She wants me to lock up and no way am I locking up with you in here. Call her and tell her you're here if you want. Or I will, but I'm not leaving you here by yourself.'

'Fine, fine. I'm going, though it's none of your business. I'll call her myself and I'll also tell her about your behaviour.'

'You do that.'

He edged past Brann, who didn't move except to turn and watch him leave. Brann followed him down the stairs and, after he'd left, slung the bolt across the door.

'Fuck's sake.' What an idiot. Maybe it was a silly attempt at being romantic, but Brann still didn't like it.

Sitting on the new sofa, he pulled out his phone.

CHAPTER TWENTY

Ophelia

Ophelia tapped the wheel as she drove towards Glenbriar. Any other Friday at this time, she wouldn't mind visiting her mum, but this was to be her first night in the boathouse. Her mum was always so busy she had to accept the windows when they opened. She needed to speak to her, but she couldn't stay long. Not with the nights closing in earlier all the time. She wasn't sure how good the lighting outside the boathouse was. And truthfully, she was still a bit freaked out at the idea of being there alone, especially in the dark. But she'd survived white-water rafting, so she could do this.

As she pulled into her mum's driveway, the hands-free rang, and Brann's name appeared on the screen.,

She slapped *accept call*. 'Hello.'

'Hey,' he said.

'What's up? I can't really talk.'

Her mum had appeared at the door; she didn't like being held up or kept waiting, as Ophelia knew from experience.

'This is important,' Brann said.

'Tell me then, what is it?' She dreaded to think. A hole in the roof? A leaking pipe? Or something worse?

'You've just had a visitor.'

'Who?'

'Sean.'

She gaped at the screen. 'Are you being funny?'

'Unfortunately not. Listen, there's no easy way to say this. He came in here and snuck upstairs with a bottle of wine.'

'What?'

'You heard me. He told Harrison you were his girlfriend, then I went up to kick him out, and he told me he wanted to surprise you. So be warned. I don't think he'd do anything awful. He's too wet for that, but I doubt you want him hanging about.'

'Oh Jesus Christ. That's horrendous. I'm calling Jacinta for his number. How dare he?'

'Yeah. Idiot.'

'Listen, thanks for kicking him out. Don't let him back in again and when you lock up, take the key away. I've got my own. I don't want him sniffing around and finding it somewhere.'

'Ok, I will.'

'Right. Got to go.' She ended the call and got out of the car.

'Hurry up,' Edith said. 'All the heat is escaping.'

'Just needed to sort something out.' Why was her life never simple? And now this little shit! What was his game? Why did it seem like Jacinta was somewhere behind this?

Edith's house was always beautiful in an understated way. The country cottage style was effortless, small piles of books and magazines were in every room looking decoratively placed, flowers added colour, and the furniture was perfectly mismatched.

Ophelia inhaled the earthy smell on entering the kitchen, ducking under some hanging vegetables. Somehow, the house reflected Edith's love of gardening and everything home-grown.

'I've been tidying the garden,' Edith said. 'So many fallen leaves everywhere. I've been looking for someone who might like to do it for some extra money, but no one has taken me up on the offer.'

'That's a shame.'

'Indeed. And how's life with you? It seems a while since I've seen you. Things have been crazy busy, as always.'

Ophelia filled her in on the boathouse, the man in the woods, the dinner dance, and the rafting, all conveniently missing out Brann. In her mind, he was one of the biggest parts of those things, but she couldn't even say his name. Somehow, it was like confessing to committing a crime.

'Goodness me,' Edith said, when Ophelia told her the latest life instalment – Sean lurking at the boathouse. 'Call him this instant and tell him to stay away or you'll get a restraining order. I would. Sneaky man.' She shuddered.

'Yes, I will. That's also why I don't want to stay too long. I don't want to get back when it's too dark.'

'Quite understandable. Call me as soon as you're home or I'll worry.'

'I... Um... There's something I wanted to ask you.'

'Ask away.' Edith sipped her coffee.

'How's Nancy?' That wasn't really what she wanted to ask, but somehow, they were the words that popped out.

Edith's expression flickered slightly but Ophelia only noticed because she was watching for it.

'She's very well. She's coming for dinner later. You're welcome to stay, but it won't work if you want to get home before it's dark.'

'It's fine. Just say hello.'

'Of course.'

Ophelia took a mouthful of coffee, not sure she could get the question out.

'Is that what you wanted to ask me?' Edith said.

'Well, kind of...'

'Ok. And is there something else?'

'Yes, but if it's not true, you might be upset.'

'If what's not true?'

'Someone told me you had a partner. I wondered if it was Nancy.' As soon as she said it, she wished she hadn't. Her cheeks were suddenly too hot.

'Who said that?' Edith scrutinised her.

It must be a lie. Her mother appeared shocked. Kristalee must have made it up, but why?

'Who said it?' she pressed.

'It doesn't matter.'

'I'm just curious.' Edith rubbed her temple and her expression softened.

'I shouldn't have said anything.'

Edith got to her feet and moved to the window. She leaned on the kitchen sink and inhaled slowly 'I don't know quite how to say this, but... well, it is true.'

'It's true? You and Nancy are partners?'

'Yes. But there are only a few people who know and I'm very curious to find out who told you.'

'But...'

'I've never really told anyone. A handful of women know, ones I've been... in relationships with, but that's about it.'

Ophelia's heart slipped. Her mother had been in relationships and never said a word. She'd met none of these people. Sometimes Edith seemed closed, but Ophelia felt she'd missed a huge part of her mother's life.

'Your father doesn't know,' Edith said. 'I didn't know how to tell my family. It's easier to talk to strangers sometimes, occasionally I've done that. I thought you would all be so shocked or horrified you'd disown me.'

'Understandable. Dad definitely would be horrified.'

'Oh, I know. I've seen so much prejudice in action, watched friends' families fall apart and seen people lose contact with loved ones. People don't always react the way you want them to. I didn't "find myself" overnight. It dawned on me gradually and I had to come to terms with it. I was brought up in a family where such things are taboo and unacceptable. I had to alter my whole mindset to realise I wasn't doing anything wrong. I wanted to tell you, but it never seemed the right time.'

Ophelia stood up, went over to her mum, and put her arm around her shoulder. 'Now's the right time,' she said.

Edith looked at her, eyes misting over. 'Really? And you don't think badly of me?'

'Of course not.' Ophelia embraced her, and Edith let out a little cry. 'I wish you'd told me before, but I get why you didn't.' She patted her back.

'I thought maybe after Nancy and I had lived together for a while and you were used to her, we could break it to you then, but... Well, it's out now.'

'I like her,' Ophelia said. 'She seems like a lovely lady.'

'Thank you, darling. Your acceptance means the world to me.'

Ophelia pulled back and smiled. 'You're like the strongest, feistiest woman I know. Be you and don't let anyone change that. If there comes a time when you want to tell people, I'll be right there for you.'

Edith smiled a watery smile. 'I think you should take your own advice. Be you and kick these silly suitors your father keeps throwing at you into the ether. Choose someone for yourself.' Edith clapped Ophelia's cheeks.

'Yes, I need to have a good think about that. Speaking of which, I should get back and make some calls, so I don't get any unwanted visitors tonight.'

'Yes. Do that straight away and let me know when you're back safe.' Edith held her upper arms for a moment. 'You're a wonderful daughter and I've done not only you a disservice by not telling you before, but also myself. So often I needed someone to talk to, and I didn't realise the answer was always here.'

Ophelia gave her another hug. 'Well, I'm still here, so if you need me again, call.'

'I will.'

As soon as she was in her car, she rang Jacinta. The call didn't connect, but she rang again. And continued to ring until eventually she picked up, when Ophelia was halfway back.

'Why have I got so many missed calls from you?' Jacinta said.

'Because you didn't pick up your phone.'

'I was busy.'

'Have you cooked up some scheme to get me together with Xander's friend Sean?'

'Oh... Do you like him? He's very well off, I understand.'

'Can you hear yourself? He's a university student. I am not dating him. Did you also know he went to the boathouse this afternoon and seemed to be planning to wait for me there? Doesn't that set any alarm bells ringing for you? Or do you think that's perfectly acceptable? Maybe you'd be happy for Xander to behave in the same way and lie in wait for unsuspecting single women to come home.'

'Really, Ophelia, you're blowing this out of all proportion. We suggested he went around to chat to you, maybe take you some gifts.'

'Oh, he brought wine apparently and took it with him up to my bedroom.'

'Don't be silly. You're making that up. He said you weren't even there when he went in.'

'I wasn't, but thankfully the builders tipped me off because they thought it was suspicious behaviour and they're not wrong, are they?'

'Alright, calm down. And what builder are we talking about? He told us a story that he'd met you at a party where you were dancing rather closely with someone called Brian, who was also at the house pretending to be the builder.'

Ophelia let out a silent groan. She should have known that would come back to bite. 'No one was pretending to be a builder. Where is Sean now?'

'He's still here with Xander, and don't worry, I'll make sure he doesn't call around tonight.'

'We're doing more than that,' Ophelia said. 'I don't want him calling around, ever. You can get this right now. I am NOT dating him. Now, put him on the phone.'

'Who?'

'Sean.'

'But...' Jacinta seemed to be huffing and puffing. 'What will you say to him?'

'None of your business. Just put him on. I insist.'

'Oh, for heaven's sake.'

Some scuffling sounds told her Jacinta was on the move. Voices spoke and then a clear male voice said, 'Hello.'

'Who's talking?' Ophelia said.

'Sean.'

'I know what you did this afternoon.'

'Look, that builder was—'

'Telling the truth. I'm not daft. He wouldn't phone me out of the blue and make up a story like that. You shouldn't have been in my room.'

'Yeah. I get that, but I was just looking around.'

'My bedroom? What were you planning? Jumping me when I got home? Not exactly romantic and not exactly behaviour that'll make me want to date you. If you'd done that, I'd have knocked you out with the nearest heavy object.'

'Look, I wasn't going to do that. So, yeah, I didn't think it through, but those builders were there, and I didn't want to get in their way. Who knew the guy would follow me up?'

'I'm glad he did. Because it tells me you and I have completely different ideas about what's romantic. And I don't like your way. So, I want you to understand there's no future for us. And nothing will make me change my mind. Don't come around my house again. If you do, I'll be calling the police.'

'Yeah, yeah, ok. You've made your point and really, no relationship is worth this much grief.'

The call ended abruptly, and Ophelia gulped a large amount of cold air, not wanting to imagine the scene. Would Jacinta be flapping around Sean, trying to apologise? Silly cow. How would she feel if it had been Francesca who Sean pulled that move on? Something told her that would change Jacinta's opinion. But the woman was such a narcissist, there was no point trying to tell her any of that.

Ophelia drove to the boathouse, glad there was enough light to see clearly. The light above the door was on. She unlocked it and went in to find the small hallway was lit up too. Something told her Brann had left it on for her and not by accident. He had the ability to infuriate her, but she trusted him. Of all the men she'd ever known, he was the one she knew she could ask to do anything, and he would. He'd looked out for her today when he could have turned a blind eye or laughed it off as a silly prank.

She closed the door and bolted it again. Sitting on the new sofa, she let out a sigh and texted her mum to say she was home. Who'd have thought she'd ever say this? But thank god, she'd met Brann. She rubbed her hands up and down her arms. It wasn't warm in here and with darkness closing in, she was lonely and isolated. If only Brann was here now. She could do with some company. His was the face that kept coming into her mind. Over and over again. Maybe if she willed him to come, he would. But that was stupid. Why would he? It was Friday night. He'd be busy with his family or out at the pub, doing whatever he did. He certainly wouldn't be calling around here anytime soon. She'd just have to suck up the loneliness and deal with it.

CHAPTER TWENTY-ONE

Brann

Brann threw some mince into a pan for the bolognese. The smell made him queasy, but it wasn't the cause. Ever since he'd left the boathouse, his head had been full of worries. Was Ophelia ok? Sure, she could look after herself, but he was uneasy after that little idiot showing up earlier. Part of him had wanted to hang about until she got back, but he didn't know where she was or how long she'd be. None of it was really his business. But he cared. He cared so hard it made his chest want to split open. Even though he hated himself for feeling this way, he couldn't deny it anymore. He ran his fingers through his hair, still damp from the shower. If he went back to check on her, he ran the risk of being as creepy as that little dick. He could always text her... Something cheeky would do the trick.

The landline rang, making him jump. That phone hardly ever rang these days.

'Have you switched your mobile off?' Caitlin's voice rang out as soon as Brann lifted it.

'No.' Brann went to feel his back pocket. But he'd changed into sweatpants after his shower, so it was probably in his work jeans. 'Why?'

'I texted you ages ago asking if you could give me a lift to Martha's party tomorrow. It's in Perth and we're meeting for shopping and lunch first, but the bus times are like really bad.'

'Yeah, sure I could. What time?'

'Can we leave about eleven?' she said. 'I'll come to the house.'

'Yeah, great. No problem. See you then. Love you.'

'Love you, Dad.'

He ended the call, gave his dinner a quick prod and went upstairs to his room, patting the pockets of his work jeans. Where the hell was the phone? Normally, it was either in his jeans or his jacket pocket, but not today. Seriously? This was weird. He couldn't even remember when he'd last had it. Had he used it since he came home?

Maybe it was in the van. Sometimes he chucked it into his tool belt and forgot about it. Grabbing a torch, he headed out into the cool evening. The sky was clear, and stars twinkled above, bright even with the orange glow of streetlamps. He scanned inside the van, down the footwells and in the side pockets, where it had often fallen out before. Not this time.

Think! He urged himself. He turned on the engine and waited to see if the Bluetooth connected. If it was in here and still had battery, this would find it.

No devices found.

Ok, this is weird.

Returning to the house, he dished out his tea and put it on the table, trying to retrace his steps. His mind wandered through the day. *Oh shit.* He'd called Ophelia from the sofa at the boathouse. That was the last time he could definitely remember using it. Had he put the phone down and not taken it with him? Surely he wouldn't have, but he'd been angry and flustered.

A cold dread trickled through him. He could get it tomorrow. No – he was taking Caitlin to the party. And he needed it in case there was a change of plans. He checked the clock; it was just after six.

With a deep breath, he cleared up, put on clean clothes, and headed back to the van. If he turned up at the boathouse, Ophelia might die of shock thinking he was Sean. But he couldn't warn her because he didn't have his phone. *Bloody thing.* Phones were useful but exasperating objects. Crucial sometimes, almost like they were a part of the human anatomy. Something he couldn't live without.

Pitch black skies shrouded the countryside, but the moon shone high, reflecting in the rippling loch as Brann drove towards Glenvorneth. What a stunning night, and he couldn't deny that checking Ophelia was ok made his chest lighten. He wouldn't have slept a wink, not knowing if she was ok.

Finally, he reached the entrance to Glenvorneth. He turned in the main gate and took the track that led the opposite way from the main house, past the little workers' cottages. The one

Ophelia had done up had lights glowing at the window and three cars outside. Inside, people were moving about like they were dancing. Camilla, the mad artiste, looked like she was hosting a party. The place was so small it was probably a very intimate affair. Brann didn't want to think about it.

He carried on up the track past the stables until it wound through the woodland area and up to the boathouse. The lights were on, and it glowed serenely beautiful beside the little lochan. The moon behind the trees was so bright it seemed like a fake photograph. As Brann got out, he goggled at the thousands of stars, so many without the streetlights spoiling them.

He rubbed his arms. He'd left without a coat or even a jumper and there was a bite in the air. Now, he had to do this without freaking out Ophelia, though it was likely to happen one way or another. He pushed the bell and waited. Nothing. What should he do? He didn't want to shout or knock on a window. That would scare the shit out of her.

A vague outline materialised in the glass door. The door opened a fraction and Ophelia peered around. It reminded him so much of the first day he'd met her he almost laughed. Would she demand I.D. again? Her eyes widened at the sight of him, and she pulled the door wider. In her free hand, she clutched a huge kitchen knife.

'What the hell are you doing here?' She gaped at him. 'You frightened the life out of me.'

'I'm so sorry. I really am.' He held up his hands and pulled what he hoped was an apologetic face. 'I didn't want to freak you out.' His eyes lingered on the robe loosely hanging from her shoulders. 'But I think I left my mobile here earlier.'

'Where did you leave it?'

'I'm not sure. I called you from the sofa after I chucked out that little tosser. Maybe it fell down the side. I don't remember. But I've searched everywhere else.'

'Ok, fine.' She let out a sigh. 'Come in.'

'Maybe you should put that knife down...' He raised his eyebrow. 'Remember, no stabbing. You were warned about that at the rafting. And you've already had a go at me with those antlers.'

'Oh, shut up.' She let him in.

He laughed. 'What did you do with them anyway? I think you should have them mounted over the front door. To ward off bad men like me.'

'I would, except they didn't work before. You keep coming back.' She eyed him over. 'Though I could try dismembering you with this and hanging your entrails outside.'

'What a delightful image.'

'Sorry.' She burst out laughing. 'But this is just so ridiculous.'

'What? Your plans to dismember me?'

'No. You being here at all.'

'Sorry, but I need my phone. It has everything on it and if the kids call, they expect an answer straight away. You know how it is?'

'Not really, but I'll take your word for it. Go and look.' She locked the door behind him, and he nipped into the living area. He shoved his hand down the back and sides of the cushion around the arm he'd sat on earlier. A wash of relief flooded through him as he touched something solid.

'It's here.' He pulled it out and checked it, seeing all the missed calls from Caitlin.

Ophelia plonked herself at the far end of the sofa and stroked the arm. The room had an almost Alpine vibe and the moonlit lochan beyond was so dreamy. 'I'm glad you found it.'

'Me too. And sorry to have freaked you out. I'll leave you in peace.' Though he was relieved she was ok.

She eyed him up and down, sucking on her lower lip. 'Stay with me a bit, will you?'

'What?' He frowned.

She glanced away with a little shrug. 'I am kind of freaked out about being here by myself. It's beautiful but... lonely.'

How could he refuse when every bone in his body was telling him to go to her, hold her, keep her safe and make sure she was never lonely and afraid again? He pocketed his phone and walked forward. Should he sit on the other sofa or...

She patted the seat beside her. With a second's hesitation, he sat. A heady fragrance, like a midnight garden, drifted over him; its warm and slightly dangerous notes tickled his senses, teasing him with images of Ophelia bathing in the huge claw-foot tub he'd installed upstairs. She caressed her skin with soapy bubbles as she looked out over the serene moonlit lochan.

'Sean's a twat.' She thumped the arm of the sofa, bringing him back to the room. 'I'd have been fine if he hadn't called around like a little creep.'

'I was worried about you. I wanted to come back anyway, but I thought you might be pissed at me.'

A small smile played on her lips. 'I'm glad you lost your phone then.'

He let out a little laugh. 'Yeah.'

'Do you want a glass of wine?'

'Better not. I'm driving, remember.'

'Of course.'

After the months of easy banter and barely concealed attraction, he suddenly felt self-conscious. He fiddled with the neck of his t-shirt, not sure whether to relax back into the sofa or perch. Why the awkwardness?

'I appreciate you telling me about Sean,' she said. 'A lot of people wouldn't have bothered. Especially after all the grief I've given you.'

'It was the only decent thing to do.'

'Thank you. Excuse me if I have some wine. Would you like anything else?'

He shook his head. 'No thanks.'

She got to her feet and wandered into the kitchen area, pouring herself a large glass of wine. 'You're one of the good guys.' She swirled the glass as she sat back down.

'Am I? I thought I was a very bad man.'

Taking a sip of wine, she eyed him over the glass.

'I mean, to be fair, some of my life choices have been suspect.' He rested back and folded his arms. 'I'm no angel.'

'Maybe in some ways that's true, but in the places it counts, you're good.'

He'd take that from her.

'You know,' she said with a sigh. 'I've been thinking about you all night.'

His eyes met hers, and she snared him again. He couldn't look away. 'There's not a minute in the day or night goes by that I don't think about you,' he said. 'I can't stop myself.'

'Same.' She stared at her glass. 'I told you months ago to get out of my head. But you didn't.'

'Likewise. You're in here twenty-four-seven.' He bumped his fist on his forehead.

'I was willing you to come here. And you did.'

'Why did you want me here?'

Focusing on her glass, she frowned. 'I just... I don't know.'

'Why didn't you call a friend if you wanted company?'

'Whoever I called wouldn't have been who I really wanted to see.'

'And that's me?'

'It's always you.' Leaning forward, she put her glass on the coffee table and wrapped her arms around herself. The desire to do the same burned like wildfire in Brann's gut.

'Maybe living here by yourself isn't a good idea,' he said. 'It's kind of out in the sticks.'

'Do you think I can't handle it?'

'That's not what I said. I know you can handle it, but will you enjoy it? Why put yourself through something if you don't even like it?'

'That's basically my whole life. I tried to escape by setting up my own business, but it never goes away. It's about duty and expectations, not enjoyment.' She put her face in her hands.

'Then shove the duty and expectations out the window. You do you and let the others do what they have to.'

'And what about the estate? My grandparents wanted me to have it, and they were important people in my early life. My parents aren't nurturing types, but my grandparents were. They also had big ideas for Glenvorneth. Plans I'd like to carry out, but I can't do anything without money. And, like it or not, a rich partner would go a long way to solving the financial problems. Time is ticking on. We've made some progress with the estate, but it's not enough.'

'You really shouldn't have to sell yourself to save it.'

'I know, but I'm struggling to see other options.'

He threw out his hands. 'Don't ask me. If I knew how to make that kind of money, I wouldn't be a builder living in a two-bedroom semi in Rowan Way, Glenbriar's most infamous street.'

She threw him a hopeless look and, for a second, he thought she might break down and cry, but she didn't. 'Will you...?' She swallowed and rubbed her fingers across her collarbone, slightly lifting her silken robe.

'Will I what?'

'Will you hold me for a moment?'

'Sure.' Shifting closer, he leaned back and let her curl into his arms. He wrapped her in a hug, his cheek lowering to rest on her soft, sweetly scented hair.

'Do your kids know where you are?' she asked.

'Nobody knows. Just you and me.'

'Tell me about them.'

'What do you want to know?' He smoothed his fingers through the glossy blonde locks.

'Do they have the same mum?'

'Yes. Does that surprise you?'

'I was just curious. My sister and I don't have the same mother.'

'True.' He gently rubbed a circle on her back, vaguely remembering her sister's connection to Caitlin but ignoring it. Now was not the time.

'Are you on good terms with their mum?'

'Yeah. Now that we don't live together, we're fine.'

'Why did you split?'

'Because we didn't love each other. We never really did. When we got together, we were high school kids. We both came from hideous backgrounds. My parents were addicts, my father was an abusive arsehole, and hers weren't much better. They had too many kids, called them crazy-ass names, like Bellephaba – I shit you not – and lived off the benefit money. Her older sisters, who all had issues of their own, brought her up. Her younger siblings have so many problems too. All of it was a mess. We were two of the most infamous kids in the school, if we ever bothered to show. She was in the year below me, but we lived close to each other. We both liked music and had wild ideas about starting a band. She was a looker and tough too; it was an irresistible combination for me.' Maybe he hadn't changed that much. 'Our making music together evolved to making out, and one day we discovered sex. We were idiotic teenagers, who knew nothing about being safe. Or maybe we didn't care. So you can guess what happened.'

'She got pregnant.'

'Yup. It was a rude wake-up call. But we ran with it. We suddenly qualified for a council house and amazingly, we got one here. It wasn't the nicest, but it was enough. I discovered I was good at DIY and one of our new neighbours helped me get an apprenticeship. We were lucky. A stupid mistake actually led to both of us escaping the prison of our parents' houses. So, we jollied along, playing families and building our life. But we weren't actually compatible. Circumstances forced us together.

If we'd had better opportunities and more sense in the first place, we wouldn't have chosen each other.'

Ophelia ran a fingertip down his chest and nestled in even closer. 'I can't imagine anyone not wanting you.'

He huffed out a little laugh. 'I'm a lot more together than I was back then.' Having kids had made him grow up fast. He couldn't afford to be an irresponsible idiot when his family depended on him, and he was determined not to be as useless as his own parents or end up like poor old Donald.

'You made good and achieved so much from harsh beginnings.'

'Through hard work and tough choices. If I'd stuck with my ex, some things might have been easier, but I wouldn't have achieved as much because I was miserable and so was she. Once we split and we were free to go our separate ways, we did. We've both done ok, more than we would have if we stayed together. This is why I keep saying to you that you shouldn't force yourself to be with someone because of the circumstances. It doesn't work. You'll thwart yourself because you'll feel depressed and boxed in.'

Ophelia looked up at him with a pained expression. Brann ran the pad of his thumb over her cheek. Such soft skin. Such a beautiful face. But sad. Such a waste. Would she find a man who'd love her the way she deserved? The way he would.

'You shouldn't have to settle for anyone. You deserve someone who'll properly take care of you. Someone who'll tell you they love you every day for the rest of their life and mean it.'

She froze, still gazing into his eyes, but her expression clouded. 'Brann... You know that we... you and me can never.'

'I'm not that stupid. Brann the builder might not always be the sharpest tool in the box, but he's not thick enough to imagine himself shacking up with the lady of the manor.'

'Don't,' she said. 'You're not stupid at all. You're more intelligent than most of the people I know.' She sat up and held her finger to his lip to stop him from speaking. 'You hide it, and that's what you're good at. As well as woodwork and knocking down walls.'

He raised an eyebrow. 'I've certainly knocked down a few of yours.'

'You have. I wish I could say I'd done half as much for you as you've done for me.'

'You've woken me up, Princess.'

'How?'

'It's hard to explain, but before we met, I was kinda numb. You and I have similar energy, and when you're around, it gives me a lift, you know? Even when we're fighting.' He smirked.

She scanned his face, her eyes dropping to his lips, and tilted her head slightly like she was working out what she'd like to do with them. 'Do you remember the first day we met? It was in this very room. There was definitely some kind of energy pinging about then.'

'There sure was. I'll never forget it. You were such a cow.'

'And you were an arrogant dick.'

He laughed. 'I didn't try to run you off the road or attack you with a set of antlers, though, did I?'

'No, but you made me want to both kill you and have you right there and then.'

'How could I *make you* want that?' He shook his head.

'I don't know, but you did, and I hated you for it.'

'The feeling was mutual.'

'I know.' She ran her fingers down his neck and across his shoulder. 'I hated that I wanted you then, and in the stables, at the cottage. Even when I was riding at the games, all I could think about was you. I wanted you on my birthday, when we went rafting... And now.'

'Now?'

'I still hate how much I want you.'

'Me too. Shall I tell you just how much I hate it?'

'No.' She slipped the edges of her flimsy robe apart and let it fall open to reveal a very skimpy red lace negligee. 'Show me.'

Chapter Twenty-Two

Ophelia

Brann's lips met Ophelia's with such intensity it knocked the wind from her, and she couldn't breathe. She wrapped her arms around him, kneeling on the sofa, and he pulled her close. The heat from his body was incredible.

They'd kissed before, but this was off the charts, deep, hot and urgent. Her lower belly spasmed and a throbbing need for him built inside her.

'I hate how you're always on my mind, even when I'm trying to be mad at you,' Brann muttered into the kiss. She felt his smile.

'And I hate how you turn me into such a desperate woman.'

With a little laugh, he tucked some stray loops of hair over her shoulder; she slung back her neck, and he kissed it like she was a goddess. He worshipped her some more, igniting fires all over her.

'Well, who would have thought it?' He ran a warm palm over her breast, thumbing the nipple through the lacey fabric of her negligee, making her moan. 'The princess wants a bit of action.'

'Needs it more like.'

'Listen.' His voice turned grave. 'I'll do anything you want... Most things anyway, but only if we're safe. I don't carry protection on me. You may think I'm the kind of guy who goes out ready for action wherever I am, but I'm really not.'

'I've got three packets of condoms in my make-up bag.'

'Er... Ok... You're very well prepared.'

'My friend Florence bought them last year when we went to Cyprus together. She decided it would be fun to see who had used the most by the time we came back.'

'Who won?'

'Neither of us used any. But she's engaged now, so she's probably finished her three packets.'

'Well, you need to make up for lost time.'

'And I suppose you're happy to oblige?'

'No suppose about it.' He unfastened his belt and unzipped his jeans. 'That's better. Things are getting a bit tight in there.'

She lifted her hand to his face, curving it around the sharp cheekbone beneath his stubble, drawing him back to her. Her lips found the corner of his mouth and she spoke against it. 'I despise how hot and bothered you make me.'

His lips parted, but he didn't return her kiss. He ran his hands over her shoulders, down her back, and cupped her bottom. Having his strong body surrounding her like this made her thrum with pent up tension.

'You despise me, do you?'

'You know I do.'

'Then we need to do something about that.'

'Yes, we do. Please, do something about it right now.' She dropped her forehead to his broad shoulder and rested against it. Her body ached, and only he could ease the tension.

He shifted back, crossed his arms, and pulled off his t-shirt, revealing his toned abs. She traced her fingertip over the celtic knot tattoo on his left arm.

'I suppose you hate tattoos?' He raised an eyebrow.

'Naturally.'

He huffed out a laugh. 'Wouldn't have it any other way. Now, tell me, do you want to do this down here or on that rather magnificent bed of yours?'

'Bed.'

'There's something poetic about us christening that mattress together, isn't there?'

'Sure is.' She scrambled to her feet, and he followed, turning off the lights as they got to the stairs.

When they reached the bedroom, he closed the door. The light from the moon was almost dazzling. If she'd been trying to get to sleep, it would have thoroughly annoyed her, but it seemed perfect for this.

She located the condom packets and sat them on the night-stand.

Standing by the window, Brann wrestled off his jeans. Even in silhouette, he looked utterly incredible. She pulled him close, his muscles tightening as she glided her palm over his warm velvet skin. He had a smattering of coarse hair over his hard-planed muscles. She moved her hand lower, exploring the firm ridges of his stomach, then around to his back.

He took in a sharp breath as she slipped her fingertips inside the waistband of his boxers. She pressed herself against him with a moan, feeling everything he had to offer through the flimsy fabric of her negligee.

'You're a big boy, aren't you?' she said, as his hands framed her face, his rough fingers knotting in her hair and angling her head.

'You bet.' He began to ply her with kisses, so strong and sure. It was like being back on the raft, sweeping into the rapids, leaping high, then plunging low, though less stressful and a lot more pleasurable.

She pushed her hand inside his boxers and took hold of him. He groaned as she touched him, still kissing her until her brain was about to combust. The rapids would drown her any second. He caught her by the thighs and lifted her, so she was forced to release him. She wrapped her arms around his neck, and he carried her to the bed. Lowering her gently, he kept his eyes on her.

'You're loathsomely beautiful,' he said, and she smiled.

He moved in beside her and lifted her negligee, making the throb intensify tenfold.

'Let's get this off.'

She obliged, pulling it off and tossing it away. He slipped off his boxers and lay beside her. She pressed against him, kissing him as he ran his hands over her body, cupped her breasts, and used his thumbs to tease her nipples. She was aching for him now.

He wrapped his fingers around her wrists, lifting her arms up high, nudging her onto her back and moving over her. 'You still think I'm a good guy?' he murmured against her lips.

She arched against him, trying to ease her desire. 'Not right now. Right now, you're very bad.'

'You don't like this?' He linked his fingers through hers, hands over her head.

'I do, but I need more.'

'Then more it is.' He moved his body closer until the heat was intense. His fingers slipped between her legs, gently parting them as he kissed his way down.

'Oh, god,' she said. 'No one's ever...'

'I'll only do it if you want me to.'

'Do it for god's sake. I'm dying here.' She lay back and closed her eyes, only to open them sharply again as his tongue touched her most intimate parts. Were these sensations real? It was too much... But not enough. *Holy mother of god.* She grabbed hold of his hair and clung to it as the rapids surged around her, carrying her away on a wave of ecstasy.

There was foreplay... and there was Brann. She should have known he'd exceed everything.

'That good enough to start with?' He shifted up the bed, moving in beside her.

'It'll do.' She smiled dreamily as she regained her breath, then she pushed him onto his back and straddled him. 'But I'm not done yet.'

'I'm very glad to hear it.' He threw his arms wide, lying fully open, like he was surrendering to her. 'Because I have lots more for you.'

She leaned over to the nightstand and lifted the condom packet. 'Give me what you've got.' She handed him a condom and moved so he could put it on.

'You should have brought that riding crop of yours,' he said.

'Is that your kink?'

'I can definitely see it being yours.' He pushed himself into a sitting position, slipped his hand around her cheek, and pulled her in for another deep kiss. Her body started to tingle again. Soon she and Brann would be together, utterly and completely. No going back.

He put his hands on her waist and gently lifted her. She eased herself onto him, lower and deeper until they were together. Inexplicably, a wave of emotion swept through her and she let out a little sob. She didn't mean to. And worse. She might actually cry, though she wasn't sad.

'Are you ok?' Brann said. 'Does it hurt?'

'No.' She shook her head. 'It's not that.'

'What then?' He crossed his hands on her back, pulling her slap against his hard chest. 'We're only doing this if you're ok with it.'

'I'm ok.' She held him, savouring the deep heat of his skin on hers and rubbing her cheek on his shoulder. The sensation of him inside her was so all-consuming it overwhelmed her. She needed to hold on to this moment. 'It just brought it home to me.'

'What do you mean?'

'That I can't have you.'

'You can have me tonight.'

She glanced at him, smiled, then kissed him with an urgency, like it was the last night of the world... and it kind of was. 'Yes. Tonight, you're mine.'

'I am. I give myself to you.'

'And I'm yours,' she said. 'For this night only. We belong to each other. And we're the perfect fit after all.'

'We really are.'

'But once it's done... That's it. Yes?'

'Then let's make this a night to remember.' He brought his lips to hers and cupped a hand around her bottom, holding her as he gently thrust. The need inside her built again, and she smiled at him in between kisses.

'Oh god, Ophelia.' He let out a groan, thrusting harder and faster. 'I hate how fucking good you are.'

That was possibly the first time he'd called her by her name, and it sent bolts of crazy desire through her.

'I'll never forgive you for how good you make me feel. Ahh...' She let out a cry as she lost it all over again.

The moon's position changed as the night went on. It shone through the bedroom window at the boathouse, the only witness to Ophelia and Brann's night together. Ophelia's emotions were all over the place, but she buried further tears. Why the hell had she let him see her like that? Not that it had done any harm – or it didn't seem to have. His empathy and care were as strong as his passion.

He stroked her hair as they lay together in a deep embrace, bodies sated and warm, so entwined Ophelia wasn't sure where her body ended and his began. His palm moved downward, stroking a rhythmical circle on her back. Scarcely above a whisper, he hummed a soft tune. She heard it more from the vibration of his Adam's apple, where her head rested, than anything else. At first, she thought it was the tune of 'Windmills in Your Mind' but then it wasn't. Something about it was familiar. Now and then, it took an unexpected course, but always gentle, almost melancholy.

Words joined the melody, barely even whispers. So low, she couldn't properly make them out. Was he singing in Gaelic?

'I hate it that I know. That I know it won't be me. I hate that someone else will take my place right here.'

Ophelia frowned, not sure if he maybe thought she was asleep, and these words were only for him, but the song went on.

'I hate that I can't love you the way you should be loved. I hate that we must part and never meet again.'

'Brann...'

'Uh-huh?'

'Are you ok?'

'We should get some sleep.' He tightened his hold on her. 'Would you like me to leave?'

'No. Please stay. I can't face the night alone.'

'Ok,' he whispered, turning the word into a soft kiss on her forehead. 'Sleep soundly. You're safe here.'

I know. This was the safest place in the world. With him. Everything they'd said and done tonight added to her reasons for wanting him. What she hated wasn't him, just the fact she couldn't have him, and how much she craved him. Now she knew he felt the same, it was even worse. Words weren't necessary. She sensed it in everything he did. But it had to stop. She wasn't meant to be with him. She had to do what was best for Glenvorneth, and sadly that would mean marrying someone who could solve the problems. This was the final fling. Now she had to put it to bed for good.

Her head was heavy, so were her eyes. His chest was warm and his arms strong. She could sleep here.

Someone was moving around. The sound was disturbing, but far away. Ophelia opened her eyes and sat up abruptly. Brann was wandering around the bedroom, picking up his clothes.

'Are you leaving?' she asked.

'I have to.' He scanned her over.

She jumped out of the bed, not caring she was still completely naked. So was he. Who was to see them out here? Unless Camilla Woodcroft was taking an early morning stroll, had climbed a tree on the other side of the lochan and was sitting with her binoculars out.

Ophelia wrapped her arms around his neck, and he pulled her close. The skin-to-skin contact made her tingle. 'Do you have to go so soon?'

'Pretty soon. I'm taking Caitlin to a party this morning.'

'You're a good dad.' Ophelia glided her hand around his cheek.

'I do my best.' He gave her a quick peck. 'Do you mind if I use your shower?'

'Of course not.'

'Where are the towels?'

'I'll get you one. I could even help wash you if you like.'

He smirked, and she eyed him over. His body had replied even if his mouth hadn't. 'How can I refuse?'

She went to the loo in the small en suite while he started the shower in the main bathroom. The towels were in the large closet in the hall, and she fetched two fluffy white ones on her way to join him. On top of them, she laid another condom. *Really should message Florence and thank her.*

Steam billowed around as she entered.

Brann was swigging mouthwash. He watched her for what seemed like an age, then spat out the mouthwash, rinsed it away and strode towards her. Gently, he nudged her against the wall, caging her with his arms and kissing her until she turned to jelly. His need pressed into her lower tummy, and she couldn't wait to steal this time with him.

Half an hour passed as they lathered each other in scented shower gel, kissing beneath the huge shower head as if in a tropical rainstorm. Brann brought her to another incredible climax before he reached out and grabbed the condom. Ophelia's back streaked up the steamy screen as he lifted her. The glass door jangled, registering every rhythmical jolt, the gushing water drowning their unrestrained cries.

All too soon, it was over. Brann was towelling himself dry and pulling on his clothes. Ophelia's heart was ready to crack, but she'd brought this on herself. She knew this had to stop. It couldn't go on indefinitely.

'Listen.' Brann clamped his hands on her upper arms. 'If this is as unbearable for you as it is for me, then you know how I'm feeling. I don't want to leave you like this, alone and cold.

We should be curled up together in front of the woodburner downstairs.' He pulled her to his chest. 'If I could, I would. I'd love to be that guy, but I can't be. I'm not your rich man. What I have wouldn't even buy that giant bed or the fancy bathtub.'

'I'm sorry,' she whispered, barely able to speak.

'Well, that was a bit of an exaggeration, obviously. But you know what I mean.' He drew back, giving her an appraising look. 'I understand your need to do what you believe is right, and I support that. But it doesn't mean I have to like it.'

'Thank you.' Tears were close again, but she must keep them down at least until he'd gone.

'Remember, I'm not leaving the country. If you need me for anything, call me. And I don't mean just for work.'

'I don't know what to say.'

'Don't say anything.' He bent in and kissed her on the cheek. 'That was one of the best nights of my life.' His hand trailed down her arm. 'Now, I need to go. See you sometime.'

'Yeah... And Brann.'

He was heading for the door.

'Uh-huh?'

'You won't tell anyone, will you?'

He was on the doorstep, ready to leave.

'No one will ever hear about it from me. Now, I really must go.' He was across the driveway in the van. Going down the track. Gone.

Ophelia stood at the door and breathed. A solitary tear fell from her eye, and she pushed it away. She had to battle through this and keep going. Crying over spilt milk wouldn't help. Brann was only ever going to be a fling. Now she'd had it, and it was over.

Perhaps the best way to stop herself from thinking was to go somewhere she'd be distracted. Her first thought was to take a ride, but if she went off on Conker, she'd start thinking and overthinking.

She got into her car and drove down the track towards the main house. Picking a fight wasn't a good idea in her current mood, but Jacinta's handling of the situation with Sean still irritated her.

The grandfather clock chimed as she entered the hallway. Why did it always feel deserted here? She made her way along the hallway and into the drawing room. No one was there, so she headed down to the kitchen. Before she got close, she heard Jacinta talking and other voices. The door was open, and Ophelia marched in, coming face to face with her father, Jacinta, Xander and Sean.

'You're still here?' she said to Sean.

'Yeah. I'm staying with Xander.'

Ophelia shook her head. How unbelievable that this boy she'd met once had the audacity to think she'd consider dating him, especially when he behaved like a twat.

'I think you're being a little unreasonable to the lad,' Rupert said with a smile.

'Of course you do. Unfortunately, I don't find his actions endearing. Also, the age difference is disturbing for me. I'm not interested in anyone that much younger than me.'

'That's a bit narrowminded. Look at Jacinta and I. We wouldn't be together if I discarded everyone younger than me.'

'Yes, but we all know that women mature a lot faster than most men and I don't have time to waste waiting for them to catch up.'

Jacinta made a weird nasal sound, like she was trying to clear dust from her nose. 'You've wasted quite a bit of time this year,' she said. 'Look at what you did to poor James.'

'I did nothing to him. And if you want to discuss this, then fine, but not here and not with those two as an audience.' She nodded at Xander and Sean.

Xander shrugged like he didn't have a care in the world; his face had the same easy arrogance as his mother. 'Let's go.'

'Xander,' Ophelia added. 'I have to thank you. Your efforts to set me up with someone were very thoughtful. Next time you get the urge though, maybe you should look for someone for Francesca.'

'Hang on,' Jacinta said. 'She's too young to be dating someone their age. I don't want any of that.'

'Don't be narrowminded, remember.' Ophelia flicked her a look, then turned back to Xander. 'Though it's probably best if you keep away from matchmaking altogether,'

'Sure. Whatever.' He clapped Sean on the back. 'Let's get out of this dusty old cavern and back to the fun.'

Jacinta flapped after her son, saying goodbye.

Rupert drummed his fingers on the table as though not sure what to say. 'Lovely weather for the time of year.'

The weather? Ophelia almost rolled her eyes. 'Oh, yeah. It's wonderful.'

Jacinta returned. 'I wish you hadn't shooed him off. I hardly ever get to see him these days.'

'It was his choice.'

'What is it you want to talk about anyway?' Jacinta muttered, picking up plates and ramming them into the dishwasher.

'We need to establish some rules. If you get the urge to set me up with someone again, then I might be up for meeting them, but none of this forgone conclusion stuff or telling people we're already dating. If I'm committing to it, I want it to be with someone I like and respect. Not someone thrust upon me, or who the two of you have already told the world is your future son-in-law.'

Jacinta rolled her eyes at Rupert, who was wearing a somewhat shocked expression. Ophelia knew it well – the one where he tried to deny he'd ever done anything of the sort.

'With hindsight, James was actually ok,' she went on. 'We just weren't a good fit for each other.' Unbidden, an image of her and Brann locked together in her bed sprang into her mind. Quickly, she hustled it out. 'Sean most certainly was not ok. Do you realise what might have happened if he'd been waiting for me when I went home last night?'

'He said he didn't mean any harm,' Rupert said.

'I wouldn't have known that. I might have knocked him out before he had the chance to explain.'

'Fair point. I admit, he wasn't a good choice.'

'So, no more. You can introduce people to me, but with no expectations. Understood?'

'Loud and clear,' Rupert said. Jacinta turned away and was doubtless rolling her eyes.

'Who is Brian, by the way?' Rupert furrowed his brow. 'Sean kept talking about some man called Brian you were out with at a dinner dance, who's apparently now working as a builder here.'

She stared into the near distance, willing this conversation to go away. 'Sounds like he's got his facts all muddled. I don't know anyone called Brian.'

'Very odd,' Rupert said.

'Who *were* you at the dance with?' Jacinta asked with a slight raise of her eyebrow.

'Friends. And none of them were called Brian.'

'Well,' Jacinta said. 'I was talking to the Countess of Dairvin the other day.' She paused, no doubt waiting for Ophelia to swoon at the name drop. When she didn't, Jacinta went on, 'She told me about a very eligible young man by the name of Rafe Harrington.'

Ophelia recalled the countess mentioning him before, but she sighed. Jacinta had a one-track mind.

'He lives in Glasgow, but his roots are here. I wonder if he might be the man.'

Ophelia held up her hand. 'I told you, no more. If the chance to meet him comes up, then fine, but I don't want to be out somewhere tomorrow only to hear rumours I'm engaged to this man before I've even met him.'

'Fine. Whatever.'

But how could she? Even looking at other men made her ill. The only man she wanted to see was Brann. The one man she couldn't have.

Chapter Twenty-Three

Brann

Brann drove around the lochside on Monday morning, heading for the boathouse. Harrison had rattled on nearly the whole way about a flat he was viewing later in the week with his girlfriend. Brann tried to listen and be cheerful about it. Because he was. His son was growing up, moving on with his life. *God knows how that helped me at his age.* Hopefully Harrison would never cite his parents as a negative influence in his life the way Brann had. He and Kristalee had done their best. They'd never be Mum and Dad of the year, but they'd tried and surely that had to count for something.

'Is her ladyship likely to be in?' Harrison asked as they pulled up in front of the boathouse. Brann's mind had never been far from Ophelia since he'd left her on Saturday morning. Whatever happened today was likely to be nothing short of torture.

'No idea,' Brann said. 'But we should stop calling her that and be nice.'

'Look who's talking.' Harrison gave him a filthy stare. 'I've heard you calling her worse to her face.'

'Yeah, well.' He pulled out his phone and saw a message from Ophelia.

OPHELIA C-B: Use your key to get in. I'm in Edinburgh today.

Convenient. And sensible. Probably for the best.

'She's not here,' Brann said.

'Is that her messaging you again, aye? Still going after a bit of rough, is she?'

'Shut it and get moving.' He unlocked the door and went in, forcing himself not to look at anything too closely, or remember what had happened there on Friday night.

'We can probably get all the snagging finished in here today, maybe tomorrow, and then we can work on the garden fences the rest of the week. Hopefully, there won't be a big freeze or anything.'

'Ok,' Harrison said. 'Then are we done with this place?'

'There's a whole load of work here, but our current contract only covers this work. Unless they renew it quickly, I'm going to put us down for some other jobs up until Christmas.'

'Good,' Harrison said. 'This place is doing my head in. Too many nobs hanging about.'

'Yup.' Way too many of them. People from a different world. A world Brann didn't fit in, which meant he'd never have the one woman he really wanted. He needed to talk to her though, because if there was nothing else to do here, he wasn't hanging around. Quickly, he thumbed out a message.

BRANN: Hey. When we're done with the snagging, we'll do the fences, but after that, do you want to renew our contract and I'll move on to the next thing on the list? I need to know soon, so I can arrange the guys for next week. Thanks.

He was already managing a couple of smaller jobs and had his contractors at other places, but much as his heart and soul wanted to be close to Ophelia, objectively it would be better if he wasn't.

OPHELIA C-B: Apologies. I should have sorted that with you sooner. Do you have other jobs you can go to? It would make sense to finish at Glenvorneth for now as most of the other things on the list are outdoors and would be better done when there's less chance of bad weather. If you don't have other jobs, let me know and I'll see what we can do. The cash flow situation isn't much better than usual, though hopefully by spring it will be.

His heart sank. Did that mean by spring she'd be engaged to some rich guy who'd bail them out? If that was the case, he wasn't sure he wanted to be the one carrying out the contract. How could he stand it? The torture of seeing her around with another man and having that man telling him what to do, lording it over him. *Ugh.* Made him sick.

BRANN: Sensible plan to put the list on hold. I've got several other jobs I can do, so no worries there. Take care.

Stupid way to end the message really, because it was nothing like what he really wanted to say at all. But telling her he loved her would change nothing. He'd pretty much told her on Friday.

He'd definitely shown her. Sadly, unlike the movies, love didn't conquer all. Not in his world anyway.

OPHELIA C-B: Thank you. I'll message Barbara and ask her to come up with your contract and sign off the work in case I'm not back before you're done.

He read that to mean she wouldn't be back. With a sigh, he strapped on his tool belt and worked through the short list of snagging, deliberately being in a different part of the house from Harrison. He didn't want to talk.

Around midday, he was adding a missing piece of skirting board to the stairs when a knock sounded on the door. Expecting Barbara, he made to get up and answer, but the door swung open and Rupert strolled in clapping his hands.

'Bally cold weather today.' He glanced around. 'Left the dogs in the car and they're not pleased, but Ophelia would string me up if I made a mess of it. Stunning place. Meant to come up before, but you know how time runs away.'

'Sure do,' Brann said, still on his knees. He didn't think Rupert worked, so god knew what he did with his time.

'I've brought some contracts up. Barbara would have done it, but she's got her nose in the books and I thought I really should see the place. Quite something, isn't it? Very impressive.'

'Yeah. It's a cool place.' Brann dusted off his hands and got to his feet, coming down the stairs to the hall.

'Now, these contracts.' Rupert pulled out a folio from under his arm. 'Shall we take a look?'

'Sure. In here?' Brann suggested, opening the door to the kitchen area. Harrison was in the living area, so this would save him an encounter with one of 'the nobs'.

'I say, this is all very impressive.' Rupert peered around. 'You're very good at this.'

'Thanks. It wasn't just me.' He'd brought in extra workers to put this place together, helping his business to grow.

'Ophelia has the grand ideas,' Rupert said. 'You have the practical skills.'

Brann frowned. Had Ophelia designed this place? He followed the plans but hadn't asked where they came from. 'Was this all her idea?'

'Oh yes. All the designs were hers originally. She does this kind of thing for her business. I believe it's quite successful, though it's all over my head. Barbara got planning permission on this site and at the Factor's House with Ophelia's plans. The stables were her designs too. I assumed you knew that.'

'She never said.' Brann ran his fingers through his hair. Why hadn't it occurred to him before? Even when she'd told him she was a designer and ran her own business? He'd assumed she came in at the end and put on the finishing touches. Not for a moment had he clocked the enormity of what she'd done. But it all made sense now. Her plans had been perfect, and he'd understood them just like he understood her. 'If I'd known, I'd have thanked her. They were the easiest plans to follow I've ever had. I don't think I had to ask for clarification once.'

Teamwork makes the dream work.

They were like two halves of one person. When they were together, they fitted perfectly and worked seamlessly. The annoyance and enmity rose from the tumult of knowing they weren't allowed to be together.

Brann read the details on the contract, though he'd already signed it at the start. Rupert signed off the work and Brann added his name beneath it.

'Barbara tells me you're back in the spring to do more work.'

'Possibly. Let me know as soon as you can. I'm a busy man and the calendar fills up fast.'

Rupert let out a huge sigh, and his lips flapped. 'It all rather depends on money unfortunately. Which is something we're a bit short on.'

'Yeah. It's never easy,' Brann said through gritted teeth. The man had no idea what it was really like to have no money. 'I suppose a lot of it went on this.'

'This was all Ophelia's own money. She's done well for herself and she's rather laid claim to the place.'

'She paid all our wages for doing this?'

'Yes. And bought all the parts. We just didn't have the means.'

Brann's jaw almost hit the floor. It must have cost thousands. No wonder she was laying claim to it. She owned it. Her family might be the so-called upper class, but they weren't better than anyone. For all Rupert's airs, he let his daughter pay for his upkeep while he did nothing but swan about spending the money he claimed not to have.

'Well, I hope she's happy here. She's got a beautiful house now,' Brann said.

'She does. It'll have to be let out to holidaymakers, of course. To make money, but she can enjoy it for a few months. We're really hoping she'll marry soon.'

'Yeah?' The reality of her predicament was even more repellent to Brann now. Even if she married a rich man, she wouldn't benefit from his cash. Her father and his wife would be the ones living in luxury, while she settled for Mr whoever-he-was.

'You don't happen to know a Rafe Harrington, do you?'

'Should I?'

'Bit of an entrepreneur. Made a lot of money in the travel industry with some new approach. I don't understand it all. But apparently, he's a good match for Ophelia. Jacinta is trying to come up with an organic – her word – way to meet him. But he's not easy to pin down. His father's big in business too, but I've never met him and am not sure how to bring about a meeting without inviting him.'

'Sorry, can't help you.' And he wouldn't anyway. No way did he want any part in choosing some random man for Ophelia. Sure, he knew the Harringtons, though not this guy in particular, but his mouth was zipped.

'Right. I'll skedaddle and let you get on.' Rupert reached the door, then turned back. 'By the way, you don't happen to have a Brian working for you, do you?'

'I don't think so.'

'Very odd. Can't get to the bottom of this one. We had a visitor at the weekend who told us he'd seen Ophelia at a dance with someone called Brian, who was also working here as a builder. She said she didn't know any Brians, but the boy was so adamant.'

Brann silently counted to ten. With any luck when he finished, Rupert would leave. If Ophelia hadn't blabbed that he was actually 'Brian', then he wouldn't either. They'd been stupid to think that little episode wouldn't find its way back to her family.

'Righty-ho! I'll be off.'

Brann closed the door on him and let out his breath. The sooner he was out of this place, the better. He couldn't go yet though. The work had been signed off, but he wasn't dishonest, and he wouldn't go without finishing the fencing around the garden area.

A low mist hung around the lochan as he drove the post into the ground. Not the best weather to be doing this, but better than frozen ground. Once this was done, he was gone, and he might never see this place again.

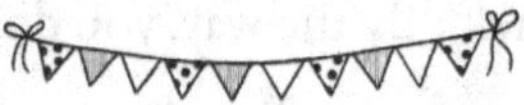

November

By Friday afternoon, the fences were up, and Brann only had the gate to hang and the hinges to set. It was something he could do himself, so Harrison checked the posts, then went for a walk in the woods. Brann had no doubt as soon as he was out of earshot he'd be on his phone to his girlfriend. He'd been itching to get away all morning to call her. Oh, young love... If only he had the same luck.

The crisp late autumn breeze chased piles of leaves around the newly fenced-off garden area. Brann secured the latch on the gate, clicking it open and shut a few times to ensure it was working properly. A car pulled up and his eyes were drawn to it. Was it Ophelia? Perhaps she thought he'd be gone already. But he didn't recognise the blue Freelander. Two women got out, both looked late fifties and one of them was vaguely familiar. Brann had worked for so many people in the town it was easy to forget some.

He dusted his hands together as the women approached.

'Hi. Can I help you?' he said, partly to draw attention to himself, as he wasn't sure they'd seen him on their way to the front door.

The taller of the two women stepped forward with a smile. Her face reminded him of someone. She was well-dressed in a belted chocolate brown coat and boots, fitting perfectly with the style of people who usually hung around Glenvorneth. 'Good afternoon. We're here to see Ophelia. Is she in, do you know?'

Brann shook his head, a frown growing. 'No, I think she's away at the moment. She's been in Edinburgh, I think.'

The woman nodded, glancing at a gold wristwatch. 'She's back from Edinburgh and she's supposed to be meeting us. But we are a bit early.'

She was back. Brann needed to pack up and get the hell out. He didn't want to be here when she arrived. Things were awkward enough already.

'You're Brann, aren't you?' the other woman said. 'You fitted a kitchen for me last year.'

'Yeah, that's right. I recognised your face but couldn't place it.'

'You're the builder who has been doing all the wonderful work here,' the first woman said.

'Well, I'm definitely the builder, but I'll let other people decide how good the work is.'

She smiled and looked up at the boathouse. 'Well, if this is anything to go by, I'd say it's very good. And Ophelia spoke highly of you and believe me, that's something, because she can be rather hard to please. Gets that from me, I reckon.'

'Are you her mum?' Brann raked up his hair. That explained who she reminded him of.

'My apologies, I should have said. Yes, I'm Edith, Ophelia's mother, and this is Nancy, my partner, who you've already met when you fitted her kitchen.'

Brann smiled, recalling what Ophelia had told her about her mother and how she'd been reluctant to be open. This must be quite a step for her, publicly declaring Nancy as her partner.

'Well, I'm about to leave, but the door's open. I usually lock up before I go, but I'm sure Ophelia wouldn't mind you waiting inside where it's warm.'

'She might not want us to see until she's ready to do the grand tour,' Edith said.

'Well, let me know what you want me to do. I can leave the door open if you're going to be here.' He had to find Harrison too.

He shifted his weight from one foot to the other, fidgeting with his screwdriver.

'We'll let Ophelia do the big reveal,' Edith said. 'But maybe we could see the garden before it gets dark.'

'Sure, take a look.' Brann opened the gate. 'There's not much there yet.' He lifted his tools out of the way and shoved them into the box. He needed to leave. Now. But where the hell was Harrison?

CHAPTER TWENTY-FOUR

Ophelia

Running late was something Ophelia hated, but she had a list of things she wanted to discuss with Stella at Wood 'n' Chic. She nipped in on her way back to Glenvorneth. This way, it would get done. Checking the time on her phone, she entered the shop. She still had half an hour to get back before her mum and Nancy arrived, though her mum had an annoying habit of always being early.

The little bell above the door tinkled. Ophelia glanced around at the beautiful furniture. Everything was so festive, with twinkly lights and little wooden or stitched decorations hanging everywhere.

'Hey,' a voice said from behind the counter and Ophelia realised it wasn't Stella, but Kristalee. She was in another quirky outfit with a long black lacy goth skirt that came to points at the hem, showing off red and white striped tights funnelling into her Doc Martens.

'Good afternoon,' Ophelia said. 'Is Stella about?'

'No, sorry. It's just me today.'

'Ah, ok. I might need to call back. I've got a lot to discuss with her.'

'Anything I can help with?'

Ophelia sucked on her lower lip. 'Not really. It's about the pieces she wanted from me. I need to sort some deliveries and find out when would be best for her. I'll ring her another day. Just thought I'd pop in while I was passing.'

'I'll leave her a note to say you called in.'

'Thanks.'

Kristalee scribbled something on a pad of paper on the desk. Just seeing someone taking a note on paper was nice. People so often used their phones for everything these days. And really Ophelia could message Stella and arrange this, but it was so much nicer seeing people in person... And it avoided Brann. Or did it? It was Friday afternoon. Would he have left? Her tummy swooped. Once he left this time, he might not be back.

All for the best.

'I wonder.' Kristalee tapped the notepad with a black finger-nail. 'Does your sister still go to the theatre club?'

Ophelia frowned. 'I, um, don't know. Why?'

'She and my daughter had a bit of a fall out. Caitlin is quite insistent your sister was... well, bullying her. I wish there was a way for them to make up because Caitlin really loved that club.'

'My sister was bullying your daughter?'

'I don't mean to accuse her.' Kristalee put her hands up. 'I know there's always two sides to every story, and teenage girls have their dramas. God knows, I certainly did.'

'And your daughter's called Caitlin?' Not that it mattered. It was a fairly common name, but Brann's daughter was called Caitlin, and she was a teenage girl.

'Yeah. Oh, I forgot,' Kristalee said. 'You know her dad. He's been working for you.'

Ophelia cringed. Small town syndrome. And not only that, but she also had one of the most recognisable names in the county. Nowhere for a Chattan-Blythe to hide. 'Do you mean Brann?'

'Yeah. I don't know if he's still working for you guys, but if he is, please don't mention that I told you about Caitlin and your sister. Brann doesn't think I should talk about it to anyone, as it's Caitlin's business. I get where he's coming from, but problems don't sort themselves without talking sometimes.'

'I won't say anything.' How could she explain she wasn't close to her sister? 'But I'll see if I can find anything out just generally. I really don't like the idea of bullying being associated with my family.' Though if Francesca was anything like Jacinta, what hope did they have? Jacinta was one of the most entitled narcissists Ophelia had ever met.

The drive to the boathouse seemed to take forever. Ophelia's head was bursting with thoughts about Francesca and Caitlin, then Brann and Kristalee. Why did it disturb her so much that Kristalee was his ex? She seemed a nice enough person and was striking and confident. Brann had confessed to never really having had the depth of feeling he should for her, but they'd been together long enough to have two children.

What kind of woman did I think Brann usually went for?

Someone like me? Unlikely. He and Kristalee were much better suited. Both unconventionally good looking, and tough.

Her mum's car was outside the boathouse and not only that. So was Brann's van. The man himself leaned on a new gate, laughing as he chatted to her mum and Nancy. The old charm was back, the twinkle in his eye.

Ophelia got out, and all eyes landed on her. 'Hello,' she said. 'Nice and early as always, mother.' They bumped cheeks before Ophelia turned to Nancy. 'Lovely to have you here.'

'It's a beautiful place.'

'Brann's been giving us the tour of the fence,' Edith said. 'But we're waiting for you to do the house tour.'

Ophelia cast Brann a look. 'He could have done that too. He built the place, after all.'

'It's all yours,' he said. 'I just did the manual labour. You designed it and did all the fancy stuff.'

She watched his face for a moment, pretty convinced she'd never told him she'd designed it. Maybe she had. But his expression was a half frown, like he was surprised but impressed.

'Sounds like you're the dream team,' Nancy said. 'One does the designs; one brings them to life.'

A little smirk played at the corner of Brann's lips. 'Oh yeah, that's us alright.'

Ophelia rolled her eyes. 'Right, let's get in and do the tour.' She opened the door and hung back as her mum and Nancy went in. Keeping half an eye on them, she beckoned Brann over. A low buzzing started in her tummy as he drew close.

'Yes, Princess,' he said in a low whisper.

'Why are you still here?'

'Just finished. I need to wait for Harrison though.'

'Where is he?'

'Went for a walk. I just had a message. He's on his way back, but he got lost.'

'Wait there.'

He lifted an eyebrow. 'Why?'

'Just do it.' She went inside and took both her mum and Nancy by the arms. 'So, this is the downstairs, as you see. Take a look around and make yourself at home. If you don't mind giving me ten minutes. I have something to discuss with Brann and it's easier if I do it now rather than wait until Monday.' And come Monday, he wouldn't be there anyway. Who knew when she'd see him again? Which meant she had to do this now.

He was still waiting outside the door, toeing the gravel with his hands in his pockets.

'What's going on?' he asked.

She beckoned him and walked around the side of the boathouse. In the oldest part of the building was a small woodshed that had been left pretty much as it had been, though it was much tidier than before. She held the door for him, and he ducked inside. When she pulled the door shut, it was almost pitch black except for a sliver of light from a tiny, very narrow window.

'Why are you locking me in a shed?'

'Because I need you.' Her hands found him, and she wrapped her arms around his neck.

'Still?' He pulled her close.

'Always.'

His lips were on her, hungry and desperate. She clung to him, dragging him in deeper, closer. His hold was so strong, she couldn't have got out even if she wanted to. But she didn't. This was exactly where she wanted to be.

Breaking off the kiss to draw breath, she moaned as he carried on kissing her neck.

'When I leave today, I'm not coming back,' he said.

'I know.'

'I might never be back.'

'I know.' She took his face and kissed him again.

'So... If you *need* me again like this. It's tough luck.'

'I know.' The words were jammed on repeat. Of course, she knew. But if there was a chance for one more crazy kiss, she wasn't going to miss it. Running her hand around his lightly bearded cheek, she drew him towards her again. Their tongues met, causing a furnace to ignite in her. She wanted to rip off her clothes and have him, but they couldn't do that. Not here. Not now.

At the sound of his van door slamming closed, they broke apart. 'That must be Harrison,' Brann said. 'I should go.'

'Ok.'

He took her face in his hands and kissed her again. 'I'll go first. Don't come out until I've driven away, or this really won't look good.'

'Right.' She listened as he crunched across the gravel and his van door closed. With shaky breaths, she straightened herself out and smoothed down her hair. His van motored down the track and Ophelia came out, closing the door softly behind her.

It was starting to get dark. The lights inside looked warm and inviting. Her mother and Nancy were visible through the window, standing in the kitchen talking. Ophelia needed to go in there, smile, and pretend to be delighted at showing them around. She couldn't let on she'd just let the love of her life drive away and she had no idea when or if she'd ever see him again.

CHAPTER TWENTY-FIVE

Brann

The streetlights glowed orange as Brann and Harrison arrived outside Kristalee's house in Kirk Lane, a quirky little street that ran along behind the village church and the manse. The houses looked cute, if a little higgledy-piggledy, but they were all small inside and always needed work done on something, from the roofs to the locks.

Brann spotted several windows already sporting Christmas trees and flashing lights. They hadn't quite reached December yet, but Kirk Lane had a very festive feeling, like something out of a storybook.

This was the half-time changeover. Harrison was spending the weekend with his mum and Caitlin was coming back with Brann. The days of pre-arranged visits and sharing weekends were all but done. To be fair, they'd handled that bit well compared to some couples, who were constantly fighting about access rights or quibbling over drop-off times. Brann had heard it so often on jobs, bitter couples fighting over twenty minutes here and there. He and Kristalee had rarely argued about stuff like that. Once they'd stopped having to pretend to love each other, they got on well. Now Harrison and Caitlin spent their time wherever they wanted. Harrison and his girlfriend were moving into a flat after Christmas and Caitlin didn't seem to mind whose house she was at.

Harrison marched straight into the house and Brann followed. 'Hey,' he said, more to announce his arrival than anything else. If one of his kids wasn't with him, he wouldn't have walked in without knocking.

The faint aroma of cooking lingered in the tiny hallway, and Kristalee poked her head out the kitchen door.

'Oh, hi. How's it going?'

'Ok, thanks.'

'Caitlin's at Aria's, but she's on her way back.'

Brann thrust his hands into his pockets. Caitlin could walk around later herself. His house wasn't that far from here, but he didn't like the idea of her walking about on her own in the dark. He heard her scoff even inside his head, but he didn't care. He couldn't help it.

'I'll wait,' he said.

'You want a cuppa?' Kristalee said.

'Yeah, please. If that's ok.'

'Sure. Come through.'

He followed Kristalee into the cramped kitchen at the back of the house.

'Have you been working today?' he asked.

'Yeah, just got back not long ago. The shop was quiet today. What about you? Are you still at Glenvorneth?'

'Yup.'

Kristalee poured the water from the kettle into a mug with a tea bag draped over the edge, stirred it, and handed it to Brann.

She busied herself making another one, then sighed, her heavily pencilled eyes fixed on the mug between her hands. 'I think I might have put my foot in it.'

Brann's brows furrowed. 'What do you mean?'

Kristalee met his gaze. 'I talked to Ophelia Chattan-Blythe. She was in the shop today.'

Brann shifted in his seat. 'Um... Right. What did you talk about?'

Kristalee pulled a side pout with her burgundy lips. 'I mentioned the bullying.'

'Seriously?'

'Yeah. Sorry. I just want to get to the bottom of it. Caitlin really misses the club.'

'What did she say?'

'Who? Caitlin?'

'Ophelia.' Even saying the name made him too hot.

'Nothing much. Just said she'd see if she could find anything out.'

'She never mentioned it to me.' But then why would she?

'I asked her not to. I knew you wouldn't want me to say to anyone.'

'Well, I doubt she'll be able to do anything much about it.'

'She seems a nice woman. Talks posh, but she's ok. Is she horrible to work for?'

Harrison came in and went straight to the fridge. 'Are you talking about "the heiress"?' he asked.

'Is that what she calls herself?' Kristalee raised an eyebrow.

'That's what she is,' Brann said. 'Though I don't think she refers to herself as that.'

'Ooh, very fancy.' Kristalee smiled.

'That's definitely what Dad thinks.'

'Harrison,' Brann warned. 'Don't let's go there.'

The main door clicked open and shut and Caitlin called, 'Hello!' before joining them. Brann put down his mug. This was the moment to make a very sharp getaway.

'Go where?' Kristalee said with an obvious smirk, not dropping the subject.

'Dad fancies her rotten,' Harrison said.

'Seriously?' Kristalee covered her mouth, but it didn't hide her laugh.

Brann cast Harrison a disgusted look.

'Oh yeah, totally.' Harrison winked. 'It's been going on for months. And she fancies him too. It's so frigging obvious.'

'That's enough.' Brann's eyes landed on Caitlin. Her brow was furrowed, gaze darting between him and Harrison.

'Who are you talking about?' she said.

'Madam Ophelia Chattan-Blythe.' Harrison adopted a snooty tone.

Caitlin gaped at Brann. 'Her? You and her?'

'No, no. Stop.' Brann put his hands up. 'He's just ribbing me. It's not...' How could he say not true? Because it was true. He'd fancied Ophelia for months, and she felt the same. They'd shared so much, kissed, had sex, for Christ's sake. Yet, how could he admit that? Caitlin would be horrified to discover her dad had slept with the sister of her bully. *Fuck*. He was horrified himself. How could he have let her down like this? Even now, her expression had fallen, and her eyes were full of uncertainty.

'It's not what?' Caitlin said.

'Not anything to worry about. You know what your brother's like.' Brann clapped Harrison on the shoulder. 'Got an overactive imagination and gossips worse than the girls.'

Harrison smirked. 'Yep, that's me. But I'm not wrong.' He gave Caitlin a little wink. 'You see if I'm not.'

Kristalee put down her mug. 'Caitlin, are you ready to go?'

'I still need to put some stuff in my bag.' With a brief glance around, she left.

'Harrison, stop stuffing your face before dinner.' Kristalee chivvied him out of the kitchen. 'You've always been terrible for that.' When she returned, she looked at Brann. 'Is any of that true?'

He gave a little shrug. 'I can't help it if she fancies me.'

Kristalee snorted. 'I wouldn't have thought you were her type.'

'Well, it doesn't matter anyway. It's not like anything can happen there, is it?'

'Do you want something to happen?'

'Are you crazy? And why all the questions?'

'Who doesn't love a bit of intrigue?'

'Let's close it down for now. I don't want Caitlin to be upset. The Chattan-Blythes aren't exactly her favourite people right now, and talking like this won't make it any better.'

Kristalee nodded, but Brann still read the grin on her face to mean she was suspicious. He couldn't wait to leave.

Caitlin was quiet in the van on the way home. What to say? It seemed like she was holding back from asking him about what she'd heard in the kitchen because she wasn't sure she wanted to know the truth. And he sure as hell didn't want to bring it up. He hated lying, especially to his kids, but how could he face the truth?

Now, if ever, he needed a cool-off period. And he'd get it because he wasn't going back to Glenvorneth.

'Listen, about what Harrison said.' Brann finally got the courage to speak as they got to the front door. 'Ophelia and I flirted a bit. But we're not seeing each other or anything like that, and I won't be working at Glenvorneth for some time... Maybe ever.'

'Right.'

'But... Well, there might be a time when I might have a relationship again. Mum might too. I know that won't be easy for you, but I'm not sure I want to be single forever.' Though if he couldn't have Ophelia, he couldn't imagine himself with anyone else. No one had ever been such a perfect fit.

'Yeah, I know. It's just kinda scary. What if it's someone who doesn't like me?'

Brann put his arm around her. 'If it's someone who doesn't like my kids, then it won't be the right person for me. Ok?'

'Ok, Dad.'

'You and Harrison will always be my number ones.' He kissed the top of her head. Hopefully Caitlin would accept that, but it did nothing for his shredded heart.

February

Brann survived three months with nothing but memories of Ophelia and no chance of seeing the woman in person until he got an unexpected call one frosty February morning, when he was working on a new-build office with Harrison and a couple of other guys he'd hired to help out.

'This is an emergency!' Barbara said down the phone. She always had a flair for dramatics. But Brann didn't want to go back to Glenvorneth. He'd gone this long without seeing Ophelia. He couldn't say without *thinking* about her because that would have been an out and out lie. Surviving two minutes without some crazy thought about her shoving its way to the forefront was impossible.

'There's a leak coming through into one of the bedrooms?' Brann asked.

'Yes. And it's Francesca's room, so she's had to move into one of the spare rooms which is very cold and dusty, so you can guess she's not best pleased.'

Brann didn't restrain his eye roll. Barbara couldn't see him. So one of the princesses had to move rooms! Oh dear. Hardly an emergency. If it had been in a house like his where a child's bedroom was the only bedroom, then fine, but in a house that had several to choose from, did it really matter? Still, Barbara was just the messenger. It wasn't her fault if she was getting pressure from above and the fact it was her calling him and not Ophelia suggested that Ophelia wasn't there. Perhaps she was back in Edinburgh.

'Ok. I've got a lot on, and the guys are busy with other jobs, but I'll come over and have a look.'

He returned to the half-assembled office area and told the guys he was off to check a leaking roof.

'I need to see if it's an emergency or not.' He didn't say where he was going. How could he stand the expression on Harrison's face?

Guilty conscience.

Happened every time he even skirted the place in his mind.

Barbara met him at the main door of the house, which cemented the idea that Ophelia must be elsewhere, and that was good.

Wasn't it?

His gaze roamed over the opulent interior in the main hall, and he caught a glimpse of a fancy seating area through a door before Barbara led him up a wide stairway.

'There's a large patch of damp on the ceiling,' Barbara said. 'I'm worried, in case it collapses.'

'Let's see it.' Brann stepped into the room and looked up, spying a brownish tide mark immediately. 'Hmm.' He rubbed at his cheek. 'Can I get up above it? Is there an attic?'

'Yes. I can show you how to get in, but I don't like going up the ladder.'

'That's ok, I can do that bit myself, but I might need a torch. Let me nip back to the van.' Once he had it, he returned to Barbara, undid the trapdoor with the long hook, and a ladder folded down.

He hoisted himself in and put on the torch, scanning about until he located the source of the problem.

'I think there are a few loose slates,' he told Barbara when he came down again. 'I'll have to look outside, but it might be too high for me to see.'

'And can you fix it?'

'Yeah, but if it's slates, you'll need to hire a cherry-picker. This roof is too high for me to go up on a ladder. There's quite a bit of damage to the woodwork inside. I can do a temporary cover inside and replace the woodwork if you want. And I'll call up about a cherry-picker, but I can't guarantee when one will be available. Once all that's done, I can re-plaster the ceiling, but everything will have to come out of that room. Plastering is messy.'

'Ah, yes, ok. Let's do all that. Jacinta was quite insistent she wanted it done. Can you cost that out for me and hopefully you can start straight away?'

'I'll try and fit it in, but I've got everyone contracted out, so it won't necessarily be quick.'

'Well, ok. Just as long as it gets done.'

It threw him out of kilter and added this to his workload. But a job was a job. And he felt a bit sorry for Barbara.

Harrison sniggered when he found out where Brann would be working for the following week, but Brann shut him up by telling him he was coming too. Two of them were needed to work the cherry-picker. Luckily for the Chattan-Blythes, the hire shop had one available. Brann and Harrison worked in the drizzly rain, fixing the loose slates and ensuring everything was watertight.

Brann then had the job of working in the dusty, cobwebby attic, hacking out rotten beams and replacing them.

Every so often, he needed to come down for air; it was cold and fusty up there.

'A little birdie told me you were here.'

Brann spun around from the bottom of the ladder, coming face to face with Ophelia.

'I thought you were in Edinburgh.'

'I'm halving my time between here and the boathouse.'

'I see.' He clenched his jaw, trying not to look at her too closely. She messed with his head. Still so beautiful, smelling of a spring garden. She was in those tight trousers and a white top again. Brann flexed his fingers; they itched to reach out and tug her close.

'Jacinta must have arranged all this.' She pointed at the ladder. 'Because she didn't mention it to me.'

'Does that mean I won't get paid again? I should have demanded upfront payment. Here's me being too trusting for my own good.'

Ophelia pulled a slow shrug and an apologetic face. 'This is all her doing. And... bollocks.'

Voices were approaching. Brann looked around.

'I need to get out of here,' Ophelia said. 'She's invited some bore of a man she was at school with to visit. I know she's trying to get me to marry him, but he's too old for me and I'm not interested. I told her to stop this.'

'Go in there.' Brann opened the door to Francesca's room. 'If she tries to get in, I'll say she can't, as it's not safe.'

'Thanks.' Ophelia darted in and closed the door.

Jacinta and a handsome man of around her age came strolling along the corridor a second later.

'We have the builders in.' Jacinta sailed past Brann as though he was invisible. 'Ongoing renovations with a house this size. Your room is just along here. I put you close to Ophelia's old room. Hopefully she'll use it while you're here, though you could always join her at the boathouse.'

Jacinta opened a door and showed the man in. Brann wanted to disappear up the ladder out of sight but didn't want to risk Jacinta making her way into Francesca's room after he'd said he wouldn't let her.

She returned a few moments later as Brann was searching around his toolbox.

'Ophelia hasn't passed this way, has she?' Jacinta asked.

'I don't think so.'

Jacinta pulled a face. 'You know, that girl is the bane of my life. From the day I met her father, she's been beastly to me. I'm only a few years older than her.'

Brann didn't react. A few? As in twenty plus, surely.

'She didn't require a mother figure. We could have been friends, but she sees everything from her point of view and never considers how hard it was for me.'

'I'm sure it was hard for her too,' Brann said. 'It's never easy for kids when their parents remarry.' He recalled the look in Caitlin's eyes when she'd thought he might be seeing someone else. The fear that nothing would ever be the same again. The sadness that someone else might steal her father's love.

'She wasn't that young. And believe me, I tried for a long time, but nothing I did ever made any difference. What was the point? I wasted years of time and energy trying to include her in everything. I was always rebuffed or sniggered at behind my back, so I gave up. She has a selfish, spiteful side.'

'She's also hardworking and generous. She paid my wages out of her own pocket when the estate couldn't.' He didn't openly name Jacinta, but the look on her face told him she understood him.

'No doubt that's what she told you.'

'Yes, she did. Because that's what happened.'

'She always has a way of putting things that make her sound good and me sound bad. I know we need her to marry well to save this estate, but I really hope it's to someone who already has their own children. Then she'll discover how difficult it's been for me over the years.'

'I doubt it's been a picnic for her either.'

'Hmph,' Jacinta muttered, stalking away. 'You don't know the half of it.'

True, he didn't. But he also knew Ophelia, and no matter what Jacinta said, he knew she wasn't as bad as all that. Maybe this time last year he'd have agreed with her, but not now.

CHAPTER TWENTY-SIX

Ophelia cautiously stepped out from the bedroom, her heart still pounding from the conversation she'd overheard. What kind of bitch was Jacinta? Not that Ophelia didn't know that already, but for her to talk to Brann like that. How galling. No doubt that kind of conversation was standard fare for Jacinta. Ophelia didn't like to think how often her name had been called mud by that woman.

'Thank you for hiding me,' she said.

Brann gave her a somewhat flat look, his expression giving nothing away. 'No bother,' he replied, his tone as neutral as his face.

Ophelia studied him for a second, searching for a sign of anything. But his demeanour remained impassive.

'I'd get out of here sharpish if I were you,' Brann added. 'Your next suitor is along there.'

'Oh, Jesus,' Ophelia said. 'Just what I need.'

'I better get back to work. Enough hide and seek for me today.' With that, he scaled the ladder and disappeared into the attic.

Ophelia watched him for a moment, without voicing any of the words she wanted to say. Jacinta's words weighed heavy on her shoulders. *Why do I never measure up to the expectations placed on me?* Was it just Jacinta's thinking, or was she actually to blame? Maybe she was as bad as all that.

As she walked away, Brann's defence of her echoed in her mind. He understood. He'd tried to defend her – called her hardworking and generous. She should have thanked him for that. But there was so much she should have said to him at some point or other and yet, she hadn't.

She strode through the estate grounds, the brisk February air doing little to dispel the lingering tension in her chest. Maybe it would never go away. Was this how she'd live from now on? Always on edge? What if she married one of these rich guys and hated him? Would she be coming out here every day to escape him? How stifling would it be? The sprawling stable came into view. Brann and co had built this. Such incredible workmanship. She pushed the heavy door open, the creak echoing in the spacious interior.

Conker whickered softly as Ophelia approached. The familiar scent of hay and leather calmed her. She'd spent so much time here – in the old building anyway – as a teenager when everything had seemed so messy and complicated after her parents split. It had been a safe haven, along with the boathouse. These days she didn't do half as much as she'd like here, but it was still a happy place to come to.

'Hey, Conker,' Ophelia murmured, her fingers brushing over the horse's velvety nose. She collected the grooming brushes. 'Fancy a massage?' She held out the brush.

The repetitive motion of it against Conker's coat was calming, and the tension started to ease from Ophelia's shoulders. Brann's words lingered in her mind – he'd defended her, seen who she really was, even when others didn't.

Conker's contented posture made her smile. 'You're a good boy,' she said. 'I just wish I knew what to do.'

He nudged her shoulder affectionately.

'Yeah, I know.' She started brushing again.

The stable door opened, and Ophelia glanced over the partition to see who had come in.

'Oh, hello.' Dagmar flicked her long plait over her shoulder.

'Hi. How are you?'

Dagmar didn't look at Ophelia but turned her back to her and opened a feed box. 'Not too good actually.'

'Oh? What's wrong?'

Dagmar sighed, turned and sat on the feed box. 'Your father wants me to leave.'

Ophelia gave Conker a few treats from her pocket, then came out and sat next to Dagmar. 'Why did he say that?'

'Apparently there's no money to pay me and I'm too expensive.'

Ophelia balled her fists. 'We pay for quality and you're the best at everything equine. I'll keep paying you if I have to.'

Dagmar cracked a little smile. 'Thanks, but that makes me feel guilty. Your father thinks volunteers can run the whole place and save him some money.'

Ophelia massaged her forehead and let out a sigh. 'My father is so out of touch. I honestly don't know how he stays alive. He's so clueless. Let me talk to him. There's no way this place can run with volunteers alone. In fact, we need more staff, not to get rid of the only person we have. This place is just starting to make money and if we're to give riding lessons, we definitely need you. No way can I do that.'

'You're not that bad,' Dagmar said.

'Maybe, but I'm not that good either, and I don't have the time. Leave it with me. I'll go and talk to him.'

Just what she needed. Yet another ridiculous situation to deal with.

Her father wasn't about when she got back, but Jacinta and Francesca were in the drawing room. 'Have you seen Father?' Ophelia asked.

'He's gone out with Anthony,' Jacinta said. 'Who was a bit miffed not to have seen you, by the way. I think they've gone to the boathouse to look for you.'

Ophelia did an internal fist pump. She'd dodged that bullet for now.

'Listen, while I'm here.' Ophelia took a seat close to Francesca. She'd kept this quiet over Christmas and even now wasn't sure how to broach it, but after Jacinta's verbal bashing, she wanted this out. 'I need to ask you about the musical theatre club.'

Francesca blinked, looking taken aback. 'What about it?'

'I met someone whose child goes there, and they told me some people had been bullying them. Your name came up.'

'How dare you,' Jacinta said. 'You can't come in here throwing allegations about like that.'

'I'm not. I just want to know what's going on. We have a very well-known family name. I wouldn't want stories going about. I'd like to at least know what we're up against.'

'I'm not a bully.' Francesca jumped up and balled her fists. 'Who would say something like that?'

'I can't tell you who it was.'

'Well, it's just rubbish. Someone trying to get me into trouble. People always do this to me. They think it's funny and laugh about it. I hate it.' She looked close to tears and stormed out the door, slamming it on the way out.

Jacinta closed her eyes, her face set. 'Do you have any idea how many hours it'll take me to get her out of that now?' She slowly opened her eyes again.

'I had to ask. Maybe she's telling the truth and if that's the case, then it sounds like someone is bullying her too, but if she's lying, then she needs to know it's not ok.'

'And none of it is any of your concern.' Jacinta got to her feet. 'I'm her mother.'

'We're a family, Jacinta. Like it or not. This kind of thing affects all of us.'

The door swung open, and Rupert and Anthony walked in.

'Dear, dear,' Rupert said. 'Is there a problem?'

'The usual one.' Jacinta nodded in Ophelia's direction. 'This time she's gone too far.'

'Oh for god's sake,' Ophelia muttered. 'I don't need to listen to this.' She stalked out of the room, passing her father and Anthony without a second glance, then climbed the stairs up to her old room. The ladder to the hatch was still down and scuffling noises told her Brann was still working up there. Stupid as it seemed, just standing here with him nearby relaxed her. Her shoulder brushed the ladder, and it clanked. Brann peered over the edge.

'Oh, it's you,' he said.

'Hi.'

He came down the ladder. 'Gotta go to the van. I need something from it.'

She swallowed, and a heavy weight filled her chest. 'I need to thank you.'

'What for?'

'Sticking up for me to Jacinta.'

He stared at her for a long, hard moment. His face, which had been so neutral earlier, now looked pained and unsure.

'It was the only thing to do,' he said. 'She was out of line.'

'It took guts though. Most people would just let her rattle on and not try to stop her. She could have sacked you.'

'She still could.'

'I know. That's why I'm grateful, even though I'm not sure why you did it, when you could just have ignored it.'

He slipped his finger under her chin, gently stroking her. 'Because I love you.'

Ophelia's eyes almost popped from her head, but before she could make any sense of the words, Brann strode past her, and she heard his heavy footfalls on the stairs.

He loves me?

What in the name of god?

Brann loved her. Shit. Shit. Shit. This was not good... Really. Because she loved him too. When it had been harmless flirting, it was pretty bad. When they kissed, it was stupid. When they slept together, they'd reached dangerous territory... But love?

Oh god. She wanted to sit down and cry. It had always been love. In her heart she knew it, but to hear it so bluntly was something else. Her head was buzzing. So was her phone. She pulled it out and saw her father was calling her. She snuck into her old room to take it.

'Yes?'

'Can you please come downstairs and talk to us? Jacinta is very upset. And all this in front of Anthony too. Very embarrassing.'

'No. I don't want to discuss that now. We need to talk about Dagmar Ingenfeld. We can't let her go. We'll never get a good enough replacement.'

'There's no choice. We're practically bankrupt. Speaking of which, you'll have to tell the builder to leave. There's no money to pay him and Jacinta says he was rude to her earlier.'

'What? He wasn't rude to her. She was rude about me, and he stuck up for me. That's why she's annoyed.'

'Well, whatever happened doesn't matter, but I can't keep him on if he's upsetting the family like this.'

Ophelia sank onto the bed. This had to be a bad joke, didn't it?

'I can't tell him that. Do it yourself or get Barbara to do it.'

'I'm afraid that's not possible either. I had to let Barbara go too.'

'You what?' Ophelia flung herself back and lay sprawled on her old bed. If she closed her eyes and opened them again, could she wake up elsewhere or discover this had all been a nightmare?

Except that wasn't going to happen. This was her reality, and there was no escaping it.

CHAPTER TWENTY-SEVEN

Brann

Brann stepped out into the biting February chill, the cold air slicing through the light fabric of his t-shirt, seeping into his bones. He made his way to his van, the rhythmic thud of his footsteps echoing in the stillness of the estate grounds. The hint of rain hung heavy in the air.

Love! Oh my god! That word. Since when had he loved anyone? Other than his kids. But this wasn't like that. This was so different and like nothing else. Kristalee hadn't been a true love, not really. Because of his kids, he'd deliberately steered away from love for the long-term. Now he knew what love felt like alright, but there wasn't a happy ending waiting in the wings.

As he reached the van, he sank into the driver's seat, the door closing with a muted thud. The interior might not be the tidiest, but it was a sanctuary, a temporary reprieve from the storm inside him.

He ran a hand through his hair, niggles gnawing at his insides. Why had he let slip those three words? What kind of idiot was he? What must Ophelia think of him now? Though if she had any wits about her, she would already know how he felt. Confessing so bluntly however was a dumb move.

Leaning back against the headrest, he closed his eyes, his confession weighing on his skull like a concrete slab. He had no illusions about the reality of their situation, but that didn't make this any easier. Pressing his fingers into his brow, he kneaded it, trying to assuage the ache.

Raindrops began to fall in a steady patter against the windscreen. He fell into a daydream where he had a magic fishing rod. He cast it out, and it came to land over three little words.

I love you.

He hooked them and reeled them back into safety, back inside him where they should have stayed. He didn't even need to know Ophelia's response. She didn't have to say the words. He already knew. She'd made it so obvious. All the times she'd come searching for him, pulled him into secret places and stolen kisses. Maybe it had started as lust, as it had done for him, but latterly it was different. The desire for a physical connection burned strong, but now there was more. A need for comfort. He sought it in her and sensed it when they were together. The way she relaxed in his hold like she'd come home, and everything was ok. They dropped their barriers for each other and it was good.

Except it wasn't.

Opening his eyes, he stared at the mansion through the rain-streaked window. She was in there. Inside a house that was bigger than the whole of Kirk Lane, where approximately ten families lived. He wouldn't want that. It was obscene, when friends of his struggled to put food on the tables for their family. This was her life and where she had to stay. Or so she thought. Maybe he'd feel the same in her position, though it was hard to imagine. Make that impossible. He had no loyalty to places or history. Only to family and people he loved. But then, part of her mindset came from grandparents she'd loved dearly.

And there it was again. Love.

Only love wasn't enough.

Ah, screw this nonsense. Just go back in there and finish the job you're being paid to do. What would he say if she approached him again? Who the hell knew?

As he crossed the courtyard, his phone vibrated in his back pocket. He jogged under the cover of the huge stone doorframe and pulled it out to check it.

OPHELIA C-B: We need to talk. It's important.

He raised an eyebrow. So he wasn't getting off the hook easily. *Great.* He went straight for the stairs, ignoring the sounds of chatter and laughter coming from the drawing room. Rupert's blustery chortle set him right on edge. Something about it was fake and blind. The man lived an outdated lifestyle and had no idea what it was like to be in the real world.

Brann returned to the attic before he replied to Ophelia.

BRANN: back in the attic. Where are you? Do you want to talk now?

He'd started levering off a tricky piece of timber when he heard her voice.

'Brann? Can you come down a moment?'

He downed his tools and lowered himself through the hatch.

'So, what is it?' *Play this cool. Act like I tell people I love them every day.* Which he did. He told Harrison and Caitlin all the time, to the point where they rolled their eyes or grumbled.

She looked away and took a deep breath, like she was steeling herself for something.

'I'm really sorry, Brann. But you have to leave.'

'What?'

He hadn't expected that.

'Sorry.'

'Why? Is it because I said—'

'It's nothing to do with that. The estate is basically bankrupt. It doesn't seem to matter what money comes in, somehow there's always more going out. Father's let Barbara go and now you have to go too.'

'Ok. Whatever. But if I go this time, this is it. I can't work like this.'

'I know that. And you'll get paid for what you've already done.'

'By you?'

'If I have to.'

'But you shouldn't have to. Your family needs a good hard kick up the backside.'

'Are you volunteering?'

'If it helps you, then yes. I don't know how you stand it.'

'Because I want more for Glenvorneth, but I can't just throw them out. They have the right to be here, but I also can't sit back and watch them let this place go down the drain.'

'Why not? Live your life now. Do it for yourself. Forget everyone else. Forget the past and the future. Let this place die before it kills you.'

She sucked on her lower lip and for a moment he thought she might cry, but she mastered herself with a deep breath. 'I can't, Brann. It's not who I am. This is not just about me, but my heritage, my grandparents, my future.'

'Yeah. Ok.' He stalked up the ladder and started throwing the tools back into the box. He was done with this place for good.

Chapter Twenty-Eight

Ophelia

Ophelia trudged through the estate grounds. Rain drizzled over her, soaking her usually immaculate hair until it was sticking to her face. She needed to be alone with her thoughts. And boy were there enough of them to keep her company for a long time. The estate was ruined. Brann gone. The heritage she clung to was slipping through her fingers. Centuries of history lost. If only she could do as Brann suggested and switch off to it all, forget the past, not worry about the future of the estate and concentrate on herself and her own life. But she couldn't. It wasn't her way.

She plodded towards the stables again. If she sat and cried, at least the horses wouldn't pass comment or judgement. They'd just let her peacefully coexist, and that was all she needed right now.

The rain fell rhythmically on the stable roof, beating steadily like a living heart. That's what this estate should be like. Not the stone cold, dead place it was. She'd made an attempt at breathing some life back into the place, but it was impossible. Her father and Jacinta were too set in their ways. If she couldn't change them, nothing would change here. And that was impossible.

The horses were all in for the day, munching at their hay nets or standing in their stalls. Another sound caught Ophelia's attention. A movement at the far end.

'Francesca?' she said. 'Is that you?'

From the end stall, her younger sister emerged, wiping her eyes and flicking her hair with the same silent nonchalance Ophelia had herself.

'What's wrong?'

'Nothing,' Francesca muttered, with a creditable attempt at unconcern.

How alike they were in many ways. Ophelia could break down this moment and cry buckets if she let go, but if anyone asked her what was wrong, she wouldn't say.

She slumped onto the feed box and sighed, resting her elbows on her knees and putting her face in her hands. Maybe they both needed a place to be quiet in.

'Are you upset about what I said earlier?' Ophelia let her hands fall.

'Of course I am,' Francesca said. 'Have you any idea what it's like for me? Whenever I go anywhere I either get people hero-worshipping me because I live here or calling me names like posh girl.'

'Yeah. I have a good idea of what that's like.'

'Well, then. Do you believe me that I didn't bully anyone?'

'Why don't you tell me what did happen then?'

'I know what it's all about. It was Caitlin, wasn't it?'

'I can't say but go on anyway.'

'She was actually my friend. She was nice, and we arranged to meet in town. Then this other girl, Hope, messaged me and said Caitlin had called it off because she thought I was really snooty, and she was just using me. Then she said this boy we knew from the club had asked if I could meet him instead. I said ok. Then I got messages from Caitlin, saying she was blocking me because she was really upset I'd cancelled on her and started going out with the boy she liked. I didn't know Hope had taken photos of me and Kyle and sent them to Caitlin. It was her messing about, not me.'

Ophelia let out a sigh. She didn't miss these teenage dramas, though sometimes she'd give anything to go back to those days because adult dramas were so much worse. 'Do you still go to the club?'

'Yes, but Caitlin left.'

'And what about these other people? Hope and Kyle? Do they still go?'

'Hope left. Kyle still goes, but we're not like dating. He's ok, but we didn't hit it off like that, you know.'

'Yeah, I know. Just like me and James and all these other men your mother wants me to marry.'

'I wish she'd stop that,' Francesca said. 'It really freaks me out that she'll start doing that to me.'

Ophelia didn't like to say, but she was sure Jacinta would do exactly that. 'So, about Caitlin. Would you like to make things up with her?'

'I don't know. I guess, but she won't reply to my messages. I can't even get in touch with her. She's blocked me everywhere.'

'I know her parents,' Ophelia said. 'I can arrange something if you like. She's always fancied horse riding, from what I understand. Maybe we could invite her for a lesson.'

'Well, ok. If you can arrange it.'

'I'll try.'

'Thanks... And for listening. Sometimes I can't really talk to mum. She's difficult, you know. She doesn't really hear what I'm saying.'

'I understand.' Only too well. 'If you ever want to offload, feel free. I know what it's like growing up with certain expectations.'

Francesca smiled and Ophelia returned it with a little sigh. *This is unexpected.* Making a connection with Francesca hadn't been on her to-do list, not when she was as wretched and low as this. Maybe putting things right with Francesca and Caitlin was the best she could do right now. When she got to arranging it though, it wouldn't be with Caitlin's dad. No. That ship had sailed. She'd go to Wood 'n' Chic and talk to Kristalee and leave Brann out of it.

March

Ophelia took a deep breath at the door of Wood 'n' Chic. Checking through the window, she saw Kristalee at the till, but no other customers. She let herself in.

'Hey.' Kristalee looked up and smiled, though she still maintained that somewhat intimating aura.

'Hi.' Ophelia approached her. 'I've got something to ask you. I hope you don't mind.' She explained about Francesca and Caitlin. 'We're wondering if Caitlin would like to come around for a visit at the weekend. They could have a riding lesson together and hopefully make up.'

'Sounds brilliant.' Kristalee toyed with a skull pendant at her throat. 'Thank you so much. I'll check with Caitlin and if she's happy, I'll message you.'

'No probs. I'll give you my number.' Ophelia took out her phone.

'Just one thing though. I can't drive. So we'll have to check if her dad's free to bring her over.'

'I can come for her. Dagmar will be teaching them. She's one of the best.'

With a combination of what was left in the estate funds and Ophelia's own money, she was keeping Dagmar on, but Perthshire was a very horsey area and if Dagmar chose to work elsewhere, they were screwed. Ophelia wouldn't blame her for leaving. All it would take was for someone with more money to come and snap her up.

Francesca came with Ophelia to collect Caitlin and Kristalee. Ophelia had suggested they didn't shout about what they were doing to Jacinta. Francesca obviously hadn't, as Jacinta seemed to think Francesca was simply cadging a lift into town and didn't ask any questions.

The satnav led Ophelia to Kirk Lane, and she turned into it, edging down the narrow space between the pavement and the church wall. Was this close to where Brann stayed? Would he see her car? Had Caitlin told him where she was going? So many questions rattled through her head, but she pushed them aside. This day wasn't for her.

'Hello.' She got out of the car as Kristalee and Caitlin came out of one of the cute, little terraced houses. The one next door had a narrow curving staircase leading to an upper floor that looked almost Dickensian. Caitlin was skinny and half hid behind her mum. Ophelia smiled at them. 'We met before,' she said to Caitlin. 'You might not remember.'

'I do,' Caitlin said.

'Nice car.' Kristalee opened the backdoor. 'And you must be Francesca.'

'Yeah. Hi.'

Caitlin jumped in the back beside her. 'Hi.'

'Hi,' Francesca said, her cheeks slightly pink. 'Did your mum tell you about—'

'She told me everything. And I'm sorry about what happened.'

'Hey, you don't have to be sorry. I'm sorry.'

Kristalee smiled at Ophelia as they took their places in the front.

'Sounds like you should close the book on it,' Kristalee said. 'And look forward to this lesson. Caitlin's been pestering us for god knows how long to go riding.'

'Well, I'm glad we can bring it about,' Ophelia said. 'Dagmar is a very good teacher, and she's great at matching people with horses. We've only got three to choose from and they're all very placid, so it shouldn't be a problem. Conker is mine. He's really good and very able.'

'I can't wait to see this,' Kristalee said.

Francesca and Caitlin chattered all the way to the stables. No one hearing them would ever know they'd had a falling out. They sounded like best friends, catching up on all the gossip. Ophelia asked Kristalee about her work at the shop, and they chatted about that and Kristalee's large extended family, who seemed to have all sorts of bizarre issues and set-ups. Some of it was soap opera or Jerry Springer worthy, and the chat easily carried them all the way to Glenvorneth. When they arrived, Ophelia and

Kristalee watched from the edge of the paddock, while Dagmar took charge of the girls and the horses.

'I need to learn to drive.' Kristalee leaned on the fence. 'So I can take her places and not have to rely on her dad or her brother. I should have done it years ago.'

'She'll soon be able to drive herself, won't she?' Ophelia said.

'Oh, don't.' Kristalee covered her face. 'That's such a scary thought. My baby being able to drive.'

Ophelia smiled. 'Yeah. That must be strange.'

'I was just a bit older than she is now when I had Harrison. Seems crazy now. She's so young. So was I. I didn't know what had hit me. I'm not even sure how we survived or how we kept them alive.'

'Looks like you've done a good job.'

'It's one day at a time and a lot of hoping and crossing fingers.' She crossed two of her black nails and held them up.

Ophelia huffed out a laugh.

'Don't you fancy having your own kids?' Kristalee asked.

'I do, but I have to find the right man first and that's a bit of a problem.'

'Is it? You seem like a nice person to me and you're so pretty, so I don't see why.'

'It's all about family expectations unfortunately. They want me to marry someone with money to save this place.'

'And are there a lot of rich blokes going about? Coz if there are, can you send them my way?'

Ophelia laughed. 'There aren't that many, which is part of the problem. The ones they find are... Well, not suitable. Or I don't like them. And that's where I have to stop being so picky and just do it.'

'But that's crazy. What if you get stuck with someone horrible?'

'Grin and bear it, I suppose.'

'I wouldn't advise that. Not after what happened to my sister.' She pulled a face. 'She got stuck with a right bastard. And what if someone else catches your eye before you meet a rich guy?'

'I'd hate to fall for someone and not be able to...' The words fizzled out. She was talking about Brann, and she had a weird sense that Kristalee had been talking about him too. Did she know? Would he have told her? She needed to stop talking before she gave something away.

'Sorry.' Kristalee nodded. 'I shouldn't have asked. Just couldn't help myself. Harrison told us his dad had a bit of a thing for you. I don't think he meant it seriously, but I suppose I kind of wondered, well...' She shrugged, but her eyes flashed with intrigue.

Ophelia's cheeks heated. How awkward was this? She cleared her throat. 'We had a bit of banter,' she said. 'I suppose that's what he saw.'

'Probably. Brann's a funny guy and he has a way of turning heads. I thought he'd find someone else almost as soon as we split, but he hasn't dated much. Not at all really.'

'Maybe he hasn't met the right person.'

'I think it's more because of Caitlin.'

'What do you mean?'

'She gets really anxious if she thinks either of us is dating. I tried for a while but it's hard. Brann doesn't want to risk losing his little girl. He's worried she'll not visit him if he's with someone else or be too upset to meet his new partner. Or worse, do harm to herself.' Kristalee let out a sigh. 'She did that before and it was scary. We've got a lid on it just now, but who knows what might trigger it?'

Ophelia frowned and sucked on her lower lip. In the back of her mind, she'd almost arrogantly believed if she suddenly had the means to save the estate, she could go to Brann and he'd tumble straight into her arms, but maybe he wouldn't. Not that it mattered. She didn't have a winning lottery ticket and didn't have the means to save the estate on her own.

CHAPTER TWENTY-NINE

Brann

Brann scrolled through his digital banking app. His wages from the Glenvorneth job were in, no doubt paid for by Ophelia. She was nothing if not honourable. Perhaps too much so. Maybe it was that which made her feel wholly responsible for her family and the estate.

Ugh.

Brann shoved his phone into the pocket of his jeans and returned to scheduling the jobs for the week ahead. Since when had he become a pencil pusher? Still, he wasn't complaining. As his business grew, so did the admin. And he was in demand. He could fill his weeks twice over the job requests. The loss of the Glenvorneth job didn't hurt in that respect, but it stung in so many other ways.

Had they really run out of money, or was Ophelia using that as a reason to get him away? No doubt he'd freaked her out by saying those three little words. Her family didn't seem the type to let those words out freely, so she probably hadn't heard them too often.

'Hey, Dad.' Caitlin bounded into the kitchen, where he was sitting at the little table he'd made himself from repurposed wood. Was that the time? He checked and sure enough, it was after four. How quickly admin days flew by.

'Hi.' He got to his feet and wrapped her in a hug, then planted a kiss on her brow. She pulled a face, but he could tell she wasn't really annoyed as she grinned. 'How was your day?'

'Fine, yeah. You will never guess what I did at the weekend though.'

'Tell me.'

'Look.' She broke free of his hug and pulled out her phone. 'I got a riding lesson.' She angled the phone and swiped through the photos for him to see.

He frowned. 'Where's that?' Because it was uncannily like Glenvorneth. But then, maybe all these horsey places looked the same.

'It's at Glenvorneth. That place I went on work experience with you.'

'I thought it looked like it.' Brann rubbed the back of his neck. This was weird. 'Why were you there? I thought you didn't like the Chattan-Blythe girl.'

'I didn't, but I found out it was all a mistake. We were both totally screwed over by Hope. She was behind it all.'

'Who?'

'She's like this other girl at the theatre club. I guess she was jealous of me and Francesca. Anyway, Francesca's sister, that posh woman, set the whole thing up for us. She even came and got me and mum and took us there. It was so cool, and they said I can do it again any time.'

'Was it expensive?'

'No charge. Because we're friends.'

'Wow.' Brann sat back at the table with a sigh. 'And Francesca's sister set this up?'

'Yeah. The one you like.' Caitlin smirked. 'I thought she was a real toff when I first met her, but she's actually like really nice. She took us all for lunch after. Even mum said she was nice, and she was like really worried before about spending time with her in case she was dead snooty.'

'Oh well, that's good.' What else could he say? How unexpected in many ways. Not least how gushing Caitlin was being about her. Might be a different story if she discovered exactly what had gone on between them.

'Did you know she's a really amazing designer?'

'Who? Francesca?' Though he knew that wasn't who she meant.

'No, silly. Ophelia. We googled her and you should see the business she runs. It's called Timeless Butterfly Interiors, and she has a shop and everything. Her stuff is gorgeous but super expensive. She's done these beautiful renovations in Edinburgh and in some big, fancy homes. I'm going to visit the shop with Mum one day.'

'Really?'

'Yeah, look her up. Go on.'

Brann switched screens on his laptop and typed in Timeless Butterfly Interiors. Caitlin jumped in behind him to show him which pages to click. Even the website had an expensive elegance about it. Brann clicked through the photos and testimonials. Wow. No wonder she'd done such a great job in the boathouse and the workers' cottages. Also, no surprise why she was frustrated at the big house. She could work magic if her creative power was unleashed. What was holding her back? Money? Fear? Her family? Why had she never told him? She'd kept her light well hidden. She should be shouting about this and using her business skills to save the estate, not letting her family trample her into the ground.

'You and her should go into business together,' Caitlin said. 'You could be like those fixer upper people on TV. You do the building stuff; she does the designs and interiors.'

'I'm not sure that's a good idea.'

'Why not?'

'We're not compatible.'

'Oh yeah? Harrison thinks you are.' She giggled.

'I'm not sure that's what he means when he says shit like that.'

'Language, Dad. And I know what he means. I'm not stupid. You said it yourself. You flirted with her.'

'So what? It happens.'

'Maybe. It would be funny if you got together with her.'

'Funny?'

'Well, yeah. You'd be like Lord Duthie or something.'

'It doesn't work like that.'

'Kind of does. Because you wouldn't exactly live here if you got married.'

'Got married? What are you on about? How have you gone from working together to getting married?'

Caitlin doubled over, laughing.

'I thought you hated the idea of me or mum dating anyone else.'

'I kind of do, but if it's someone I like, I suppose I don't mind.'

Brann put his head in his hands and groaned. Sometimes his life was a strange place.

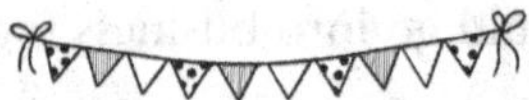

Brann and Harrison stopped for a breather on the second-floor landing as they manoeuvred the sofa up the staircase on the way to Harrison's new flat. Just one more floor to go. These old flats were among some of the best priced in Glenbriar, but they were worn and tired.

'Tell me again why you had to pick a place on the third floor,' Brann grunted, adjusting the weight of the sofa.

Harrison snorted, sweat glistening on his forehead. 'Because I'm poor. Otherwise I would have got one of those riverside places.'

'Life goals. You can build up to it. This is a good starter flat.'

'Yeah, and it's practically a workout every day getting up these stairs.'

Finally reaching the third floor, they stood before the door of the flat. Brann wiped his brow and looked at Harrison. 'Right, let's see if we can get this thing in. I'm not sure I fancy starting your life here by having to remove the door and knock out part of the wall.'

Harrison laughed. 'I guess I brought the right parent along if we need to do that.'

'Glad I've still got my uses.'

'Let's go for it.'

Brann bumped open the door with his foot, and it thudded against a side wall.

'Oh my god,' a voice from inside said, and Harrison's girl-friend, Colette, skipped into the hallway. 'Will that fit in here?'

'Dad's already planning on knocking down walls if it doesn't, so it's going in one way or another.'

Colette clutched her cheeks. 'Ok. Let's hope.'

'I don't think sofas existed when these places were built. Or the people who owned them couldn't afford them,' Brann said. As they were originally built in the nineteenth century to house mill workers, the owners probably had very little.

With a lot of pushing, pulling and lifting, they finally got the sofa inside and along the short, oddly angled hallway into the living room cum kitchen space.

'This place has so much potential.' Brann tapped on the wooden floor with his trainer. Harrison had the skills to do it up and make it worth more, so hopefully it would prove to be a good investment.

Colette beamed and flopped onto the newly installed sofa. 'Feels like home already.'

Brann winked at her. 'Home is where the heart is. It's not where you are, but the people you share it with.'

Harrison joined Colette on the sofa, wrapping an arm around her. 'We're all set then.'

'Get a room,' Brann muttered, but he smiled as he made his way back to the van. This was a new start for Harrison, and he was happy for him. A little tinge of green clouded his vision. Ok, so he was a little jealous too, but no way would he let it show. Just because his own love life was a tattered mess didn't mean he couldn't enjoy seeing someone else's happiness.

CHAPTER THIRTY

Ophelia

Ophelia and Hayley turned into The Back Wynd and headed up the hill. For a Sunday afternoon in March, the weather was great. The black clouds from the previous day had hurried away on a gentle breeze, leaving only a fluffy aeroplane trail to part the bright blue sky.

It had been a long time since Ophelia properly walked around Glenbriar. Hayley knew all the streets and shortcuts better than she did, and after having had a nice lunch together, they'd decided to walk back to Hayley's house.

'I can't wait for you to see it,' Hayley said. 'It was Oliver's house before we got together, but I never want to move from it. It's on the Fairways Estate.'

'That's quite new, isn't it?'

'Yeah. Oliver bought his house before it was even built.'

'Sounds amazing.'

'It's not as brilliant as the boathouse, but I like it.'

'I'm sure it's just as good.'

'Well, I quite like being near other people. I don't fancy living in such an isolated place.'

'Hmm.' Ophelia was getting used to it, but the night she'd spent there with Brann still stood out as the best night she'd had there, not just because of the sex they'd had, but because she'd liked his company.

'How's the husband hunting going?'

Ophelia sighed. 'I meant to tell you. I had a message from James the other day.'

'What? I thought you and him finished before you got started.'

'We did. But he asked if I wanted to meet without any family pressure and take things from there... Without telling his parents, or my father or Jacinta, that is.'

'And are you going to?'

'Maybe. I said I'd think about it.' And really, she should. James was by far the best of the people she'd met that year, but it still didn't solve the problem that she didn't actually fancy him.

They passed by a row of old boxy-shaped tenement houses, much smaller than the ones in big cities, but with the same tiredness about them. They had tiny little patches of gardens on either side of the paths. Some were overgrown or littered, but others had daffodils bobbing in the gentle breeze. This area was like a forgotten part of Glenbriar, hidden behind the fancy shops and restaurants in the main street and masked by the tourist attractions and hotels.

'Hi, Ophelia.'

Ophelia lurched into the present. Who was talking to her? She didn't know anyone here. Her gaze landed on another row of boxy tenements on the other side of the road, where a young girl was waving to her.

'Oh, hi.' She waved across, recognising Caitlin.

A silver van was parked at the kerb. For a thrilling moment, Ophelia thought it was Brann's van, but it wasn't. His was white.

Caitlin beckoned, and Hayley gave Ophelia a quizzical look. 'Who's that?' she asked quietly.

'Er... Caitlin. A friend of Francesca. Let me go and say hello.' They crossed the street, Ophelia's heart doing somersaults. This wasn't where Kristalee lived. She knew that as she'd picked them up for the riding lesson from Kirk Lane. So... Did Brann live here?

'How are you?' Ophelia asked.

'Yeah, good. Harrison's new flat is up there. I'm just here to nosey, but they've sent me to get stuff from the van.'

'The van?' The thrill returned. Ophelia's head flicked to it. There it was, large as life – Brann Duthie & Son, Joiners. He had a new van. She couldn't linger here any longer. They had to walk on. She couldn't risk an encounter. Not here in front of Hayley.

'Great. Sounds like you're really busy. I should let you get on.'

Hayley had clocked the van too. 'Are you Brann's daughter?' she said, and Ophelia's heart sank through the pavement.

'Yeah. He's inside helping.'

'Oh, I know him,' Hayley said. 'We both do.'

Caitlin's lips twitched, and she glanced at Ophelia. 'I know.'

'This is Hayley,' Ophelia said. 'We're just on our way to her house.' If she started walking, would Hayley follow? Voices approached from the close. Ophelia fidgeted with her sleeve.

'When did he move in?' Hayley asked.

'Yesterday. But there's still more stuff to go in. Dad took all the big stuff in already.'

Ophelia didn't register anything else of what they said. Brann and Kristalee were walking down the path. Could this get any more awkward? He stopped.

Ophelia couldn't focus on any part of the conversation between Hayley and Caitlin. She might faint if she looked at Brann, but her eyes didn't want to go anywhere else.

'Oh, hello,' Kristalee said. 'What brings you here?'

Thankfully Hayley explained in her bubbly way. Maybe she'd met Kristalee before. Either way, she was chatting to her like an old friend.

Ophelia caught Brann's eye, and he lifted his eyebrow slightly. Then he edged past her. 'Excuse me, ladies. I need to get some more boxes.' He walked behind her towards the van; she could see him out the corner of her eye.

The heel of her suede ankle boot clicked reflexively on the pavement, and she forcefully stopped it, but her legs were restless.

'Are you ok?' Kristalee tapped her on the upper arm.

'All good, thanks.'

'Can I come riding again soon?' Caitlin asked.

'Sure. Just arrange it with Francesca. I can give you a lift most weekends.'

'I've suggested she does some volunteer work to pay for the lessons. She could help muck out and that kind of thing.'

'Absolutely,' Ophelia said. 'Dagmar would be delighted with some help.'

Brann came out of the van with his arms full of boxes. He barely glanced at them as he passed by and headed inside. *Hell.* Why could she not stop looking at him even when she was trying to look the other way?

'Why don't you come in?' Kristalee was watching Ophelia. 'Have a look around. I'm sure Harrison won't mind.'

'What?' Ophelia blinked and her heart tremored again. 'We wouldn't want to intrude.'

'Not at all. Come on.'

'Have you met his girlfriend?' Caitlin asked.

'Er... no.'

'Colette, she's really sweet.'

'Colette?' Hayley beamed. 'Of course. I work with Colette. I didn't realise Harrison was the boyfriend she was moving in with. She always calls him Harry.'

'She's the only person allowed to call him that. He normally hates it,' Caitlin said.

Now there was no getting out of it. Hayley was champing at the bit to get upstairs and see her work friend.

They followed Kristalee and Caitlin up the stairs. Ophelia hung back, her pulse drumming like crazy.

'Hey, Colette, you'll never guess who's here,' Caitlin said.

'Oh my god.' Colette screamed when she saw Hayley and Hayley laughed, disbelieving that she hadn't put two and two together and worked out Harrison was Colette's boyfriend. Ophelia recognised her too from her salon appointments, and maybe there was a flicker of recognition from Colette as she smiled at Ophelia.

Ophelia fiddled with her fingers, sensing many eyes on her as they entered the living area.

'Lots of potential here.' She aimed to keep her tone carefree.

Harrison chuckled. 'That's exactly what Dad said.'

Caitlin glanced at him, and they both laughed. Kristalee gave a weak smile, but her eyes held a hidden warning as she looked between the two of them.

'Well, it does...' Ophelia didn't want to read anything into their exchanged glances. Caitlin's gaze moved to the door behind Ophelia, and she turned her head, following the look. She stiffened. Brann was leaning on the frame. He didn't flinch or betray anything as their eyes met.

'Great minds and all that,' he said.

'Like you've got one of them,' Harrison quipped.

'Watch it, or you can put that wardrobe in yourself.'

'Great street view.' Hayley grinned, crossing to the window. 'I used to live in a flat and I loved looking out the window at everything.'

'Haven't you got some handiwork to be getting on with in the bedroom?' Ophelia murmured to Brann, sensing him behind her.

'Maybe,' he muttered.

Hayley started talking about something funny, but Ophelia's attention was cut off by a low whisper in her ear.

'But it's not as much fun on my own.'

She shuddered. He was so close to her.

'You found a husband who does the job yet?' he murmured.

She turned her head towards him with narrowed eyes. 'Wouldn't you like to know?'

'Not really.'

Everyone laughed, and she turned back to the group. Hayley was eyeing her with a know-it-all grin.

'Do you want to stay for food?' Colette asked.

'We've just had lunch at a cafe,' Ophelia said.

'Thanks anyway,' Hayley added. 'We'll let you get on.'

Brann stepped aside, casually holding out his arm to let them pass. Ophelia gave him the briefest glance. The heat was intense, and she loosened the top button of her waxed jacket as they went down the stairs.

'What were you saying to Brann?' Hayley asked.

'Nothing.'

Hayley raised an eyebrow. 'Oh really? Say what you want, but it looked to me like you were flirting.'

'We certainly were not.'

Hayley shook her head and smiled. 'Really?'

'Why would I do that?'

'I think you like him a lot more than you let on. Why not go out with him for a bit?'

Ophelia's heel caught between two paving slabs. She wobbled slightly, before pulling it out. 'I can't.'

'But you do like him.'

'Yes, Hayley. If you really must know. I do like him.'

'Fancy him?' Her smile was annoying but infectious and Ophelia found herself smiling back despite her irritation.

'Alright, yes. But, really, you know nothing can happen.'

'So, you're going to settle for James?'

'He's not that bad. And liking him and respecting him is better than nothing.'

'Better than being with someone you love?'

'Who said I loved Brann?'

'Do you?'

'Oh Christ. Just stop now.'

'I'll take that as a yes.'

'Don't you see how impossible it is? Can you imagine a life where we're together? We don't belong in each other's worlds.'

'That's a bit insulting,' Hayley said. 'You don't belong in mine either and yet we're friends.'

'That's true, but different.'

'Not that much different. Also, what happens if you marry some rich man, and it turns out he doesn't want to spend all his money saving Glenvorneth? I know you thought about a prenup, but I bet Oliver wouldn't let anyone sign all their money over to saving the estate. So your big plan might not work anyway.'

The last remnants of her father's flimsy plan drifted away, leaving Ophelia tumbling into the abyss.

'You told me your grandparents fought for you to inherit Glenvorneth. Why did they?'

'Because they didn't want some random male relative inheriting it.'

'Then maybe you shouldn't be considering letting some random rich man save it now. They picked you to avoid that situation.'

Ophelia frowned. It wasn't exactly the same thing, but Hayley had a point. Her grandparents wanted her to carry out their plans and continue their legacy. What if she had the power to do it herself? Maybe she didn't need the cash upfront. What if all she needed was a new approach? Something that wouldn't only save Glenvorneth, but save her from signing up to a marriage she didn't want. She wasn't the one who needed to sign up to anything. The germ of an idea started in her mind. But could it work?

CHAPTER THIRTY-ONE

Brann

Brann got out of the car in the driveway of Glenvorneth. The mansion house towered over him and he ground his teeth. Was he a sucker or what?

Rupert had phoned in a flap, begging him to finish the work in the attic, and paid up front. Brann would have taken savage satisfaction in saying no, but that wasn't him. When Rupert said Ophelia had abandoned them for a 'secret project', as he named it, Brann suspected she'd gone back to Edinburgh. If she had any sense, she'd stay there and grow the design business she was obviously so good at.

Brann had agreed to fit the job in at the end of the week, but going back to Glenvorneth was not a prospect he relished. Rupert appeared at the main door and waved. Still dressed in his plus fours, he looked like he was auditioning for a period drama.

'Hello, hello,' he bellowed as Brann got out. 'How are you? Busy, busy?'

'Yup, I'm always busy,' Brann said. 'You?'

'Lord, you don't know the half of it. One darn thing after another. It's been a bad year.'

'Has it?' Brann couldn't muster a smile. This lazy man had done nothing, but he still had the nerve to complain.

'It's all about the money, isn't it? Or lack of.'

'Well, I built you a whole new stable block that was meant to bring in money. Your daughter renovated one of the workers' cottages that's meant to bring in some more. And we both did over the boathouse, which I understand was meant to be a holiday home with a fairly hefty price tag.' Normally he wouldn't speak to clients like this, but Rupert was getting on his wick with the I-have-no-money routine. This must drive Ophelia berserk.

'Goodness gracious, you sound exactly like Ophelia.'

Brann lifted his tools from the back of the van. 'Well, maybe you should listen to her. She has some first-rate ideas. Have you ever looked at her website?'

'What website?'

'Her business website. You could have her work her magic here and do all sorts to this place.'

'Jacinta doesn't want too much done, you know. She values her privacy.'

'Then you've made your choice. No point complaining about not making money if you're not planning to make changes.'

'Hmm. You really sound like Ophelia. Have you been chatting to her?'

'We've talked before, sure. We worked together on all the estate projects. Her designs were so easy to follow. I didn't realise she'd done them until you told me.'

'I know she's good at her job, but I fail to see how overhauling this house will make any difference.'

'It won't unless you use it as a basis for something else. You need to let the place out, or at least section off part of the house and have luxury holiday apartments or something. But all of it means change.'

'You and Ophelia should go into business together.'

It had been said before, but there was no need. Ophelia could do all this without him, but she came up against the family walls with everything she suggested. It must drive her insane.

Brann still had some work to finish in the attic, but when it came to the ceiling, he would contract a couple of other guys to do it. He hated plastering. That meant he'd only be here a couple of days and hopefully that would be the end of it.

He'd almost finished replacing the first beam when he heard the ladder rattling.

'Brann,' came Ophelia's voice. So she was here. *Fuck*. 'Are you up there?'

'No,' he replied.

'Very funny. Come down a minute, will you? We need to talk.'

He rolled his eyes and lowered himself out of the hatch. 'What is it, your ladyship? Have you come to sack me again?'

'No. My father is paying for this. Or at least he said he had.'

'Yes, he paid upfront.'

'Well, that's something. So, what did you say to him? He told me you had some great ideas and that we should work together.'

Brann shook his head. 'We've already worked together. Not always amicably, but we got there. On all the projects, I've seen what you've been trying to do. I just told your father everything you'd attempted and said there was no point moaning about having no money if he wasn't going to act on your ideas.'

'Bloody typical of my father.' Ophelia folded her arms. 'He'll listen to a man.'

'I doubt he was really listening.'

'Oh, but he was. He told me we should put our heads together because you're a real "ideas man".' She air-quoted.

'He has no idea what he's got in you.'

'He's certainly never taken me seriously, and if he knew about what you and I had done... Well... Let's hope he doesn't find out.'

'I actually couldn't care less if he does. Your father's opinion is worth nothing to me. I can't respect a man who wants to sell his daughter to the highest bidder to save his own skin. He should thank his lucky stars he's got a daughter who's willing to sacrifice her happiness to make sure he gets to carry on doing what he does best. I.e., nothing.'

Ophelia drew in a breath and held it for a moment, staring at Brann. Maybe he'd gone too far, but how could he help himself?

'Actually, you're right. I'm not sacrificing myself or anything else for the estate anymore.'

'Does that mean you're heading back to Edinburgh for good?'

She shook her head. 'No. I'm considering living at the boathouse and opening a branch of my business here. Not only that, I've got more ideas. Some of them are plans my grandparents started, plus I went to see Barbara the other day, and she had some ideas too.'

'Ideas that don't involve men with big bank balances, I hope.'

A small smile quirked on that beautiful mouth of hers. 'No, but they involve a man with a big heart, and a big' – her eyes travelled downwards – 'tool belt.'

He cocked his head. 'I assume you mean me.'

'Who else?'

'What do you want me to do?'

'I need to talk to my financial advisor first, but if the plans are viable, they'll involve a lot of building work. Would that be something you could do?'

'I'd do anything for you.' The words tumbled out before he could stop them.

She pressed her lips together and looked away. 'I know you would, but I hate asking for favours.'

'We'll work something out.' Dammit, he always gave in so easily. 'I saw your business online. It's quite something. You're quite something. If anyone has the business skills to save this estate, it's you.'

She sucked on her lower lip. 'You think?'

'I know. I just don't get why you didn't tell me before. Why not tell me all those designs were yours? They were fucking brilliant.'

'I've got used to not talking about my business here.'

'Timeless Butterfly Interiors,' Brann said. 'Own it.'

'I guess I got sick of the vitriolic looks and snide comments whenever I mentioned it, so I stopped. That name gets a similar reaction to swearing in this house.'

'Your family may be rich, but they're so twisted.' His parents hadn't been great, but you got things straight. 'They've no idea what they've got in you.'

'I really don't know how to thank you.'

'You don't have to. I should thank you for what you're doing for Caitlin with the riding lessons.'

'I'm hardly doing anything.'

'But you're doing something and that's what matters.'

Their eyes met, and for a long moment, they just looked at each other. Ophelia's gaze slipped to his lips, and he knew they were of one mind. He'd kiss her forever given the chance, but that road was too risky to stray onto again. 'I gotta get back to the attic. Give me a bell when you have more concrete plans. I'm happy to help.'

He climbed the ladder, hauled himself back into the hatch and sat for a moment in the cold, fusty air. Where was this going? Maybe working alongside her was the best he could hope for, but really it didn't come anywhere close to satisfying the gaping hole in his chest.

CHAPTER THIRTY-TWO

Ophelia

Ophelia watched carefully as George, the financial advisor, read down the page she'd handed him. As he flipped it over to read the next page, Ophelia exchanged a glance with Barbara.

Barbara pulled a side pout like she wasn't sure what to make of the situation. Ophelia had told Rupert Barbara was returning to their employ and hadn't hung about to hear his reply, though she'd heard Jacinta muttering about it.

'This is a fairly comprehensive business plan,' George said. 'And very ambitious.' He ran his finger down the page. 'That's fourteen different points.'

'Yes.' Some of it was an extension of the list Ophelia had given Brann to work through the previous year, but there was more. She'd revived her grandparents' plans to have an artisan quarter in the courtyard, and to use the grounds for family friendly events. She'd never persuade Jacinta to give up her control over the main house while Rupert was alive, so she'd worked around it with solutions that focused on the grounds and the outbuildings.

The concessions were that the main house would open for some weeks in the summer for special events and tours. Barbara was investigating preservation grants.

The workers' cottages and the Factor's House would become high-end holiday lets. The courtyard would be developed so Ophelia had an office to run the Glenvorneth branch of Timeless Butterfly Interiors. The other rooms would become the artisan and crafters' quarter and a gallery to be leased to artists. A Timeless Butterfly shop would be there too, with a small café and coffee shop. Food always made money.

They would work more with Stella – that brought a smile to George's face at the mention of his wife. That way, they could sell finished pieces and split profits.

'I'm still looking for opportunities to lease the estate as a location for films or TV too,' Barbara said.

'And we're working more on community involvement,' Ophelia said. 'Once the café, shop and gallery are open, that'll tie in with the livery and horses.'

'It all looks good, but where's the capital coming from?' George asked.

'We're starting with the rent money from the workers' cottages. They can be completed without too much outlay.' Camilla Woodcroft could stay if she agreed to pay the proper rent, not the 'mates rates' Jacinta had given her, and she was welcome to practise her 'mad art' in the new crafters' quarter. Ophelia wouldn't let Jacinta trample the plans this time. 'Once my business is open,

I hope to attract clients from the area and the money I make here will go directly into funding the next projects and so on.'

'That sounds workable,' George said. 'Your next step should be to expand this list into actionable items and cost each one. Once you've got that, we can talk again if you need to or if you feel confident in moving on, then go ahead.'

As they left his office, Ophelia high-fived Barbara. 'That went better than expected. But I'll be a lot happier about it once we've told my father and Jacinta.'

'I'm not sure how you can stop her getting in the way,' Barbara said. 'She's the thorn in the side of progress, unfortunately.'

'I'm going to make them both sign a contract. And you're the witness.'

'What?'

'Yup. Not only you. I've asked Brann to come along too.'

'Oh? Why?'

'Because he's going to project manage all the renovations and builds. That'll give me time to focus on my business.'

'Wonderful. He's ideal.'

Indeed, he was. And he'd agreed. Ophelia hadn't forgotten his words. *I'd do anything for you.* But she'd be paying him for this. She didn't expect favours, and she wanted it done properly, because it had to last.

Brann met them the following day and Ophelia shook his hand, holding her breath as their skin made contact. All very professional.

'How are you?' he asked Barbara as he shook hands with her.

'Oh, ticking along. I'll be happy once we get this out of the way. Jacinta is not in a good mood. She's been pestering me to tell her what it's all about and she's very angry because I won't.'

'Let's get it over with then.' Ophelia led them from Barbara's estate office into the main house and up the front steps. Without knocking, she opened the door to the drawing room and took a seat on the chaise longue. Barbara took an armchair, but Brann plonked himself beside Ophelia, so close her thighs grazed up against his dark jeans. She glanced at him and would have chivvied him for sitting so close, but when she caught the expression in his eyes, she was glad he'd chosen this seat. The warmth from him was strengthening and his look told her he was here for her and would have her back no matter what they threw at her.

'What is this all about?' Jacinta smoothed out her skirt and fidgeted with her rings.

'A bit formal, isn't it?' Rupert said. 'Aren't we just having a chat about some building ideas?'

'No, father. We've gone way beyond that,' Ophelia said. 'This may appear formal because that's exactly how I want it to be. We're not only here to discuss some building ideas. We're going to present a robust action plan for the future of this estate. It's a plan that means we can move forward straight away and something we can do ourselves without relying on outside help... Like James Charlton, for example.'

'Oh please,' Jacinta said. 'It needn't have been James. We offered you plenty of choice. Is this just an excuse?'

'An excuse for what?' Brann said. 'An excuse for her not to marry someone you choose for her so you can live off their money?' He eyeballed Jacinta, and Ophelia almost laughed at her stunned face.

'I was just looking out for her prospects.' She fanned her hand across her chest. 'I'm not even sure why he's here,' she muttered aside to Rupert.

'He's here because I invited him,' Ophelia said. 'And from now on, you don't have to worry about my prospects. You can start thinking about your own. The plans I have here have been made up with Barbara, Brann, George Wylie, our financial advisor, and me. Some of them are extensions of ideas my grandparents had for Glenvorneth. Father, you know how hard they fought to ensure the estate came to me, and I believe they did that for a reason.'

Jacinta looked like she'd stepped in horse dung.

'They wanted me to carry on their legacy.'

'And what do you think Rupert has been doing?' Jacinta stared at her.

'Not enough, if truth be told.' Ophelia gave them both a sorry-not-sorry look. 'That's why you called me back in the first place, if you recall.' She fiddled with the papers on her lap. 'At present, there are no official roles for either you, Father, or Jacinta. However, if you want to take an active role, then we can arrange that, and it would be much better for the estate if you did.'

'Wait a second,' Jacinta said. 'We already have roles here, and what roles do *they* have?'

'Barbara will continue running the estate, while I focus on the new branch of my business.'

'Timeless Butterfly Interiors,' Brann added. 'A very successful company. You're lucky to have the CEO giving up so much of her time to run this place. She's one of the best, after all.'

Jacinta's outraged face could now curdle milk, and Ophelia was barely holding back her smile. Her heart almost hurt at hearing his praise. When she recalled how delighted Lucinda was at being handed the Edinburgh office, the grin broke on her face. Though Lucinda's delight hadn't lasted long when she realised Ophelia wouldn't be there anymore. Business lunches would need to be arranged soon, so they could keep in touch.

'And what's his role?' Jacinta looked Brann up and down. 'Or have you paid him to be your cheerleader?'

'He's project managing all the new builds and renovations.'

'What new builds?' Rupert asked.

'This is why you need to read the action plan.' Ophelia got up and handed each of them a copy.

'You want me to read it now?' Jacinta asked.

'That's the idea.' Ophelia returned to her seat next to Brann. His lip quirked up and, as she sat, he laid his hand on her thigh and gave her a gentle, reassuring pat. Her insides flipped at the close contact, but she drew strength from it too.

'This all sounds quite delightful,' Rupert said. 'And definitely something to look into.'

'No. We're not looking into it, father. We're doing it.'

'When?'

'As of now. I have a contract here. Barbara and Brann have signed up to their roles. Now, I need you and Jacinta to sign up to it.'

'Sign up?' Jacinta frowned. 'What am I signing up to do?'

'To agree to work on this plan and not to hinder it in any way.'

'It's a bit much,' she said.

'Is it?' Brann asked. 'More than being asked to sign up to marry someone for their money? You were looking out for Ophelia's prospects in wanting her to sign up for a lifetime with someone she didn't even like. Now she's looking out for yours, without expecting you to do anything.'

'Well, yes, but it doesn't say explicitly what I have to do. I'm not working in a shop that's more for her benefit than ours.'

Ophelia sensed Brann on the verge of erupting. 'You don't have to do anything like that,' she said.

'And nothing she's done here is for her immediate benefit. It's all been for yours.'

'Of course I would appreciate all the help I can get,' Ophelia went on before Jacinta could speak. 'But if you can just agree not to stand in the way of the works, I'll make that do. For example, if we makeover another of the worker's cottages, you can't install a lodger who barely pays half rent because she's your friend. If we start making money on the livery, you can't spend it on a fancy holiday or sack the staff and try to get volunteers to run it. Decisions like that will be made in collaboration.'

'You make it sound a bit harsh,' Rupert said. 'None of those things were done to jeopardise the estate.'

Ophelia took a deep breath, but Brann's hand brushed her thigh again. 'That's exactly why those kinds of decisions need to be made by all of us.'

'And when you say all of us, you actually mean you,' Jacinta said.

'Ultimately yes. That's the privilege my birthright allows me. And the reason you called me back here last year, pretending my father was on his last legs. This is what you wanted. It's not the way you wanted it to happen, but it's the way I'm doing it. Now, are you going to work with me or against me?'

'Of course we won't work against you,' Rupert said.

'Then sign the contract.' Ophelia lifted two more bits of paper. 'I had George write it and you can have it checked by any solicitors or anyone you want.'

Jacinta and Rupert exchanged a look. Ophelia watched them. What would they do? Jacinta must be in internal agony. This went against everything she stood for... How she'd hate giving Ophelia the upper hand.

'She's right,' Rupert said. 'We won't get anywhere if we keep dragging our heels. Let's sign up and see where things go.' He scratched his name on the paper.

Looking like she'd just swallowed a fly, Jacinta signed hers.

April

With the signatures on the paper, Ophelia kicked her plans into action. She and Brann had lots to do, but the air between them was still foggy. She couldn't forget how he'd stood up for her during the meeting though. Jacinta may think she'd paid him to be her cheerleader, but she hadn't asked him to do anything like that. Everything he'd said had been from him, and it made her chest brim with hope.

Still, she needed to crack on. There was so much to be done. And on top of her original plans, she decided to arrange a grand opening for the new livery and stables. Somehow it grew into a family fun day.

'Think of the attention it'll bring,' Barbara said. 'We can have stalls. Vendors pay for a pitch, that kind of thing. You could have one for Timeless Butterfly Interiors. It would get people interested before you open the shop here.'

Suddenly Ophelia had a Family Fun Day to organise and run. It was the kind of event her grandparents used to arrange at Glenvorneth. She just wished it hadn't been at such short notice. Amazingly, it all came together, though she felt like she'd run a marathon every day for a fortnight to get there. She stood on the stairs and smiled at her grandparents' portrait. 'I hope this is what you would have wanted. I think I'm finally getting somewhere.' Her grandparents smiled back as they always did, and she was sure they'd approve. 'I have something else I want to do, but it's more personal. I hope you approve of that too.' And it was rather dependent on Brann. As soon as the fun day was done, she needed to talk to him. Her heart buzzed at the thought, but nerves tempered the excitement. What if he didn't want what she wanted?

Jacinta had made her contribution by asking the Countess of Dairvin to cut the ribbon on the stables and declare them officially open. Oh well, at least she'd done something, even if it was only to make sure Ophelia wouldn't get all the credit.

'I never expected it to be this big,' Ophelia told Hayley as they walked around the estate, which resembled a mini Highland Games field, all ready for the family fun.

'It's amazing. You've worked so hard. I was talking to Colette about it at work. She's coming with Harrison. I absolutely love the Timeless Butterfly stall and Lucinda is so lovely.'

'She really is.' And she'd been good enough to come along to look after the stall for the day. 'Let's see how she's doing.' They headed to the stall, which was next to a local craft stall named The Crafty Bee, dazzling in bright yellow.

'There's Lilah.' Hayley dashed off to hug the redhead who was behind the crafty bee stall while Ophelia went to Lucinda.

'Everything ok?'

'Great,' Lucinda said. 'It's brilliant to see this place in person.'

'And you met Hayley.'

'Oh, she's wonderful.'

Right on cue, she appeared back beside Ophelia and put her arm around her shoulder.

'Is something wrong?' Hayley asked.

'No.' But it was. Brann was here somewhere too with Caitlin. He deserved a break after the hours he'd put in over the past few weeks. The works in the courtyard were in progress. But she wanted to see him away from work. Away from everyone. She needed a moment of peace with him so they could talk. Not about the future of the estate. But the future for them. Maybe it wasn't possible but what if it was? Things had moved on in her life. Did he think so too? He'd said he loved her all those months ago, but what did that mean now?

'Come on. I know you better than that now.'

'So do I.' Lucinda raised her eyebrows.

'You haven't agreed to meet James or something, have you?' Hayley frowned.

'I thought he was well gone,' Lucinda said.

'He is. I told him I didn't think it was a good idea. Now that we've got the action plan, I don't need to marry anyone rich. I don't need to marry anyone. I'm free to choose what I want... And who I want.'

'And who's that?' Hayley peered at her.

'I think you already know.'

'Well, I don't.' Lucinda put her hands on her hips.

'You're about the only one.' Hayley grinned, then returned her focus to Ophelia. 'Everybody who's seen the two of you together knows. It's not like you've ever done that great a job at hiding it.'

'Who are we talking about?' Lucinda pressed.

'Brann,' Hayley said.

'Isn't he the obnoxious builder?'

'Well, he's the builder, though I rather misjudged him.' Ophelia drew in a breath. 'And it's got complicated.'

'Life is.'

'She's right,' Hayley said. 'But if you want him, tell him.'

'Tell him what?'

'That you love him.'

'Is it *that* serious?' Lucinda stared at her, and slowly Ophelia nodded.

'He told me himself months ago.' Ophelia fixed her hand to the top of her head.

'What?' Hayley stared at her. 'And what did you say?'

'Nothing. I let him go.'

'But he didn't go, did he? He's still here. If he really wanted to stay away from you, he could.'

'True.'

'Do it,' Hayley said. 'Go and get him.'

'Yes, do.' Lucinda pointed into the crowd. 'Go find this man so I can meet him.'

'Oh, there's Oliver.' Hayley waved.

'You go and have fun with him,' Ophelia said. 'I need to go. I'll catch you later.'

'And when you do, make sure you have Brann with you,' Lucinda said.

The sun cast a warm glow over the stables as Ophelia made her way through the crowd, listening to the happy buzz of chatter and kids laughing and squealing as they rolled on the grass. This was where she'd caught Brann with his shirt off last year. She smiled at the thought.

Dagmar led a pony around the paddock with a child on its back. Her job was safe, and she seemed happy about that, in her own quiet way. By the fence, Ophelia noticed two familiar figures, her mother and Nancy.

'Hey.' She leaned on the fence beside Edith.

'Ophelia, darling, you've truly outdone yourself with this,' Edith said.

Nancy nodded in agreement. 'Everything looks fantastic.'

Ophelia smiled. 'It was a bit last minute, but it's better than I expected.'

'I'm amazed you got your father and Jacinta to agree to this,' Edith said.

'They've signed a contract, which basically forbids them from meddling.'

'Genius.' Edith laughed. 'That's my girl. Your grandparents would be proud. I got on better with them in the end than your father.'

'Uh-oh. Speak of the devil,' Ophelia said. Rupert was ambling around the paddock with Francesca. Jacinta was there too, with a frown and a pout that told Ophelia she wasn't happy about any of this. But as soon as the countess turned up, Jacinta would change her tune.

Edith pulled a face as Rupert approached. 'The downside of returning here.'

Ophelia thought of Brann and Kristalee and how they put their differences aside for their children. Something her parents had never achieved.

'Hello, hello.' Rupert peered past Ophelia at Edith. 'Quite an event this has turned out to be. Just on the lookout for the countess. She should be here at any moment.'

'This is Ophelia's doing.' Edith narrowed her eyes at her ex-husband. 'She's put in a tremendous effort to make this day special for everyone. So never mind the countess. It's Ophelia who should be cutting that ribbon.'

Nancy nodded. 'That would have been fitting.'

'It's fine,' Ophelia said. 'It's like having a local celebrity.'

Jacinta pulled a supercilious expression. 'It was my idea to invite her. And it will be lovely to see her. So lucky she could fit this into her busy schedule.'

'Lucky Ophelia chose to allow it,' Edith said.

'Oh dear,' Rupert said. 'This could go on all day.'

'No. We're here to have fun,' Ophelia said. 'And there's the countess. We should go and welcome her.'

But before she could move, Jacinta bustled off and Rupert, looking taken aback at being left alone with his ex-wife, turned and followed her.

'Fine,' Ophelia said. 'I'll wait until she tires of her fan club and then go and talk to her.'

'You know,' Edith sighed. 'We all make mistakes in life and your father was the biggest one in my life. The only good thing to come out of it was you.'

'Thanks.'

'I hope with all the new things going on here, you've ditched the idea of marrying some rich prat just to please your father. I married him for similar reasons, and I wouldn't recommend it.'

'I'm not going to marry any of the people they suggest,' Ophelia said. 'Whoever I end up with will be someone of my own choosing.'

'Good for you.'

'Do you have someone on the horizon?' Nancy asked.

'Maybe. We'll see.'

'Sounds intriguing,' Edith said.

'I've definitely met the man I'm in love with... I just need to work out if we have a future together.'

CHAPTER THIRTY-THREE

Brann

Brann leaned back on a fence post, sipping a coke and watching Caitlin as she rode around the paddock.

'She's taken to that quickly,' Harrison said, with half an eye on his sister, and the other on Colette who'd wandered away to chat to Hayley.

'Yeah. She's enjoying it.'

'Weird, huh? It's like we're connected to this family of nutters, whether we like it or not.'

'They're not all nutters.'

'Don't tell me. I know the one you think isn't. When are the two of you going to admit it and get it on?'

'We already did that.'

'What?' Harrison goggled at him.

'Yeah. Ages ago. But that doesn't mean we have a future together, does it?'

'You hooked up with her?'

He shrugged. 'I guess you could call it that.'

'Holy fuck. I knew it. Then go and do it again. Jesus Christ, it's so bloody obvious. But if you marry her, please god don't start wearing that Toad of Toad Hall outfit. Otherwise I'll disown you.'

Brann folded his arms, balancing his coke can on his elbow. 'Ok, let's get something straight. I'll never dress like that and I'm not marrying her.'

'Aye, aye. So you say.'

Brann shook his head but couldn't help a smile growing on his face. Harrison's confidence was annoying but kind of sweet.

Caitlin finished her ride and made her way over to them.

'The official opening is on in a few minutes. Let's go and watch.'

Brann looped his arm over her shoulder, and they walked to the main door of the stables where a crowd was gathering.

Before long, a microphone sprang into action and Rupert's voice spoke.

'Hello. Isn't this wonderful?' he said. 'So nice to see such lovely people out and about.'

Brann looked heavenward. Why was he making the speech? He better not claim everything that Ophelia had done here as his own.

'It gives me great pleasure to welcome our family friend, the countess of Dairvin, to do the honours and cut the ribbon.'

The countess smiled and held up a pair of scissors big enough to be shears.

'Thank you, indeed,' she said. 'It's wonderful to be invited to Glenvorneth to carry out this task, and it gives me very great pleasure to declare the new stables officially open.' She made a swooping cut, and the ribbon fell away.

Brann joined in the clapping but pulled a face. This felt off. Where was Ophelia and why wasn't she up there, getting the credit she deserved?

'Before I stand down,' the countess said. 'I'd like to invite one more person to join me. None of this would have been possible were it not for the absolutely marvellous efforts of Ophelia Chattan-Blythe. Up you come, Ophelia. I insist.'

It looked like both her mother and Hayley were shoving her onto the stage. She blinked and glanced at her feet as the countess smiled at her.

'Well done, Ophelia, on a wonderful job.'

'Thank you,' she said. 'And I appreciate your words, but in all honesty, these stables weren't built by me. I made the designs and decided what I thought would work well, but Brann Duthie, the builder, his son and his workers did the hard labour. They were the ones who put all this together and if Brann's here, maybe he'd like to come up.'

A hand landed on his shoulder, shoving him forward. It was like doing the walk of shame, only it wasn't shame. People were clapping and patting his back like he'd won the tug-of-war again. He reached the front where Ophelia, the countess, and Rupert were standing on the steps up to the stables.

Ophelia looked at him for a moment, then put out her hand. He took it, and she held it tight as he stepped up beside her. 'Thanks, Brann,' she said. 'Just so you know how much I appreciate the work you did here.' Although she still had the microphone in her hand, it wasn't close enough to her mouth for the words to be very loud and it felt more like she was talking just to him.

She leaned up and kissed his cheek. Before she could pull away, he slipped an arm around her waist, tugged her close, and planted a kiss on her lips. She relaxed and smiled as she returned it. People cheered and wolf-whistled. Brann drew back with a grin and winked like he was just a lad stealing a kiss.

In the crowd, he saw Hayley almost jumping up and down. Harrison and Caitlin were looking at each other with irritating know-it-all happy faces, but they were smirking. At the Timeless Butterfly stall, Ophelia's colleague had her hand clapped over her mouth.

'Er, yes.' Rupert took the microphone, eyeing Ophelia and Brann. From the lowest step, Brann spotted Jacinta gaping with her hand sprawled across her chest. 'Well, thank you, Brann and Ophelia, for the work,' Rupert continued. 'And thanks to everyone who came out today. I hope you have a wonderful day.' He switched off the microphone and blinked, first at Ophelia, then at the countess.

'Thank you for having me,' the countess said.

'Can I get you some tea?' Jacinta asked, still half eyeing Brann and Ophelia.

Ophelia continued to hold his hand, but seemed to be deliberately avoiding his eye.

'No, thank you,' the countess said. 'I need to get back. I have another appointment later.' She turned to Ophelia and winked, then bent in and whispered something in her ear.

'Nice to meet the man behind all this.' She shook Brann's free hand. 'I daresay we might be seeing more of you in the future.' She left with a little grin.

'Well, um.' Rupert cleared his throat. 'Is everything alright here?' He glanced between Brann and Ophelia.

'Never better,' Brann said.

'Am I missing something?' Jacinta said.

'Probably,' Ophelia replied.

'And would you care to enlighten me?'

Ophelia turned to Brann and took a few short breaths. 'I love Brann.' She turned back to Jacinta. 'I don't want you to set me up with anyone. I only want him.'

'What,' Rupert said.

'You heard me. And even if nothing comes of it, I've set the estate up with a plan. I'm going to choose my own life and the people I want in it.'

'Of course, that's fine. It's just a little surprising.' Rupert stared at her for a moment, half-frowning, half smiling.

'Well, I'll let you be surprised for a moment. I need to talk to Brann in private.'

She led him inside the stables and turned to face him.

'That was interesting,' he said.

'And true.'

'I know.' He took her face in his hands. 'I've known for a long time.'

'I've loved you since forever. Even when I hated you. Maybe I never really hated you. I hated not being allowed to have you.'

'And now you're allowed. What are you going to do?'

'I thought I needed a rich man to help me save Glenvorneth, but all I need is a loving man to stand with me.'

He gazed at her. 'I want you. You know I do. I need you with me too. We're the perfect fit. But this life... How can I?'

'I can't force you to do anything, but if you want, we can try. You can learn to live with my family, and I'll learn to live with yours. Though I don't mind if we avoid mine as much as possible.'

He grinned. 'I said once before I'd do anything for you. And I will. I love you so much.'

Ophelia laughed as he dipped into kiss her.

'Who'd have thought it?'

'Well, if you believe my kids, everyone's been thinking it for months and we're the only ones who can't see it.'

'Hayley says the same.' Ophelia flung her arms around his neck, still laughing, and he lifted her off her feet. 'Let's go and find them then. They'll enjoy gloating over us.'

'I don't think I'd ever have believed I could be this happy, but I am,' Brann said.

'Me too.' Ophelia took his hand and led him out. Wherever she was taking him, he would follow.

EPILOGUE

Ophelia

Ophelia woke in Brann's arms. Beyond the end of the bed, the view of the loch from the boathouse was clear in the early morning light. The empty feeling she'd had in the boathouse since moving in wasn't an issue anymore. Not now that she had strong arms to hold her.

Brann stirred, and without opening his eyes, pulled her closer to him.

'You're not thinking about getting up, are you?' he said. 'It's Saturday morning.'

'I know, but remember, we have visitors coming.'

'Not for ages yet.'

She giggled as he kissed her brow and stroked her hair. Ok, thoughts of the visitors could wait. Brann's light stubble tickled her as he kissed his way down her body. Saturday mornings were made for this.

By the time they got out of bed, they didn't have that long to wait before Caitlin, Harrison and Colette were due to show up. Harrison had obviously seen the boathouse before, but the only time Caitlin had been inside, it hadn't been near finished. This felt uncomfortably like a first meeting. The first time Brann's children had been to this house since he'd unofficially moved in. Ophelia's body was tight with the pressure of needing to put on a good show. She couldn't afford to do anything that might upset his kids and force him not to make this official.

'Are you ok?' Brann stepped up behind her, massaging her shoulders.

Ophelia sighed. The tension eased slightly under his gentle touch. She turned to him with a vague smile. 'I'm just nervous. I want everything to go smoothly today. I don't want to mess up. Look at what Jacinta did to me. Now I'm in the same position and I haven't got a clue what to do. Maybe I was hard on her all these years.'

'No. It's different.' He turned her around, took her face in his hands, and kissed her. When he drew back, he smiled. 'You aren't Jacinta. You're a totally different person. You've already met my kids and they like you. Sure, you freaked them both out at first, especially Harrison, but now they see the funny side.'

She took a deep breath. 'But this'll be a big change. It won't be like Caitlin can just nip over here whenever she wants. It's miles out of town.'

'When she wants to come out, I'll pick her up, or her mum can bring her. She's taking lessons. Caitlin likes spending time with Francesca and volunteering at the horses, so this'll be ideal for that. It won't be the same as what she's used to, but it'll be just as good. I've spoken to her and she's ok with it.'

'I hope so.'

'Believe me, and stop worrying.' Brann wrapped his arms around her, drawing her close. 'You're an amazing woman. You're strong and determined. I know you'll never harm my children the way Jacinta hurt you. I trust you.'

That, more than anything, gave her strength. She nodded and breathed deeply. 'Ok. I can do this.'

'I know you can.' He winked.

The doorbell rang.

'I'll get it,' he said.

Ophelia waited, listening to the happy voices. Caitlin came in first, gawping around with wide eyes. 'Wow. This place is sick. I can't believe how it's turned out. Wait until I get photos.'

'Hey.' Harrison followed Caitlin in. He was hand in hand with Colette, who looked equally as awestruck as Caitlin.

'Hi,' Ophelia said. 'How are you?'

'Good.' He grinned. 'Better, now I know you and Dad are together and I was right all along.'

'Stop,' Colette said.

'Ahem, Dad.' Harrison raised his eyebrows. 'Was I or was I not right from the start?'

'You were right. Yes, son. And if you keep on being right, I'll make sure you get a sticker and the class-star award at the end of the week.'

Caitlin sniggered.

'I'd love to live here,' Colette said. 'Hayley told me it was awesome, but it's so much more amazing than I imagined.'

'Well, you've got the right boyfriend to make that happen,' Ophelia said. 'He knows how this place was put together.'

'Not sure I've got the cash,' Harrison said.

'You'll make it,' Ophelia said. 'You work hard, and your dad has a thriving business.'

He nodded. 'Yeah.'

A lot of the work on the estate Brann was carrying out himself. He scoffed at the idea of ever owning this much property or being 'lord of the manor', but he took the business side of things more seriously than her father ever had. She knew her grandparents would be smiling down on her. They would definitely approve or Brann and what he brought to Glenvorneth. And she had faith that together they could bash this place into better shape and get it ticking over to the point where it made a steady income. So far, her father and Jacinta were playing ball and keeping a low profile. If they were shocked about Ophelia's relationship with Brann, they kept it to themselves. She was pretty sure neither of them would dare say anything to his face.

'Oh, we have something for you,' Colette said. 'It's from all of us.' She pulled out a bottle of champagne.

'To celebrate the royal wedding,' Harrison said.

'Who's getting married?' Brann asked.

'You two.' Harrison winked. 'Remember, I'm always right.'

'Thank you.' Ophelia took the bottle from him and put it on the sideboard. 'Shall we drink it now?'

'Am I allowed it?' Caitlin asked.

'Maybe a tiny bit if you don't tell anyone,' Brann said.

'Yeah, because we know you never drank before you were seventeen,' Harrison muttered.

'Don't do as I do, do as I say.' Brann pointed at him. 'Dad's privilege.'

Ophelia popped the cork and poured the fizz into five glasses. Beside her, her phone lit up, and she saw Hayley's face on the screen with a message. She flipped it open and read.

HAYLEY: would you and Brann like to come for dinner one night? I still can hardly believe the two of you are together. It's so amazing. I'd really love to have you here. Xx

Ophelia smiled. She'd reply later, and of course they'd go. She'd also love to have Hayley back here. Hayley's only visit had been one Sunday afternoon when Ophelia had still been on her own, and that seemed like a different world now.

'Thank you,' Caitlin said as Ophelia handed her a half-full glass. She handed the full ones to everyone else.

'Here, I meant to say before,' Brann said. 'I emailed the homeless shelter we took old Donald to, and they got back, saying his family found him. He's gone into care, but it's better than trying to survive out here.'

'Certainly is. I'm glad he's ok.' Ophelia took a seat next to Brann and smiled. 'This has been one crazy year. When I came back last winter, I would never have predicted anything that's happened here. The day I met you' – she looked at Brann – 'it was surreal.'

'The day you thought I was the moped thief and tried to attack me with the antlers?'

'The very same. Who'd have thought we'd have gone from that to this?'

Harrison raised his hand.

'Except Harrison, of course.'

He gave her the thumbs up.

'Well, I'd just like to say. Here's to us all and to many more crazy years.' She raised her glass.

'And no more antler attacks.' Brann clinked his glass on the side of hers.

'Or you two sneaking off round the back to do whatever,' Harrison muttered.

'Sorry, can't guarantee that.' Brann grinned at Ophelia, and she smiled back until it broke into a laugh.

'We'll never guarantee that.' Leaning forward, her lips met Brann's. She closed her eyes and ignored Harrison's groan. When she pulled back, she kept her eyes on Brann. 'The only thing I can guarantee is how much I love you.'

Brann reached out and stroked her cheek. 'It's all I ever wanted.'

'Aw, guys,' Caitlin said. 'You're making us all a bit emosh.'

'Or wanting to vomit,' Harrison said. Colette slapped his thigh.

Brann put his arm around Ophelia's shoulder, and she took a sip of champagne. While the others chatted and took photos on their phones, Ophelia whispered to Brann, 'It's been quite a ride, hasn't it? But we're good, aren't we?'

He squeezed her gently. 'Never better. Sometimes, the most unexpected people turn out to be exactly the ones we need.'

She nodded. Yes. He was right. In so many ways. She'd never have put a relationship with Brann the Builder down as an item on her life plan, but here it was, and now it was the only plan that really mattered. As long as they were together, everything else would fall into place. Silently, she raised her glass to that thought, clinked it against Brann's and they both took a sip. She kept her eyes on his, safe in the knowledge that together they were strong, loved, and finally whole.

The End

More Books by Margaret Amatt

Scottish Island Escapes

1. A Winter Haven

2. A Spring Retreat

3. A Summer Sanctuary

4. An Autumn Hideaway

5. A Christmas Bluff

6. A Flight of Fancy

7. A Hidden Gem

8. A Striking Result

9. A Perfect Discovery

10. A Festive Surprise

The Glenbriar Series

1. Stolen Kisses at the Loch View Hotel

2. Just Friends at Thistle Lodge

3. Pitching up at Heather Glen

4. Two's Company at the Forest Light Show

5. Highland Fling on the Whisky Trail

6. Snowdown at the Old Schoolhouse

7. Starting Over at the Crafty Bee Barn

8. A Surprise Proposal in the Rose Garden

9. Cutting it Neat for the Wedding

10. A Classy Affair in the Country

11. Mix Up under the Mistletoe

12. A Fresh Start on the Bridle Path

13. Last First Kiss at the Village Church

14. Fight or Flirt on the Scenic Route

15. Love Match on the Road Home

Love on the Edge – Barra Series

ACKNOWLEDGEMENTS

Thanks as always to my husband, Ian, for supporting my dreams and helping me think up some of the place names in the book (as well as all the bonkers ones I'll never use but are good for a laugh!). Also to my son, whose interest in my writing always makes me smile. Although romance books aren't exactly his thing – he keeps asking me to add outer space elements or at least elves – he's always ready to cheer me on!

Throughout the writing process, I have gleaned help from many sources and met some fabulous people. I'd like to give a special mention to Stéphanie Ronckier, my beta reader extraordinaire. Stéphanie's continued support with my writing is invaluable and I love the fact that I need someone French to correct my grammar! Stéphanie, you rock. To my lovely friend, Lyn Williamson, thank you for your continued support and encouragement with all my projects. And to my fellow authors, Evie Alexander and Lyndsey Gallagher – you girls are the best! I love it that you always have my back and are there to help when I need you.

Also, a huge thanks to my editors at Leannan Press!

Of course a huge thank you goes to the readers who continue to support me in so many ways. I appreciate each and every one of you and hope that I can keep bringing you more books to enjoy! Big love.

Margaret XX

ABOUT THE AUTHOR
Margaret Amatt

Margaret has told and written stories for as long as she can remember. During her formative years, she spent time on long walks inventing characters and stories to pass the time.

Writing books is Margaret's passion and when she's not doing that, she's often found eating chocolate, walking and taking photographs in the hills around Highland Perthshire. Those long walks still frequently bring inspiration!

It's Margaret's pleasure to bring you the **Scottish Island Escapes** series, **The Glenbriar Series** and the **Love on the Edge – Barra** series. Each series features interconnected stories for those who enjoy inhabiting Margaret's world but each and every book can be read as a standalone if you'd rather dip in and out.

You can find more information about Margaret on her website or by signing up for her newsletter

www.margaretamatt.com

www.ingramcontent.com/pod-product-compliance
Lightning Source LLC
Chambersburg PA
CBHW011217190726
48287CB00008B/2653